Flying Dark

A Novel

By Colin W. Sargent

HellBound Books Publishing LLC
Houston, TX

**A HellBound Books LLC
Publication**
Copyright © 2023 by HellBound Books Publishing
LLC
All Rights Reserved

Cover and art design by Tee Arts
For HellBound Books Publishing LLC

No part of this book may be reproduced, stored in a retrieval system, or transmitted by any means, electronic, mechanical, photocopying, recording or otherwise without written permission from the author This book is a work of fiction. Names, characters, places and incidents are entirely fictitious or are used fictitiously and any resemblance to actual persons, living or dead, events or locales is purely coincidental.

www.hellboundbooks.com

Flying Dark

Chapter 1

Hopewell Township, New Jersey, March 1, 1982

1) *Aviate.* 2) *Navigate.* 3) *Communicate.*

HUNTER FOLLOWED HIS HEADLIGHTS as he drove along the east side of the Delaware River, then eased up the slope of the Sourland Mountains. The evergreens fell away as he penetrated more deeply into the scene of the unimaginable horror.

Just ahead, the gate for 188 Lindbergh Road leapt into view: leafy estate, anonymous mailbox under the trees' canopy, slashes of forgotten stone walls.

Time check: 2:44 a.m. In the ringing silence, he entered the mile-long driveway and listened as his tires crunched along the gravel toward the place that revolted him to the base of his senses.

It was here, on the windswept, rainy night of March 1, 1932, where twenty-month-old Charles A. Lindbergh Jr. vanished. The baby was stolen from the country estate Lucky Lindy built with his prize money for that first solo flight from New York to Paris. Lindbergh and his bride had barely furnished their dream house before their dreams were ripped to shreds. When little Buster's remains were discovered, the lovebirds promised themselves they'd never sleep here again. They made a gift of "Highfields" to the State of New Jersey in 1933.

Now, The Albert Elias Home for Delinquent Boys was temporarily deserted due to a convenient heating-system failure. No clueless guards, no harried social workers, no belligerent students, no tremulous faculty, just the unluckiest spot on earth.

This was by no means Hunter's first time here. In fact, it was his second time today.

More than three decades ago, he'd been packed off to Elias after a disappointing first year at Montauk Public, a.k.a. MonPu. Against all odds, he'd found an ally in Manfred, the strange German teacher who acted as a resident advisor and who introduced Hunter to the joy of flying. "If there's one thing in the world I could have, it would be my own *flugzeug*," Manfred once made the fatal error of saying at the Saturday morning Elias flying club, supported by an anonymous donor. Of course, the other boys pounced. Ever after, they called him Fluke Kook behind his back, but Hunter, who felt calm only when he was in the sky, shared a deep kinship with the reclusive émigré.

Other than his weekly trips to the airfield, Manfred appeared never to leave the campus. He called himself an adoptee, and Hunter took it to mean that though he was grateful for the asylum he'd been granted in 1943, he'd never felt it was more than an arm's length embrace, and that the American dream was always held just out of reach. Occupying a small dependency just steps from the home's back door, Manfred turned off the single lamp on his desk set in the window promptly every night after the 10 o'clock news.

Hunter hadn't heard from, or even thought of, Manfred for decades, but the voice on the answering machine was unmistakable. "Mr. Schunning here. Manfred. I know this sounds very out of order, but I do not know who else to turn to. I am in a pickle." He coughed. "Let me explain. My contract has not been renewed. I must have my name cleared. A student has made some mischief, and now some of the parents claim I am a…Communist." Another cough. "That I was a Communist agitator in Berlin. That I lied on my application for citizenship. Of course, this is nonsense, but I have nowhere to go. I've heard you've been making a name for yourself in cases proving people aren't who they say they are. Might you do the opposite? I am exactly who I say I am."

Hunter's instincts told him this was a rare case of the truth. Clearing his old friend would be a piece of cake. And it nearly was.

But when Hunter knocked on the cottage door with the report of Manfred's activities in Bamberg (there were no surviving family members, they'd all perished at Buchenwald, and Manfred had gone on to teach in Switzerland, just as he'd always maintained), it was too late. Manfred had suffered a massive hemorrhagic stroke and was dead before he even hit the floor.

Hunter felt a rush of sympathy for his old friend. But it occurred to him that maybe this was what Manfred wanted. Hunter had found Manfred's birth certificate.

Manfred's parents never married, so his surname Schunning was his mother's. But his father's name was Hauptmann.

Holy smokes. Bruno Hauptmann, the monster, the child kidnapper. So, Manfred didn't end up here by accident. He must have been searching for something. Absolution, perhaps?

Well, at least they wouldn't have to discuss this 'unpleasantness,' a Manfred word. It didn't take a genius to see why Manfred couldn't take care of this himself. There would have been no explaining this to the board.

An ambulance arrived, and Manfred was taken on to the morgue. When Hunter asked the head social worker who should be notified, she just shrugged.

Hunter felt an icy chill in the parlor when he sat down. Had it always been this cold and damp here? The janitor came in and said, "I'm sorry, but we're going to have to evacuate the building." The old furnace had finally failed, and it was going to be four days before heat would be restored. Hunter nearly made it back to the airport when he turned the car around.

Manfred's lonely death had struck a match, throwing an eerie light on feelings Hunter had long since pushed aside. Something else bothered him about this place. From the very first night he'd spent here, listening to haunted tales from the other delinquents about the shallow, mucky grave–the dismemberment, the wild critters and bugs beginning to feed (no detail was too grisly for the boys to discuss at length)–Hunter had felt there was something else unspoken buried under the leaves with the innocent child.

He couldn't say he wasn't lucky to have been sent here–after all, the school was in Lucky Lindbergh's home–but he could never shake off the sense of unfinished business here, even though he'd graduated with honors before leaving all of this behind. He'd received a congratulatory letter from Manfred when he finished at Harvard, followed by a card when he got his Navy flying wings. When Hunter sent a wedding invitation, he received Manfred's regrets by return mail just as expected.

Hunter passed the empty sentry hut, having made sure the caretaker had hied himself to Hillbilly Hall, three miles away in Hopewell, playing that third game of pool (from a corner table in the shadows, Hunter had watched the poor guy lose the first two). The driveway got two shades darker before the glow of a clearing opened to reveal the whitewashed brick French Provincial mansion with gables. This was his first midnight back in 30 years.

Two fifty-two a.m. The windows of Highfields were black. They stared at him. When he turned off his engine, he could feel his heart beating through his chest. It wouldn't do to get caught here now. There would be questions. Hunter preferred to be the one who asked all the questions.

He slipped to the ground and took a deep breath. Listening for the sound of approaching steps–few could listen more intently–he donned a set of cotton painter's gloves. Grasping a pair of shears from his pocket, he walked to a nearby telephone pole, pried open the steel box–a pen light between his teeth–and snipped the wire to the security system. He hoisted down an aluminum extension ladder from the roof of the janitor's Suburban. Best to keep quiet and focus on the job at hand. He brought the ladder neatly to his shoulder and carried it to the south pavilion.

Counting four windows back from the maison's façade, he ratcheted the ladder to full length against the north wall. Then he angled it above the first-floor library and set it to a point just below the nursery window.

As a teenager, Hunter had often wondered idly how odd it was for the exquisitely sensitive Lindbergh to have been, by his own account, reading in the library when the kidnapper crashed a ladder against the wall directly beside him, clambered up, forced open the nursery window, and spirited his namesake son from his crib, sometime within the span of four hours, 6 to 10 p.m. Nor during these looming hours was the Eaglet's mother within earshot of her sleeping child. Nor the paid nurse, summoned to help the little baby through a head cold, nor the butler/caretaker, nor even Trixie, the black Scottish terrier puppy notorious for yipping "loudly at strangers." From this house without ears, Hauptmann had left a crude ransom note, splintered the bottom half of the homemade ladder as he fell while descending, muffled a cry in the dark, and dragged the child away.

The world, along with the Lindberghs, lost its innocence. Now, it calmed Hunter to see the undulations of gray roof slates devised by Lindbergh to crest and trough on their ridges like the Atlantic waves he'd flown over in the *Spirit of St. Louis.* "The kind of stipulation only a genius would dream of," Manfred had marveled. Remarkably, they were pitch perfect.

Time check again. Two fifty-nine a.m. Moonlight caught the ladder rungs as they rose from the blackness of the damp grass to the window. Let's see what the local newspapers will make of this. Fifty years slipped away when he closed his eyes. Breathing softly, he hiked deeper into the five-hundred-acre estate, determined to follow the path the kidnapper took with the precious bundle.
Hunter's Red Wing boots plashed in the wet meadow. The ladder grew smaller as he walked a serpentine four miles into the wizard-dark woods, barely a shriek below the Princeton-Hopewell Road. It was here the boy's shallow grave was found two months later. Hunter dropped into a ravine, found the little black patch that seemed to repel all growth, and stared into the abyss.

Chapter 2

Manhattan, New York

Don't fly with your hands, fly with your head.

HUNTER STOPPED BY HIS SUITE at the Waldorf Astoria, made a quick phone call to a pilot buddy from the old days, and packed his bag. Boarding the Pan Am red eye to West Berlin, he settled into First-Class Seat 2A. Wasn't that what friends were for? Picking up the Jaguar waiting for him at the airport, he took the Kurfürstendamm into the business district. So early in the morning, the boulevards were nearly empty.

Inside the Deutsche Bank building, he made his way through the marble lobby to the elevator. A discreet sterling plaque whispered the law firm of Schröder & Neumann occupied the penthouse.

As he whisked skyward, Hunter surveyed the other Hunters in infinite recursion, mirrors upon mirrors. "Sixth floor, everybody out." A few steps down the hall, a nervous group sat on the edges of its chairs.

"*Guten Morgen*, Herr Dauger." John Abel Smith, Esq., had coiffed hair and a precise British accent, even when he spoke German.

"*Wo ist der Kaffee*?" Hunter said.

"Sylvie will take your coat. They're all waiting."

"I'm on time."

"Yes, but you're expensive."

"I'll wrap this up as quickly as possible." He studied Smith, whose eyes were rocking. "What is it you're not saying?"

"This one's different. It involves a worldwide hero. You were familiar with the Lindbergh name before you got the files for this case?"

"I was a pilot in the U.S. Navy a million years ago."

Smith dropped his voice. "We need to keep a lid on this. Lindbergh died in 1974, but we haven't been able to close the estate yet because new spiders keep crawling out of the woodwork. Right now, at least seven German and Swiss claimants insist they're Lindbergh's rightful heirs. They're complicating"–he waved quotation marks with his middle and index fingers–"closure of the estate for the five Morrow/Lindbergh children."

"Six," Hunter said, "counting Buster."

"The dead only inherit earth. There's always been interest in the flying fortune. The marriage to the Morrow family brought J.P. Morgan money to the table. But it's the magic name Lindbergh that's now the gold coin for entreé. These are strange days when celebrity is eclipsing family and wealth."

Hunter grasped his suitcase. "If you can't be famous, at least be infamous. Let's get on with this."

Inside the conference room, a lawyer type in pinstripes and a matron in a hat with a net veil flanked an adventuress chatting easily. She was urban, dangerous, sophisticated, and girlish all at once. Hunter was completely captivated.

Just beyond her fingertips, a cut-crystal glass of ice water reflected her motion and her lovely face.

Those eyes. When he opened the door, she did not stand, though her attorney and her aunt jumped as though there were a bomb scare. Hunter took a seat and tapped his pen on the desk, getting a grip. In order to keep his eyes off the prize, he addressed the aunt.

"Why don't you tell the story, and I'll follow with my questions?"

"My sister and I were both in college when the War broke out. Our house in Schultzdam was bombed. We never found our parents. We lived there, just the two of us, hand to mouth, fear our only guest. For a time, we worked as waitresses. By the early 1950s, we'd found work in a U.S. government typing pool and were so grateful. We were offered positions in Italy, and we were really excited to start a new life. There, we befriended two other sisters, Brigitte and Marietta Hesshaimer. We were introduced to 'Careu Kent' at his apartment in Rome. When he got drunk that night, he felt me up! His hand was on my back, warm. The others couldn't see. Then he grasped my buttock, and he wouldn't let me go."

"A gentleman's gentleman," Hunter said. "Some things don't deserve to be remembered."

"I found him repulsive, but my sister fell hard. When she became visibly pregnant, suddenly the Americans no longer needed her services. Her position was eliminated. Pia was born, and my sister gave her the last name of a local bricklayer who'd been killed in the war. A month later my sister was killed in a train accident." She licked her lips, then looked down at her hands.

"So, I'm assuming your claim is that your sister dated Col. Lindbergh and no other man in Italy in 1952," Hunter said. He turned to Pia. "Pia, may I call you that?" He plunged on, not allowing her to object. "Now I have some questions for you. Oh, by the way, how do you feel about a lie-detector test?"

Her lawyer lit a cigarette and crossed his narrow knees. "I don't see what gives you the power."

"Mr. Dauger has our complete confidence," Smith said. "You yourselves have acknowledged his expertise by signing the release that allows him to question this young lady in private and submit her to a lie-detector test. You agree you will accept his well-considered determination. He is the world expert in these matters, with over seventy cases upheld for legal descendants and their assigns against frauds." He looked quickly at Pia. "I hope you'll forgive me for speaking plainly."

She fingered some droplets at the top of her glass and smiled.

"And how many have you ratified?" the lawyer demanded of Hunter.

"Your client can't be acknowledged the daughter of Charles Lindbergh just because she claims to be such," Hunter said lightly, watching her. "While DNA testing may one day storm across deductive reason, we're not there yet."

How lovely you are, and how well you hold your head. Don't you have your hands on the tiller. If those were the only determinants, everything would point to a yes here. But for Lindbergh's heirs and business partners in the United States, it wouldn't do for it to get out that he had three shadow families in Europe to immortalize his heroic strain, his Social Darwinism an unforgivable, and oddly unconsidered, experiment. Not yet. "Besides, if she's the real deal, questions, research, and logical conclusions are her allies. Let the truth be her North Star."

"Why are you speaking about me as though I'm not here, Mr. Dauger?" the beautiful stranger asked.

"Because you might have worn some undergarments. If you were my client, I would have suggested it."

Her eyes did not flicker. Her breathing remained even. Her attorney gripped her hand and said, "I'll be right here for you."

"Let's get this show on the road," Hunter said, opening the door to the conference room.

"You understand I'm her counsel," the lawyer said. "I'm used to accompanying my clients."

"Yes."

"Yes, what?"

"I understand."

"It's all right," she said. "I've got nothing to hide."

"When there is something to hide, one becomes an actor," Hunter said. "It forces all the people round one to act as well."

"Lawrence Durrell, *Justine*."

Now this was something. An educated thief. Hunter closed the door and marveled at the quiet as he watched her glance at the black box on the table. Look at you, with your daring eyes. How calm you are, as though you know this goes deeper than a mere sexual encounter. More intimate than that.

She looked straight into his eyes. "A polygraph," she said. "I thought they'd been debunked. Will I feel anything?"

"No, only it will. It senses emotion." He unsnapped the top of the box, took off the lid, unraveled its long cord with the four-in-one universal adapter, and plugged it in. The Haas-Krämer hummed as its two blue lights flickered on.

Outside, the attorney and aunt glared at him. Smith pressed his ear to the glass, an unnecessary pantomime since he'd had the conference room bugged. A new place this time. Balancing on a chair, Hunter magnified his height advantage by placing one foot on the Biedermeyer table as he unscrewed the air-conditioning vent and detached the microphone as Smith's face fell. See, how he pretends to be surprised.

Hunter wondered why he himself hadn't taken the trouble to remove it before bringing her inside. To impress her? The thing about an interrogation was, sometimes you forgot which side you were on.

Hunter took his seat. You're looking relaxedly at me, with the perfect blink rate. You are, I must admit, rather sensational. I wish you weren't just another poseur.

"Have you ever been to Geretsreid?"

She shook her head.

"Or Baden-Baden?"

"I left when I was six, so I don't remember much."

His machine's dials looped the loop. Was there such a thing as a perfect lie? "What do you remember of Lucky Lindy?"

When she glanced at the watchers outside the window, he added, "Reaction time is key here. You must respond without delay."

"I never knew such a person. When you think about it, what's so lucky about someone who's fallen to secret assignations and shadow families? It was he who was the imposter, impersonating a hero. He should have been called Skillful Lindy, or Sly Lindy."

Her hands were in repose, open. She carelessly picked up her glass of water, took a drink, and put it down so it no longer blocked the open space between Hunter and herself.

"But of course, you'd have known him as Careu Kent."

"Well, apparently, I didn't know him. What father could have loved his children if he'd never revealed himself to them? At least the Lone Ranger had the decency to wear a mask." Another sip. "Did the Lone Ranger just come to the screen in costume, or are we just supposed to understand he had a life before, some backstory like an accident? Probably a sexual deviant." She reached into her purse and pulled out a blurry, scratched photograph of a tall, balding figure bending over a dark-haired child with a faerie-like intelligence in her eyes. "This is all I have of my father and me."

The dials stalled, then did an aeronautic maneuver not unlike an Immelmann. The machine was just a prop, anyway.

You haven't once touched your hair to adjust it, or moved your glance from mine.

"At least you took the trouble to make up a good lie," Hunter said in Italian. And still, you don't flush. He looked deeply into the deckle-edged Kodak as though he were falling into a mirror. "I'm making a copy of this." Before she could answer, he put it into the photocopier and pushed the button.

As the machine crackled and a light beam danced across the ceiling, she said in a low voice, "That won't damage it further, will it? If you're using it against me, you should have given me a receipt."

"I keep a collection of such things. Even if I haven't determined their authenticity, they're of interest." He removed an envelope from inside his pocket. "Look, I like you, but we don't have much time. I have a cashier's check for 50,000 francs, along with a release. If you sign the release, foreswearing any further attempts or claims to descent from Col. Lindbergh, the money is yours. You'll walk out of here a rich woman. Otherwise, this process could take…years. You won't have to worry about the wrinkles on the photograph then."

"You don't believe my aunt's story, do you? How large the American family's fortune, and how small of them to doubt me. Obviously, there's credibility to my claim or you wouldn't be offering this. Are you concerned that maybe you'll never be able to prove I'm not his daughter? Is this just about the headlines: 'The Lindbergh Anastasia'?"

"That'll be good for about fifteen minutes. The thing about Anastasia was, the Bolsheviks made sure her dental records were lost so no real princess could turn up with a verifiable claim. In your case, there's no evidence you ever existed, so there are no dental records to destroy. But there is blood work. It's that easy. There is no match."

When he reached into his valise to pull out a file, she looked at him a moment and then began to sign. "Smart girl," he said and handed her the check. He shook her hand, surprisingly warm, and waved the others in. "The results of the test were inconclusive. I am most sorry I can't confirm this young lady as a matter of legal responsibility." He turned to her. "I know this must be disappointing for you and your aunt, and I haven't the slightest doubt that she is absolutely convinced she is telling the truth. I am grateful you've taken the sensible course toward settlement, and in all candor, it's better for you in the end if you truly aren't related to Mr. Lindbergh, because anyone deserves a better father. He was a big man, but the smallest family men."

"No editorializing is called for," Smith said.

The aunt gave him a funny smile. "After he married my sister, Herr Lindbergh told me that when he was young, he used to barnstorm. To drum up interest, he'd visit a village and fly over the *platz*. Then he'd push a straw 'man' from his *flugzeug* so the crowds below would think someone had fallen. It whetted their taste for blood."

For a flash Hunter thought of Manfred.

"We're done here," Smith said. "I thank you all for coming."

Hunter walked to the window and scratched his sandy crew cut, shifting his weight as though seeking balanced flight in a rudderless universe. It was now nearly noon. People were walking quickly; cafes rose from the sidewalks. Looking down, he saw the lawyer and the aunt enter a waiting car without Pia. Skipping the elevator, he ran down the stairs and chopped through the lobby, scanning. He spotted her retrieving a faux mink jacket from the coat check and caught her with her hand on the door.

"Can I interest you in lunch, Pia?"

"Are you for real?"

Hunter watched her flush and look at him hard, her disturbing eyes boring into his skull. She lifted her chin. She was an orphan like himself. That train had killed *both* her parents. He still wasn't sure what happened to his. According to his research, she'd done some acting in Valle d'Aosta, though she'd trained as a musician. What would it be like just to close your eyes and fall into that hair.

"You're still scoping me out?" Pia said. "If you're so sure you've undone me, why follow me? What do you get, a loser's fee? What a way to make a living. What kind of man wants to go out with someone he's convinced is a liar?"

"Better the liar you know," Hunter said.

Chapter 3

West Berlin, Federal Republic of Germany

One peek is worth a thousand instrument cross-checks.

THERE WERE SEVEN Cuban restaurants in West Berlin, but once you knew your way around only one was worth the trouble. Since it was a Tuesday, he and Pia might just slip in for a bite at Havana Sexy, the best of the dives.

He grasped the door handle, vibrating with tango music from within.

Same old waiter, the leering cod. Already yelling 'La Tropical!' to the barkeep as the door wheezed shut behind them. At least he kept his mouth shut as he led the way to the last booth on the left, stepping silently past the tankful of shellfish. In the dusty painting below the black lights, a solitary skier in a gaucho hat stared from his Alpine mountaintop, surveying the savage beauty of the gorge below. *Strength through Joy.*

The waiter placed the beer in front of Hunter. Pen poised over pad, he turned to Pia. "And for the lady?"

"You might want to try the *canchachara*," Hunter said.

"I might," Pia said.

She turned to the waiter. "Daiquiri, please."

When the waiter returned with her drink, she surgically resected the blue plastic marlin from it and tossed it on the table. "This is intriguing. I've never been here before." She scanned the menu on the chalkboard.

"This is pretty familiar country to me," Hunter said. He'd forgotten the waiter was still there, waiting.

"She'll have *Langosta a la Cubana*," Hunter said, "served hot over rice."

"I'm allergic to shellfish," Pia said.

"No, you aren't."

The waiter looked from one to the other.

Pia leaned forward. "That's right. You're sure you know everything about me."

"Then what would you like?" Hunter asked.

She addressed the waiter directly. "I'll have the *Langosta a la Cubana*."

"*Ropa Vieja*," Hunter said.

"Anything else?"

"I'll let you know if we want anything more later."

"It's a bit early to be talking about 'we,' isn't it?" Pia took a sip of her drink. "Or are you referring to Lindbergh's first autobiography, *We*? How telling that the 'couple' he's referring to is himself and the *Spirit of St. Louis*."

Hunter couldn't look away. When she opened her eyes she drove straight through him. In a Porche 924, maybe? She veered and accelerated, navigating a corniche cut deep into the Alps. Then she pulled over, slammed the car door shut, and stepped outside, removing a red and white cellophane-wrapped pack of Lucky Strikes. She shook it in front of him. "You just can't get away from it," she said.

He drained half his beer without either of them speaking, or needing to speak. What was true for flying was true about life. Any pilot knew the descending order of priority was *aviate, navigate, communicate.*

"Why did you really invite me here?" she asked. "Don't tell me you have more questions."

"Why'd you sign the papers?"

She exhaled. "Because…I was ashamed of myself."

"That proves it. Shame is not a Lindbergh trait."

"For the me who just wanted the money." She batted her eyes and slipped into a stage persona. "But the real reason is, I just wanted a chance to meet you."

Hunter realized he wished this lie were true. What had gotten into him? "You know, you really are a good actress."

"You already know that."

"You're free of Lindbergh. Do you know what that's worth?"

"It doesn't solve my daddy issues." She looked him right in the eye.

"You're still working with the independent film?" he asked, though he knew she knew he knew the answer. In her lamentable underground farce *Deutscher Tabakgegner*, young people dodged bullets racing up dizzy stairways while trying to ban tobacco in Germany against a government conspiracy bent on promoting smoking, for the tax revenues. In the chase scene, hapless suits (dressed, unfortunately, like Hunter himself) fired automatic weapons at the Pia character while two long-haired Greenpeacers assisted her in winding her way through an endless glass building. Cut to the next morning with all three of the young bohemians waking up together (shockingly) before going out for their loathsome jogging, taking deep draughts of young, muscular air.

Hunter allowed his eyes to take in her slender form, her inky eye shadows direct from Bertolt Brecht and the *Neue Sachlichkeit* movement. *Du bist sexy.* 'Sexy' was German slang long before it ever became English.

"I saw you lurking about our set last week," she said. "Before you were you."

"What's your movie about?"

"Must everything be about something?"

The lobster tails were bright red, curled, hot. "Oh!" she said. "I didn't think the ghost pepper would be so intense."

"It transforms anything it touches."

"This is so. I don't think I've ever had Cuban food I've enjoyed so much."

"You haven't," Hunter said.

He idly turned over the top card of the illustrated pack that decorated every table and put it down quickly. He wondered if Pia had seen him glance at it.

AS THEY LEFT the restaurant, they passed a gentleman in black. The specter seemed elderly but strangely erect, as though recalling an earlier life where military bearing was demanded. He lifted his umbrella, tipped his hat, and bowed, clicking his heels the way the aristocratic Prussians did in the Great Before. Was he really there or had Hunter just imagined him?

"Do you know that man?" Pia asked. "He seems to know you."

"No."

Hunter hadn't known him in Bonn, Frankfurt, or Munich, either. But this ghost of a ghost still tickled somewhere in his memory's memory. Though they'd never met, he sensed—what can one sense about a bum you'd just pass by on the street—he'd always been watching him, since boyhood. From out of the corner of his mind he'd seen him, in dreams. What could they mean? Could Pia tell this fellow was carrying a pistol? For that matter, had she seen his own? His jacket might very naturally have fallen open while he was plugging in the Haas-Krämer. For the first time in a long time, Hunter felt uncomfortable that someone might have seen his weapon.

The *òrìṣà* spirit card had whispered bad news. It was the Nine of Air.

"You know, all of a sudden, I'm feeling jet-lagged," Hunter said. "I'll walk you to the train."

Chapter 4

Flughafen Berlin-Tempelhof, West Berlin

If you push the stick forward, the houses get bigger.

T HE NEXT MORNING, aboard an executive charter, Hunter sipped his scalding coffee and willed himself to get a grip. He couldn't keep his mind off the events of the day before, even though Smith had seemed perfectly satisfied. The Mirage turbofan hummed. As the jet eased toward the takeoff runway, the stew (Hunter knew better than to call her that) ran through her safety instructions.

"Ladies and Gentlemen, welcome aboard our flight from New York to Paris. Please make sure that all carry-on items are stowed either in an overhead compartment or completely beneath the seat in front of you. If you are seated in an emergency exit row…" She pantomimed a landing over the sea, gently swinging two fingers down.

She brushed a yellow oxygen mask, tubes drooping, in front of her face, a plastic effigy of sex. How routine it had all become; there were no more Lindberghs to render it holy. Her captive audience was bored with the miracle of aviation. At least she managed to surprise him when she delivered orange juice in a real glass. It stared up at him from his seatback tray.

Landing at Charles De Gaulle Airport was calming. In the blinking sunshine he debouched at Orly, checked into Hôtel de Crillon, and hurried to Vitry-sur-Seine. This was the morning light painters loved best, softly warming the budding sycamores along the river. The elevator in the Beaux Arts *gratte-ciel* lifted him gently to the executive floor.

All this paneling, the music a cover. If everything's carpeted, aren't we all sneaking up on each other? Not that it mattered much here. Some debunking cases were high stakes. From what he'd seen of the file, this encounter was more of an *amuse-bouche*.

Swinging into the office of Beringer, Sauvage, and Tremble, attorneys at law, he smiled to see Toulos Verdere lower his reading glasses.

"Hello, Yankee," Verdere said. "Give me some skin."

"Moulting again?" Hunter asked. "I didn't know you shed this time of year."

Dark leather chairs, black walnut paneling. Another law office where nothing changed, even through two World Wars and an occupation. The only updates to the décor were an African Campaign snake-bite kit in its original green pouch below signed photographs of writer Michel Butor, cigarette dangling precariously from his lower lip, and Rudy Guernreich cupping the sharp elbow of a starving model in a monokini. No doubt these deliberate additions were secret signals to impress entertainment clients. Beringer, Sauvage specialized in the fabulously undead.

"You've brought the machine?" Verdere asked, looking at Hunter's briefcase. "I do so like the machine."

"You Parisians give me the crepes," Hunter said.

Two minutes later the Haas-Krämer had its two blue lights on. Outside the window a barge pushed its way down the misty Seine, following the curve toward where the Eiffel Tower ought to have been. Had someone moved it? You'd think you had a glimpse of it, then you'd turn around in your car and find it was following you. For now, its presence was only theoretical.

He watched as a tall blonde clipped in, accompanied by a white-haired consul in grave cravat, wringing his hands.

"This is Mr. Dauger," Verdere said.

"Rica Chanel," the woman said, extending her hand for a kiss.

"Yes, of course," Hunter said. "Is it miss? Please take a seat over here." He waved the consul away.

"Interesting you're wearing Guerlain if you're Coco's granddaughter," Hunter said to the claimant. "Eau de Joy."

"It was on sale. Chanel never is."

"Never?"

She smiled. "So how do we do this?"

"Let's start by your describing a goatee for me."

She frowned.

"You know," Hunter said. "A Van Dyke."

She straightened. "You mean a Mandyke. Where are you going with this?"

"Sometimes a slip is just a slip," Hunter said. "But you must hurry. Reaction time is important to me.

"Me, too," she said. "Doesn't a slip also hide something that is meant to engage?" She drew her fingers along her chin, pulling forward. "A Van Dyke–it grows out here."

Hunter made a jot into his notebook. "A liar, that is, one who misrepresents, often exaggerates with gestures."

Her hand dropped to the table.

"Also, anyone who isn't a liar." Hunter went on with his scribbles.

"For my next trick, I'll describe a spiral staircase," she said. "Is this going anywhere, because I haven't had breakfast yet."

"Then I'm all for an early lunch." Hunter stood up abruptly, unplugged the cord of his machine, coiled it, and stuffed his notebook into his valise. He lifted his voice. "Someplace with a good view?"

"Another insult," she said. "No, no, let's get on with it. Since we're both here."

"As you wish, mademoiselle," Hunter said. "And if you listen attentively, I know a way to secure a great amount of money for you." This was all too easy. He had three endorsed *cheques* in his bag; without a doubt this interrogatee was going to accept the first offer (barely enough to cover pommes frites and steak au poivre).

"You know," Hunter said, "the funniest thing happened to me on the way here from Deutschland." With the Haas-Krämer back online, he scanned the dials and recorded peak amplitudes when she put her chin on her hand, then faked a smile. "Call it a presentiment." He leaned forward, doubled his eye contact. "I want you to know that somehow, someway, I knew this would happen. Are you ready to hear what I have to say?"

"It's your machine."

"When I checked out of the hotel in West Berlin, a Filipina woman was at the desk. An Indian taxi driver took me to the airport. At the counter, an Arab took my ticket and showed me to the concourse. I flew to Paris. An Arab airline agent welcomed me. An Indian taxi driver drove me to the hotel, where a Filipino clerk checked me in. I thought, wait a minute. I didn't have to take this trip for this to happen. I might as well have stayed in West Berlin. My reality was turned inside out, like I'd disappeared into the beveled edge of a mirror. Maybe, like you, I didn't exist at all."

A nasty smile. "Maybe you disappeared entirely. You're the invisible man."

"I wouldn't want to play the Invisible Man. If you do a good job on the show and hold out for more money, the producer says, 'I'll just get another invisible man.' Just like you aren't the granddaughter of Gabrielle Chanel at all. You weren't born anybody's daughter." Hunter took a deep breath and picked up his notes. "Raoul Morgandraz, Algerine. At twelve, you ran away to Cairo. They took you in at The Dar al Areej orphanage in the El Tawoon section of Giza, but instead of making good, all you learned there was deception. It was there you crossed that final line and one hundred percent of the time dressed as a woman, maybe your true self but an imposter to the bones."

"Actually, that was my first step into the truth," Morgandraz said. She probably didn't realize she was snarling.

Hunter thrust his hand into his valise, reached past the book he was halfway through, and slapped a thick folder in front of the pretender, who stared at it in dumb fascination. Forgotten doctors' appointments, laundry tags, traffic tickets, an orange citation in condemnation of her dance as an "*affreuse juive*" slave girl in front of open windows for the Royal Scots Dragoon Guards. When a blue passport damp with the past rose from the packet and hovered in the air, the transpontine seized it.

"I've been looking everywhere for this," she said. "Where did you get this?"

"A friend of mine on the police force recovered it from a strip-club robbery," Hunter said. "I thought you could use it."

"I've been looking everywhere for this. Not having it cost me three nights in the nick. They called me a vagrant and shipped me out to Sidi bel Abbes."

Hunter nodded. "It was there you became a lady of the evening. For a time, you impersonated the lost Englishwoman Mordessa Soules, countess of Camaryon …" *A gentleman in black keeps following you, though you don't know who he is. And you're becoming involved with an imposter when that's a very dangerous thing to do. This girl Pia is creeping into your every thought.*

"You mentioned there might be an honorarium," Morgandraz said.

"Yes, 10 francs for a more suitable blouse. Sadly, that isn't real Chanel, either."

Chapter 5

Geneva, Switzerland

No matter what else happens, fly the damn plane.

I T HAD BEEN a productive month. There was enough money showing in the bankbook that Hunter felt he'd earned some time off to pursue his hobby. Taking the high road, he looked outside his driver's-side window–Lake Geneva raced the other way. High above the slash of blue were the Alps, lofty in the fog like Supreme Court justices. Downshifting, he curled into a narrow road lined with paranoiac buildings and entered a hamlet in Vaud.

Of all the cantons in Switzerland, Vaud was the most eccentric–every window a set of crystal-clear eyes. All the inhabitants, even the domestic animals, maintained the same opaque expression, an orderly degeneracy he'd always found comforting because it never changed.

At 55, Lindbergh chose one of its bijou towns, La Tour de Peitz, as a sexual hideout. His mind was bicameral, divided between the world he knew and the world he dared himself to enter–a trait he shared with Thomas Jefferson.

One side was filled with sycophants and the *Spirit of St. Louis*. The other was moist and indiscreet, unscheduled, consequences be damned. Say you were Lindbergh in 1961. Hell, you'd made it, hadn't you, but you had no private life to call your own. Once you'd accepted the Service Cross of the German Eagle from Hermann Goering (the four swastikas decorating it enhancing the misunderstanding), you were suddenly deemed and doomed a Nazi in the U.S. Putting 'America First' didn't have to mean you were giving aid and comfort to the enemy. Never mind the force from inside your own country that climbed up that ladder, reached through the darkness, and stole your first-born son. After that, you owed nothing to Roosevelt's Amerika. Dr. Alexis Carrel, the genius, the Nobel laureate, your partner in invention, had told you Switzerland was freedom in a skirt. Imagine the relief of slipping through the world anonymously, ripping through lesser peoples' moralities like the *Übermensch*, Nietsche's Superman, in search of the next Lois Lane.

His private research sliding into obsession, Hunter had sought out a Pan Am inflight menu bearing Lindbergh's signature and picked it up at auction, a steal because it was marred, according to the catalog, by "a mark where Scotch tape was removed." What he'd really been after was the single sheet of blue stationery folded inside. Dated December 20, 1969, it was enlivened by the shy handwriting of a young woman who'd had a flier for the flyer:

"I was working as a Pan Am stewardess in first class on a flight to Frankfurt when Mr. Lindbergh, who was on our board of directors at that time, voluntarily signed postcards and menus for all the crew members. I watched him signing them. He was very gracious and friendly. During the flight he showed me his cockpit pass so I could let him in with my key. When he exited, I happened to be sitting on the jump seat and he sat down beside me, and he asked my opinion about what I thought Pan Am could do to improve conditions between management and crewmembers. I was fortunate enough to have him as a passenger twice on this Frankfurt flight."

Once in the powder room and once in the Ritter Hotel.

It took no time at all for Hunter to track the stewardess down to a gated subdivision in West Hartford, Connecticut, all white and disturbingly so ("It's better not to drive through *East* Hartford," she'd whispered on the phone) and prime her with questions to discover elements of her encounter with Lindbergh. During Hunter's last vacation in Germany, he'd checked into the Ritter in the guise of a traveling executive for Merck. The hotel's brochure had proclaimed "Seventeenth-century charm amid the half timbers of Frankfurt's *Alt Sachsenhausen* district, with all the modern conveniences that the discerning traveler requires." Happily, hoteliers love their guest books as a shameless form of advertising, though Hunter knew he had to be on guard as there was no code against counterfeit celebrity signatures. But there it was, darkened by time, the instantly recognizable, tellingly childish scrawl "Careu Kent." How many guest books had Lindbergh signed like this? The silly cover name was a conflation of Dr. Carrel's surname and Superman's latent alter ego, Clark Kent. His Yankee fame repressed during the act of seduction, the Eagle was free to expose his silk cape and fly over the dismal cities bombed to brick-stacked silence during World War II. Was Lindbergh aware he was doing this, or was it a psychotic break from reality?

Hunter had booked the same mini suite where Lindbergh and the stewardess stayed, No. 312. No, thirteen years later, the couple had left no clues. What nonplussed Hunter about the Ritter was, none of the beds had headboards, the result a headlessness to the whole establishment. In the arms of Morpheus, he'd fallen headlong into a nightmare: Lindbergh and his stew of the moment sitting knee-to-knee in the cockpit of a Boeing 707, sharing their private drink–a Seagram's 7 & 7–with both their heads raggedly decapitated. Spouting blood. Which didn't stand up to scrutiny, like so many dreams, because how could you sip something if you don't have the cardinal advantage of a head? No doubt Lindbergh had come by his predilection for Seagram's after chumming around with Joe Kennedy before the War, serving as British Ambassador.

HUNGRY, HUNTER PARKED in front of the Vaud Inn, strode through the lobby, and slipped down to the rathskellar.

"Would you like a beer, sir?" the St. Pauli girl asked in brisk English, her blue eyes the same shade as the lake. What, had he dreamed her up, too?

His first wife had dressed up as a St. Pauli girl once for Halloween on Long Island. A world away. "Did you learn to speak like that in the international school?"

"Yes, Mr. Cliburn. I blush to tell you, my mother saw you in 1958, in Frankfurt, after you won the Tchaikovsky competition."

This is the way the human mind works. You're tall, you're American, you look importantly familiar, you have slightly sandy, curly hair. Here among the cuckoo clocks, there's an alienating shock to you. So naturally you're Van Cliburn.

"Was that at the *Alte Oper*?" Hunter asked, warming to a smile.

"Yes!" the waitress said. Stumbling, she threw in a curtsy. She stared into his eyes as though searching for the young pianist, though it was her mother, and not she, who had seen him. Fascination once removed. "You do remember..."

"Oh, no, I'm sorry, miss. It's simply a case of mistaken identity. I'm not Van Cliburn. I could prove this to you very quickly. Have you a piano?"

"Are you pulling my leg, Mr. Cliburn?" With a laugh, she hiked her skirt to show her knee. "Everyone's entitled to his privacy, but some people go too far."

"No," he said. "I should have spoken sooner." Attack privacy. But this was getting interesting. She no doubt mentioned her leg in order to draw his attention to it. A lot of the younger girls weren't wearing slips anymore. He was reassured to know she was.

"I'd like some Glann ar Mor," he said, Swiss law having outlawed Swiss whiskey. "Barely an inch–just enough to add some color to the water. And the *table d'hote*."

When he turned to look at his newspaper, she grew more bold, increasing her eye contact and admonishing him with a tap on the wrist. Maybe she'd known all along he couldn't tickle the ivories.

Neither was she too discouraging when she visited his table too often and too many times picked up his glass as though to gauge if he needed a refill.

"What's your name?" Van Cliburn said finally. If you're not careful, you'll start to believe in your own lies.

"Maude."

"Maude from Vaud. Can you wink, blink, and nod?"

Before long she'd pulled up a chair in the jump seat beside him. So, Lindbergh's trick actually worked. Let your quarry come to you. Make sure to take the shallowest of interest in people, however humble their lot in life, to learn how they behave in their element. Talk frankly with those below your station to find a devastatingly simple way to keep yourself down to earth. Or attract prey.

Lindbergh had written another letter that Hunter now had in his private collection. Accounting for a fortnight's disappearance, the aviator mused, "I don't require entertainment. I am primarily interested in people's routine ways of life–more the ordinary than the spectacular."

For all Hunter knew, this waitress was yet another of Lindy's daughters.

"As for who I am, keep it dark, won't you?" Lindbergh finished. "You don't get to know soldiers if you have stars on your shoulders when you meet them." Not bad for a guy who's barking mad. They should have locked him in a room and thrown away the room.

The next morning, Hunter descended the stairs to the rathskeller, sat at the same table, and savored a plate of fried red tomatoes, eggs, and Tête de Moine cheese.

Where was the gentleman in black, or Maud for that matter? No time to think about that now. He walked out to his rental car, gray as a dove's wing, got in, and read a French newspaper. The world started to move again outside his window.

He drove slowly to the International School, Les Monts-de-Corsier. Wealthy wards in uniforms played outside, drowsy with recess. An intent blonde girl walked alone past them and sat under a tree. Hunter took a few notes, then pulled out his Pentax. Whenever he hit the shutter, it was so loud it felt like a grenade going off.

"Sir, you're not supposed to take photographs of the children," said a voice behind a rake. Hunter didn't even bother to turn around.

"I'm not on school property." This, by the way, was not a guess. He'd looked into the lot lines. With a shrug, the groundskeeper moved on.

When he was a Navy attaché with the Diplomatic Corps a dozen years earlier, he'd bumped into camera-shy Kenyans at the Nyali Beach Hotel in Mombasa. When he'd swung the lens toward their eyes, they'd murmured and ducked, sure their spirits would be trapped in the silver box if they didn't dance away before his shutter clicked. Or so they professed. But this Swiss miss took her fame with more equanimity. In fact, she turned directly toward him and stared. Far from feeling strange about it, it was as if she knew his lens was trained on her. As if, instead, she were taking pictures of him.

He kept snapping. She opened a book, then put it down and started on another. She tucked a golden strand of hair behind her ear. After a few moments, she looked up.

"You might be a perv," she called out. "Tell me, are you a perv?"

"An enlightened question," Hunter said. "Young people are cruel geniuses at making the rest of us irrelevant. If you have a problem with people watching you, don't stay out in the open."

"I knew it," she said. "A perv."

HUNTER ARRIVED at the Beau at dusk, just as the lights were coming on. Walking through the lobby to his usual suite, he nodded to the ghost of Noël Coward. For over a century, the Beau-Rivage Palace in Lausanne-Ouchy was a favorite of the notorious and noted seeking camaraderie and shelter. Mussolini, Dietrich, Chaplin, Garbo, and Princess Gortchakov had touched down here. In brooding exile young King Michael of Romania had been regent du jour after the War. Depending on the night or the light you might see the shades of Pablo Picasso; Somerset Maugham; the Aga Kahn; CIA director Alan Dulles; and Alonzo XIII, King of Spain. Freddie Mercury.

Taking the private elevator to his rooms, Hunter set his valise down for the invisible attendant to unpack and walked to the balcony. The ink beyond his porch rail disappeared into nothingness until it regained focus as sparkles on the far side of the lake. The easiest way to enter the spirit world this time of day was through cognac–a sip of Pierre Ferrand Ancestrale at $735 a snifter and then the lucid dream that he was watching a couple in a boat halfway across the lake; he could see the lights. Two figures, center stage, with shotguns. Hunting at night? He heard but did not see a flock of wild ducks flapping up from the water.

For an instant the racket rushed his hotel, banked along the façade, and disappeared.

Hunter brushed his teeth, slipped into bed, and drifted back into his book, short stories by Luritz Kahn. Kahn drowned in Lake Geneva. The authorities had dragged the lake with a rusty hook to recover the suicide, but Kahn perplexed investigators by shooting himself after he drowned. In the story Hunter was reading, a writer was in the clutches of a vignette that had somehow come alive and begun to write itself. Each morning the hero would wake to find a new chapter rolled into his typewriter more frightening than anything he could have imagined. Was somebody stealing in while he was asleep to write the new material?

What a waste of time ghosts were. Grab hold of a ghost and pretty soon you were looking in the mirror. Hunter kept reading. Recklessly, the story dropped its hero into a sleek Graf & Stift convertible careening unseen through the woods. A sensuous traveler rode shotgun in the passenger seat, her face out of view.

Chapter 6

West Berlin, West Germany

Pilots without fuel become pedestrians.

THREE DAYS LATER Hunter stirred, lifted his eyelids, and woke from the flowered chaise in Pia's tiny flat in Prenzlauer Berg, West Berlin, where he'd waited. He picked up his glasses from a side table that held a framed snapshot of Pia in one of those self-belted, untailored shirt dresses that were dragging all of Europe into a state of general slovenliness. A brass Peace-sign brooch.

The latch rattled. The bolt slid open. Framed in the doorway, Pia stared at him. Her eyes widened.

"Hi." He stood to greet her.

"You again. You Yanks, with your 'hi.' Well, at least you're not the Stasi. What's so hi?"

"From the looks of things, you are."

"How funny, your showing after all this time."

"Pia, you never answered my postcard."

"Who sends a postcard of Copenhagen that plays like a record?"

"For your information, it's the national anthem."

"Well, what now, doubting Thomas?"

"Please, call me Hunter." How young she was. Too young. "Do you even know who doubting Thomas was?"

When she walked to him, he grew even taller. Now he was a full six foot seven, towering over her.

"Spoken like a true seminarian," she said.

She wore a turtleneck, black capris, and black flats. The capris did not inspire surety, if only because of their intermediacy. Neither were they full length slacks nor cutesy shorts. No matter how good they looked on her, and they looked unforgivably good on her, there was something duplicitous about an incomplete garment. A lie, a true 'fabrication.'

He nodded to the battered piano in the corner. It shifted to the left and glared at him. "Do you play often?"

She walked into her closet kitchen outfitted as a galley, bereft of Norwegian wood. Two glasses of Dubonnet. "Drink some of this and I'll play for you."

"Play the Chopin. I like it best."

A quick inhale. "Where did you catch my show? Were you stalking me?"

More than two dozen times, in a dozen dives (he always chose the table in the shadows, next to the gentleman in black) and outside her window in the dark. Research and stalking were one and the same. He was a shrub. *How do you do. Shrub here.* He was background, outside the lights. She'd finish brushing her hair, and then she'd slip into the Chinese gown with the dark blue trim and wrap it tightly under her chin. She'd flip through the sheet music, crease open a page, change her mind, and close the book. She'd dissolve into memory. Slowly Chopin's first nocturne, the sexy one, would take shape and set the room in motion. Maybe she sensed his watching, or had he crossed some line where the hunter became the hunted, and she was drawing him in.

"No big deal. Don't play it, then," he said.

But she slipped back into the nocturne, deeply and richly, while Hunter closed his eyes. Abruptly she stopped, shattering the illusion of a domestic tableau. "I don't have to be a private investigator to know you've been married before."

"Do you really want to hear this? Dido entered my life out of nowhere, like the song, but she only stayed through two verses."

"The joker of serious things," Pia said. "I'm the investigator here. So go on."

"One night I was playing craps at the Casino Across the Sound on Long Island, and Dido was holding up a slot machine. We were both winning. *Voila*. Pretty soon she and I were celebrating our winnings in our birthday suits."

"So, you picked your wife up in a bar. Bullshit. Tell me what really happened."

"It's un-happened," Hunter said. "It was a long time ago."

She drew closer, a little shadow. "Dido was a fool."

He studied her for a minute and decided to take a chance. "We were just about your age when we met. A buddy from my Navy days and I started a charter company; I was a private pilot."

"How private?"

"We flew out of MacArthur Airport in Islip. My wife worked in the tower at Martha's Vineyard, whispering about glide slopes on the UHF. I fell in love with her voice before I met her. I flew toward it like a homing pigeon but never found her at the end of the wireless. Then one time I was filing for an instrument flight plan at the tower, and I heard that voice again." He shrugged. "She'd been reassigned to flight planning at my home base. I heard her behind the counter and walked toward the voice. I asked her out."

"So, she was an actress, too."

He closed his eyes. "You could say that. There was only one Cuban restaurant in my part of Long Island. I didn't have much choice. I remember the muffler on my car was almost falling off. We came in low and loud."

Pia reached quickly and touched his shoulder. "I'm sorry. You're still in love with her. But she isn't alive, is she?"

"What makes you say that?" He'd stopped searching for Dido ten years before, but she'd slipped away long before that.

"As little as I know you, I have the sense you could never let anyone go."

She flushed, then brightened barely a second later. He noticed her eyes were strangely unfocused. What would the young ones do without their drugs. But with proper guidance, you can kick them. She stepped back gently when she caught him looking at her pupils. Then she raised her voice, so very Dido-like.

"People shouldn't be allowed to get…as controlling as you."

The way she stood, like a bow being slowly drawn, with those thin strong arms. The way she walked, just the way Dido, irradiated with her own youth, used to walk. Is that what this was all really about? The way she drew closer. The way she lifted her chin, kissed him. Environmental theater.

She reached around him and drained her glass. Then she started to pull her turtleneck over her head. He caught her shoulder.

"Hold on," Hunter said. "We don't really know each other."

"That makes one of us," she said.

"Let's start this evening again. We can go out and get some dinner." Then, if you want to invite me back, it's off my conscience. I won't have broken in. I won't have intimidated you into aggressiveness. We'll be like two children, with no one the wiser for it. We'll pull the darkness over our heads, skin divers in the night.

"You perv," she said. "Well, at least it's a free meal." She shook out that hair. "Take two."

"I'll drive. I hope you don't mind, but you probably will," Hunter said and reached behind a chair to produce a red TWA inflight travel tote. "I've packed for you."

"Where are you taking me?"

"Switzerland."

"Whatever."

As they sped through the darkness, Pia examined the contents of her bag. "I won't wear Shalimar. Dido's, right? Now I get it." She held out a sheer garment. "I should be able to get a few marks for this at the flea." A throaty laugh. "And Pepsodent. You'll wonder where the yellow went."

"A universal sentiment."

"You like to stay ahead of people. So, you'd know I only use baking soda. Haven't you dissected me enough?"

"I'll celebrate and protect you."

"Well, there's a motto–for a Central American police force. Isn't it you I need protection from? I think you're insane."

"Can't you just relax and have a good time? It's Friday night. We'll have you back from Vaud by Monday morning."

"Did you bring your little box?"

"I never travel without my box."

"Oh, great," Pia said. "Because I have some questions for you. What are you really after?"

"You're the unexpected."

"How old are you?" she asked.

"In some parts of the world, I'm still age-appropriate enough to be your boyfriend. Except I have a file on your boyfriend." Hunter leaned back and looked at her. "I'm fifty."

"Radu is not my boyfriend. We met on the set of *Death under Glace*. I mean, we're not…" She reached inside her TWA bag, unable to find the bottom.

AT THE BORDER, the guard scuffled through Hunter's papers until he hit one that appeared to be white hot. He put his reading glasses on to consider it more acutely. Then he picked up a telephone, speaking quickly. Slowly he smiled. When he handed the documents back, he snapped a salute.

"Who *are* you?" Pia asked.

"I am the Hunter Gracchus."

The road was dark with curves. In a sense, the road was driving the car. Slowly they climbed to a higher altitude. Black mountains folded into higher, snowy peaks. From up here, he could see Vufflens-le-Chateau, where he'd once dined with the so-called 'great grandson' of Ferdinand de Saussure, who'd died here in 1913. Before after-dinner coffee he'd guided the scruffy imposter to the wisdom of accepting the usual settlement (somewhere below .1 percent of the potential loss–Hunter's take was twenty) in exchange for dropping his claim.

"Hear that? Geese are on the wing," Hunter said.

"I don't see anything," Pia said.

"You can't see them, but they're over the top of the car. Flying in perfect formation just above the clouds."

Maybe it was Hunter who'd slipped away, not Dido. To what extent had her…vanishment determined who he was today? Even his own partner had stopped looking him in the eye. In the numinous eight-ball where his fortunes were suspended, inky with black liquid recording fluid, what had summoned the word "formation" just now? Was it the girl, so Dido-like, the geese, so Navy-like?

"What's with you and Switzerland?" Pia said. "I've never trusted it. One part of Switzerland thinks it's Germany, the other Italy, the rest of it's convinced it's

France. It's like you, Hunter. There is no you." She paused. "Welcome to the club."

Chapter 7

Lausanne, Switzerland

A check ride should be short enough to be interesting, but still long enough to cover everything.

HUNTER WATCHED PIA open the French door to the balcony to feel the *geist* of Lake Geneva rush in. With unconscious sexiness she stretched and walked to the rail, unaware of all the other girls mirroring her action past and future. She may have sensed she resembled Dido, but she was different than anyone he'd ever met. Maybe it was better she lived in the moment. Otherwise, she might wind up remembering things that never happened. As he did.

"What's over there?" she asked.

Beyond the black nothingness was a twinkle of lights. So indistinct were they, they emphasized the reality of this rail, this girl, right now.

"How often do you stay here, Hunter?"

"You should know, I have bit of a psychic connection. A place like this just sort of feeds into it. Top of that, I like the food." Hotel Beau Rivage wasn't just a Bermuda

Triangle for disappearing chaps from the 1930s, or polite corpses fathoms deep, for that matter. "Since Lausanne is the capital for all people running away from something, it's a center for international fusion food–black truffle wanton."

She looked up from the menu. "Anything Caribbean?"

"The sous chef here used to work at La Bodeguita Medio in Old Havana," Hunter said. "But let's try something different tonight."

He pushed the annunciator and drifted into French. "Hello. Just for a few days. Two of us. We'll have champagne cocktails and the bitter salad. For dessert, burnt orange."

Pia stood on tiptoe to pull out a copy of *Lady of the Lake*. She flipped through the pages so quickly she created a little breeze.

"A Scottish delicacy," Hunter said. "Rare is the orange tree in Scotland, so when the ships began to import them, a cult following started. They marinated the fruit, decocting to magnify its taste times three." His focus dropped to her lower lip. "Bitter, but somehow better. An orange fetish, to my way of thinking."

"So, they set them on fire?"

Was it possible he had a separate awareness, a separate self that existed only if she were staring at him? He tried to swallow without letting her see he was doing it. For a while they said nothing. It was half past midnight by the time the white table was wheeled to the loge. Wind lifted the corners of the tablecloth. "How's the new movie going?" he asked. She seemed to hold her answer until the waiter, her age, touched his match to the blue phantom hovering over their oranges and left.

"*Wet behind the Years.* That's where I got this black bra." She peeked inside her shirt to see if it were still there. To make sure, she unbuttoned her top button.

"It takes a leap to see you in vacation bible school," Hunter said.

"*Au contraire*, I play the chaperone." She grinned. "You'd like my black glasses."

"There are no chaperones at vacation bible school."

"And you would know this…how?" She lowered her voice. "Who's the expert now?"

He flashed back to the blonde imp at the International School. What the hell was he doing? He speared an orange and mixed it with the lettuce.

"Radu has set it in the American South," she said.

"He's quite a rascal, your Radu." The coffee smelled good. He poured some into his cup. Then he spilled the cream into the black and watched it turn into phantasms before stirring it. It looked so lovely he feared he might disappear into it.

"He says it has a certain 'otherness' to it."

Hunter said nothing.

"Just when the girls are innocently comparing their bodies, there's a 'disjuncture,'" she said, half becoming the voice of Radu as his diction slid inside her. "An interruption. In which one of your American skunks sprays the church dog. Astonished, the girls rise from bed half-dressed and try to clean him with tomato juice. Then I come in, my robe half open. My remedy is to take Snickers out into the snow and rake the snow through his fur with my fingers."

"A Yankee skunk?" Hunter asked. "In winter vacation bible school. Your Radu again?"

"The snow isn't wet; it's like dry-cleaning. Then I come in with the secret solution, Massengill Disposable Douche."

"You may have forgotten, I'm unshockable. I've heard every lie there is," Hunter said.

The lake seemed to be breathing. Hunter peered into its distances. Blue and indigo slipped into purple. "David

Hemmings isn't in this flick, is he?" He stretched. "Is the chaperone ready for bed?"

Pia reached over and touched the back of his hand.

DAWN WAS GREEN RAIN and fog, spectral as it burned away to reveal the sleepy lake. Beside the rail, breakfast awaited. Rashers of bacon, grilled tomatoes, and pineapples. The invisible Serge had brought the German, Swiss, and Italian newspapers and fanned them on the table, too, along with a gym bag half spilling over with Hunter's mail, stamped gaudily from far-flung ports of call. All of which mattered very little, since Pia was wearing nothing but a bed sheet.

He rubbed his eyes, then opened them quickly. Directly exposed above her left hip was the scrawled curl of a little scorpion. So odd he'd missed the tattoo the night before. "There was no reason for you to defile yourself like that."

"So now you own me?"

While her November 7 birthday made Scorpio her astrological sign, it was insufficient to account for this…impulse.

"Hunter. That was nice last night. But do you never remove your socks?"

"Dido didn't like the socks, either. But she liked it even less when I took them off."

"What are you hiding?"

He unrolled a sock and stuck out his foot.

"Interesting."

"Repulsive, you mean." He fingered the purple membrane that webbed between his toes. "*Syndactyly*. The surgeons said my mother must have smoked during pregnancy. It was much more pronounced before my surgery. It almost kept me out of flight school."

"Does it hurt?" She caressed the knotted scars, then withdrew her hand. "If you can fly, what led you to this line of work?"

"Flying wasn't risky enough for me. And I don't investigate for free."

"Not what I asked," she said gently. "It's just, what do you have against," she ran her hand down her silhouette grandiloquently, "imposters?"

"Actually, I'm fascinated by all of you."

"How many of us do you see?"

He looked behind her, as though counting. "You're coming fast and furious."

She looked at his foot. "Do you have a matched set?"

He put the sock back on. The conversation was over. He reached inside the gym bag and retrieved three days' worth of the Hopewell Township newspaper. He flipped to 'Night Beat' in local news and found the police report: "Possible Burglary Attempt at Highfields Discovered by Caretaker." He'd returned from a Saturday evening church service to find a ladder leaning against the house, the story went.

"What've you got there?" Pia asked.

"It's kind of a crossword puzzle I'm working on," he said. "It has to do with a particular subset of Pretenders. You're not the only imposter who claims to be a Lindbergh. Some are actually convinced they are the kidnapped Lindbergh baby."

Carefully he clipped out the news item, then shifted to the next day's edition and clipped two short letters to the editor related to the ladder. He'd check them out later.

"You'd be crazy to claim you were a dead baby. Wasn't his body discovered, and didn't they execute somebody for his murder?"

Hunter thought back on the deep file he'd put together about the remains of a boy found about six kilometers from the house, in the woods.

The photos weren't flattering. The corpse looked every bit the charred voodoo doll he should have been after six weeks in the woods. The back of its skull was caved in. Small animals had eaten away at its black, leathery skin, which though cold and wet looked smoked. So foolish to kill this golden goose when it might have been worth, by orders of magnitude, dazzlingly more as a ransom. It must have been an accident. The police brought Lindbergh down to identify the remains of his son, and instead of being distraught, he was as calm and objective as if he'd detected a pool of oil under the *Spirit of St. Louis*. He considered the death-scorched figure of his little boy, its rotten silhouette discovered face-down, its jaw and lush lips eaten away. Hi, Daddy. No left hand, no right arm. Wild creatures had rendered it gender-indeterminate, its eyes eaten to the sockets. How the police would admire Lindbergh's cool. He counted its teeth. Perfect. He matched the dirty baby shirt fragment, below which the Eaglet had no heart. The rats had eaten it. There was a sense of the right leg still being visible, though the left had been chewed off below the knee. Lindbergh's eyes flew embarrassedly toward its toes. Twenty-one hours later, he'd mercifully have it cremated before it suffered the further indignity of a forensic autopsy, scattering the ashes. Leave it to the senseless to make sense of things–the dark hordes without wings.

"Each Pretender has his own exotic narrative," Hunter said. "But this isn't very romantic talk, as your Radu might say." He cut one of the grilled tomatoes in half, speared it, and held it toward Pia to eat.

"He's not my Radu," Pia said. "But now that you mention him, I guess this is as good a time as any to tell you he just came in." She looked out the window toward the parking lot.

Hunter sliced another tomato and let his scan drift to the pile of unopened correspondence spilled from Serge's delivery. Though he hadn't seen it the night before, he now noticed the red and blue hash marks of a No. 10 Air Mail envelope from the States. It was over-posted with twenty-year-old Dag Hammarskjöld invert stamps–the more rare because they had no rills.

Hunter already knew what was in the letter. Ned Dauger, his adopted father, would never have permitted one of his precious plate blocks to be used for anything so useful.

A FEW HOURS LATER, Hunter opened the elevator door to the lobby and spotted Pia sitting with Radu. A flash of bright pain traveled up the bridge of his nose, then exploded in the middle of his forehead. Had he imagined all of this? Had he imagined taking her to this hotel? Best to handle this carefully.

With the airmail envelope aflame in his vest pocket, he walked to the couple. Radu stood. Turtleneck, jeans, not even an update of Yevgeny Yevtushenko–just a cheap copy.

"Good to meet you," Hunter said. A quick nod. "How'd you get here?"

"I specialize in coincidences," Radu said.

"Yes, I've seen your films. I mean, what brought you here?"

"A car."

Did "a car" really mean fuck you in Romanian? Hunter knew what "Radu" meant, at least in the Securitate sense. Enemies of the Ceausescus were asked to walk through a room that was filled with radioactive isotopes, code named Radu. A fatal passage. It was a running gag in Bucharest–"Watch out, or they'll introduce you to Radu."

He looked at the director. There was something radioactive about him–he had the air of a postwar mutant. Radu was what they called a Frankie. Frankies, or franks, slid in and out of leather bars in Berlin and Stuttgart where your claim to fame was you had just one testicle. The typical compensation was to carry a Glock .40.

"We were just talking about your American poet Gary Snyder," Pia said.

Radu smiled and adjusted one of his cup sleeves. "I'm sure all of this would just be boring to you."

"You bet. He's barely a poet. In stuff like 'Mid-August at Sourdough Mountain Lookout' he's doing nothing more than recording qualia. Everything else is just," a dismissive wave of the hand, "Apache Marxism."

"You know poetry," Pia said.

"I know Gary Snyder. Through my wife. My specialty is frauds." Hunter fastened his eyes on Radu, who busied himself with lighting a Pall Mall.

"Radu is a friend of Ilie Nastase," Pia said.

"Any friend of Ilie's."

"I love the smell of testosterone in the morning," Pia said.

And there, across the room, was the gentleman in black in the corner, drinking a Pappagallo-colored refreshment. Hunter raised his hand toward his neck, then dropped it. Yes, what if he were making all of this up, if all of his shadows had converged and assumed the lark of this dark spirit. He looked at the man and decided he liked him even less than the first time he didn't see him. "Excuse me," Hunter said.

Radu shrugged.

Hunter walked briskly toward his quarry, who with unhurried style turned round the corner. All the while it was as if the lake outside were watching him. When he reached the corner, he saw the man turn right, step into a shaft of sunlight, and disappear.

Chapter 8

Geneva, Switzerland

Don't drop the aircraft in order to fly the microphone.

THE FLIGHT FROM GENEVA TO LONDON was sapphire with rain, the Seagram's unsettling. Hunter switched planes and landed at Kennedy at twilight. He walked past the hopeful stares of limousine drivers holding signs (you look familiar, are *you* my fare?), bought seven newspapers–everything but the *New York Post*–and rented an invisible silver Jaguar XK-E as he unkeyed the darkness. Leaving Manhattan in his wake, he released himself into Long Island as the turnpike became more dreamy, leading deeper and deeper into his past.

"Why do you do this kind of work?" Pia had asked him.

"People pay me to think about the things that scare them." He hadn't been down this road since he was a kid. Old creosote poles lined the way–had they been here before? Beyond, the Atlantic Ocean opened up ahead of him, stars decapitating the night.

He skirted Roosevelt Field Mall, sparkling with department stores instead of the wing and tail lights of the *Spirit of St. Louis* taxiing for takeoff from New York to Paris; turned right by the old HoJo's; navigated the simplicity of Route 7 along Great South Bay past the unlit mansions and their service roads; descended to sea level below the golf course; and hit the beach.

How can you start humming a tune you don't even like? Somehow, the old foxtrot "When We're Alone" slipped into the car. *"Cuando Estamos Solos."* It was Dido's favorite.

> *Just picture a penthouse way up in the sky,*
>
> *With hinges on chimneys for stars to go by,*
>
> *A sweet slice of heaven for just you and I*
>
> *When we're alone.*

He rolled both windows down and felt the moist salt air burnish the red interior, dampening the burled wood front of the glove case. Waves jumped out of the darkness when the high beams hit them, crashing with light.

> *We'll see life's mad pattern*
> *As we view old Manhattan*
> *Then we can thank our lucky stars*
> *That we're living as we are.*

Dido was five-foot seven with abrupt dark hair she brushed out of her eyes when she was painting. Even friends close to her were so sure she was Italian, but she was *la mitad Cubana.* Her reporter dad had cubbed at the Kansas City Star before making the big move to the Miami Sun Sentinel. Two weeks after he proposed to her mom, a music student at *Universidad de La Habana*, Batista's secret police shot him in the *Plaza Vieja*. As famous for her maroon beauty as for her weapon of choice, the oboe, she followed her lover in death during the birth of their daughter, leaving Dido to grow up with begrudging, inadvertently neglectful relatives in New York.

Dido's subject was Brooklyn, chasing its lost glamour and decay like a war correspondent. Sometimes she'd slip into the city with Lee Krasner and Diane Arbus and disappear into forgotten brownstones and uncharted tenements for days. More like hours. *Your truth is above glide slope, slightly below glide slope, on glide slope.* Why the devil lie to Pia that you met Dido while shooting ground-controlled approaches at MacArthur muni? She was a pilot. To celebrate their engagement, instead of looking at starter homes like their cohorts, they scouted two-seater seaplanes. They bought the sweetest little yellow Piper Cub outfitted with aluminum pontoons. Hunter learned the true meaning of joyride when they took impulsive, stolen picnics along the shore of crystal lakes and made love on the plaid lap blanket spread on pine-needle floors. Dido filled her sketchbook with stylized versions of her little monoplane which she chatted about silk-screening onto the floaty scarves she sold at a friend's boutique. The license suspension she received for substance abuse nine months later crushed both of them because it meant she should no longer take the controls of the *True Love*.

Let's get this straight. If you were a serious painter, you had no manicure. Dido's fingertips were perfumed with turpentine. In spite of the burn (or maybe because of it), she bit her nails bright red to the quick, just as she did everything else.

The night of her first show, when the curious of Amagansett filed into the Stephen Talkhouse ("If it's good enough for the Rolling Stones"), she greeted them in a filmy dress she designed herself for the occasion. At the hem were the silhouettes of forest evergreens. When you looked up, a twilight layer of pink turned to the softest of greens, then blue. The blue darkened to cobalt. Near her neck was midnight blue with a spray of stars. The girl who would disappear was wearing a sunset.

Hunter shadowed her in an invisible blue suit.

"I don't want to speak to them," she said.

"I'm sorry," Hunter said, "but I've talked to Rudy and Mike from the gallery, and they both say you have to. They believe in you like I do–do it for them. Look, now Diane's waving you up."

Dido sold seven of her paintings and two etchings, but when the photographer from the weekly newspaper turned up, she slipped away. Hunter found her at the back of the nightclub kitchen, staring at clean glasses, the rubber-tubing tourniquet having left an angry red ring on her arm.

"Why? You've done so well."

"Then you'd want me to do *more* well. I'd have to come up with more ideas, and then more. Do you know what a death sentence *more* is? And then where would I be?"

He held her that night in bed. "You're still shaking," he said.

"Feel the back of my neck," she said. "I'm perspiring."

It was one of his favorite places. He pushed her hair up, playfully licked the pearly skin below it, and closed his eyes in pleasure, sensing her pulse and inhaling her fragrance. "I love every single part of you," he said. When she didn't answer, he said, "There isn't anything in this world we can't do, if we do it together."

"You don't understand," she said. "I love you, Hunter. You know I do. But I can't be here. If I don't do something fast, I think I'm going to go crazy. I feel my heart racing. Put your hand there."

He put his hand there, between her small breasts, and felt the vibration thrum through his fingers. "You have the heartbeat of a hummingbird."

"Go to sleep, honey," she said and rolled away. "You have an early flight tomorrow. Can you just hold me?"

Hunter put his arms in a great circle around her and nestled his face on the back of her neck.

"I'm so cold," she said. "I'm freezing."

Hunter got up and found a blanket. When he covered her with it, her form was so frail he was afraid her bones might break. But she was opening and closing her hands fiercely. "I love you," he said into the back of her neck, but she shook her head. Five minutes later, she bolted up and walked to the fresh white canvas on her easel, a sheet around her waist.

"Is anything wrong?" he asked.

"I just have to get this," she said. "If I don't do it now, it's gonna get away." She had a bottle of vodka at her side. In the dark light, Hunter imagined the label had the grin of an S.S. skull.

Outside, he heard dogs barking. Not far from the rose bushes outside their window, sharp as turpentine, the smell of an American skunk bloomed. "Jesus, Dido, how much of that are you drinking?" He rose and headed to her. "You're shivering. You're shivering all over."

"Don't look!" She stood in front of the canvas. "Please."

All Hunter could see was black. Gently, he grasped her bottle. "May I have some of this?" Maybe the best thing to do was drink the rest so she couldn't get her hands on it. Four gulps down, he felt the burn. His face started to flush. He kept drinking while she forgot about him. He sensed her moving around, painting, stepping back. Later she slipped into bed with him and stared at the ceiling while sipping something new. Where and how had she gotten it? He thought he'd cleaned the house out. He felt an anvil on his own forehead from what he'd drunk. She was so wan, barely 100 pounds. How could she abuse herself like this?

When he woke, the room was empty. All the blinds were shut, something she never permitted. Because she'd thrust the windows open behind the blinds, they danced in the light breeze. Her canvas was gone. Only the lingering smell of the ocean, paint, skunk, and the vanished sense of Dido filled the room. He remembered her kissing him on the forehead, or had she? Where was she off to this time? She left a note, held down by her glass. "I'm off. X, D."

At the dock, the *True Love* was missing.
Because of her rising fame, word spread quickly. The newspapers, fishing boats, and helicopters rattled the sky loose of its bolts from the Labrador Current all the way to the Grand Banks, looking for her. Experts from the National Oceanographic and Atmospheric Administration guessed at her course and drift, and for Hunter, who flew back-to-back searches himself until he dropped thirty-five pounds, every night got darker. Seventy days later, the community came together for a candlelight vigil. Dido was lost to him forever.

THEN, EMBARRASSINGLY, she came back–vacant eyes, her hair matted and distant. She smiled and kissed him, they reassured the neighbors, the newspapers took disappointed note–good news gets fewer column inches. Three days back, over a spinach salad and a carefully measured four-ounce glass of wine, she said, "I can't take this anymore–the constant surveillance, the watching, the waiting for me to slip up. I'm suffocating."

"C'mon honey. Let's give it a week. If you still feel this way, I'll move into the club."

"I want a divorce."

Hunter tried to be soft. "How can you divorce me if you're not yourself?"

"I'll pick my own apartment. My own. I can see it. Cattails outside. The sparkle of water."

He saw it, too. The shades pulled down. Empties strewn all over the floor. This was bad, very bad. "Okay. But I get to check in to make sure you're all right. I still get to care for you." Even if she was too hurt to love him, he'd still get to love her. "Those are my conditions." He watched her momentarily light up, like a filament flaring before the bulb went out entirely.

"Yes, sure, wonderful," she said. "I know where." When she smiled his heart scuffed a dance. Even this Dido was better than no Dido at all.

Finally, they put $750 down a few blocks away for a broom closet with a twin bed and a hurricane lamp. He moved her in, feeling he was tossing an anchor and chain into the water without it being connected to the boat. He watched the chain sizzle down to blackness. Had Dido's eye color permanently changed to black? "I love you," he said. She looked away as he kissed her. "I know I'm saying all the wrong things, but please give me another chance."

Two weeks sped by. Sometimes she had company, lonely blades she met at Tequila Mockingbirds, and he hated himself for being aware of how much she hated her life. Were these drug deals, dates, or both? He hated himself for spying on the love of his life, but somehow, he'd always known this was going to happen. If she had a life-or-death need to be without him, shouldn't he love her enough to allow her even this? He went back to flying, but listlessly. At five-fifteen p.m. on the last Tuesday in July, he rang her up, but she wasn't in. The next afternoon she telephoned and left a message on his answering machine. He called her back, but no one picked up the phone.

He went to her place the next morning. Her Karmann Ghia wasn't there. All the lights were burning, the windows thrust open, rectangular screams.

"Dido?" He pounded on the door. No one seemed within.

He climbed through the living-room window. A single black couch. Her TEAC vibrated with the Ramones, ringing the stemware. Dick Cavett was interviewing someone in the din.

He could smell vomit in the bathroom, the shower still running cold. He started breathing heavily. No sign of her in the bedroom. Desperately, his mind made ridiculous compensations. Maybe she'd run over to the corner store to get something. Or was she still here? The closer you got to Dido, the more she seemed to be both the seer and the seen. All right. He'd checked everywhere for her but the closet. With a sense of dread, he walked up to it. Touched the handle. It swung open. A black hole. Nothing stared back at him.

The hole got blacker still. A dark force clawed at his heart. He kept swallowing, his mouth dry. This was a pivotal point, the beginning of a new career. He'd call his partner later and tell him he'd sign away all claims to the business. He'd found his true calling, investigation. The search for the closest thing you could get to truth. It was up to him now. As much as they'd try to care, other experts wouldn't be able to help him where he was going. *Aviate, navigate, communicate.* Calling on his old Navy skills after calling the police, he drove a sector search to all her haunts. He stopped in with her friends. No joy. The more he talked with people, the more they averted their eyes as if it were his fault, as though he should have known about this all along. Wildly he stepped up the visits, called more distant friends, set the darkness in motion. To find her, he'd follow her into whatever portal she'd stepped through, make her darkness his own. From then on, it was *investigate, navigate, communicate*.

HUNTER KEPT DRIVING. That was ten lost years ago. How could he have misplaced a decade? He'd promised himself he'd never return again. It was unlucky to return unbidden, but now he was hard bidden. The lights of Accomac Variety Store flashed through his windshield; he pulled over and jangled the door open. Nothing had changed. The jar of boiled eggs still ticked uneasily on the counter as though waiting for permission to explode. Dusty Kellogg's variety packs lined up disconsolately below a faded picture of Venice to the right of the air-conditioner. And Giovanni Montebello, the store owner, still sat behind the counter on the same wooden stool, the bottles of Black Seal and Absolut behind him, safe from thieves.

"Hello, Gio." Hunter stuck out his hand.

Montebello looked into his eyes, calibrating time and distance. Slowly his mouth tightened. "Hunter. Long time no see. It's so good to see you."

The 'you' fell from his lips and sank in dark water.

Montebello had worked among the hardest in the searching party. Hunter remembered him saying, again and again, "Everyone who knew her loved her." Somehow it rankled him. Montebello now seemed worried for him. "You're still looking for her, aren't you?"

Hunter nodded. "Of course, Gio. I'll always be looking for her, but I guess only she can find me." He felt dead inside. Having slipped into the same darkness to find her, he'd barely found his way out. Because honestly, if someone you love loses her mind and steps into the darkness, have you any alternative but to follow? It was one thing to be a moist system, but quite another to be so low-pressure, scary. Dido, even the idea of Dido, was so low the bottom dropped out of the glass. She'd haunt you with those dark eyes that told you she'd never come back–worse still, that she was never here. Dido, there was no you.

Why did you go out alone like that? Maybe it really was his fault. He'd left her in her unstable condition for weeks on end to fly all those charters, some as far away as South America. Maybe everyone who wasn't garroting someone was nonetheless a latent murderer. It was what made the Germans itch.

His extended executive shuttles had engineered Dido's disappearance as surely as Louis Althusser had murdered his wife. In Vaud, naturally, something Hunter had turned up while debunking royalty claims from Althusser's younger half-sister, who, having declared her brother incompetent, sought a fifty-percent return from his published work.

"I was lovingly massaging my wife's neck," the philosopher said during his deposition. "I looked down and saw someone had strangled her."

Years of electroconvulsive therapy lay ahead for Althusser, while Hunter's guilt was far more clear. He had no desire to go back to piloting when his "disjuncture" with Dido was what led her to "redefine her existence"…elsewhere. What had he done in all the years since, really?

Push comes to shove, he couldn't remember. Sometimes he could so easily bring back the most intimate details about how they'd met, the crinkle her cigarette packages made when she took a smoke from one, the flare of her match.

So easy to unravel yourself if you're your own pretender. The nightmare made fresh. Everyone was sure Dido was dead somewhere. But he knew she wasn't.

Dido knew, too.

Chapter 9

Montauk, Long Island, New York

To go up, pull the stick back. To go down, pull the stick back harder.

THIS CLOSE TO MONTAUK, the mansions were fragrant with noble rot. Hoary turrets buckled into collapsed roofs, salons cantilevered over the spume, portes cochères disintegrated into rocks above the stink of seaweed. Everywhere, the deep ocean watched him, knowing everything, remembering everything.

He rolled along Old Montauk Hi-Way above the gray sweep of beach past the neon detritus: The Beachcomber; The Breakers on the Ocean; Hartman's Briny Breezes; and, towering over everything, Montauk Manor. Beyond that, the bathhouses rose out of the sea until the road stopped to deposit his adopted father's two houses on the rocks.

To the left was "Naiad," the wreck the first generation built in 1922. To the right was the low-slung modern affair Ned Dauger commissioned Walter Gropius to design in 1968, "Witchcraft," after the song. Bold and disturbing, Witchcraft was, without apology, Berlin Meets the Hamptons. The second floor was sheer glass, creating the illusion it floated over the waves. Neighbors and even family members wondered how Ned could have come into so much money so late in life. He hadn't earned it while researching for the Navy or Raytheon. Hunter hadn't wanted to think about it, but he knew it was something he'd have to face sometime. Was it really the lottery, as Ned suggested, or the stock market? Then, too, why had he chosen something so unaccountably beyond his taste?

Not a big talker, Ned.

"It's beautiful, Dad," Hunter told him.

"Check out these plans," his father shrugged, as though he'd never seen them before.

Now it was Ned who'd checked out.

The window of Witchcraft was filled with mourners, a larger crowd than Hunter had ever seen inside. With no room in the driveway, he parked on the beach, crossed the street, passed a wave of prickly rosa rugosa, and stopped to look at the Big Dipper as it came to rest over the gambrel roof of Naiad.

How many storms had exploded against this porch, waves dark as nightmares. How frozen the feeling of looking at a place once warmed by Dido's presence. Naiad was the oldest cottage on the spit. As a child, he dreamed of winterizing it and living here year-round, walking the beach below the sweep of stars. "Do you think we could just stay here?" Dido asked him one July night.

He allowed impatience to creep into his voice. "Forever, until the end of time?"

And there it was. That look of defeat in her eyes he was destined to relive for the rest of his life. Or was it disappointment in him?

Heat lightning bloomed on the horizon, reflecting against the walnut-stained beadboard partition. It was sticky hot, no way to sleep. Pig hot.

She'd smiled, but the loneliness in her eyes cut him.

"Well, it's an old house, way too dark," he said, trying to fix things. "But as long as you and I are together and there's air-conditioning, we'll be fine."

Hunter felt a lump in his throat. He knew it wasn't such a good idea to come back to this place, so Dido like, but this time it wasn't his choice to make. He turned from Naiad, cut through an overgrown path in the roses that turned into an expensive curve of crushed white oyster shells, and crossed to the forest of I-beams that supported Witchcraft. Dwarf lights directed guests to white stairs that jumped out of the darkness.

The whispering wealth–the jolt of it. Where had it come from?

He stood in the shadows, waiting. The night so starry and malignant it seemed to rush toward him and swallow him whole, connecting him backward to other black moments best unremembered, the past and future tunnels that drain into the same inky well. The front door shivered open to reveal a face from the past.

It was Tina, his adopted or "real" sister, depending on what manner of address you preferred. Tina the improbable. Tina, short for nothing.

"You're here," she said.

When doctors told Ned and Helen they'd never have kids of their own, they adopted Hunter and covered his questions with the sweet story that they'd found him just like they'd found their black kitten,

Caliban, in a cardboard box. "You are our greatest joy," they said. "Our prize."

Then the surprise. When Hunter was barely old enough to cut his first lawn, little Tina was born, the blood daughter–a previously inconceivable miracle of nature. It was Hunter himself, the son of strangers, who'd joined the family under more unusual circumstances, sometime in the dark Before. The way he remembered it now, overnight his father went from Dad to Ned.

"Hi, Tina." Hunter bounded up to hug her. "It's great to see you!" Wrinkles raced across her skin like tiny spiders. The deadly curse of too much sunbathing.

"You're too late," she said. "You've missed the funeral."

There was a time when Tina would have been too cool to speak like that. Back when she was too much in demand to have time to cut people down. Hunter turned back the black pages of red-eyed summers until he could see himself working at a nearby hotel, putting out beach chairs for guests from a little cart for tips only.

Even then he was so tall he was nicknamed Tiny. Once he'd seen a fully clothed interloper, had to be in his mid-forties, pull his Rolls Royce to the curb, walk to the beach's edge, and look down at his sister, sunning on a striped towel in her sunglasses, her transistor radio blaring beside her tanning lotion.

The guy jumped down onto the sand, walked to her. Hands in his pockets, casual amid the dunes, he'd cast his shadow down. "I just had to tell you. I saw you from my car. I wouldn't forgive myself if I didn't tell you, you're the most beautiful girl I've ever seen in my life."

Tina flashed her frozen *Goodbye Columbus* smile, the one Hunter suspected she practiced in the bathroom. "Thank you."

His constatation received, the man drove away. What then? So, this was then. Loves dying on her, four husbands vanished like topaz.

"I'm very sorry," Hunter said in an easy, deliberate voice, the best kind to use if you were dealing with Tina. "Where is Dad right now? May I see him?"

"Not unless you have a shovel."

The room pricked its ears.

With a note of surprise, Hunter realized he was still outside. Tina was standing sentry at the door, barring his entry, not welcoming him.

"I'd forgotten how cold it gets out here," he said, "even in late March."

When Tina didn't step aside, he angled in past her. He pulled the storm door behind him more briskly than the pneumatic closing mechanism desired, and it shrieked. Now he had the room's full attention.

"You look good, Tina. I wish I'd made it in time. I guess I've been away so long that being here or missing it is the same thing. Can you forgive me?"

"Well at least you didn't wear your uniform. Thank God."

Her Long Island r's sounded like a closet full of black, rusty hangers. Hunter smiled. "I haven't been in the Navy for fifteen years." He waited. "Is there prescribed dress for missing a funeral?"

"When was the last time you saw that shrink?"

"Close to ten years ago," he said. "I've stopped seeing Dr. Feelia."

Tina shook her hair and adjusted it behind her ear, revealing a sparkler with a round brilliant cut.

"You've been drinking," she whispered. "How could you do this?"

More accurately, it was she who'd been drinking. Had he been drinking, Hunter might have replied that listed ahead of 'manliness' and 'sobriety' in *Charles Lindbergh's 59 Desirable Character Traits* was the virtue of 'balance.' Keep your balls in the center.

He scanned the sea of wistfully friendly faces and the hardscape of a spread—Triscuits, brown bread, champagne crackers, luncheon pickles, and Underwood Deviled Ham. If anything here had ever seemed familiar to him, it no longer did. "You know, that's a beautiful fire," he said. Skirting the Seagram's, he selected a glass of ice water.

Some of Ned's cronies drew back as he neared the flames and looked above the mantel at Warhol's *Silver Car Crash (Double Disaster).* That must have set somebody back a pretty penny.

Hunter felt a flood of relief when Ned's best friend, Harrison Vine, the former Navy captain, tapped his shoulder.

"I wondered where you slipped off to," Harrison said. "I thought, maybe we lost you to the Afternoon Effect."

"Last I knew, that was still classified Secret," Hunter said.

Hunter was suddenly 12, listening to Ned and Harrison's stories about hush-hush maneuvers off Woods Hole. The two researchers had stumbled upon a dark space where submarines could hide from enemy destroyers and their depth charges. Sonar-invisible. An honest-to-goodness shadow zone. Hunter dropped his voice. "Did you get to talk with Dad toward the end?"

Harrison put his hands in his pockets. "I'm sorry, I didn't." He hesitated, then drew closer. "You know, with all our research, and in spite of all the technological advancements we've made, sometimes you should still only believe what you can see with your own eyes. I want you to know, you're welcome here."

"I'm glad!" Hunter said. What was he getting at?

"You flew in from…Austria?"

"Lausanne, Switzerland."

Harrison eyed Hunter's water glass. "Are you sure I can't improve on that somehow?"

Hunter saw Auntie Ruth's hull numbers and running lights bearing down on him. When Ned lost Helen to melanoma, Helen's sister Ruth lost her husband, too. Ruth and Ned had obviously reconnected and bonded at the spousal support group. She wore a two-piece wool Pendleton suit of armor, wrinkles, loud lips, stockings. There was barely time to brace for the bow wave. To block her, Hunter hoisted his glass in a toast while she crushed him with a hug.

"How your father would have loved to see you so strong, and poor Helen, God rest her soul. You seem completely recovered! So marvelous in your good health and smashing civilian clothes. Look at him, Harrison!"

Harrison bowed and withdrew.

"Come here with me, darling." Flashing eagle irises, she motioned Hunter to a corner. "You've got to understand, dear, you're in a bit of a touchy situation."

"I didn't know touching was allowed."

"It's just the condition of Naiad. We've been so embarrassed for you. If your father were alive, he'd turn over in his grave!"

Hunter said nothing.

"The blinds are askew. Half the roof has blown away, with more leaks than you can say grace to. There's a rusty old boat trailer by the garage. The roses are going crazy. It's just a shame you let it get this way."

"Beautiful Naiad," Hunter said.

"Your father was in no condition to keep it up, so, and I say this with all good intentions, it's just–an insult to your family what you've let happen. Everyone feels the same way."

"If only I'd known." Hunter brightened. "I can take a few days. I'll have a look at it."

"Well, I don't suppose it matters now."

"Sure, it does. I love the old place. I'll make a little time. It'll be fun to spruce it up a bit before I head back to Europe. I guess the ladder's still in the garage. It'll be great to get up in the salt air."

"Then you don't know."

Hunter turned to see his sister. "You wouldn't like me to fix up the cottage?"

Tina's eyes rolled skyward. "You miss your father's funeral. Then you want to talk about bequests during his wake? His corpse is still warm."

Hunter imagined underground fires along the highway caused by buried tires spontaneously combusting in the moist darkness.

"Not to worry." Hunter held up his hands. He flinched inside when Tina took a quick step back. "I don't really like to own things. I couldn't possibly take something on like Naiad. I never expected to inherit it. Give me credit for that, at least. I'm unattached. I don't have a family. And maybe I won't have to climb up that ladder with a bucket of creosote after all!" Relief blew in like a sea breeze. "I was just offering to help with some repairs while I'm here."

"We're going to meet together tomorrow if you can wait that long to talk about the money."

"If it's about money, I don't need to be here at all."

Compact and brawny, a Gila monster in a suit with fold marks on his trousers stepped beside Tina and blew up his neck to intimidate. "Is everything all right, honey?"

"Boyfriend?" Hunter grinned, stuck out his hand, and remembered Ned's letters. "Ronnie, right?"

"We can press the flesh some other time," Ronnie said. "This is a wake for your father."

"During my vacation?" Hunter was so close to being free–nearly completely off the hook.

"Maybe we should take care of this outside," Ronnie said. When he swelled his chest, his scripted name rose above the pocket of his dress electrician's shirt. The little tramp's cheeks reddened; his frame vibrated. Threat level zero.

"You never knew Ned," Tina shrieked to Hunter– almost a whoop, like a crane. "You haven't seen him for twenty years. When you came and brought that drug addict…"

Dido again. There was no reason to bring up Dido. Hunter felt himself dissolving, disappearing.

Another depth charge. "I lived with Ned all those long nights when he was so lonely after mummy died," Tina said. "What did you do? I earned this. I put in my time."

Hunter looked out the window toward the sea and thought of Ned getting into his rowboat at night.

"He was such a private person," Tina said, looking around.

Ned lit a yellow whale-oil lamp on the transom, then expertly poled himself over the breakers, lifting beautifully over the swells. He started to row with his short, courageous arms. Hunter watched the oil lamp rise slowly into the stars.

"He was incredibly lonely," Tina said. "And you, all you've done here is drive here in your car…"

"It's true, I drove here in a car."

"…To collect what's yours."

"I don't follow you." Actually, it was easy to follow her. She was climbing straight up with him until he stalled. Then she'd do a wingover and dive in on him.

Tina balled her fists. "You just want your cottage, don't you? You just came here to get what's yours. Well, Jimmy Lord says the new will is uncontestably binding."

"Jimmy?" Hunter scanned the room, unable to recognize Lord among the dozens of silver heads. Lord was Ned's real-estate attorney. So odd to hear Tina toss his first name around with nostalgic familiarity, as though she, too, were of Ned's generation, one of 'the old gang.' Lord had to be in his late seventies now. Hunter shrugged. "I didn't know about the old will." What an ecstasy of wasted time.

Tina looked to Ronnie for strength.

"How could you miss Dad's funeral?" she said to Hunter. "How could you be doing this?" She whispered to Ronnie, then started to cry. "This is a wake, you know."

"All right," Hunter said. "But I want to see the wake rule book."

"He's blaming me," Tina sobbed to Ronnie. "I was there when Dad signed it. And you," she said to Hunter. "It's completely legal. I told you this is not the time to talk about legal things." She softened her tone. "Really, if Daddy wanted me to have the cottage, too, as well as this house, how was I to stop him?"

Hunter held up his hand and laughed. "I really love the cottage but won't accept it, no matter how hard you try to make it mine!"

Tina darkened. "You asked for it. I remember it so clearly, it's like he's saying it right now. Daddy said,

'I am deeply disappointed in my son, who has failed in life. Because of your steadfast loyalty, Tina, I want you to have Naiad, too, after I cross to the Great Beyond, because you're so reliable you'll make sure it's kept up the way it should be." Tina crossed her arms. "I am my father's daughter."

"Well, he's gone now," Harrison said.

Hunter looked for Auntie, but she was nowhere in hearing.

For a moment Hunter was nowhere in speaking. Finally he said to Harrison, "Would you like to see my car?" They walked down the stairs toward the roaring night surf. As they looked across the water, the temperature dropped five degrees. "No fishing boats," Hunter said.

"It's been a cold spring." Harrison rubbed his hands.

They turned to the rental car and discussed it softly while their bodies disintegrated, cells dying like lights on the houses on the far peninsula.

Tina crossed the street carrying something stiffly in front of her. It could have been the coffin of an infant. "Where are you staying?" she asked.

Another surprise. In the vacant, leaking Naiad, was his room filled? No one was living there, if you could judge by the boarded-up windows.

"This is our home," Tina said of all Long Island. "You could have stayed here, but you went away with the Navy to the other side of the world. You never once came to visit your father."

Harrison looked down.

"That is my fault," Hunter said. "Of course, we wrote to each other." Ned had never sounded unhappy.

"He'd never complain to you in a letter. After mummy died, he just got smaller and smaller. Night after night for the twenty years you were gone, I've consoled him. You broke his heart."

Hunter laughed, not knowing why. "I don't want any trouble. I love you. Everything's happening for the best."

"How dare you criticize my life, you, who never came back from Vietnam."

He tried to pull her into his ten-mile stare. So hard to focus on these people when they were in your face–like that.

"I did come home."

"Only to meet…that person."

"You mean Dido, my wife?" Hunter studied Tina's eyes, looking down their hallways to see if she knew anything new. Nothing. Dido was top secret now, mothballed and unspeakable. "Anyway, I'm glad to have met your…Ronnie," Hunter said.

"He's looking for a job. People don't understand what he has to offer just because he was prevented from graduating high school. He's wired a little differently. Do you have any problem with that?"

"It's not so cold," Hunter said. "I could stay one night in the cottage, in the room with the little propane stove. Tomorrow we can meet with the lawyers, and if you need me to sign anything, I'll be glad to sign a waiver of future claim if you like."

"There's no need for that," Tina snapped. "We've already met informally, since I'm the executrix. And you won't be staying in Naiad. It's all cleaned up to be shown this week. The real-estate broker's coming for a first-in tomorrow."

"Oh, you're renting Naiad?" She'd need to unboard the windows before a tenant came in.

Tina burst into tears. "I can't take these interrogations anymore. I've been out straight cleaning both houses and caring for my dying father, but that isn't enough, is it? That isn't enough!"

Hunter looked over the water toward Ned, his rowing father. He tried to see the whale-oil lamp, the light. He hoped he was rowing hard.

"You've come here questioning everything we've done. Well, I have to sell the houses. They're too much pressure for us! Ronnie and I want his little Jennifer and Nicole to grow up away from these pressures. *That's* Ronnie's job. He works full-time to look after the finances so that little Jennifer's and Nicole's futures are secure. We've picked out a house in the country."

"Both houses are for sale?" So much for Ned Dauger's legacy.

"Here is the paperwork. You want all this legal work done so quickly. Daddy wanted it this way. He told me before he died."

"You know, I still love that funny smile that lifts your lip like that," Hunter said. "Let's ease up a bit. I really am glad to see you." He stepped back a yard and took a big breath.

"Still playing chess?" Harrison asked.

"Young man's sport," Hunter said. "Like fencing. I can feel it fading. The one-hundred-yard dash is a better carryover sport than chess."

Harrison couldn't fathom it. "You don't play at all? Weren't you ranked in the top–"

"No." Hunter smiled. He turned and beheld the window full of people, Auntie still bedizened in her wicked New England tartan. Flashes of red, black, yellow, and green scintillated down the razor pleats of her skirt, then connected with the tartan socks, neckties, and accessories throughout the room. The surface of the window misted over, covering a harbor of dead teeth.

"He did leave you something," said Tina with disaffection.

"Yes?"

"Here." She handed Hunter the stiff object wrapped in a red trader blanket. He opened it carefully and saw it was a box containing a heavy glass decanter marked "Wardroom, USS *Semmes*" and a key with a Bakelite tag inscribed N-X-211. "Who's the psycho bitch now?"

"It's a shame you don't still play," Harrison said.

Hunter refolded the blanket around the decanter, stepped into his car, and put it on the passenger seat. He tossed the key into the glove box.

"Be careful," Tina said. "These were Daddy's things. It's so cold, that glass could crack. And thank you for your service. Now that you understand me, maybe it's best if you never come back here again." She stared at him. "Where's your famous sense of humor now?"

Chapter 10

Long Island, New York

A pilot is the first to arrive at the scene of an aircraft accident.

HUNTER STARTED DRIVING along the water's edge. More dark shapes slipped away, lost haunting grounds. Scanning the passenger seat, he gazed at the trading blanket with six black slashes sewn into the wool near the label.

The slashes stand for six beaver pelts. He could still hear Ned Dauger saying it. Ned gave it to Helen during their honeymoon in Maine after the War. At least now they were together again.

Hunter could fold this evening over as easily, toss it in the back of his car. In the cirrus layer above he saw an airliner flying a Great Circle route, to London, probably, following the Northeast coast until it took the big right turn into the dark.

Steaming into the stars, it occurred to him, what was Tina getting? The two houses, sure. On the other hand, who'd want to live between the devil and the deep blue sea?

Ned Dauger was way out beyond the horizon, his yellow light winking in the distance, looking for Helen. Hunter trolled slowly along the water, past dark towns and variety stores, bumping along the coast. When he reached the Amagansett lighthouse, he pulled over and shut off the engine.

Leaving his car, he walked through dead sea brush to the tower and leaned his head against the cool stones. You knew it when the gentleman in black was walking toward you. Tonight, he seemed a little jittery. Maybe he had Huntington's Correa. Or he might just be a jive dancer listening to the music in his head. In that case, every day would be a transatlantic crossing for him. The gentleman held up his left hand, as though requesting silence.

"You're someone special," Hunter said. "I just don't know who you are."

"Have you ever considered," the man replied, "that all this time, I've been imagining you?"

"No sense chaffering like this." Hunter looked beyond the man into the whistling dark.

"You don't have a smoke, do you?" the man asked.

"Why not?" Hunter fished in his pocket, gave him one, and lit it for him. Then he saw. The man's right hand had no fingers. Where fingers had been, skin smoothly covered the severed digits at the root. "What happened to your hand? I hadn't noticed it before."

The man held it up. "My wife was in a wheelchair. I was loading her into our van, and I caught my hand in the cable."

"I'm sorry."

"The worst thing was, I had dismemberment insurance," he said. "But the insurance company said because my whole hand wasn't taken off, I wasn't dismembered. Though they wished they could help me, they couldn't help me."

"Is your wife all right?"

"Since I wasn't home to help her while I was in the hospital, she went to a nursing home where she died barely a week later. You don't happen to know anyone who's looking for a van with a ramp that needs some adjustment? It's not my aim to trouble you about this, but I suspect she blamed herself for what happened to me."

"I'm sorry," Hunter said. "Do you think maybe it's time to stop following me?"

"I had to give up bowling," the man said. "You're all I have left."

"Well, I have to go," Hunter said.

"Yes," the man said. "I know." The slightest pause. "Any word about your wife?"

Hunter scratched his head. "No." It echoed into blackness.

Hunter realized this wasn't the man he kept seeing in Europe. He wasn't the same person he kept seeing all the time. This was a guy who'd visited Ned at least five times. They'd always go into the library and close the door, but not before he'd give him a magic trick or even a trinket and say, "Hey, Buddy." Sometimes Hunter had wished the visitor were his own father. He realized seeing a person like this was a perfectly normal phenomenon. It was his unconscious trying to push something forward, saying, 'This is important. Take note of something you're forgetting.'

"They were wrong," the man said. "Your father was really proud of you."

HUNTER DROVE THROUGH the throat of Long Island, crossed the Williamsburg Bridge into

Manhattan, battled the cabs on Bleecker, then turned onto Fifth and Park. At the Waldorf he gave his car keys to the valet and rode the elevator to Suite 712. This was his home in New York and had always been available to him when he needed it except for that one time during the unpleasantness of 1979. Neither the staff nor the Shah of Iran's bodyguards had seen fit to alter anything, so during his next visit Hunter had allowed himself a moment to relax into the security of familiar things. Then it hit him. The drapes had changed.

He dropped his battered Vuitton duffel on the luggage rack and grabbed the telephone receiver off the nightstand. "I need a 6 a.m. wakeup call, please. And the usual from room service." He removed a bottle of Angel's Envy from the mini bar. Some of the old crowd was there and remembered.

He took out his flight-school ditty bag and laid it on the marble counter. He knocked back a swig of the bourbon and began to brush his teeth. He couldn't avoid the face in the mirror. While he might still have the shy aspect and diffident grin of a Viking hero once removed, his eyes were bloodshot enough to make any flight surgeon frown. Those couldn't be Lindbergh's eyes looking back at him. Soft streaks of silver stole into his hair, so in any case he wasn't going to be as lucky as Lucky Lindy, whose blond Nordic locks had kept their color until his death. Or maybe Lindbergh's hair was a fake, too.

The room grew darker, and Hunter realized he was getting cold. New York was no place to be in March. Maybe he could interest Pia in a trip to the Canary Islands or Florida–someplace warm. Hawaii was spectacular in March. It was also where Lindbergh spent his last days.

Lindbergh no doubt craved the anonymity of the Pacific. After FDR slapped him for his anti-war radio speeches and refused to re-activate his Army colonel's commission in the wake of Pearl Harbor, Lindbergh was lost, denied a uniform during a war, his wings clipped.

Branded a traitor and a coward, he conducted his own version of *The White Feather*. He'd be damned if he wouldn't prove his patriotism in spite of Roosevelt blacklisting him as a Nazi lover, an anti-Semite. Though Lindbergh lost his lucrative board seats with aviation firms, his old friend Henry Ford, rumored to have Nazi sympathies of his own, opened a tiny door to the 'club' when he gave him a job as a civilian advisor, test pilot, and instructor, which led him into the cockpits of F-4U *Corsairs* and P-38 *Lightnings*.

Sent into the war zone in Guadalcanal, Biak, and Palau as an "observer," the stranger at first astonished then irritated the Navy and Marine pilots when he strode into the wardroom. How novel. Here was a specter from the past–like John Wilkes Booth walking onto a Hollywood set.

Then they watched the odd duck fly. Overnight Lindbergh was invited to join the 475th on its missions– a ghost, invisible, an undercover member of Satan's Angels.

Officially, MacArthur knew nothing about this. FDR was kept in the dark. If the Navy brass were discovered to have given their blessing, heads would roll. In secret, Lindbergh was allowed to sweep over the palm trees, into the clouds, and engage the enemy.

It was Hunter's guess that the Pacific Theater was the birthplace of 'Careu Kent,' where in utmost privacy a privileged American male might get away with anything. Warming to the invisible man in the war zone, Navy and Marine officers treated him like an older brother.

Lindbergh taught the young aviators how to save gas as he had with the *Spirit of St. Louis*. Their flying average radius grew from 475 to 707 nautical miles, enabling them to reach targets that were impossible before. Ditching from fuel starvation was no longer an issue. Beyond being a mechanical genius, it turned out Lindbergh was a gifted stick at dogfighting, too. His fellow pilots marveled at his courage–he set up countless Japanese targets and gunned down a Zero on his own. Not to mention, they loved the old man's easy manner when he knocked off for a little R & R. He really listened to tales of their adventures, their families, their girls waiting for them back home. Or at least he put on a good show of it. He entertained them by shooting a flying fish midair with his Navy .38 from the deck of a PT Boat slaloming through palmy islets at 30 knots.

Had Lindbergh seduced any women in the Pacific? Hunter had to wonder how many exquisitely reflexed Solomon Islands claimants were out there now–more future Pretenders for him to shoot down.

Next morning, Hunter dined in Peacock Alley (two eggs, sunny side up; a single piece of unbuttered toast; and a tall, cool tomato juice. Black coffee). He walked through the lobby, slipped through the revolving door, turned left, and started along Park toward Grand Central Station in light rain.

It was raining when Lindbergh's ticker-tape parade guided the flyer along Broadway, Park Avenue, Fifth Avenue, and Wall Street. The boulevards vibrated with four million people waving from buildings where, two years later, some would jump to their deaths because their fortunes had been reversed during the Great Stock Market Crash. Maybe Dido had jumped to her death. Where was she right now–did she even call herself Dido? She could be just blocks away.

But then she'd have worked so hard to be undetectable, he'd be flattering himself to think she was doing it all for him. Get a grip. Dido is dead. You don't want to picture what lonely room she ended up in at the bottom of a bottle of Five O'clock. He'd found a fifth of Virginia Gentlemen inside the toilet tank when he cleaned out her apartment after she disappeared.

Hunter patted the pocket of his sport coat to feel the key and its tag. To Tina, the runic letters N-X-211 meant nothing. The "N" was the letter assigned to the United States by the Commission Internationale de Navigation Aerienne for wireless radio call signs during the Paris Peace Conference of 1918. The "X" stood for 'experimental.' The numbers 211 denoted April, 1927, the time of aircraft registration.

The noise grew to a roar as he passed through the doors of the train station and entered the huge lobby. Like a great umbrella, the vaulted ceiling covered him, its sheltering girders converging at the apex of the vast central arch. Circular skylights alternated between rectangles to relieve the gloom, some of the panes flickering in Pacific blue. Above the pillars, a monumentally stoic clock seemed to stop time as crowds, trains, and red caps rushed below. *Tick.* The mural above the great doorway at the end of the hall glowed with a "Map of the Atlantic Ocean," scene of Lindbergh's Great Circle triumph. The Lone Eagle had scuffed through this marble hall many times to board trains.

The platforms splayed out ahead, digital schedule boards winking with departures and arrivals. Candy stands, tobacconists, and the smell of newsprint flooded Hunter's senses with fragrant confusion. It was still rush hour. As many as five thousand souls surged here in their restlessness, their lives and deaths, their cough-drop urgencies, their comings and goings. This relentless, gullible 'us.' Which left out 'them,' the missing ones, the sick ones. *Tick.*

Hunter stopped to have his shoes buffed, nodding to a man in an apron sitting beside an empty oak throne. He took a seat.

"You're a tall one," the shoe shiner said. "Name's Joe."

"Hunter." They shook hands. "No wax, please. Just a brush."

"Where you headed?"

So much of where he was headed was uncharted. "My next stop is Switzerland."

"Hard to get there by train."

"From this stand, you probably always know what's going on around here," Hunter said. "Are the baggage lockers still right off the main concourse?"

"Yessir, but not for long. There's talk of phasing them out because of the bombings at LaGuardia." He winked. "Personally, I think it's a union thing. 'DIY lockers' means fewer handlers on the payroll."

Hunter looked quickly past him and saw his old friend, the fellow from his dreams. The gentleman in black tipped his Homburg as though they were both in a Magritte painting. Then the crowd engulfed him as it ebbed and flowed, moving toward the concourse through motes of light pouring from demilune clerestories that lined the grand hall and made the station's interior a strange gray heaven. *Tick. Tick.*

"He'll be back," Hunter murmured.

"How's that, sir?" the shoe man asked.

Hunter paid for the shine and strode into the throng, growing closer to the bright rails. How like clouds crowds could be, concentrated and brilliant, then dispersed. The dusty arch labeled "lockers" was exactly where it was supposed to be–he'd have to get a new plan. When Hunter sneezed, the young woman at the counter said, *"Gesundheit!"* This all felt way too strange, way too watched. Too still. Hunter had sensed crosshairs trained on the back of his neck before, and now he whirled and dropped to the station floor as the first bullet whizzed over his shoulder. The crowd screamed, streamed, zagged back and forth, and blocked his view.

Was he in one of Pia's movies? Two more bullets whizzed by and cracked into the marble behind him.

Psstwhack!

Two figures in black trenches ran toward him through the crowds as a policeman's whistle shrilled. Hunter shot to his feet and flew up a wrought-iron staircase to a maintenance floor that led to a glass staircase that rose over the central clock. *Psstchew.*

He ducked behind a cement pillar and raced down the stairs on the other side, but his left leg felt mushy. Better not to think about it, particularly if you're a target.

Now the crowd on the main concourse raced left and right like rabbits on a runway. *Tick.* His chest started to pound. He jumped down four stairs to a platform and collapsed amid police whistles screaming above him, hitting his forehead on the floor.

"Sir, are you all right?" he heard a voice saying.

"Sure, fine," Hunter said. He tried to get up, but it was as if a lead hand held him down. The front of his head hurt like hell.

"But you're bleeding," the voice said as he was loaded into an ambulance. The voice softened, and he lost consciousness.

Chapter 11

Manhattan, New York

He who sees first lives longest.

IN THE HOSPITAL, a crowd in scrubs hovered. Didn't anyone wear white anymore? Hunter drifted on a cloud of disinfectant. "Sweet Jesus, that must hurt. That bullet nearly passed right through your leg." The wound was cleaned and wrapped, and he was sent to a recovery room. The next morning, one of New York's finest buttonholed him at the discharge station.

"How you getting on? Luckily, it's only a flesh wound. It's that concussion they'll have to watch. You nearly split your head in two." He handed him a card. "We'd like to talk with you at the precinct. I can give you a lift there and back to the Waldorf. Okay?"

"Sure, thanks," Hunter said.

At Midtown Precinct South, West 35th Street, he was guided to the ops desk. The sergeant stared down. "Your name?"

"Hunter Dauger. Was anyone else hurt at the train station?"

"Just you, buddy. Please have a seat. How's the leg feel?"

He seemed so sincere Hunter took a moment to answer.

"Where were you headed? I mean, you were in a train station."

"Commuter run," Hunter lied. "To Long Island." A breath. "Did you get the guys?"

"Who we caught was you."

"Did your officers see the two men shooting?"

The sergeant raised his hand. "Settle down, buddy. Come on in. The lieutenant wants to talk with you."

A door swung open and Hunter entered. He realized if he reached to his left temple he'd feel a bandage there.

"Dick Snark," the lieutenant said. "It's good to see you again, Commander Dauger."

"Have we met?"

"I was in the fuel crew at NAS Key West. I was just a peon, a petty officer second-class. You wouldn't have noticed me."

But Lindbergh would have.

"We see you have a license to carry a concealed weapon for five different countries." He touched the file on his desk. "I see stamps for Berlin, Paris, Naples..."

None of which were countries.

"Why would you need to do that?" the lieutenant asked.

"I work with lawyers as a consultant. What I have to say frequently disappoints clients."

"Can you tell me what happened, Commander?"

"Two people were chasing me and shooting."

"It'll take a while for ballistics to analyze the slugs we removed from the marble. One witness said he saw a wild man running around, climbing stairs, and shooting himself in the leg. Maybe trying to kill himself." He lifted his chin and looked at Hunter's forehead.

Do not reach up and touch the bandage.

"You've been in rehab, right?"

"Not in quite some time."

"Also treated for depression."

Hunter nodded.

"Depression is a dark doorway. You're lucky. Some people never make it back out." He flipped back into the file. "Harvard, United States Navy. Deep selected for commander. It isn't every day I talk to someone with both the Navy and the Distinguished Flying Cross. They just didn't give those out in the early 1960s. You'd have had to fly an SR-71 to pull that off..." He looked into Hunter's eyes. "Hmm, Florida's just 90 miles from Havana. I remember none of you guys was a big talker."

HUNTER'S FIRST LOOK AT HAVANA was as a distant glow through palm leaves in solo pursuit of a secret stranger. It would have been beyond embarrassing to the State Department if another Yankee had slipped into Cuba in the dark to assassinate Castro. So, when intelligence surmised that a former Navy pilot named Richard Streak had decided to take matters into his own hands, rented a boat, oiled up, and swum the last two miles into the coast, stealing into the heart of the *selva* at night, he had to be stopped. And quietly. Hunter was sent in because he knew him.

"Contain the situation." Hunter's footsteps grew louder in the darkness like Abacuoa drumbeats as the silhouette ahead of him kept running. Hunter tripped over the root of a mangrove, kicked his boot free, and kept chasing. His agile opponent ran helter-skelter, rounding the dead stumps of spirit trees, never stopping for breath, Hunter slowly closing in. Another fall. Splash. The banana canopy was so thick there was nothing but green hell in front of them. Caracaras and merlin birds exploded from their nests.

In the end, the shadow suddenly stopped and turned to Hunter. Streak, his old roommate from flight school, flashed that familiar grin Hunter had seen so many times above the collar of his service dress blues in the Capital Grille in Washington, D.C. at Somebody's hail and farewell party. But this Streak was in rags, and a gash in his leg dripped onto his bare foot. His eyes rocked in the night forest.

"*I know you*," Streak said, bent over and drawing deep breaths. "Hunter."

"Come on, Streak. You shouldn't have come here. This is over."

"Not for me, it isn't."

"Give me your gun."

"Where's your famous sense of humor? I thought the CIA wanted Castro dead."

"There's dead and there's dead. Your plan doesn't meet the test of… plausible deniability. Way too much blowback."

"If you're going to talk like Bobby Kennedy, you'd better shoot me now." Streak looked at the palm trees and banana fronds darkening their spot as if to memorize them. "You've hunted me like a leopard. Kill me like a man."

Wild and gnarled at their bases, the trees rushed in. A shadow settled in front of Hunter's face, as though someone had painted it directly in front of him so he couldn't see.

"Come on, Rick. There's no need for that. Come back with me. We've all been there. I'll get you some help."

"Any longer is torture," whispered the voice. Streak drew his knife and rushed.

A shot echoed from behind Hunter and Streak fell, first to his knees, then face down in the mud.

I know you.

Hunter didn't know who fired that shot. Was somebody just trying to save his life, or had Hunter led a more dangerous assassin to his prey?

"BUDDY." Hunter felt the police lieutenant at his arm. Was he everybody's buddy? "Buddy. I'm not suggesting you shot yourself. It's just that this is the second case of yours that this precinct is involved in." He pulled out a much larger file. "According to this, we called you down here about your wife's disappearance. Do you think these cases are related? She's still missing, isn't she?"

Hunter knew the time would come when he'd have to be straight with Pia and tell her he'd really met Dido at Alcoholics Anonymous.

"We have a description of the two shooters, although it doesn't help us at all," the lieutenant said. "Two white men, dark hair, black raincoats. Thirteen rounds were fired from what appears to be a Benelli CB M2, though a handful came from a Sauer P-226. Your description would improve on anything we have."

"Five-foot eight and a quarter, five-foot eleven and a half," Hunter said. "I saw flashes as they moved inside the crowd. I was surprised they didn't close on me while trying to shoot me. But that's all I remember."

The lieutenant gave him his card. "Call me if you think of anything else."

Chapter 12

En Route from Manhattan to Nuuk, Greenland

See that propeller? Everything behind it revolves around a pile of money.

FIVE DAYS LATER, HUNTER WAS BACK AT WORK as he looked through the passenger windows of a de Havilland Canada Dash-7 on final descent. The single runway grew larger. Behind it, glowing with the turquoise and purple aurorae of the night sky, the cut-crystal peaks of Quassussuaq and Ukkusissat startled as the background for Nuuk, the tiniest national capital in the world. Few foreigners imagined Greenland as even having a city, but this well-kept secret, with its budding international airport, spatter of lights, and bars, seemed content to sleep safely within its perfect harbor, sheltered from the Atlantic inside a scorpion's tail of ice.

Exiting the aircraft, he crunched into the terminal for a scalding cup of coffee and a salvo of three aspirin, then made his way across black volcanic cinders toward his driver's car. Though the overcoat covered his slight limp, his leg felt stiff from the frigid temperature. The fedora and scarf did a ludicrous job of hiding the skin-colored bandage near his hairline. *"How dashing!"* Dido would say. Then she'd smile and fix the mess he'd made of himself with her warm hands.

"I know you," Hunter's driver said as he stepped into the taxi. Jamming into reverse, she spun the wheel hard before heading downtown, leaving the Air Iceland terminal behind them. "Where to?"

"Attaveqatigiinnermut Siunnersorti–Nordamerika & Misissuinermut Siunnersorti." Hunter caught her eye in the mirror. "How's my Inuit this time?"

"You've been practicing. But 'Nuna Relationship Management' would've been easier on both of us." She pointed ahead. "Let's see what you can do with that Danish sign."

"Well, the first word's easy," Hunter said. "Nuuk means Nuuk." He rubbed his chin. "Okay, let's see. 'The Heart of a Nation. Fueled on Fresh Air.'" Actually, steam. This would have been right up Lindbergh's alley. Greenland's heat and electricity were tapped from an energy source rising through cracks in the permafrost into underground fuel cells. This far off the New York grid, at least a person could be out of sight, protected by geographic isolation. So, whoever was chasing him would have a hard time avoiding notice. For the average killer, traveling here would be…unimaginable. But then, the 'unimaginable' was a safe haven for monsters. It was the biggest hiding place in the world.

"You could have just read that from the guidebook," his driver said.

"I'm not going to stop at the law firm today," Hunter said. "Just drop me off at the Hans."

"You've got it, boss." She turned toward the Hans Egade, Nuuk's *komfortabelt konferencehotel*. As they rounded the corner, she asked, "Are you here again to see Aniq?" She raised her chin to listen.

"Yes."

"You know, it may be hard for an outsider to believe, but Aniq's becoming a bit of a folk hero to us."

"Have you seen him lately?"

"Not much. He's in jail."

The sky above Aqqusinersuaq Street had turned bright pink, streaked in green. They passed Parliament, the University, and the Stadium, still stubbled with signs left over from the 1982 Arctic Winter Games, a pale gesture to civilization. On this glacier, survival was never a game. Hunter lightly touched the gunshot wound on his leg. It was still tender, but cooler.

"I don't suppose you're going to tell me why he's in jail," he said.

"I believe the charge this time is fomenting."

"Ah."

Hunter paid her, checked into the penthouse on the sixth floor, and dropped into the skeletal restaurant for dinner. Salmon, imported capers, vodka from Iceland, Pringles.

THE NEXT MORNING, it was kippers and ketchup, with a side of seal. It was an easy walk to Nuna Law Firm, where Aniq Peary sat on one side of a conference table with a court officer. Facing them were two Washington D.C. lawyers. Hunter had met them six months earlier when they hired him to debunk Aniq's claim to descent from the famous polar explorer Admiral Robert E. Peary. When they stood, Aniq was closest to Hunter's height. Built like a basketball forward, Aniq had quick eyes and deep, full lips. He'd grown his dark, glossy hair longer in the last six months, like a rock star. Straight from the sagas, he moved and acted like a prince, his strength fresh as snow. He shook the chains shackling his wrists in lieu of offering a handshake.

"You didn't bring your lie detector," Aniq said in perfect English. "It must be bad news, or you wouldn't have come in person."

There was a soft knock on the door. A young woman came in with four coffees on a tray. With every movement, she cast quick glances at Aniq.

"How do you take it?" she asked Hunter.

"Black."

The two lawyers asked for cream and sugar, while Aniq kept his eye on Hunter's spoon.

"You haven't always taken it black," Aniq said, "because you're stirring it now. When did you stop taking sugar?"

"So, you're the detective," Hunter said and took a sip. "What got you in the slammer?"

"Inciting a riot," the court officer cut in. "If I had my way, he'd still be in there."

"Love you too, Luki," Aniq said. He turned to Hunter. "I'm not sure if you know about the infamous Blok P."

"What about it?" Hunter asked.

"You can see it from your hotel, and from outer space. It was supposed to be our savior, the first modern apartment complex built in Greenland, vintage 1965. Miles of cement with tiny windows to save us from the Stone Age. Our great Socialist experiment, the megalith from Denmark. The structure itself may be cool, but we're just not into it. Because we are Inuit. You don't take working savages and box us into a European floor plan. The architects forgot we're nomads, fishermen. When they moved us in, we couldn't haul our whales up the tiny stairwells to cut them. In no way would our marine equipment fit in the teensy closets, mod for Copenhagen but just a bust here. So, we started piling our red whale and seal blubber on the balconies. Years of blood running down the pipes have stopped up our waste system. Our nets and cables fill the hallways, inviting disaster. It could have killed people." He called out to the corridor, "You know, Sana, my friends and I will have some more coffee."

The two lawyers looked up, surprised at the commanding tone Aniq assumed and the effect it had on the staff, who brought it quickly. The shorter lawyer looked to his peer as if to say, this isn't going the way we'd planned at all.

Aniq closed his eyes. "You'd think they would've given us red bathtubs, because that's where we do the hacking and deboning." He shook out a spirit. "Fishy *Psycho*. I just wanted to see what the place would smell like if I set fire to it, with two hundred of my closest friends."

"Never happened," the court officer said. "Aniq is good at a lot of things. Arson isn't one of them."

"But he's in custody," Hunter said.

"He's an honored guest here until he tells us who really started the fire."

"Luki," Aniq said gently. "No one was hurt. It really was all me."

"Please call me Lieutenant Luki," the man said, trying to regain control.

Hunter had seen pictures of the interior of Blok P, because Dido had showed them to him in *Art in America*. The benighted place had become a performance art space when the 'ghost writers' decorated the hallways in blood with nightmare imagery. *Shark, Devil Whale, Seal 7, Patuktuq.*

Decorators from Paris and Milan flew in to steal the patterns.

Hunter studied Aniq as though making his final decision. "Now I know you're not descended from Admiral Peary," he said, looking hard at Aniq and tuning his every sense for a reaction. "Peary knew how to grease his skids, but he didn't dare to set the world on fire."

"I've always been proud of being part *Eskimo*." Aniq leaned back in his green leather chair.

Hunter turned to the two lawyers. "Let's step outside a second."

A room away, Hunter drew them closer. "I've got some information that isn't going to make you happy."

"You're working for us," the shorter one demanded. "Just shut him down."

"I don't work for you. I work for the truth–and my commission."

"We thought everything was all arranged."

"Prepare for a *derangement*. As I see it, there's really just one choice: damage control with a stab at settlement, though I don't think money is what floats his boat."

"Then your work isn't worth anything to us."

"*Au contraire*. I get my percentage of what your clients save if Aniq takes a settlement. But if he doesn't, I still get my base rate. One million dollars."

"Money always talks," the shorter lawyer said. "Let's offer him the lowest settlement we can. You may be on retainer, but you're not running the show."

"I think we're in a whole different longboat," Hunter said. "I'll do what I can, but we're going to lose this one."

"YOU'RE GOING TO VERIFY ME," Aniq said when they returned. "I knew it this morning when I woke up. I thought,

'That which has been expected has arrived.' In Inuktitut, it's *Asuilaak*."

"Delusions of grandeur," Hunter said as he wrote in his notebook. "Near total detachment. Now I guess you're going to tell me you went to Stanford instead of Cal Tech. The first sign of any pretender is an education."

Aniq folded his arms and grinned at the suits. The lawyers squirmed. "Do you see? He's going to tell me I'm me."

"If I were to ratify you as a Peary descendant, it's not as though you'd be looking at a vast inheritance," Hunter said, his voice growing distant, even to his own ears. "I guess there's a small island in Maine. He's a disgraced explorer. He lied about making it to the Pole."

"We already made it to the Pole centuries before, so that's not news to us. Only you of lower latitudes bought that myth. This need to be declared 'first.' Now you're hanging onto some guy on a snowmobile in the 1960s as the real and true discoverer of the North Pole. We prefer to share."

"There is no money here," Hunter said and pulled out a file from his valise.

"Isn't who and what I want to inherit my business?"

"It's your move, gentlemen," Hunter said to the attorneys. "I haven't said anything yet."

The older of the two, in a plaid tie, said, "Young man, are you doing this just to hurt a family–people you don't know who live in Washington D.C. and scattered across New England. Just to set something else on fire."

"Not a family, *my* family."

"One hundred thousand dollars U.S. is a lot of blubber and vodka," the shorter attorney said. He fell into a whisper with the taller man. The whisper carried the two into the hallway.

"It won't change anything if you take it," Hunter said to Aniq.

"If you want me to disappear, I'm very expensive," Aniq said.

"Maybe others need it who are dear to you," Hunter said. The jailer looked away. "You could run for president or something."

"The Snow Child." Aniq looked past him as if he were fishing.

Hunter left Aniq and joined the lawyers in conference. "It's your call," he said.

The three returned. "They'll go to five hundred thousand," Hunter said. "It's not my purpose to recommend whether or not you take it. The settlement records will be sealed, so no one will know."

"I'll know."

Hunter looked past Aniq. Outside the window a gooney bird started a slow bank over the dental arts building. He yawned. *If you show the lawyers you admire him, you'll hurt him.*

"You lost your chance," Aniq said. "Now there's no amount of money I'll take."

"One million dollars," the tall man said.

"I thought my family had no money," Aniq said.

"None to speak of," the tall man said.

"Any more advance?" Hunter said. "Going once, going twice?"

The lawyers shook their heads. Hunter gave Aniq a long look, though he didn't flick an eyelash. *Tick.* "Then, sold, a barren ignominy and frustration without a cent to your name. You are the real deal, Mr. Peary. I have some documents for you."

"Hold on a second!" the short lawyer said. "We weren't finished, Commander! This is not the outcome we felt we were entitled to from your services. I mean, Jesus Christ."

"Up here, the word is *Jisusi Cristusi*," Hunter said. He looked at Aniq. "Did I get that right?"

HUNTER FLEW TO REIKJAVIK, then took the night plane over the Great Circle to Paris. "Please close your window shades," the attendant said. Why, because the black waves below were too frightening for passengers to see? At least when you saw them, they were thinkable. Reluctantly, he closed his shade, too.

He liked the Icelandic stewardesses, with their elfin ears and long, slender legs. He sipped on spectacular vodka, ordered a second drink, and slipped into a dream.

In the dream, two women walked down a dark forest road with a slow curve. He guessed they were in their mid-twenties. They were talking in low voices, so he drew closer to hear and detected low-register English, just this side of cockney. But they wore bobbi socks and sweaters American style. The year seemed more 1932 than 1982.

The moon shone on their legs, and he could see they differed in musculature. The one on the left had stronger legs, clearly less feminine. Both wore nets in their hair and kitten heels wildly inappropriate for a jaunt like this.

Behind him he felt a flash of headlights rise over his head and cut through the shadows. The car drove through Hunter's vanishing form and up to the two girls…ladies…creatures before him. Now they turned to face the headlights. Their faces started to melt.

THE ICELANDIC ELF grazed his shoulder with her snowy hand. She had to be at least six feet tall. "Are you all right, sir?"

Hunter looked up at her as the dream faded. Or was she a dream herself? "Yes, I'm fine."

"I thought you might like a pillow," she said. "Another vodka?"

"No, thank you." He'd already set his watch to Paris time, so he didn't bother to check it. But he figured they were roughly…halfway across. He looked at the other passengers, all sound asleep, some snoring. Where did they go when they were asleep? His heart began to race, so he gripped the arms of his seat, though he tried to do so without her seeing it. Slowly he relaxed the fingers of his right hand.

She smiled. "It's such a long flight, it's best not to think of where we are. I'm just hoping you can find a way to get some rest before we get to France. Are you traveling to meet someone?"

Chapter 13

Paris

In thrust I trust.

L ANDING AT CHARLES DE GAULLE, Hunter slipped into the usual rental Jaguar and drove to Vitry-sur-Seine. Swinging into the office of Serra Leavy Cazals, he waved at Toulos Verdere as he again passed by the dark leather chairs, the black walnut paneling.

"Let's get on with this," Hunter said. Outside the window a barge pushed its way down the foggy Seine, the Eiffel Tower phenomenologically impossible, its sparkling lack of existence subordinate to his desire for coffee and therefore subject to debate. Why were then and now struggling for the same spot in his mind? His wounds whispered him back from his trance.

Hunter did not stand as Napoleon VII walked in. "Le Prince Noir" was very slight, with café-au-lait skin and blue eyes that danced away from contact. Red gums hinted at cocaine. The kid looked a little sleepy, a little girly. He slipped out of his backpack and carefully placed it on the conference table in front of him.

"Would you like some coffee?" Verdere asked.

"Your line of descent, please," Hunter said to Le Prince Noir.

In a rehearsed voice, Le Prince said, "We might start with my great grandfather, Napoléon IV, Eugène Louis Jean Joseph Bonaparte, prince impérial de France, son of Napoleon III."

"Yes, yes, the disgraced great grandson of Napoleon I, exiled to London," Hunter said. "I'd have spotted you that. Tell me why Napoleon IV would bed a Zulu camp follower."

"Please speak more kindly of my great-grandmother. She was a celebrated entertainer."

"How convenient that he was entertained by her just months before Zulus killed him in a clash in 1879. It's unlikely you have documentation from a tribe that wasn't known for its writing. There are no records in *isiZulu* until 1883. Or perhaps you can produce a love letter in English?" Hunter leaned back and gazed out the window. Then he saw Verdere and two of his administrators spying on them through the conference room's glass wall, their eyes locked on the dials of the Haas-Krämer. "Perhaps the information was conveyed to you by song."

The kid's eyes flashed. "It's what I was always told. I don't care if you believe it."

"But you care most terribly that I pay you for it," Hunter said. He looked at a piece of paper. "Three million guineas to drop your claim."

"Money is the only thing you people understand. In his teens, Napoleon IV (everyone called him 'Loulou') fought bravely with his dad in the war with Russia and survived withering fire at Saarbrucken. Our family was exiled. We moved to 1 King Street near St.

James's Square in London. Loulou found life in London stifling, so at 23 he set off for Africa with his manservant, the legendary Xavier Uhlmann, last of the *valets royaux et imperiaux*. Those who loved Loulou were upset. Queen Victoria, his godmother, sent word to him not to be rash and strictly prohibited him from fencing, though he'd excelled at the Royal Academy. Gossips whispered of his one day marrying Her Majesty's daughter, Princess Beatrice.

"But when the Zulu war broke out, something changed in Loulou. Before anyone in the house of Bonaparte could object, the child who'd been born in the Tuileries to the Emperor Napoleon III and Empress Eugénie de Montijo was commissioned a Lieutenant and dressed in the uniform of the British Royal Artillery. In Ulundi, he was determined to show his mettle. As a member of a royal family, he'd sworn strictly to play it safe, but in secret he headed up a patrol that was a mixed lot from the 17th Lancers and an African guide.

"In the lonely twilight, tending a fire, he first saw my great grandmother, the daughter of a tribal leader. In the months that followed, they met many times. His fellow officers begged him to keep his distance. Mr. Xavier argued with the prince, but the couple had fallen in love.

"My great grandmother was barely fifteen. The lovebirds were married according to Zulu custom, with Mr. Xavier as witness. A child was expected."

"Very pretty," Hunter said. "Loulou and the Zulus. Are you sure you've never worked at Madame Tussauds?"

Verdere looked quickly at the dials on the machine while Le Prince plunged on.

"Against orders, Great Grandfather went on patrol again. He and his men drew into a circle and were having coffee. At night a superior Zulu party rushed them. Loulou's men scattered. When Royal Artillery scouts found him the next morning below a pile of birds, they discovered multiple stab wounds through his heart and through his eye. He'd turned to fight the warriors off himself.

"Mr. Xavier sailed with Great Grandfather's body to London, where there was a scandal resulting in court martial. An officer from the 17th Lancers was dismissed for letting Loulou venture into danger. But the romance touched Xavier deeply. He returned to South Africa and looked up my great grandmother. 'He'd have wanted you to have these,' Xavier said, handing her this black bag."

Le Prince Noir lifted a silk sack from his backpack, its edges lightened by time, and set it reverently on the conference table. "There are three items inside." He plunged his hand within and produced a dagger, its scabbard encrusted with rubies. "This was passed down to me directly from Napoleon IV. His initials are on the blade."

Hunter pulled it from its sheath and held it to the light. The rubies' shade was pigeon's blood from India, probably Mysore. The escutcheon had the bee, the eagle, the imperial mantle, the hand of justice crossed with the scepter, and some initials scratched beside the chain of the *Legion d'honneur*.

Le Prince reached more deeply into the bag and withdrew a tiny stuffed leopard, mid-Victorian, its mouth sewn into a smile. Behind one ripped ear, time skipped like a sky wave and the cat's fur looked brand new. Its entire coat became young and plush, as though a supernatural breeze were ruffling it. Hunter refused to take the oddity when Le Prince thrust it toward him, it seemed so full of *ilumbo*.

Le Prince unwrapped some tissue to reveal a smoky daguerreotype. It showed *L'Enfant* Napoleon IV clutching the same toy. "Xaviar said Empress Eugénie owned it before Loulou," Le Prince said. "It is said the leopard watches over children at night."

"With just the one eye?" Hunter asked. "I'm sorry, but your story miscarries. For starters, this knife won't cut it. While it's *Manufacture de Châtellerault,* it's been made by a machine; you can tell by the soft plate marks. Though superintendent Chassepot resorted to machines in 1869, the firm made a point of forging all its blades by hand till 1913. Maybe you've been taken in by some *forgerie*? The daguerreotype can't be five years old. No, I was hoping you might produce something 'written in Britain.'"

A roll of the eyes. "Of course, the Zulu side has no such thing. My British relatives will not share anything with me. I've heard of your famous research. I put it to you, why do you expend so much energy in proving a negative?"

Hunter stopped himself from stirring black coffee. "I'm asking the questions. I'm not the one petitioning for money based on things my ancestors did, real or imagined. I don't let ghosts tell me what to do." He lifted his head and called out to the glassed-out ones, with their glassed-out eyes. "Could we have some more coffee, please?"

The kid looked at him. "Can't you see what happened? I'm the kind of history no one wants to talk about."

"In sum, you have nothing. When all else fails, resort to the truth." Hunter reached for his forehead; he couldn't believe he was the one perspiring. "If I can't even predict the present, with all its ephemera, what chance do I have with the past?" Best not to rattle. "I am prepared to give you a check for £2,100, likely twice your legal fees. I will not refute your story, but this is the very instant you have to believe there is no one else on this earth who will pay you more, much less listen to you. The truth is nothing more than what people believe. You seem okay. Do you have a girlfriend or whatever? You should seize the moment, 'Prince.' Take a deep breath and start living your own life."

Chapter 14

Flemington, New Jersey

A smooth touchdown in a simulator is as exciting as kissing your sister.

THE LITTLE THEATER GROUP had performed this re-enactment for twenty-five years. Hunter had seen it once, when he was twenty-five, and sworn he'd never return. But here he was. Pia had sent him the briefest of notes. She was to star.

"You'll see. It's...vivid," she wrote. "You like surprises, don't you?"

So, he'd flown from Lausanne to Newark; rented a Jag; checked in with the hospital surgeon (copacetic) and the Manhattan police (no leads); and with a relaxed mind driven sixty miles south to the lost borough of Flemington, New Jersey. While walking past the Union Hotel toward the theater, Hunter had nodded to a woman surrounded by reporters, a crowd of people, and two police cars. Mrs. Anna Hauptmann had been trying to clear her husband's name since he was electrocuted in 1936. Hunter wondered if she knew about the woman Bruno had loved and fathered a child with in Germany. Not that she needed more grief. By a malignant coincidence, Anna's own son by Hauptmann was named Manfred. Did she know there was an earlier Manfred with a different mother buried under the leaves of time?

The courtroom stage was set with chestnut benches, tables, and boxes. Stark white cards with black lettering denoted the witness, counsel, judge, and defendant–all for the benefit of the newspapermen. Incriminating incandescents hung with the same eerie indifference they glowed with while suspended above the real-life participants. Hunter took a back-aisle seat.

Lights Out

THE BLACK CURTAIN STIRS behind the judge's bench. It parts slowly, revealing a single spotlight shining on the director sitting cross-legged in a gruesome electric chair–charred wood with an iron head cap, its rusty wires dangling. The crowd gasps. Abruptly, he grips the chair's arms and stands. 'Old Sparky' glides backstage on a track, out of view.

"Welcome to historic Hunterdon County Courthouse." The director pushes his glasses back on his glistening forehead with his index finger. "My cast and I are pleased to bring you this year's performance of my play *Crime of the Century*. The events you will see tonight really happened."

The spotlight zigzags across the crowd, then darts to an oak witness box. Growing in brilliance and intensity, the light stays still.

"This is the very testimony station used in the murder trial of Bruno Hauptmann. The year is 1936, and the international media has rushed here to make uncountable newsreels and provide 24-hour radio coverage of the mass hysteria that gripped not just our nation but the world.

Audiences of that day couldn't get enough of what you are fortunate to witness for the next two and one-half hours. You will be able to eavesdrop, as it were, on the dreaded and thrilling events that resulted in the conviction and ultimate execution of Hauptmann, accused of kidnapping little Buster, the toddler son of the famous aviator Charles Lindbergh."

The director peers into the audience, seems to catch a friend's eye, and gives a little wave.

"While the re-enactors and I have been rehearsing this special public-service educational event just for you, please remember we are amateurs." He wipes his forehead. "What is novel about this production is, it's real. It really happened. If you'll just let yourself forget *when* you are for the moment, you, too, will be swept up in the tumult of events."

HUNTER SINKS back in his seat. Before the beginning of any show he attended with Dido, he loved listening for the sound of her rubbing her hands together. It was because they were so icy–but he also liked to think it was out of anticipation. He'd fold her into his arms to warm her up. In her somewhere of somewheres, in that black lacuna she was flying across, was she thinking about him? The curtain falls again, and the theatre is in darkness for a full sixty seconds.

Act 1. "Footloose."

Sound of crickets. The curtain slowly rises on a spare stage lit by a crescent. Moonbeams cast eerie shadows through silhouettes of trees staggered from back to front, suggesting a dense forest. From the left curtain, two figures stroll into view. The first is a jouncy girl in an overcoat with large patch pockets. She turns to the audience and her sister downstage:

Emily: "I hope we don't have to wait long—it's as cold as a witch's tit!"

Violet: "Shhh!"

Hunter is so familiar with this pair they might as well have been his babysitters.

Violet, in a bright red, close-cropped jacket with a faux mink collar, turns and looks up the aisle toward the audience as if gazing up a dark road. She spots something.

Violet: "What was he driving?"

Even though she's prepared him, it startles Hunter to see that the actress playing Violet is Pia.

Emily: "You must have seen that car. You were the one who gave him your telephone number. Well, the Morrows' number."

Violet: "Yes, but you flagged him down."

Emily: "It was a Nash, dear."

Violet (squinting): "Emerald?"

"Greenish, anyway."

Violet raises her hand to her head, but Emily taps her wrist.

Emily: "Don't keep fiddling with your hair. It makes you look desperate."

Violet: "We are desperate. Why else would we be here?"

Emily: "Speak for yourself." *She draws out a flask from a coat pocket, takes a gulp, and hands it to Violet.* "He's not much of a gentleman, asking us to come here unescorted through the dark like this."

Violet: "A man with a car is a man with means."

Emily: "But what does he mean? I think you should have asked Septimus Banks to come along. He comes to your whistle."

Violet: "I wish he wouldn't."

Emily: "I still think you should have accepted his proposal. Husbands don't grow on (she looks up and waves toward the branches), well, trees."

Hunter leans forward to hear better. Pia seems so remote.

Violet: "I'm the maid, so naturally I must marry the butler. Coo, there's got to be something more. You'd think a girl might deserve a little excitement." She lights a cigarette, then inhales it deeply, cupping her elbow.

Emily: "What do you expect from this guy, this 'Ernie'?"

Violet: "Maybe a movie. Maybe more."

Emily: "Everyone in Mrs. Morrow's household is sure you're Septimus' intended."

Violet: "He's at least seven hundred years old. If you find yourself in a runaway train, shouldn't you jump off? I don't want that cold fish in my bed. Imagine his blue toes."

Suddenly Hunter is back at the Beau Rivage, unrolling his socks. Pia looks on.

Headlights flash across the stage. Like a pair of Siamese cats, the two sisters turn on tiptoes to see. Recorded sounds of an automobile approaching. Its tires stop on gravel. Sounds of a car door opening, then slamming. The Unreliable Alibi strides onstage in a dove-gray overcoat, gray fedora, and gray suit. He frowns at Emily.

Ernie: "There's room for just one."

Emily needs no coaxing. She turns to walk away.

Emily: "Be careful. Remember, the Morrows lock the doors at midnight."

Violet takes Ernie's outstretched elbow.

Ernie: "I've got some friends I want you to meet."

They walk offstage. We hear the roar of the Nash starting up. With two quick toots of the horn, it drives away. Lights out, curtain.

Act II, Scene I: "The Peanut Grille."

The curtain rises. The crescent moon has been replaced by the neon script Peanut Grille, *hung over a bar. The trees have been replaced by café tables and chairs. Ernie and Violet sit in a back booth with a Mysterious*

Couple. She wears a veil over her face, he a fedora pulled down low.

Violet: "What movie are we going to see, Ernie?"

Veil: "Aren't you the shy one?"

Fedora: "I haven't finished my 'tonic' yet. Just joined us and you're already running the show?"

Ernie looks round the empty room. Not even a barkeep in sight.

Ernie: "Change of plans. We're parking right here at the Peanut Grille for a while."

Violet: "Oh. My sister doesn't know where I am."

Ernie: "Nobody does. Just be a good scout. How about a quick one? Looks like our drinks are going to be free tonight."

Lights out.

Act II, Scene II. "Nighthawks."

Lights on. Interior, Peanut Grille. There are a bunch of empties on the table.

Ernie: "Another beer?"

Violet shakes her head.

Violet: "I'd really like some coffee." She looks in her lap.

Ernie: "Unless you're planning on making it yourself, I don't see that in your future."

Veil: "How long have you worked for Ambassador and Mrs. Morrow?"

Fedora: "And who's taking care of the baby right now?"

Violet looks up very quickly.

Violet: "Are you talking about the Morrows' grandson, Col. Lindbergh's baby? What are you interested in him for? We must not talk about him."

Lights out. Curtain.

A spotlight picks up the director as he walks to the edge of the stage.

Director: "Ladies and gentlemen, I hope you will pause to understand this moment. You have just experienced Violet Sharp's Alibi. *This* is the exact moment little Buster is kidnapped."

Act III, Scene I. "The Police Station"

Violet sits at an oak table in the hot lights of an interrogation room. A detective sits on the corner of the desk, close enough to look down Violet's blouse.

Detective: "Your references, please."

Violet hands him two folded letters, which he scans and slides under a brass paperweight of the Statue of Liberty. Then he pulls out his own folder, flips through it, and thumps at a page.

Detective: "You were born in England, right? Your own mother ejected you for being salacious?"

Violet is calm, unruffled. She shakes out her hair.

Violet: "Of course not."

Detective: "Did you fake your references?"

Violet: "You're barking up the wrong tree."

Detective: "Tell me about the right tree. The ladder. Reaction time is key here. You must respond without delay."

Violet: "I don't know what you're talking about."

The detective peers deeply at her.

Detective: "You might have worn some undergarments. If you were my daughter, I'd have suggested it." *He leans back and studies her from head to toe.* "But tell me, are you anyone's daughter? That's quite the jawline you've got there." *He rubs his own Adam's apple.* "Tell me, are you a natural woman?"

Violet raises her chin.

Violet: "I will not dignify that with an answer."

Detective: "There are some very simple ways to find out. I could have the matron strip you right here, or maybe you'd prefer to tell me about how, for money, you conspired with other confederates to steal the child of Charles Augustus Lindbergh. We know a lot about that night. We can prove you were *not* at the Morrow House, as you should have been. You disappeared from view. In our timeline, you are the only one who drops out of sight. You have no alibi."

Violet: "Ask at the Peanut Grille."

Detective: "They say you were never there. I want you to think about this long and hard tonight before you return tomorrow. Maybe like a good little maid you'll find a way to sweep up the loose ends of your story and tell us the truth. You know something. If you know what's good for you, you'll tell us what it is."

Lights out, curtain.

Act III, Scene II. "Snack Time"

The curtain rises to show the kitchen interior at 'Next Day Hill,' the Morrows' mansion in Englewood, New Jersey. Violet walks distractedly this way and that. Behind her is a huge jar emblazoned with a skull and crossbones and the words 'Silver Polish' visible from the deepest seats of the theater. The director comes onstage. Violet's motion freezes.

Director: "The next day, Violet will be in for questioning by the police. During this interrogation, without telling her, they will ransack her lodgings for clues. What they will find is the pathetic trousseau of just another girl. In England, Violet's mother rejected her for being a wild child who encouraged bold looks from men. Crossing the sea in search of love, Violet toiled in Toronto before landing a position in Mrs. Morrow's service. If you're close to the limelight, you might end up with some of it, right? In 1932, Anne Morrow and Charles Lindbergh were the world's most lustrous couple, and Highfields had just been built for them. Buster's nursery was in an upstairs bedroom. Violet had *many times* cared for Buster and knew the little knacker's intimate routine. How she must have basked in the reflected glow when the handsome pilot and his wife in a shimmering gown stepped out for receptions in Manhattan and Princeton, leaving her to look after the little one. Surely, she had a right to a bit of the stardust she was so tantalizingly near. Stranger still, why was it that no one stepped forward to corroborate her alibi, even her sister? She was such a nobody, no one will bother to follow up her story and track down the owner of the green Nash. Is this a case of the truth, with its tiny red taillights, disappearing into the dark?

"Violet was able to keep her composure the first day while the detectives, under the direction of investigation leader Major General Norman Schwartzkopf, Sr., head of the New Jersey State Police, grilled her to a crisp. But now that she's learned she has to come in for more questions the following day, she drinks herself to sleep with bourbon she pinches from the Morrows' liquor cabinet. The next morning, she slips down the back stairs through the Morrow's tall kitchen, outfitted with all the modern appliances (no expenses spared), to the pantry."

As he speaks, Pia follows his directions. She takes two slices of pumpernickel from a bread safe and lines them up on a marble counter. She prepares a tomato, tears watercress from a head, places them on the slices, and adds pepper from a grinder. She picks up a sterling silver knife engraved with the letter M. With a flourish, she slathers on a thick layer of silver polish from the jar. She studies her sandwich for a moment, takes her first bite, then a second. Resolutely, she finishes it all. The director drops to a near whisper.

Director: "Cyanide is the active ingredient of silver polish. The lethal dose she has ingested will shut down her body's ability to turn the cyanide into thiocyanate. With the red cells' ability to produce oxygen blocked, she will suffer chemical asphyxia."

Pia begins to convulse.

Director: "Nausea, dizziness, and wild gasping follow about twelve minutes in."

Pia falls to the floor, thrashing.

Director: "An unconsidered life is not worth living, but how much worse the unconsidered death. Her heart will race as her breathing stops. Her eyes are X's when they find her as though softly electrocuted–her face the distinctive cherry red."

Hamming it up, sticking out her tongue in a lampoon of a death scene, Pia is suddenly bathed in a red light which gives her the telltale hue of cyanide poisoning. She rolls her head to the side in a grimace, eyes bugged, her tongue hanging out.

"Is this for real?" Hunter hears a voice behind him say. "This is worse than dinner theater. What's for dessert?"

The director peers out at the crowd.

Director: "Bruno Hauptmann's defense is never allowed to suggest Violet's suicide creates a reasonable doubt about his guilt. Violet went by many names."

A severe photograph of a woman in a pigeon hat looking more like the director himself than Hunter's Pia is projected over the entire stage.

Director: "Violet could certainly have revealed Buster's location to these people. Forget about the timeline and look at the crime."

Hunter has seen it many times–the head shot's angled jawline, hawk-like nose, gash of lipstick, and pearls.

The producer stands in the audience and shakes his fist. "Now, wait just a minute."

Director: "But for all of our exoticizing of Violet, a bigger fact remains. We're so caught up in Violet's strange behavior while being questioned, her devouring the silver polish, her incriminating suicide. But incredibly, Colonel Lindbergh himself is never directly questioned about *his* whereabouts during the night of the kidnapping before the trial. The police don't dare ask. Nor do FBI investigators. Had they plied Lindbergh with questions, they might have discovered another suspicious timeline. Lindbergh wasn't even supposed to be at Highfields the night of the kidnapping. He was supposed to be speaking at the Waldorf Astoria hotel in New York. Unaccountably he was a no-show. Instead, inside man Henry Breckinridge made apologies to the crowd. The true white gentleman's alibi is never to need one."

Producer: "That's enough. "You agreed not to bring this up in exchange for my backing."

Director: "I reserve the right to change my mind. Your pay-to-play proposal is so unethical it frees me to do whatever I want."

Producer: "You can go to hell. We will not hear of an American hero defamed like this."

Director: "What prevented us from asking the great man where he was the night his son disappeared? How is it that Lindbergh calls his advisor Breckinridge to the scene ahead of the State Police and FBI? Why do some of us fly above suspicion? The *Spirit of St. Louis*, that's why. Lindbergh's fame quintuples after Buster disappears. When you factor in his narcissistic love of risk, isn't that motive enough?"

Producer: "No father would do such a thing."

Now two other Thespians emerge from behind the curtain, dressed as stagehands. In the mock scuffle, punches are thrown. The crowd gasps.

Is Pia in any danger? Hunter rises and quietly walks up the center of the aisle. He vaults onstage. The curtain abruptly closes behind him as the crowd applauds. Hunter addresses the back of the room: "Another re-enactment disaster. This is what happens when history and entertainment have a torrid affair."

Chapter 15

Manchester, England

Gravity is the killer of young adults.

WAS TRAVELING FINALLY losing its charm? The idea of spending years trying to forget his life, only to have it remember him, was keeping Hunter awake at night, along with the gentleman in black, who'd become an increasingly frequent visitor. He'd had a brief respite in Pia's arms, but that was over before he knew it. His schedule was a jealous mistress.

Hunter debouched at Manchester Airport, breezed through customs, hopped on a train, and headed northwest to Kent's Bank Railway Station, just south of Scotland on Morecambe Bay.

Cyril Manthorne, the Queen's Guide to the Sands, met him at the station.

"It's good to meet you, Commander."

So, Cyril had done his homework, too.

Hunter shook his hand. Now here was a grip. You'd have to be strong to pull someone out of quicksand.

Seventyish (he could pass for 60), Cyril wore an iron wool cable-knit sweater that still carried a whiff of mothballs, even though it was early April. Gray curls sprang from below his threadbare Harris tweed hat. He leaned on a four-and-one-half foot brob–a carved walking stick finished at the top with an ebony handle and blue duct tape. Though it bore no auspicious jewelry, it was the scepter of his office, ratified by the investiture of Queen Elizabeth II.

Hunter glanced beyond the rickety rail station to check the Bay at low tide. The extreme reach of sand made its boundlessness almost desert-like, a glow on the horizon, except this wasn't Araby, it was Jolly Old England at its most antic and magical. In the distance, eddies sparkled like a mirage. He looked harder. Though there were miles of mud flats, there was barely a glimpse of the Irish Sea.

"Hungry?" Cyril asked.

His warmth was a surprise, since he knew very well that Hunter had been hired to find dirt on his claim that he had the right to pass his position as Guide down to his son.

"I could eat," Hunter said. "Is there time?"

"There's always time," Cyril said. "I've got something on the stove at home."

They reached the mouth of the Kent River estuary and the stone cottage that was accorded as a perquisite to the Queen's Guide to the Sands. Like Cyril's hoary hair, wildflowers roared up and down heathery footpaths around the property that dropped to a fringe of eel grass and then, infinitely, the eternal salt flats. Hunter listened. Still no sound of the sea.

"Just you wait. It'll come in like a freight train," Cyril said, leading him to the kitchen with sliding doors facing the water. "Meanwhile, we'll have lamb, with potatoes and carrots." A wink. "Don't worry, there'll be no black pudding. I loathe the stuff. Besides, it's too dear." He walked to the pot and started stirring. "When I first took my turn as Guide, money wasn't the object. It still isn't–the stipend is £15 sterling a year. But with the honor comes this old place, Guides Farm, a royal privilege since it's owned by the Queen. The Duke and Duchess of Lancaster have kept it up for the Guides and their families since the mid-16th century. It's the only home I've known for nigh twenty years." He took a flask off the shelf and poured a slug of Lanky Black whisky into the stew. "My secret ingredient."

"So, what does the Duchy get from you in return?" Hunter knew the answer. He listened intently for the way Cyril would handle it.

"Once upon a time there were no railroads or airplanes. To cross the sands from one village to another, you had to take on enormous risks. It's a 45-minute race against the tides, and a wet passage. Even if you're fast, you're going to end up walking in water. If the tides from the Kent River don't get you, the quicksand will. So many people perished, the neighboring towns got up a petition and the King created the appointment. Before then, monks from the Priory of St. Mary and St. Michael at Grange-over-Sands risked their cassocks to save imperiled travelers. Do you know the Cistercians? Their abbey's been around for 800 years. They wear white choir robes below the black scapulars. From a distance they seem like flocks of sea birds."

St. Mary, St. Dido. Hunter had playfully given his wife that nickname in happier times. Sometimes a coincidence was just a coincidence. "Who helped before the monks pitched in?" he asked.

"No one. We have the skeletons to prove it. From the beginning of time, people have been in a rush to get from there to here, or here to there—folks from Bolton-le-Sands or Slyne-with-Hest must conduct their serious business at Flookburgh Point or here at Grange-over-Sands. People think these tides are strange, but how could they be strange if they've happened forever? We're the strange ones. If fools didn't always rush around, there'd be no need for a guide. For hours on end, you can't hear or see the Irish Sea. Suddenly you're drowning in it. But that's not the big deal. The big deal is, my son doesn't want to take over as Guide after me."

With a lump in his heart, Hunter felt Cyril's extravagant loneliness. Certainly there was no recent sign of a woman here, beyond a well-thumbed copy of a book by Djuna Barnes. His research had turned up lovely Rebecca Manthorne, but she'd left the picture during the summer of 1969 and returned to her native Jamaica, leaving her newborn behind. "Did your son tell you this himself?"

Cyril's eyelids flickered. "Six years ago, we pulled up a crew of Mandarin cockle diggers who'd drowned. So, what did the local newspaper do? They ran a photo captioned 'Queens Guide and Black Helper retrieve bodies.' Ian has thick skin, but in this case, the editor was a friend. They went all twelve years to local schools together. Now he might as well have been a stranger. Ian said, "I've never seen Hong Kong, Dad. I think I'd like to visit the Far East." He went right to Lancaster University and got started on his economics degree. He's been in Hong Kong two years now."

"I hope you don't blame him," Hunter said.

Cyril pressed his lips. "There's no law says a son has to take over his father's work. I know Ian won't accept the post because he knows he'll never really be accepted here. I just want him to be asked. I'd feel free to see him go free. But the Duchy, speaking for the Crown, says they won't ask him if there's a chance he might not refuse."

Hunter closed his eyes. "So, you're fighting for his right to refuse."

"Yes. It's mine to give him, and his to take it or not."

"You must love him very much," Hunter said.

Cyril straightened. "Like any man his son."

Hearing the knock at the door, Cyril tightened. "That must be your barristers." His face reddened. So sure handed at guiding poor souls through burping pots of quicksand or electric tides, he seemed lost in his own living room. How like a blindfold anger was. Worse still, Cyril aged ten years as he guided two attorneys to the living room and chairs.

One took a long look out the windows while unbuttoning his coat.

The other fussed with her briefcase in lieu of shaking hands.

"So, you're up from London," Cyril said, an accusation. "Where are you staying?"

"The Travelodge on King Street," she said.

"Of course, you are," Cyril said.

She looked at Hunter. "At the Travelodge, you can be sure of what you're going to get. Are you there, too?"

"No, I'm at the Sun Bar and Grille."

"Oh, how quaint," she said. "But it sounds like a restaurant."

Her partner stepped in and slapped a writ in Cyril's hand. "You serve at the pleasure of the Duchy, Mr. Manthorne. Your work is welcome until the day you die. But if you choose to retire, this will serve as a 30-day notice to vacate. Your honor is not passed by descent. You're not the son of the last Guide, are you?"

"When the Duchess of Lancaster visited me, I asked her about this," Cyril said. "I asked her when I presented her a bowl of red roses I grew in this garden right here, as sure as you're standing before me. She promised me the job was Ian's."

"Ah," the woman said. "I suppose you have this in writing?"

She'd echoed Hunter's own words to Le Prince Noir. He felt panic–a starling caught in his chest. Or was it a black-headed gull.

"A promise is a promise," Cyril said.

"It's a pity she's dead," the man said.

"A pity you're an arsehole."

"Mr. Manthorne. Sir." She took a deep breath. "You can ask the young man who claims to be your son to follow you until you're blue in the face, but that doesn't give you the right to convey the title of Queen's Guide to the Sands. Ultimately only the Queen has that right."

"He is my son, body and soul. A son is a son is a son."

A sigh. "You never married his kaffir mother," she said. "I understand she ran off when he was a baby."

Cyril jumped up. "I will not have you speaking of my son's mother as if she's a whore. I mean it." He clenched, then relaxed, his fists. "What you just suggested. Think of that tonight in your Travelodge on King Street. Just the one room for the both of you?"

She flushed. "The decision has been made." She turned to Hunter. "We trust your research will back us up."

"This is not over," Cyril said.

"We've said all we have to say," the man said.

"But I've not yet told you what I've found," Hunter said. "Manthorne says his son is going to refuse. Why don't you believe him? If he were saving you in these tricky tides, you'd believe him, wouldn't you?"

Outside, the Irish Sea had come in, big as a wolf. It boomed on the shore. Spume burst onto the windows, rattling the thick glass in a hail of tiny stones.

"It's not Mr. Manthorne's title to give, even as a gesture." She turned to Cyril. "You can't give what isn't yours."

"Have you any idea how many lives his son has saved?" Hunter asked.

Cyril shook his head in disapproval and bristled like a porcupine. "It's bad luck to keep score!"

"Seventeen," Hunter said. When he'd reached Ian by telephone he wouldn't say, so he'd had to investigate it on his own, cribbing a tally from rescue accounts in church newsletters and fishwrappers from the Lancaster *Times* to Fleetwood, Ulverston, Heysham, the Westmorland *Gazette*, and records from the Abbey. There, he'd examined holographs itemizing the descent of every guide at Poulton-le-Sands.

Hunter opened his briefcase, pulled out a file, and handed it to the woman. He risked a glance at Cyril. "As for lineage, Ian's is corroborated by his mother."

"You've talked with Rebecca?" Cyril leaned forward. "I didn't authorize you to do that." He rubbed his eyes. "Did she say anything else?"

"She said you rescued people who went into the Bay in inappropriate footwear."

"There is no appropriate footwear for Morecambe Bay," Cyril said. "Barefoot may be the only way for a tourist to go." He looked out the window as if it were calling to him.

The Irish Sea was now calmer but even closer. It entered the stone cottage, slipped into the kitchen, and made itself a pot of tea. "Sometimes the Bay coughs up its 'clarty corpses.' In 1727, the mud flats yawned and exposed the perfectly dressed bodies of a horse and rider from Medieval times, the gentlemen all in coattails and finery just like that, whip in hand just-so. Minutes later, black sea birds feasted on what used to sit atop his shoulders." Cyril paused. "There's no better successor than my son, or more rightful. He knows these flats like the palm of his hand."

"We have someone more suitable in mind," the woman said.

Cyril trembled, then brightened. "Can the 'suitable' scramble over the glassies like a sea spider? Ian should be asked, is all."

"There is no lawful history of one guide choosing his successor," she said. "The job goes to a white male of good moral character between the ages of twenty and forty. No exceptions."

Hunter waved to the file. "There have been exceptions. While Thomas Orloop did not pass it on to his son in 1574, he did pass it to his daughter Altash. In 1616, she died, and her son carried on the post. Would you like me to keep going? The Guides continued their line of descent through the Wars of the Three Kingdoms. There was a gap after World War II, when the two Guides before Mr. Manthorne had no issue. But otherwise, the passage from father to son was virtually unbroken. I found all of these in London in the National Archives. I thought you folks were from London."

"We'll have to review these," she said, shuffling through the folder. "Whether or not these documents are proofs will require further study. I find this very disagreeable, Mr. Dauger, as I find you. We're paying you. This act of charity is going to be another black mark on your reputation." She caught his eye. "Oh, yes, we've heard about Greenland."

"Mr. Manthorne Jr. will receive a formal job offer–in writing and through your office–by next week, or I will notify the National Council for Civil Liberties and they will publicize the details of this dirty deal of yours. This tide will come rushing in, and I will ensure you are personally named in the papers." Hunter looked at the two. "Speaking of deals, dirty or otherwise, Cyril's instincts are good. You two are sharing one room at the Travelodge, though both of you are married, and not to each other."

The advocates raced to their car, slammed the door, and sped away.

"Your son is lucky to have a father like you," Hunter said.

"I'm the lucky one," Cyril said. "I can't ever pay you back."

"You're telling me."

Cyril studied him a moment. "Come with me. I'd like to show you something in the coal shed." It was safe to walk outside now. So near just moments before, the sea had twinkled back to a distant shimmer.

Stopping before the rustic lean-to, Cyril pointed to a foggy promontory, then drew his hand in a sweep to the north. "Far more than I, Ian has shown bravery here, such bravery. He kens these waves like none other."

"What waves?" Hunter said. The Irish Sea had disappeared.

Hunter looked west, then south. Morecambe Bay would have been to Lindbergh's left as the *Spirit of St. Louis* hurtled across the southern tip of England toward Paris. Following Cyril to the shed's door, he inhaled and smelled the pitch in the shingles still wet from the spume. Cyril creaked the door open. Light slanted in from the bright afternoon sky. Curled in a corner of the straw-lined floor, a terrier looked up while a single wiry pup slept beside her.

"Hello, you two," Cyril said. "There's a good girl." He patted the mother, reached down, and pulled up the tiny puppy, who flicked an eye open. Now he put her on Hunter's chest. "Last of the little loves."

Hunter tried to put her down, but that didn't work. Her scrambling lower claws dug into his leg and woke his gunshot wound. "I don't have to hold her," he said, raising her higher so she looked directly into his eyes, and he felt the connection of an animal communicating fiercely through silence. When she made the movement to rest her head on his shoulder, he let her. When she sighed, he knew it was all over. Running his hand down her knobby back, he marveled at her sturdy all-weather coat.

"She's yours," Cyril said.

Hunter took a breath. Here was something he hadn't planned. He felt something warm above his heart–the puppy was peeing on his suit. "This is all I need."

She looked him long and dark in the eyes and gave a tiny yap.

"Good thing. She's the last of the litter, and all I have to give you. Her mother is the pride of the Lake District. Some call her a border terrier, but this close to the border, you're safer just to call her a terrier."

Hunter surrendered. "What'll I name you, brown eyes?"

"Who gave you the birthright to name this dog? Of course, you're named Dido, aren't you, girl!"

THAT NIGHT, it took all of Hunter's reasoning and £30 to convince the housekeeper at The Sun Bar & Grille to let him bring Dido into his room after dinner–in a wicker basket he picked up at Lancaster Market.

"What do you weigh, seven pounds?" he asked when the door closed and left the two alone. "Maybe you'll like this." Dido gobbled up the poppers and kidney he'd rescued from the pub downstairs. Watching her circle round and round at his feet and then settle down, he sipped another pint of ale. Dido looked up at him, searching for the first words she would ever speak. "I will take care of you," she said with her liquid brown eyes. "And I will never let you go."

Chapter 16

Sevenoaks Weald, Kent, South of London

The future in aviation is the next 30 seconds.
Long-term planning is an hour and a half.

DIDO LIFTED HER sculpted head and closed her eyes to feel the breeze as Hunter's rented Jaguar slalomed south through the copses toward the windswept south coast of Britain. There was a sense of 'whee' to the curving roads that took the pair to the thatched-roofed hamlet of Sevenoaks Weald in Kent, a half-timbered parish trapped in the early 1500s between London and Hastings on the English Channel.

"Am I close to Long Barn?" Hunter asked the gentleman in black, who with his good hand was swinging a scythe at the side of the road.

"Yes, you're close." He nodded toward a nasturtium-covered trellis surrounding a thick black gate a few hundred yards ahead. Behind the gate, a stone mansion beckoned with time-darkened privilege. "The Lindberghs came here during Hauptmann's execution to hide from the world press. What's your excuse?"

Hunter said nothing.

"And who is this in the front seat?" the man asked.

"Dido."

"You're going to have a hell of a time traveling tethered to that."

Dido stood on her hind legs and gave the man a wary eye, then a sharp bark.

"Yes, I am. Want a ride?" Hunter asked.

"No, I'm fine right here."

Hunter drove the last quarter mile to Long Barn, turned off the ignition, and let Dido cool off on leash. Drowning in lush green shrubbery, this retreat, with its high-peaked gables and Elizabethan high-seriousness, was crowned entirely by terra-cotta tiles. Diamonded with secrets, the narrow casement windows were bolted shut against intruders.

Here and there, ravages to the design confused the Shakespearean period with the Edwardian, though at least the updates made this place easier to defend from intruders. Not so easy to scale that seven-foot brick wall.

Hunter turned a slow circle to let his research on Long Barn catch up with his eyes. Dido followed, keeping neatly from getting her line tangled around his feet.

Birdsong kept the silence from being deafening. Lurid headlines still vibrated in the air. *Lindberghs in Seclusion. Lindberghs Vanish to England. No Bairn for Long Barn.* The wildly off-kilter *Romantic Hideaway.* So much press forced its way toward this gate during the Trial of the Century for the Crime of the Century that the local bobbies set up blockades to repel strangers from entering within a one-mile radius of the estate. On the other side of that stone wall were the corn fields, so flat Lindbergh used to land here in the dark.

Dido yipped. A man in a cloak and a tam-o-shanter left the house from a side door and approached along a trellis shaded by climbing roses.

"Tom Watchman." He returned Hunter's shake and bent to rough the scruff of Dido's wiry neck. "And who is this little elf?"

"She calls herself Dido," Hunter said. "May I bring her in with me?"

"For what you're paying us, you could have brought the whole litter." To Dido he said, "As for you, little darling, you may find some amusement with Ajax, our cairn."

Lining the stone-floored foyer was an oak livery cupboard, a William and Mary library table, and a scatter of high-backed chairs with barley-twist stiles.

When they followed the long, dark hall into the drawing room, Ajax seemed reluctant to come forward. Instead, he skittered to the extreme left corner of the salon, slid below the concert grand–it had the heft and ponderous inelegance of a Bluthner–and waited for them, front paws extended, and hind legs raised, tail wagging. Dido ventured halfway under the piano until she felt the cool of its shadow, then slipped back to Hunter's side.

"Well, that's a start," Hunter said.

"We have a little something to get rid of the road dust," Tom said. Withal, his wife June appeared with frosty drinks on a silver tray. "The Ally's should be here any minute. They're walking over."

"I think I hear them now," June said. She was taller than Tom though she stooped to compensate and spoke in a halting whisper. She loped to the door.

Tom nodded to Hunter. "They're getting on. I guess we are, too. But you'll find we're all sharp as tacks."

Hunter looked into the great hall to see a Georgian Sheraton sideboard rising from the shiny black oak floors. A vase filled with gladiolas woke up the white wall. Dido stared under the piano to catch another glimpse of Ajax, who answered with his shiny eyes.

"Commander Dauger, this is our bookkeeper, Randall Ally. Sadie, here, is our very popular school guidance counselor."

"Retired, of course," Sadie said, and gave Hunter a peck on the cheek. She strayed to his ear. "You'd think you'd be the first person to ask us about the Lindberghs in ten years, maybe more. But you're the second since yesterday."

"Was it a gentleman in black?" Hunter asked as they found their seats.

His new friends looked uncomfortable. He waited for someone to answer. No one did. "You must all have been very young when the Lindberghs were here," he said finally.

"Younger than they were," Tom said, "and very much in love. We'd just been married ourselves."

"We were still graduate students," Sadie said. "We'd come in to help out after school and on weekends."

"How many servants were there?" Hunter asked, just trying to relax them.

"There were eight, I believe, including ourselves," Sadie said. "Tom and June, the two of us, Sandford, Phippie, the Latimer child, and then Henrietta, not counting the outdoor hands running the farm. Kenneth the gardener was in charge of them."

"You're forgetting Aeva," Randall said.

"Not forgetting her," his wife said. "That woman is just not worth mentioning, that's all."

"Most beautiful girl in the parish," Randall said.

Hunter watched June, who'd bitten her lip instead of joining the discussion. Her silence was growing larger and was almost becoming the controlling force in the room.

"She was dismissed by Mrs. Lindbergh after two months for getting too familiar," Sadie said.

"Too familiar with Colonel Lindbergh?" Hunter asked.

"Too familiar with everybody. But particularly Colonel Lindbergh."

"If you think it was sexual, it wouldn't be right," Tom said. "I think Aeva was interested in aviation. Starstruck. She was always asking him about flying."

Hunter nodded. "What was her position in the household?"

"Just housecleaning, windows, shine the coal scuttles, polish the silver," Sadie said.

"Does she still live around here?"

"Everybody is still living around here, unless we're in the cemetery," Randall said.

Hunter said nothing.

"Colonel Lindbergh had no time for dalliances, if you're going there," Tom said. "He was deeply grieving the loss of his child with his wife. She told him not to read the newspapers, but he couldn't help himself, all the way until Mr. Hauptmann was hanged."

"Electrocuted," Randall said.

"And good riddance." Sadie's eyes danced. "Imagine stealing somebody's child, and somebody so famous as Colonel Lindbergh's. Mister Charles did everything he could to help Miss Annie through this, but she wasn't getting over it, either. How could she? Sometimes I'd walk into a room, and I'd catch both of them just looking at each other with red eyes. Or I'd see them hugging each other, their shoulders shaking. One Wednesday evening she was just grabbing onto the corner of the mantle as if she were drowning. You'd hear her crying at night, too. I'll never forget, the sound was haunting, almost beautiful, like a dove's."

"Why Wednesday evening, in particular?"

"My guess is, you're putting together a puzzle," Tom said. "But why?"

"It's more like I'm pulling a puzzle apart," Hunter said. "To see if the old pieces can fit a new way. About the Wednesdays…"

"That's when the friends from London were invited over, like clockwork," Sadie said. "What a group. Ambassador Kennedy was the favorite, oh, so many times. 'Good old Joe' brought chocolates and some lovely whiskey." She glanced at her husband. "Then Mr. John Asquith, from the theatre. He was concerned with the way their privacy was being protected during the trial."

"Of course, the Lindberghs were devastated," Hunter said. "But did you ever see them arguing?"

Another glance from Sadie to Randall, who scowled.

"Like any young couple," Tom said.

"What did they argue about?"

"They argued about their dead child," Randall said. "He kept saying what's done was done."

"I think he wanted his wife not so much to forget about the first one, but to move on." Sadie paused. "Colonel Lindbergh was restless. Once it was dark and his family was asleep, he'd take long walks across the heath and then cut down the Blake hillock into town, maybe for a drink at the Speckled Hen. I saw him coming in very late one morning. He gave me his perfectly adorable grin, you know, and put his finger to his lips as though to shush me. I mean, he was still a man, you know. Or part god. He liked to talk with real people. He said he was a real student of human nature. He often told me how real I was."

"I just think he thought you were pretty," Randall said. "Which was no lie."

"Now you're talking," Sadie said. "Keep it up!"

"No problem there," Randall said. "I mean he loved his wife. It's just that the poor woman turned to stone when her baby was murdered. It's no surprise she became a writer. What better way to get out of looking people in the eye."

"Were there other State Department people beyond Ambassador Kennedy?"

"He wasn't ambassador until '38 or so," Tom said.

"But he was already well known in London," Sadie said, "nobbing about with the Cliveden set. Oh, yes, we had our own master race. Did you know Col. Lindbergh and Mr. Kennedy looked quite alike at the time? What they usually talked about, loud enough to ring the glassware, was the dangers of the Jews. Mr. Douglas Fairbanks would chime in with them, along with the owners when they were in town. Sir Harold George Nicholson leased Long Barn to the Lindberghs while he was chargé d'affaires in Berlin."

Hunter looked at the thudding Bluthner. That explained that monstrosity.

"Sir Harold's wife, Lady Vita Sackville-West, was a novelist, you know," Tom said.

"Before the Lindberghs came, while her husband was away in Germany, she and Virginia Woolf were in charge of their own affairs, so to speak." Sadie winked drunkenly at Hunter.

Randall plunged on. "Yes, the Wednesday get-togethers. Certainly we saw a lot of that nasty Dr. Carrel, the Nobel laureate who worked with Col. Lindbergh on the glass heart, or some such invention."

"Imagine the concept of a heart made of glass," Sadie said. "Speaking of which, mine's empty." When Randall didn't take the hint, she reached for the decanter herself.

"When Mr. Henry Ford visited from America, he and Mr. Lindbergh looked over plans for the airstrip Mr. Lindbergh wanted to build here," Randall said, "and they chatted about that. But most often they talked about Hebrews."

So much for the lost child. "So, this really was a nest of anti-Semites," Hunter said.

Tom spoke quickly but softly. "Some of them came for the gardens. Sir Harold and Lady Sackville-West designed them together when they lived here before. But yes, among many interests they shared a concern about what they called the Jewish situation."

"Is it something in the water?"

Hunter caught his reflection in his glass and looked away when he saw Lindbergh staring back. Perhaps there was such a thing as a gentle hatred. He leaned forward. "Did Mrs. Lindbergh participate in this?" Anne Morrow Lindbergh, deep in her grief, the mourning dove. "Was she nodding, agreeing, laughing, or what?"

"She gave the Colonel long looks when he started to spout off," Sadie said. "She rolled her eyes. But she didn't stop him."

"Neither did we," June blurted out. She hung her head.

"But we were just kids," Randall said. "We were servants. They didn't want any suggestions from us."

"We know now that's no excuse," Tom said. "We still ask God to forgive us for not telling them off."

"When he was around that kind of company, he'd go on and on and on," Sadie said of Lindbergh. "Just before Christmas, a whole group of them came here, the entire 'nest,' as you say. It was another Wednesday night, all of them calling the Jews a festering sore bent on destroying Christianity and all who dared to defend it. The scum who were in this parlor!"

Randall took a deep breath and stole a look at Sadie's glass. Was he wondering if there were some way he might add some ice?

"This is *entre nous*, isn't it, Commander?" Randall said. "I'd just as soon you didn't take notes in that little book, because we're just talking, you know? My wife and I found this so repulsive even then…"

"But Coco Chanel was so stylish and tiny," Sadie said. "And Lady Astor, the first woman member of the House of Commons, had the most marvelous furs…"

"They thought themselves knights of a new order," Randall said, warming up. "Hitler, they said but oh so wrongly, would make Europe great again."

"I remember standing with my serving tray right on that carpet over here, and I saw Col. Lindbergh coolly in agreement, nodding his head at unspeakable evils. Whenever he winked at me, I felt a flush. He stepped closer, as if we were sharing the moment, though I didn't feel that way at all about the Jewish people. I've always felt terribly sorry for them. Then, in front of everyone, he ever so gently ran his hand down the back of my dress."

Tom was refilling everyone's glasses, but Randall shook his head when he came to Sadie's.

"Did he take advantage of you?" Hunter asked Sadie.

"It did the Lindberghs no credit," Randall broke in. He gripped the arm of his chair with his arthritic fingers, then relaxed them. "Our little parish doesn't stand for such things. Um, are you church or chapel, Commander?"

"I went to church when I was in the Navy," Hunter said. "Strictly non-denominational. Funerals of fellow pilots. 'To those who perish in the air and sea.' I have a sense of the spiritual, but I've never felt entirely sincere in a pew, participating in very specific rituals when my head is somewhere else. To be quite honest with you, church may be the thing I'm most afraid of."

Sadie leaned in. "Do you think you could fly solo across the Atlantic, Commander?"

"Do you think there was any possibly the Lindberghs were fighting because Mrs. Lindbergh wasn't entirely sure that Col. Lindbergh had told the police everything he knew about the case?" Hunter asked.

No one spoke.

Finally, Tom cleared his throat. "I do remember there was some crazy talk that some people thought there was a possible baby swap or an accident that had nothing to do with a kidnapping. Myself, I could just imagine Colonel Lindbergh's disgust at having a child with a deformity."

This was interesting. The word deformity had not come up.

"He was a perfectionist," Sadie slurred on. "I remember he'd fly into a rage if a flower petal were left on a table, or a glass were left out of the cupboard."

"An imperfect child would have been an embarrassment," Randall said. "Almost like having a Jewish child."

"Oh, no," Tom said. "I think we've drifted off course and ventured into gossip. This is not at all our intention. You are mistaken if you think we've suggested the Lindberghs were doing anything but grieving for their boy. They were sick over him, tearing their hearts out, and they did have hearts."

"When the boy's murderer was hanged, I mean electrocuted, in 1936, they cried for hours," Sadie said. "I heard screams from their bedroom. They went months barely talking to each other. The sound of the silverware got louder and louder with every tea. Then, Colonel and Mrs. Lindbergh sat on the German side during the Opening Ceremony of the Olympics because they were invited guests of General Goering and his wife."

"The Goerings were their hosts," Tom said. "They might have thought, to refuse to sit with them would have been rude. I like to think Goering and Lindbergh were probably just two grownup boys talking together, two of the world's best pilots. They weren't talking politics; they were talking shop."

"But still," Randall said. He pulled a cigar from his vest pocket and lit it. "It was extraordinary he chose not to sit with the American spectators." A slow inhale. "Probably not a big fan of Jesse Owens. Black magic, I imagine he thought."

Hunter knew that Lindbergh's earliest forays to Berlin in 1936 were at the suggestion of the U.S. government.

Major Truman Smith, the U.S. military attaché in Berlin, was Lindbergh's secret contact with the Pentagon. It was Smith who suggested Lindbergh tour the airfields in Germany; Smith who let it slip to the smitten Goering that Lindbergh might like to meet him; and Smith who foresaw Germany was gearing up for war.

Lindbergh knew enough to keep his options open. He took up the challenge and visited Berlin as a spy, slipping undercover as himself. *Keep it dark, won't you?* With Goering boasting at his side, Lindbergh toured the Nazi *Flughäfen*, took mental snapshots of engineering facilities, memorized the newest monocoque and low-wing construction techniques, and hobnobbed with other birds of his feather in prototype plants, counting the Messerschmitts along the way.

Wherever he stopped in Deutschland, he received thunderous acclaim. Radios tuned, the Germans considered The Lone Eagle one of their own, a "Viking prince of the air." Lindbergh allowed his image to be subverted into propaganda. Hitler, who routinely suppressed the comments of strangers entering Germany, was so taken with Lindbergh that he insisted the press print Lindbergh's entire speech about the dangers of warfare and all the armament he'd seen: "Europe, and the entire world, is fortunate that a Nazi Germany lies, at present, between Communistic Russia and a demoralized France. With the extremes of government which now exist, it is more desirable than ever to keep any one of them from sweeping over Europe. But if the choice must be made it cannot be Communism."

Lindbergh found the Luftwaffe bigshots "especially anxious to maintain a friendly relationship with England." Based on his private chats with Goering, Germany had "no intention of attacking France for many years to come, if at all."

Charles and Anne stayed at Goering's high-security mansion in Wilhelmstrasse; Charles was even invited to fly a Junkers 52. How very odd. What was Anne doing during the interim, touring gardens with one of Goering's mistresses?

The next day of their visit, Hermann guided Charlie into the secret engineering caves below Adlershof. Hunter knew Lindbergh's reports to the U.S. Secret Service and the Department of War were still classified. Having read them.

HUNTER GLANCED at his own glass and wondered how much time had passed during his reverie. True, you never completely floated to the German side, Daddy, just partially. But that part was your heart. The marvel of it was, even with your racism, selfishness, and mixed sympathies, you remained an American, through and through. No, please, God. I won't be your son.

Hunter turned again to June. Now it was she who was studying him. How long had he disappeared into his involutions? When you catch yourself slipping from reality, in order of priority, you aviate, navigate, communicate.

Aviate: He stopped June from filling his glass a third time.

"You know," she said, "you could be Mr. Lindbergh's older brother as I remember him."

THAT NIGHT HUNTER DROVE into town through the ancient forests of Andredsweald, looking for the most beautiful woman in the parish.

Dido yanked her head up, reading his mind. *Think like that and maybe you are a Lindbergh.*

"Don't worry, she couldn't possibly hold a candle to you, girl," Hunter said.

He passed a silent hay harvester and looked at the stone houses, the sedge more neatly trimmed as he neared his destination. Leaves on the oak trees turned up, embarrassed by the rising wind and sensing a storm. Crows spiraled, then clung to the branches. As he continued into the parish, Hunter ran his hand over Dido's fur as she curled back to sleep. Now he was very much in the village, which grew with Kafkan intimacy. Everything was getting too close, invasive. Continue, intruder.

Chapter 17

Andredsweald, England

It's more important for a pilot to be lucky than good.

LAST CALL. The only pub with the lights still on was Riot Goat. Hunter drank in the thirteenth-century half timbers, forged-iron hinges, and brass knocker. The rest of the surrounding village was so still he paused on the stoop to listen to a horned owl before pushing open the bar's ancient door. Three hulks sat in a snug, drowsing in front of sweating pilsners.

"I'd like a glass of Macallan," Hunter told the keep.

"There's a thought," the keep said. "Along with a bevy of the King's own Scottish Borderers to serve it, right, lads?" He nodded to Hunter and poured him a Bishop's Finger.

"When in Rome. Thanks."

Well, this part of Sussex really was Rome 2,000 years ago. After the required three quaffs and a game of darts—Hunter won because the others couldn't be bothered to stand up to throw–he looked at the bartender and took a breath.

"You're about to tell me the real reason you've come here," the keep said. "Because you've clearly missed the tourist season."

"There's a woman, Aeva," Hunter said. "Lives around here?"

The keep said nothing.

"She used to be a great beauty," Hunter said.

The keep stared. "She could be your mother."

"Do you know where I can find her?"

He looked at his watch. "She lives at Rivertop Farm, with her daughter. They'd be asleep now, if the daughter ever slept. My cousin is their housekeeper. She says the young one works her eyes red every night till four or five in the morning, researching legal histories. She's a barrister but has never appeared in court. An odd one, that, but brilliant."

"Do you have her telephone number?"

"Hold on." The keep flipped through a beat-up phone book. "Here." He looked at the telephone behind him, then back to Hunter. "The booth is outside, across the street, near the chemist's."

"HELLO, MY NAME IS Hunter Dauger. Is this Aeva?"

"No, it's her daughter," a flat voice said.

"I'm sorry to call so late, but I'll only be in town tonight. I wonder if she'd like to speak to me about something that happened fifty years ago."

"It's pretty late." The phone crackled during the disapproving pause. Then the voice came back on. "She says she could talk for a few minutes. If you come now."

The lonely streetlights flashed as Hunter and Dido drove east, climbed a hill that tunneled into the dark, and broke into an oasis-like enclave, awash in heather.

Tall and built from rag stone quarried in the 18th century, Riverhill House rose above the copse and hickories, window upon window of storeys rising into the night. A single powder-blue Triumph TR-3 slept to the left of a huge turkey oak; two Land Rovers guarded the right. Hunter counted five Tudor chimneys. When he reached the ironstone black door, it opened before he could knock.

A woman in a blue sweater, her blonde hair streaked with gray, smiled. She nodded at his Jaguar. "You can bring your dog in."

"How do you know I have a dog?"

"I have eyes." She picked a single strand of fur from his jacket. "Bring her here."

Dido was only too happy for the invitation. Her nose had made a funny print on the misty glass of the passenger-side window.

"Dido thanks you, and I thank you," Hunter said.

"Ooh, you're almost too young. Look at this tiny thing. Could I hold her?"

"Sure."

Dido snuggled against her cheek, then looked at Hunter to make sure it was all right.

"You are a little love," she said. Then she reached out her long hand. "I'm Aeva. Please come in."

The first time he heard Aeva's name, Hunter sensed something hidden in the silent A. A girl cloaked in the mystery of a diphthong might be a princess in the electromagnetic spectrum. Just flick a switch and she's invisible on a radar screen. More intimately, it might be done with just a look, some downcast eyes. All these years later, Aeva still had it all: powerlessness with a core of power, understated beauty–she was a mistress of dramatic illusion, a secret waiting to be unwrapped. Perfect for a grieving Lindbergh. How different was his wife Dido's seductive interiority, wild and uncultivated like the heath listening to him a few yards away, moist under the moon. A Bathsheba who'd never invite you in. Aeva, by contrast, wouldn't declare who she was, but she might leave the window open for you.

Hunter stepped inside and followed. At the far end of the gloomy salon, he detected a harp. He'd expected Tudor fireplaces, but they were German porcelain, and valuable.

The runner was Kidderminster, in velvet pile so plush it 'remembered' the gentlest of passages. Not only was this house built for the lord of the manor, someone with cold cash owned it even now. "How long have you been a tenant here?" Hunter asked.

Aeva paused as they entered the library. "I have a life estate. I used to work here, and the Rogers family granted it to me."

Hunter looked past her and saw a gray silhouette on a ladder adding books to the top shelf as though she were sifting through unexploded ordnance. He nearly jumped when the clock on the mantel struck three a.m.

"It's all right, come in," Aeva said. "This is my daughter, Aelwyn."

Hunter was struck by the family resemblance. But in place of her mother's ethereality, Aelwyn, in her mid-forties, had a wash-and-scare haircut–a China chop. She wore torn-off sweatpants and a dirty sweatshirt. She didn't turn to greet the visitor.

"She's just reordered the library," Aeva said.

Hunter guessed at the unspoken: no doubt for the fiftieth time.

"She's an advocate," Aeva said.

"Mother," her daughter warned.

"It's good to meet you," Hunter called up to Aelwyn. "That's quite a task."

Aelwyn turned, but she avoided eye contact. "I liked it better talking to you on the telephone, when you didn't express insincerity," she said. She descended and sat in a lump beside her mother on the sofa. Stranger than strange, she grew more ravishing with the act. But her posture betrayed her. Sprawled with legs splayed, she pulled at her sweatshirt and scratched her side.

"You were gracious to let me talk to your mum," Hunter said, never having said mum before, not in that sense.

"I'm just here to help my mother with her estate, and then I'm out of here." Aelwyn spoke to Hunter, but her eyes were on Dido, who was curled quietly below the sofa table. She reached for her. "That's a pretty pup." Head down, she half-turned to her mother. "He said I could hold her," though Hunter had not. He lifted Dido and handed her over. In an explosion of resentment Aelwyn stood, nodded, and removed Dido to the extreme end of the library, turning her back to the room.

"Your daughter's asked me not to say anything insincere," Hunter said. "I'm a probate investigator, as well as a Charles Lindbergh…student or scholar or what have you. At Long Barn, they told me you worked briefly for the Lindberghs."

Aeva had lost contact with him, watching her daughter, but now she looked quickly back with keen eyes.

"They implied, somewhat unkindly, that you were dismissed," Hunter said.

"I was barely there before I was out the door," she said. "I'd turn a corner and see Mrs. Lindbergh looking at me. Unless it was late at night, and then it was Colonel Lindbergh, with his embarrassed smile. To this day I think he visited my room just to talk. I never met a man so curious, so lonely." She paused. "Lonely is not the correct word. He had a nervous sort of remoteness he was desperate to conceal. His manic curiosity sometimes seemed to come as if he were struggling to find some key to relate to people. He wanted to know about who cut my hair. He wanted to know every detail about my bicycle–even where the rubber wheels came from–and if I kept a diary. He wanted to know what kind of bird that was that didn't move on the fence. He wanted to know what music I listened to, what I thought of President Roosevelt, and what my friends in the village thought of him. He asked quite shyly if people in the village had celebrated his flight. He grew excited. He said he was almost positive he remembered flying over my house."

Hunter took a deep breath. "It seems like you learned quite a bit more about him than one would think, working just two months in his household." He looked over at Aelwyn, who'd released Dido and was now playing solitaire, lost in the faces of the cards. "Doesn't she hear us?"

"She's concentrating. She gets that way sometimes."

"Your daughter mentioned your estate. Are you not feeling well?"

Aelwyn turned to them and raised her voice. "Mother, I have autism. I am a special case. Is that what you're going to tell him next? We don't have to talk with strangers. We don't even know who he is."

"Do you mind my asking what year you were born?" Hunter asked Aelwyn gently.

"Yes, as a matter of fact, I do."

He made a note to check the records. Then he turned to her mother and looked at her with a sadness he'd never allow himself to express. Why did Lindbergh need to compromise young Aeva if his sweet Anne were just steps away and they'd been through so much together? How cruel these English strangers were to 'seduce' Lindbergh with their quiet demeanors. It wasn't Aeva's being the most beautiful girl in the county that revved him up, it was the *risk*. Not only could Lindbergh fly across the Atlantic, he could do *this*, too. And this, and even this. It's what kept the *Spirit of St. Louis* aloft, what we loved him for. Though as a poster child for autism, the concept of risk was alien to him.

Suddenly Hunter couldn't help himself. "What kind of music did you like to listen to?" he blurted.

"William Vixie and his Band." Aeva brightened. "Col. Lindbergh hadn't heard of them, but he was the only one in Sussex who hadn't."

"Who cut your hair?"

"My mother cut my hair, and for years ever after."

Hunter's breaths grew shallow. "What kind of bicycle did you drive?"

"A Royal Eggert. Robin's egg blue."

"Quickly, who was the bird on the fence?"

"He was a stuffed bird, from India. A robin magpie."

"What did you think of Roosevelt?"

"A fool. The crippled president of a bankrupt country. Everyone made fun of him."

"Where is your diary?"

Her head danced, swaying. Her daughter's eyes widened. She brought her hands to her temples, the turkey oak aflame. "My mistake. I told him I didn't believe in diaries."

Chapter 18

West Berlin, West Germany

Fly low and slow and don't tip on the turns.

JOHN ABEL SMITH raised an eyebrow at Dido. She returned his stare, then risked a yip. "Do you know how expensive that carpet is?" Smith asked.

"Yes, she does," Hunter said.

"We're not accustomed to pets. We have a rule against them. Look, she's about to jump up on me."

"You're wrong about that. She's an exquisitely trained animal. I wired you about her. She's given me good luck from the minute she was given to me. Unlike you, she's never, ever caused a problem. You're the one who made her bark."

"You brought her from England," Smith said. "I find that interesting. We have quarantines to protect us in Germany. If you reported her arrival to airport security, she should still be in quarantine. Maybe that's why you arrived in your own plane."

A rental, actually. With Dido as co-pilot, he'd flashed across the English Channel below a host of stars. Above Le Havre, he turned off his active IFF to go 'dark' at just the right moment–not so much radar deception as to spare French interceptors from needless worry. With no one the wiser, he and Dido landed at a private airport in the dead of night. If you took on a dog, you had responsibilities which might or might not agree with intrusive rules from nosy nations.

"I'm always astonished at things that upset, and do not upset, you Germans," Hunter said.

"I'm not German," Smith said.

"*Noch nicht.*"

"Not that she isn't a lovely little thing," Smith said. "Sylvie, do we have a basket for her? Or perhaps could you hurry-scurry and fetch one?"

"She has one of her own. I've brought it," Hunter said. "Dido doesn't like change."

He removed her basket from his Vuitton duffel and set it in the corner opposite the one occupied by a tall glass vitrine. "She's sensitive, so I won't subject her to your vile Nazi memorabilia." Alongside Smith's loathsome lugers were the suicide capsules. Each glass ampoule held a deadly dose of potassium cyanide. At the last moment, when all else fails, crack it open before your enemies can interrogate you.

Dido comfy, Hunter and Smith went to the conference room.

"Word is, you're cracking," Smith said. "Your proofs are too elegant, your grand delusions unhinged. Live like you're in a Chekhov story, die like you're in a Chekhov story. You might have picked a more convenient time to self-destruct."

"Thanks for caring," Hunter said. "Cracking, by definition, happens when structural integrity is lost. When did it become cracking to tell the truth?"

"We're talking about a luxury commodity. The truth might let you sleep at night, but it doesn't pay the bills. Let's just say my clients 'hope' you won't decide on caprice that this claimant coming in today is the natural son of Herr Messerschmitt."

"Just another bastard, then," Hunter said. He plugged in the Haas-Krämer. "And just another money case. Unless you tell me, why would someone spend years proving he's related to a cruel industrialist who used slave labor?"

"No worries, it's just the usual. Let's keep this short and sweet."

"Messerschmitt died four years ago, and his estate is settled."

"Let's just say his heirs find this new beneficiary unsettling."

In walked Arnauld Hemmer. Stork like and prematurely bald, he kept his depraved green eyes in eternal motion–maybe to catch a flying insect. All the while Hunter wired him to the Haas-Krämer, Hemmer bounced his knee.

"Please stay still," Hunter said. "Restlessness is the sign of a liar. From Berlin to Hong Kong, 'poor man's leg' means you're 'shaking your money away.'"

Hemmer froze.

"Here's a question to help me calibrate the machine," Hunter said. "Are you ready?"

"Yes."

"Do you believe you're the son of Willi Messerschmitt?"

"What kind of test question is that? That is *the* question."

"How instructive and fascinating," Hunter said, "that you didn't say yes."

"I have proof."

"More likely pudding," Hunter said. "Like to see what I have? What I have is new." He crossed his legs as though he were in Ned's den in Long Island. "You've told us you weren't born in a hospital, but apparently you weren't born anywhere else, either." He pulled a sheet from a folder and pushed it toward Hemmer. "Please note the signature of Xina Drivuch, your devoted delivery midwife who now declares that after all she did *not* bring you into this world."

"This is not possible. How much did you pay her?"

"More than you did, apparently. But it's not who you aren't, it's who you are. Here's a *photograph* of you with your real mother. I'm sure you'll be relieved to learn she was not one of Willi's mistresses."

Hemmer glanced at it and touched his lower lip. "That's my stepmother. Why would you think that all of his mistresses have been disclosed?"

"Here's your birth certificate."

"That's a forgery."

"Here are your fingerprints, from East Germany."

Young 'Messerschmitt' took two full breaths.

"Here are your grandparents, holding you," Hunter said. "What's your problem with them? They look okay."

"They were a cover. It's time to acknowledge who I am. I embrace the hatred."

"Finally, we agree, kid." Hunter spun a document across the table. "Simon Wiesenthal's new *Zivilklage* attaches Willi Messerschmitt's assets most directly. I've marked *Instruktion* December 30, 1943, your 'father's' call for fresh slave labor from Mauthausen-Gusen concentration camp. You know, those prisoners deserved to be paid for building his lovely Messerschmitt 262 jet fighters. Wiesenthal was one of the lucky survivors."

Hemmer's eyes wandered to the open door, finally resting on Dido, curled up in her bed. Hunter drew so close he could hear Hemmer inhaling through his nose.

"See these initials? Your 'dad's.' He's culling undesirables for mental or physical deformities and rushing them to Sarmholdt Euthanasia Centre per Direcktive W7." Hunter's webbed toes twitched. "See the number below this green stamp? It raises the Mauthausen-Gusen list of the dead to 141,211 human beings. By the time the lawsuits are settled, there'll be no funds for your benefit. Wiesenthal and his foundation will be watching you for the rest of your life. If he can't ruin you, he'll at least ruin your name. When the courts elude him, he has ways of exacting vengeance upon the damned."

Hemmer's eyes started to boil.

"How are we doing so far?" Hunter asked.

"Excuse me," Hemmer said softly. "I'd like to call my lawyer."

AFTER HEMMER BOLTED out the door, Smith said, "This is more like it. Vintage Hunter. Glad to see you're yourself again, though this has been a costly defense. Wiesenthal's consultation doesn't come cheap. Details like this put your expenses on the moon."

"Who's going to fault me for running up the Nazi expense account? It matters very little to me how much I cost your 'clients.' What surprises me is that both Messerschmitt and Merck have retained you in their defense."

"Don't pretend you didn't enjoy yourself. You frightened the poor young man to death."

"To scare someone, a little réalité doesn't hurt. The poor little Messerschmitt calveling." Hunter swallowed. In this second all the Pretenders seemed to dissolve and become one thing, himself. "Surely he was in it for the love, not money."

"Say, what happened to you in New York?" Smith asked. "There was a lot of talk about the shootings. Want to hear my theory?"

"You pay me to bust theories. In matters of the imagination, let's keep it real. The problem with you and your unsavory clients is, you don't allow for coincidence."

"It's the Carrel people."

What was he getting at? Just how tuned in had Smith become to Hunter's buried intuition, or was he just fishing? Hunter shrugged. "Why would the Carrel people be interested in me?"

"You tell me. At the American Club the other night, Boo Cunningham was going on and on about how the Lindberghs' share of royalties for inventing the world's first artificial heart could be as much as $100 million right now."

"Club facts," Hunter said. "What a bunch of hideous B.S."

"We're talking about a hideous fortune, and a hideous group of people who'll want to be part of it. Who better to play the lost heir than you? You know all the angles."

"Lindbergh's patents for the Lindbergh-Carrel glass-chambered perfusion pump would have expired in 1951, his European patents in 1954," Hunter said. "Even if he'd made modifications, he'd have had no protections after that. 'The inventor trades public disclosure of his invention for a finite lifetime of a monopoly of the product.' So, I'm not sure there's really anything to cash in on by being a new Lindbergh heir and sharing old, expired patents. The royalties earned during the lifetime of the patents could conceivably be obtained from the other beneficiaries, but that still presumes someone commercialized the patents– built a working product during the life of the patent, not decades later. It's a hallucination to imagine there's money there."

"Maybe others share in the hallucination," Smith said. "You're awfully informed for someone who claims not to be interested. Maybe you enjoy being a target."

Hunter closed his eyes, then laughed. "You're so fascinated with the money; I can't rule you out as one of my shooters." He nodded toward the vitrine.

"You know and I know, if someone really wanted you out of the way and there was enough money involved, you'd be dead," Smith said. "I am only a go-between, paid by commission, just as you are. But think–how many imposters have you unraveled? The shooters might be anyone. People get upset, Hunter. Some of them may feel the need to get even for what they imagine they've lost. By my count, you've earned over $9 million from the four Chanel defenses alone. No doubt some of your vanquished foes dream every night of taking you down."

"I'm hungry," Hunter said. "You?"

"You mean at that degrading restaurant? You mean you'd bring your dog? Dogs aren't allowed inside the nicer restaurants. Not through the front door. Perhaps they have a place for her in the kitchen."

INSIDE HAVANA SEXY, Hunter called for *La Tropical* and watched it foam into its sparkling self on the table. He ordered the *Ropa Vieja*. Quiet as a mouse, Dido slept at his feet, courtesy of a thousand-mark note slipped to the owner.

"You've made my point. Money talks," Smith said. He eyed the blackboard. "We aren't going to have the same thing again, are we?"

"What did Heraclitus say? You can never order the same Cuban meal twice."

"Having the same routine has made you eccentric, in spite of your efforts to cover for it. That's why you've substituted the dog. I've watched and waited for you to mention her, but you haven't said a word about everybody's favorite fraud, what was her name? Pia?

They're talking about *her* at the club, too."

"You're just trying to stir up trouble. Who do I have to go in and beat up now?" Hunter asked. Right now, he could use a little less of Smith and his cheery annihilation, his pencil moustache, his scarf more craven than cravat. On the other hand, Smith had just transferred $70,000 to his account as agreed. "If you want to know, I think of little else." Stalled in time, Hunter watched Pia stab her lobster tail, free it from its bright red shell, and try a bite. "In fact, there's no use denying I brought you here just to be closer to her. We sat exactly at this table." He refused to look at the pack of spirit cards.

A tiny fish in the tank flashed, then disappeared. Above the tank's black lights, the dusty painting of the solitary skier stared from his Alpine mountaintop, surveying the savage beauty of the gorge below. *Strength through Joy.*

"If you two are such an item, why isn't she here now?"

"You're not listening," Hunter said. "Who says she isn't here now? Pia enjoys an intertemporality. Unlike you, she isn't tripped up by notions of past, present, and future."

"From what I could see, she was perfectly capable of looking out for her future," Smith said.

"You're on thin ice, Smith. Still, there's an advantage to your limitations. When I get up from this table, I'm not taking you with me."

"In her cleft of time, I suppose she's thinking exclusively of you?"

"Yes. In my imagined sense of Pia, that's an absolute necessity." But Hunter knew she was likely with her director, Radu, now that the Hauptmann play had run its course. And what was Hunter himself up to now? He'd have to get back to her. The problem was (and he'd spent weeks not facing this), he wasn't ready to see her again. Seeing her too soon could be disastrous. His love for Dido hadn't kept her from disappearing. The last thing he could afford to do was rush things with Pia.

"So, really, she's a projection of your own narcissism," Smith said. "The only difference between you and Lindbergh is, he was more successful with women."

"That's the deepest compliment I've ever received from a man. This is fabulous. Slow down and realize what you've just said. You consider me his equal as a flyer!"

"Only in the sense that I wouldn't fly with either of you," Smith said. "As for discovering who's shooting at you, that's going to be a voyage in the dark."

Hunter had known Smith for years, and trusted him–about a few things. He wasn't sure he liked him.

Chapter 19

If we fly a little lower, we'll see the lights.

THAT NIGHT, HUNTER FELL into a dream. He was, yet wasn't, in Havana Sexy. Sensing dark eyes watching from the spirit world, he tried to toss the *diloggún* for good luck, but no matter how loudly his cowrie shells crashed to the table, he was coming up dead. Bursting from his chair, he thrashed outside the restaurant to find cool air. He was walking along a boulevard when suddenly the gentlemen in black floated to his side.

"Got a minute?"

"I will not dignify a nightmare with conversation," Hunter said.

The man nodded. "Some things are better left unsaid. Or undone." He held out his dismembered hand, but the fingers had grown back, like the severed legs of a starfish. The hand looked smooth and young, a 15-year-old boy's. He turned it over to show Hunter. "Like that? I'll bet it makes you feel all good about yourself inside." He looked over his shoulder. "I don't suppose you see those men over there."

"What men?"

"Those men. See, you make my point. That's how bad luck works. It's like a breeze, straight from the Ile en Bas d'l' Eaux." A sigh. "Do you see nothing from the other side? Don't you know what a warning is? Hark."

The shot slammed into Hunter before he heard it, knocking him over, but not before he watched a second bullet slide through his rib cage as slowly as a dessert spoon through ice cream. More slowly: a third bullet passed through his hand without touching it. Wrapped in the sound of wings, the gentleman in black kneeled beside him. "*La Flur s'apres former*. I'm sorry. *Magick*." Hunter's left leg jerked up. Fire raged in his neck as a fourth round slapped his throat, nakedly real this time. A hideous pincushion–spiny with bright pain–he twisted to his side and gripped his back. As the shooting stopped, a group of shadows approached him, holding hands. Far behind them was a smaller shadow. The silence grew enormous, leaden. Hunter felt the great beating of his heart grow louder and slower as it synchronized with the heartbeats of the dead. He waited for it to become completely silent. So, this was how it ended.

It was too late anyway if you'd already turned up the Nine of Air. *"Hunting and chasing has begun... Risk of death."* The illustration showed a bird flying erratically, desperate not to be shot. At the bottom of the card, the barrels of nine rifles were trained on the doomed creature. Hunter's eyelids flickered as his head fell backward into darkness.

Chapter 20

Brooklyn, New York

Probability of survival is equal to the angle of arrival.

UNTER'S HEAD REELED. How long was he out? He felt the unmoored sense of lost days, weeks of travel, but all he knew right now was, he was sitting down. *Aviate.* Dido's tongue licked his left hand. His breaths grew shallow. He held up his hands; neither had a wound. He touched his throat–no bandage. If this was another fantasy, he'd plunge into it. Don't discount the good news that you weren't really shot in your dream.

Navigate. His mind raced to fix his plot and drift. The blackout he must have just suffered didn't help. This wasn't West Berlin. This wasn't Manhattan. This seemed more like…Brooklyn. That's right. He was in an office in Brooklyn.

"Well, it's been a while." Michelle Feelia, Dido's psychotherapist, held out her hand to shake his. Hunter took in her large, tortoise-shell eyeglasses and an open-necked silk blouse. So many of her ilk dressed as though they'd just vacationed in Guatemala, but Michelle exulted in sensuality. Was that because she herself had spent so much time on the 'other' side? "I checked," she said. "You were four appointment books ago. Ten years."

It felt familiar to hear Michelle's low voice. He knew so few women who enjoyed air-conditioning–some were terrified it might age their skin or chill them to goosebumps. Michelle kept the small window unit behind her desk up at full gust, lifting her loose, wavy hair. On the yin side, she kept a kettle of water that doubled as humidifier on a handy electric hotplate.

"So, what's new?"

Dido flattened to make herself invisible.

"I've met someone. Her name is Pia." He waited for her reaction.

"Tell me about her."

"She's an actress."

"What does Pia look like?"

"She's about my former wife's height."

Her eyes widened. "Does she bear any other resemblance to Dido?"

"She could maybe be her…cousin, but younger. She could have been the ring bearer at our wedding."

"Flower girl." Michelle got up abruptly at the screech of the kettle. "The training for rigidly stylized sexual-identification roles starts early." She gave Hunter a mug of tea and took a sip from her own. She shook her hair out. "What attracts you to Pia, and how did you two meet?"

"She's quite serious about her acting. We talk. She wants to learn about everything. She likes Cuban food. She has an incredible sense of herself." Hunter paused. "She was an opponent in a lawsuit."

"Is she very much younger, Hunter?"

"Sure, I guess so. Yes. She thinks it's funny."

Another sip.

"And what do you think?"

"I think it may be too much of a cliché."

"Is that why you're here? Only you can decide that."

"I know this isn't your job to give advice, but I find myself without family and with no other counsel."

"You know, Hunter, I can wish you well, but I can't give you permission. Only you can do that."

"Ah, the head-shrink speak. Now we're co-conspirators in a cliché. Or does that sound 'hostile'?"

"How much time have you spent together?"

"Actually, I've been avoiding her."

"Interesting. But something deeper brought you here. Maybe referred pain."

"Don't bring Freud into this."

"Your brain blacks out when your injury is really to your heart."

She was getting closer to the D. word. Hunter shivered. *Don't let your thoughts travel.* Don't take this hard. Just listen to her questions. Aviate, navigate, communicate. Hunter closed his eyes.

"Are you sleeping well?"

"No, actually."

She nodded twice but seemed distracted by a snag on her sweater, which she tried to push into the yarn. Then she looked up. "Hunter, what do you see when you look in the mirror?"

"I don't recognize myself."

"Since when?"

"Since…I met Pia. That's not true. I can't tell you how long before. Pia just made me more aware of how I felt."

She made a few notes. "Maybe we need to talk about your wife. Have you seen her?"

Hunter looked at the silent fan on the opposite side of her office. Wired to the upper corner above the window, it was at least thirty years old. What made her keep that when she had the air-conditioner installed? In her bookcase, a yellow smirk of *National Geographics* lined the bottom row. He looked at her brass desk tray, filled with expensive pens. Then he looked at her silver lips. Was silver lipstick still available?

"No," Hunter said. "Have you seen her?" She'd always been Dido's therapist.

"No," she said. "Enough time has passed that I feel I can tell you my greatest professional regret is that I was not able to help your wife."

"Have you heard from her in any way?" Hunter asked.

"I can see Dido is still very much with you, in her absence. All I can say is, she's very much with me, too." She reached over and touched his hand. Then she leaned back in her chair. "Can you tell me again, because a decade can sharpen some recollections, or at least distort in an interesting way: how did she disappear?"

"The more I think of it, the more it was, 'I woke up, and she was gone.' Like a big black curtain coming down."

"Had you fought?"

"No." If only. He might have drawn her close. He could have told her he was sorry. "I got lost myself."

"That happened when you started searching for her, Hunter," she said gently. "Like Lancelot in *King Arthur*." She smiled. "I'm reading it to my son, who's six. Here you are, you've lost your Guinevere. Neither of you took it very well. Lancelot disappeared for a year. No one could find him. Sir Thomas Malory writes, Lancelot 'went wood.'"

"Crazy, you mean."

"Hunter, as your friend, not as your doctor, because I will not take you on as a client, I need to tell you, it's important to keep clear in your mind what's real and what isn't. What wood have you disappeared into? I saw your interview in *The New York Times* magazine."

"Then you know I have a job."

"A quest, you mean. Inserting yourself into other people's problems. You want to make sure it's not only about not facing your own."

"It pays well."

"Take me back. When Dido disappeared and you stopped flying and started investigating, what did you feel?"

"I felt lostness in all that black, like I had disappeared."

"What did you do about it?"

"I threw myself into my work and it slowly went away. You'd probably say I papered it over."

"So, this is really what you wanted to talk about? If I remember correctly, you're an orphan, right?"

"Is that like a thing with you?" Hunter asked. "Dido told me you asked her that once."

"Some people believe if you can't find your parents, you'll never find yourself. I personally don't think that true."

"Identification, friend or foe. I'm not sure that's my radio frequency," Hunter said. "It's more like this, Michelle. What if people you were missing were easy to find but they swore to the world *you* didn't exist?"

"That would keep me awake."

"I have these dreams."

"Tell me what you mean."

"It's not like I can tell them. They're so real, it's like they happen to me."

Chapter 21

Naples, Italy

The unknown is a distracting co-pilot.

THE HOTEL EXCELSIOR–illustrious for hosting guests from Clark Gable and Giancarlo Giannini to Sophia Loren, Alfred Hitchcock, Lena Wertmuller, and Mussolini–was renowned for its views. Hunter looked past the gauzy curtains billowing from the floor-to-ceiling windows to see the slow purple slopes of Vesuvius rising to their seductive twin peaks. To the east, he watched the silhouette of Capri rise from the water like the head of a crocodile. Welcome to sunny Italy.

"It's good, your bringing me here, Marcello," Pia said.

"The name's Hunter."

"Whatever," she said, and rose from the bed. Hunter shifted his eyes from Vesuvius to Venus.

"Can I come along this time?" she asked, leaning over to give him a deep kiss.

"Is this bring-your-daughter-to-work day?"

"I want to see how the actors stack up against me."

"Sure, come along. You can drive."

"Hunter, this is so healthy for you. You are relinquishing control." There was a knock on the door. "Although you did insist on ordering breakfast for both of us without consulting me."

A smile. "You're going to love it."

She slipped around the door while Hunter admitted the room-service cart. Everything was in season. Lemons so yellow they drove you mad. The porter was a bit too curious. Unable to catch a glimpse of Pia but inhaling her fragrance, the young Lothario withdrew, pulling his cart as he departed for his dungeon.

Hunter donned the wheaton Kiton jacket Pia had picked out, while she wore azure, her forehead and the back of her neck still glowing. This was going to be a good day.

"Have you ever been to hell before?" Hunter asked her when they settled into their rented Ferrari 512. "I mean, outside of Germany."

"This isn't my first time to Naples, if that's what you mean."

Hunter gripped his seat, unobserved, he hoped, as Pia rocked on her spiked heel and jammed her pointed toe into the accelerator. The Ferrari growled. Dido flattened herself into the back window ledge. Darting around cabs and Vespas, Pia whizzed by the palm trees and turquoise water that cuddled the restaurants around Borgo Marinari and the Castle of the Egg, downshifted as she threaded the needle up the narrow streets of the Spanish Quarter, and stopped at the Vomero.

Hunter looked at his watch. "You realize, we're not shopping."

Pia put on her sunglasses and zoomed past Grand Hotel Parkers along the upper shortcut that dropped down to Mergillina. Just before she started to climb the hill along Via Petrarca, she took a hard right and pulled over. "Now where?"

Hunter looked at his map. "Take this road," he said. "Now take this one." The touristy restaurants and post card stalls turned into drug stores and then desultory tenements. It almost seemed the weather changed from a perfect sunny day to a gloomy atmosphere of dreary disappointment. Then, between two walled estates, a narrow road took them inland for hundreds of yards.

"Can't you feel it?" Hunter said as they spiraled lower, following the signs toward Lago di Averno. "We're approaching the portal to the underworld."

When Lake Avernus finally burst upon their vision, it was black, dejected–a spectral disappointment. Ringed by sulky tall grasses, it was just as quiet as the moment before the meteor slammed into Napoli from space eons ago and connected the surface of the Earth to Hades.

"Here Dante, guided by Virgil, descended to the lower depths to write the *Inferno*," Hunter said.

"It's chilly," Pia said as she slowed beside the edge of the lake and parked. "I do so love it when you lecture me. You can't pretend you don't know I studied the classics." Dark-lidded strollers studied them, then turned away. "Where is your meeting?"

Ahead was a grocery store at the gateway to hell. Across the lake, just 500 meters wide–a stinkhole, really, gasping with volcanic gas–were Roman ruins so insubstantial and dissolving the painter Turner might not have been able to capture them.

A nightingale chased by a swarm of larks flew toward the lake and then banked, as though an invisible wall of repulsion directed their light hearts away.

"Jesus," Pia said.

"Maybe not exactly Jesus," Hunter said. He scanned the lake, the dead grass, the collective sigh of Averno. "Let's head left and follow the lake around."

As Pia backed, turned, and drove slowly clockwise around the Stygian Lake, Hunter felt the weight of its dreary aspect. The few cottage yards that abutted the road were shielded by tall fences and grape vines.

Far from being a tourist attraction, Avernus was now a tourist repellant that was slowly being choked by tendrils and roots from the surrounding farmland. As Pia continued her circle, Hunter saw a deserted, locked, dilapidated motel. He translated the Italian: "Motel Hell."

"Do you remember what a sunny day it was when we started out, Hunter?"

"This won't take long," he said, and scooped Dido below his left arm. The hair was straight up on the back of her neck. "It's okay, girl."

"Is she all right?" Pia asked. She slowed the car but still ventured forward.

"No."

Finally, a stone wall appeared on the right. Looming ahead was the parking lot of a nightclub and bar, which did indeed face the black lake, shielded by weeping willows. "Lovely," Hunter said. "Attention weary pilgrim. Stop here for a quick one before you abandon all hope."

For years, this was rumored to have been a safe house for the Camorra. Dozens of cars were abandoned here, some dusty with time. There wasn't a soul in sight.

"This is something I have to do alone," Hunter said.

When he emerged from the Ferrari, a black dog approached, blocked his path, and gave him the eye as he headed for a sign in flickering neon scripted into "Lounge."

Inside, Hunter's client was waiting–dressed to kill. Opposite him, a small, angry man in a rumpled suit was sunk into a corner, as if he'd been waiting there for a thousand years.

On the telephone, Hunter's client had made the situation succinct: "The pay is not great, but you might find this amusing. Someone thinks I'm the devil. He's suing me for what he's sure I've done to him, though he's done it to himself."

"The devil always says he's not the devil," Hunter said.

"But this time I'm not lying."

"That's a sure sign you're lying."

HUNTER WALKED BRISKLY to the pair. "*Buongiorno*," the two men said and stood.

"I was hoping you'd bring the lady in," Hunter's client said. He spoke so elegantly it was alarming. He wore a van Dyke, a narrow black suit, and a half smile. Was that Tartini's *Sonata in G Minor* playing in the background? "Your *bambola* looks delectable in that car, if you don't mind my saying so. What a doll. *Bellissima!*"

Better wrap this one up quickly. "I've brought some documents," Hunter said.

The tiny man in the corner, having taken his seat, shot back up. "Let me see those."

Hunter shrugged. "They're notarized. They prove this gentleman is not the devil."

The little man tore at his hair. "How can you prove a negative? He's ruined my nightclub, murdered my clientele, devoured my livestock! My wife's spaghetti…no longer sticks to the wall."

"I can prove a negative if the negative never existed in the first place," Hunter said.

"I am not the devil," the client said. "Nor have I ever been the devil. I was not the devil yesterday, nor will I be tomorrow. Signor, you don't just get to be the devil because you want to be the devil." He stood and slowly rose from the floor, but no one saw it. He spread his van of scarlet wings.

Hunter glanced at the door.

"Why must heads turn to me when something starts to go wrong?" the client said. "I bid you good afternoon. You have represented me with distinction. I suggest you and Dido head back to your room at the Excelsior and finish what I started. Or do you insist on calling her Pia now? Tell her *Ciao* for me."

Chapter 22

West Berlin, West Germany

If a pilot screws up, the pilot dies. If ATC screws up, the pilot dies.

"Y OU'VE HAD A CAKEWALK so far," John Abel Smith said. "But this will be a little different. The ultimate claimant."

"Yeah, a cakewalk." *If you consider recounting nightmares in which your new girlfriend appears to your possibly dead wife's psychiatrist a cakewalk.*

"So that's why you're offering me more money," Hunter said. "As far as I'm concerned, a pretender is still a pretender."

"The thing is, this guy is for real. And he knows everything."

Through the glass partition of the law office, Hunter watched the interrogatee sitting alone inside the conference room. "I thought he'd retained Snazel and Lipcritz." Hunter had faced Snazel before.

"He's saying he doesn't need them," Smith said. "In perfect English. I'm afraid you've met your match this time."

Hunter opened the door to the conference room. Tall and wiry, with a lean, tanned face, the young man stood with the clear-eyed grace of a natural leader.

"Hi, I'm Rolfe Renner. Pleased to meet you."

He was in his mid-thirties and blond, with a lanky Scandinavian physiognomy and sleepy blue eyes. He looked at Hunter as though from a great distance. As though he'd just stepped from the cockpit of the *Spirit of St. Louis*.

Hunter took a slow breath, then hit the toggle switch. The Haas-Krämer hummed as its two blue lights flickered on. While he put the armband around Rolfe's bicep, he felt him staring at him.

"You know, we could be brothers. Or half-brothers," Rolfe said.

"While I get this set up, just talk about anything you'd like," Hunter said. "I won't interrupt you."

Rolfe didn't need to relax. He seemed born that way. Far from being irked by the Haas-Krämer, he seemed solicitous of it. "Am I staying still enough for it to work properly?"

"You're fine," Hunter said. "Free-associate, though in the fullness of time no doubt we'll be devolving upon the single question, can you touch upon your claim to be Charles Lindbergh's son?"

"Careu Kent's son," Rolfe said.

"You can be Careu Kent's son all day long. How is it you're Charles Lindbergh's son?"

Not only did he look like Lindbergh, he did seem devastatingly like a younger version of Hunter himself. Hunter's own resemblance to Lindbergh so disturbed him he often shaved with his electric razor while looking out a window, rarely into a mirror. Growing up, he routinely ducked photographs. In high school, and later in his college flying club, more often than not, the caption was *Not Pictured*: Hunter Dauger.

"My mother's name was Vera Renner," Rolfe said. "She died of breast cancer when I was eleven."

Hunter glanced at Smith, who looked from one to the other.

"I've sent you the letter my father wrote to her from Connecticut," Rolfe said to Smith, who nodded. "It was among the private things she hid behind a sliding shelf in her bookcase. She kept more letters from him below a panel in her jewel box."

"You found them after she died?" Hunter asked.

"She was quite alive. I was ten."

"So, she spoke to you about them?"

"At first, she was quite angry. She told me I had no right to snoop. Just before she died, she received this last one, which she shared with me. She told me, 'Someday these letters may mean something to you. But they no longer mean anything to me.'"

Hunter took the photostat from Smith.

> *My dear Vera,*
>
> *I am so distressed to hear of your illness. Why haven't you told me about it? So many individuals of merit, I suspect because of the contaminated environment that afflicts so much of this World, have had to contend with enormous grief at such a young age. You did not deserve to have this happen to you. I cannot express my frustration at the inadequate research programs, not only in the United States but in Germany and Switzerland. Once leaders in...*

Hunter studied the handwriting–cramped, narrow, big initial caps and descenders, the slant remarkably to the right. It was genuine. He noted the small "d" in the salutation. Only Charles Lindbergh could speak to a lover, the mother of his child, with such savage detachment.

> *I know it has been more than a long time since I drew near to you. The demands on my business travel have made it impossible to do better than I have done, but I know that is not an excuse. So often I wonder what you are thinking, and determine to visit you if only you would let me, only to find myself out straight with the unimportant affairs of men in meetings as close as Hamburg, but you and I have always known that schedules are a devil I must obey. I convey my deepest regard for you and your son, the thought of whom is such a tonic to me. For now, consult the doctors and follow their guidance. You are ever in my regard. Yours, CK, Darien, January the seventh, 1958*

Smith rolled his eyes. "I must say, I like the signature. Now that we've had the opportunity to test the original, I can confirm the paper was manufactured in 1953; the ink dates to 1955 or 1956." He lifted an eyebrow. "Of course, this proves nothing. Nor is your matching blood type persuasive."

The three men were quiet a moment.

"Anne Morrow Lindbergh has never acknowledged you or your mother," Smith said.

"Nor we her," Rolfe said.

"What is your objective, beyond money?" Hunter asked.

"I hate my father. But because I am a surgeon myself, I am interested in my father's invention, a temporary substitute for the human heart."

"You mean you're interested in the royalties," Smith said.

"My father's brash ignorance, his mechanical knack for tinkering, was exactly what his inspiration Dr. Carrel was missing. Maybe his charm, goddamn him to hell for it."

"It's a waste of time, son," Smith said, "to hate your father, whomever he may be. Where could that possibly get you?"

"Dead, apparently," Hunter said, thinking of the scene at Grand Central. He took a long look at Rolfe. "None of which makes you Lindbergh's son. If you were, it would still be a spider's path to unravel the expired patents to cash in on the millions you imagine would be coming your way. You'd waste your own life trying."

"With its vacuum chambers, the Jarvik 7 is directly indebted to my father's glass heart. If nothing else I could sell my claim, to Carrel's people."

"Don't you think Lindbergh's uncontested Yankee heirs have looked into this?" Smith asked.

"Lost in their involutions and guilt," Rolfe said. "Among my siblings, I'm the only doctor. Think of what good it might do if I were to dedicate any share I might derive to research. This is a long shot, but I'm here to earn the right to try."

The Haas-Krämer stirred and hummed at a higher pitch. The red needle pegged to the right and nearly burst from the dial. Hunter looked at the ultimate Pretender, IQ of 175. You are the prince of liars. Ghosts attend you. You are…so very nearly me.

Smith rose. "If you'll excuse us, Doctor, I'd like to speak to Commander Dauger in my office."

When Hunter started to rise, Rolfe touched his arm. "Is it all right if I speak with you first in private?"

Smith shrugged and left.

"You've been ducking some lead," Rolfe said. "I'm glad to see you made it here, seeing you're a target yourself.

How's your leg feeling?" He looked at the sutures healing near Hunter's hairline. "You ought to be more careful."

"What would you know about that?"

"You wouldn't expect me not to have researched you," Rolfe said and grinned. "I own a telephone. And I'm used to using the microfiche machine at the library to look up periodicals."

"Tell me about myself, then," Hunter said, looking carefully into his eyes.

"Not an easy task," Rolfe said. "Like me, there is no you."

Hunter poured himself a glass of water, took a sip, and lowered it to the table, tremor-free. "Tell me something I don't know."

"Perhaps we could talk… about your man in Havana. The one who got away."

Hunter grew silent. "He didn't get away. We lowered him into the ground. We buried him. We covered the tracks. I'm not proud of this, but we sat and quietly emptied a bottle of rum, just to make sure. Dead men don't climb out of the grave."

"Not just any bottle of rum. A good choice, by the way. Cuba Zina is sweet and dark. Let the guys in the pickup boat drink the Ron Palma Mulata."

"I'd love to know who you questioned to learn this."

"It wasn't so much an investigation as a reunion. The members of your crew–Swann, Blethen, Spencer, Driscoll, Fitzpatrick–were brave men, sadly all dead. But Fitzpatrick was in the hospital when I reached him."

MIRRORS ON MIRRORS. The Haas-Krämer's needle shifted and pegged sharply to the left. It was one thing for Lindbergh's magnetic compass to have lost its direction over the Atlantic. Here, across the azimuth of personality, there were fewer guarantees. How could it be that Rolfe's galvanic skin resistance was nearly zero. Hunter adjusted the gain.

"It's reading all over the place," Rolfe said. "I have something of a gift with gadgets. Let me see what I can do."

"What exactly do you know about Lindbergh and Carrel?" Hunter asked.

"So, you believe me?" Rolfe asked, as though a bargain were being struck.

So, the doctor needed more validation. Hunter watched him look through the door Smith had left open. Catching Rolfe's eye, Dido jumped from her basket and trotted in. She lifted her front paws to Rolfe's knees as she wagged her tail.

"Hello, little friend," Rolfe said. "I just might have a little something for you." He looked at Hunter. "Is it all right?"

Hunter nodded. He watched Rolfe give Dido a tiny biscuit. The most disarming thing about interviewing your younger self was, you seemed so nice.

"Just tell me, leaving nothing out, what you know about Lindbergh and Carrel," Hunter said.

As Rolfe began to speak, Hunter gathered his energies. The more closely he looked into his pretender's eyes, the more anxious it made him. This was not happening. He tried to stay below the level of screaming.

"Well, as you know, our father shunned the glow of celebrity," Rolfe said. "Turn on the lights, he'd run for the dark. He was a very private person."

Our father. Hunter shook his head. "The jury's still out on that. John Q. Public may have bought the myth that Lindbergh was just a farmer's kid from Little Falls, Minnesota, but he was really born in Detroit and grew up in Washington, D.C., the wealthy son of a fully inflated congressman. Rep. Charles A. Lindbergh Sr. was a master manipulator of the backstory. He hosted more fund-raising parties than you could shake a lobbyist at. Money flowed in. Revolving around that was vaulted ambition, not to mention women of all types, while Lindbergh's mother, Evangeline, tended the home fires. The 'introverted' Charles Lindbergh. Maybe Superman went to high school in Smallville, Doctor, but young Lindbergh went to Sidwell Friends with the children of other Senate members and ambassadors. He was born with a silver spoon in his mouth."

"I'll take your point, but he still disliked crowds, even when the world was at his feet," Rolfe said. "St. Charles. When they ran toward his plane at Le Bourget, something changed in him, deeply. Whatever illusion of boyish modesty he emanated was magnified a millionfold. After the ticker-tape parades, he had entrée to the salon of any distinguished human in the world. Mahatma Gandhi, Pablo Picasso… Imagine being the dear friend of every president, emperor, scientist, artist, or plutocrat you could think of, however swell, however cruel. Oddly, his world got smaller. Trouble with your phonograph? Contact Tom Edison. Fancy a loan? Dwight W. Morrow, the U.S. Ambassador to Mexico, was a partner at J.P. Morgan. When Lindbergh married Morrow's daughter, he deepened his luck and became more of an insider. But what might he do next? He'd already stood the world on end. People were so in awe of him they stammered in his presence. He walked through echelons of flashing cameras wherever he went, until they became a roar in his ears."

"Was that the man you saw as a child?"

"I'm one of the lucky ones. I never saw him."

Hunter swallowed and looked away.

Rolfe held up his hand. "When he died, he left me with my curiosity. I grew intrigued with the scientist, not the pilot, he might have been. From 1928 to 1930, he kept an apartment in Manhattan, but he also lived with his wife's family in New Jersey while his house was being built. His star burned so bright it wasn't long before he bumped into

Albert Einstein and Alexis Carrel, who won the 1912 Nobel Prize for his vascular sutures. Though his writings were unhinged, Dr. Carrel's sutures revolutionized medicine. As a boy, he was inspired by the miniature stitches he saw seamstresses using in Sainte-Foy-les-Lyon, the French hamlet where he was born. Their embroidery is world famous."

"Dr. Carrel the eugenicist," Hunter said. "Not everyone is impressed with his 'work.'"

Rolfe nodded. "The seeds of anti-Semitism were latent in Lindbergh. They were passed down to his father by his grandfather, and more before. Nurtured by his new friend Dr. Carrel, they woke in him and grew, racing up walls and covering the windows, a hideous, smothering kudzu."

Hunter glanced at the Haas-Krämer. The needle was too quiet. "What was *your* childhood like, Rolfe? Is there a secret handshake for anti-Semites?"

"You've lived in Germany," Rolfe said. "I don't have to draw a map for you. Lindbergh's first brush with Carrel was social and might not have been improved upon had Lindbergh's sister-in-law Elizabeth Morrow not slipped toward death from a damaged heart valve due to rheumatic fever. Few know Lindbergh was in love with Elizabeth first before he proposed to her younger sister Anne. Elizabeth was taller, more elegant, just a lovely girl. At some level he might have wondered, was there a way he could have them both? If only he could take advantage of his friend's breakthrough suture techniques by taking Elizabeth's heart outside her body so her system wouldn't collapse while Carrel repaired it. Well, there'd never been a heart transplant before. But it was Lindbergh, so distant personally, so scientifically immature to the point of rudeness, who had the negligent spiritual…irresponsibility to dream of such a thing. The unscalable wall, of course, was how *do* you take a heart out of a body and keep your patient still living? Only a monster with superhuman detachment would consider it."

"Wouldn't some people just call it luck?"

"Where you come from, yes," Rolfe said.

"So here they were, Tom and Jerry."

"Lindbergh first visited Carrel at the Rockefeller Institute Laboratories in Manhattan. Then, when Carrel's racist ideals were no longer tolerable in New York, the Rockefeller Institute banished him to the Isle Saint-Gildas. Lindbergh was a frequent visitor to Carrel's Elba. They savored their shared interest in engineering–sometimes Lindbergh even made entries in Carrel's private notebooks. Lindbergh could take the stiffest calculations and make them elastic somehow."

Hunter darkened. "I'd be interested to see Carrel's notebooks. I've spent a lot of time trying to track them down." He took a risk. "I say you're bluffing."

"I got them from my mother. She was trained as a researcher, but Dr. Carrel would only allow her the title of laboratory assistant. There was no love lost between them when Dr. Carrel had his heart attack, and she was asked to preside over closing the clinic without any compensation. She felt she had a right to them."

Rolfe opened his briefcase and took out a stack of four black Morocco notebooks. Hunter seized the one on top and began to read.

Chapter 23

West Berlin, West Germany

Pilots read checklist items to each other every flight and recite from memory those they need every three years.

As HUNTER SLIPPED into the notebook, the room got smaller until everything around him grew dark, then disappeared. The first memo entries were spattered with fluids of unknown origin. Hunter was drawn into the snapshot glued near the top of the second page. *Surgical Amphitheater, July 7, 1935.* One of Lindbergh's early visits.

His piercing eyes framed in black glasses, Alexis Carrel looked back at Hunter–and Hunter alone–from the operating room in his laboratory on Isle Saint-Gildas. All the walls of the room were mirrored, as was the ceiling, to magnify the light. Draped in black gowns, black caps, black masks, black-rimmed goggles, and black rubber gloves, he and his surgical team of five were multiplied by the mirrors' reflections so their individual movements were the movements of thousands. Under his exacting direction, the apprentices–a murder of crows–clustered and bent to pick at the live insides of their patient.

Hunter loosened his tie. Why did he feel so hot? In all his research of Carrel, he'd never felt the surgeon's poisoned essence swim up to him like this, surrounding his senses.

Captured in the moment of writing these microscopic scrawls, the madman was muttering to himself.

Carrel turned toward a knock on the glass. The door glided open as though it floated free of hinges. Carrel signaled to the team and stepped into the anteroom.

"Yes, yes, welcome, Charles. We've been waiting for you."

Lindbergh, in flight suit and tie, cradled a padded box. "I've brought the new design. This one's made of a more heat- and pressure-resistant glass."

"Ah! We may have an opportunity to test it out in the next 24 hours."

Lindbergh looked beyond Dr. Carrel into the surgery, where the team hovered over a gray-skinned man with blue lips who was laboring to take a breath. "Is that the patient? Do these people just wash up on shore for you, Alex? Why don't we do another animal trial? We have the langur."

"That would be a waste of time. This patient has signed a waiver for us to do anything we can in the name of science to save him. We've told him this operation could save his life. If we're lucky, he'll live at least a few hours. His family will honor him. We'll wait until no later than 5:30 tomorrow morning. Would you like to join us?"

A pause. "So, he can't know what he's getting into."

"None of us does, really. Beyond problems of the heart, he has multiple deficiencies like so many of his race, in this case the defect of syndactyly. What you're holding in your hands is our only chance, Charles. With luck, our de1vice might save him. And if not him, at least he's ennobling himself. Why are you looking at me like that? It's your scruples could kill him."

"Is he even strong enough to survive the initial transfer? How are we to handle the blood loss?"

"His heart is failing. But he's 46, a good candidate. We'll remove his heart, keep his circulation going with your glass chambers and my pump, repair the tear in the muscle, and reinsert." He looked at Lindbergh perspiring. "Anything worthwhile is a risk." He turned the faucet to bright hot and plunged his hands in to wash them. Clouds of steam rose toward the mirrored ceiling.

"As far as how we'll handle the potential blood loss, I have that covered with a willing donor. It's not my first choice, because he's a mental defective. His parents have kept him hidden for most of his life, but it's as good a backup plan as I could conceive. Since I don't believe our patient will have any issue, I'm not concerned with defects being passed down through the blood."

"Jesus God, Alex. You're a regular Frankenstein. Anne says hello. She says she's sorry for having called you 'beastly' the last time she saw you. She won't make it in until Wednesday."

"We'll have a few days, at least," Carrel said. "Not to put too fine a point on it, but I hope you'll take my advice about other women. With genes like yours you have a responsibility. You and I understand things that not everyone understands. I say this like a father to a son: I would like you to meet young Vera. A brilliant physicist in the making. Very healthy, very intelligent. Perfect genetic history. All I'm asking is that you meet her, not in a hidden way but proudly. She is your destiny."

"I would never do anything that might hurt Anne."

A red light over the surgical door started flashing.

Carrel left, came back, and whispered to Lindbergh. "Tomorrow's patient has gone into cardiac arrest. The attendants are doing Dr. Crile's chest compressions now.

We have no time to lose. Over there is the closet. Put on the gown and shoes, but shower first."

"It will be an honor, Dr. Carrel."

HUNTER FLIPPED TWO PAGES ahead in the notebook. The patient survived barely three hours. All but the man's family considered it a great success. Before they'd finished washing up, Carrel and Lindbergh were making plans for the next trial. Grabbing a few hours sleep, they agreed to debrief in the breakfast room. Their voices grew louder.

"Permit a little jealousy from an old man," Carrel said. "Poor Charlie. Why do you offend me? You're everything I can never be. Great men are gifted with intuition. They know without reasoning or analysis what they need to know. You are such a man, Charlie. But pretty as it is, your new glass gadget hasn't really worked yet–not truly–in spite of its promising debut. If it does, who knows? Maybe I'll give you a heart."

"You sure have a way with words," Lindbergh said.

"*Ne pas deranger*," Carrel said. He tapped his forehead, then bent down to read some notes. "You know, at some point, we're going to have to talk about finances."

"I'm not interested in money," Lindbergh said.

"Like hell. You're not interested because you are money. The moment you darkened my doorstep, the grant funds came flying in. Suddenly *Time* magazine comes calling, sure your great-American-hero status will sell copies. If the great name of Lindbergh weren't on these patent applications, none of this money would be coming in now. I have three more for you to sign. One for the centrifuge, and two for the perfusion pump."

"So lovely," Lindbergh said, looking at the glass heart, "but too late for some."

Carrel whistled through his teeth. "Remember, my young friend, in the very beginning I confessed to you over cocktails it would be too late to save your sister-in-law because we couldn't operate on heart patients without stopping the heart from beating."

"Alex, she had a name. Liz Morrow."

"God rest her soul. But once Miss Morrow was lost, she became your inspiration. She kept you awake at night when you weren't distracted by her pretty sister. You worked on the engineering problem to save she who was now dead and buried. You couldn't stop, what do you call it, trouble-firing."

Lindbergh sighed. "It's troubleshooting."

"It was you who found a way to let the heart keep beating outside the body while we worked on it. Yes, you were too late for some, but just in time for the rest of the world. You know where this will lead, don't you? The day is not far away when our surgical teams will be able to put a strong, fresh heart in place of a devastated heart. Through science we will arrive at a supreme race of heroes like you."

"Hopefully not wearing these creepy black gowns."

"You've opened the door to eternal life."

Lindbergh peered at his glass heart. When he lifted its convolutions of chambers for Carrel to see, the little man looked stunned afresh at its enchanting balance of vacuum and gravity, the breakthrough more stark for its lack of moving parts. "Any pilot could have come up with this," Lindbergh said. "One, isolate the misfiring heart on a test stand; two, connect it to the rest of the aircraft systems by wire and hose.

"The centrifuge was far easier to imagine. Just combine the washing and plasma isolation into one step instead of two. It's a variation on Dr. Moss's superchargers in West Lynn. I've been consulting on the new turbo-superchargers they're working into the B-17s at Boeing, and it's helped me to realize one man's dynamometer stand is another man's gurney. Like a high-performance engine, the heart is a combustion chamber. Intake, compression, ignition, exhaust. Not everyone understands that an aircraft actually breathes, articulates through its flaps and ailerons, sees through its instruments. You ought to come flying with me sometime."

"Intuition eavesdrops on clairvoyance; it appears to be the extrasensory perception of reality." Carrel scowled. *"Tu me fais peur."* He pushed the papers into Lindbergh's chest and departed.

"Like I said, you talk funny, Alex."

Lindbergh *père* flipped through the documents while Hunter, leaning in to hear him splash the nib of his pen into the ink and scratch his signature, fell all the way in. Unable to stop the sensation, he felt himself rushing into quondam immediacy, love's lost moments aroused and seduced, the walls speeding behind him, backwards and black. Dr. Feelia wouldn't understand. *But look at my arms.* Hunter stared at them while 'then' devoured now. Holding his hand up against a bright light suspended from the ceiling, he made a shadow before he was born. When he brushed his fingertip against the naked bulb, he jerked it back. Carrel's ears pricked. The Frenchman wheeled at him, smiling with sharpened Vichy teeth.

"You," he said to Hunter. "I'm thirsty. Get me something. Get him some, too," he said of Lindbergh. "The wine is in the drawer."

Hunter barely opened his mouth. He looked down at his shoes dissolving on the floor, still not quite there. Then, almost like tearing a muscle, he risked a first step, then a second. The drawer opened unbidden as he reached for it.

"It's now or never," Carrel said. *"Une verre de vin."*

Dragging his suit coat in (the last part of himself) from the conference room with a sucking sound, Hunter left Rolfe alone.

"You shouldn't give him too much of that," Lindbergh said to Hunter as he donned the black gown. "With a mind like his, he's already pretty high. Say, I don't think we've been introduced. I didn't see you come in." He held out his hand. "Charles Lindbergh."

"Hunter Dauger."

"Where do you hail from?"

"I grew up in Long Island."

Lindbergh cocked his head. A wistful sparkle stole into his eyes. "Hark, what part?"

"Way out there. Montauk."

"That is way out there." Lindbergh looked enviously into the room where Carrel disappeared. He handed Hunter his untouched wine glass as if he were a servant and started into the surgery. Outside the window was the royal blue of the Breton coast. Dancing in the waves was the second, more petite, island Lindbergh would buy in 1936 for $16,211, the better to hide from the world and draw closer to Carrel. Just six hundred yards apart, Carrel's *Île Saint-Gildas* and Lindbergh's *Île Illiec* were joined by a sand bar that vanished at high tide. A drop in the sea, *Île Illiec* was four acres small with a single windswept stone castle nestled among the cliffs, the perfect fortress of solitude for the future Careu Kent.

"Tu me fais peur," Hunter called after him.

Lindbergh stopped. "Say, isn't that what Dr. Carrel said?" Lindbergh had a way of staring at you as though you were Venusian.

"Yes," Hunter said. "It means you scare me."

Chapter 24

Garden City, Long Island, New York

If we are what we eat, some pilots should eat more chicken.

HOW LONG CAN you be unconscious without knowing it? A day, a week, two weeks? Hunter's blackouts were lengthening and getting more exhausting. Soldiers and heroes went to see The Elephant, but psychotics and alcoholics saw elephants, too. *Aviate.* Hunter rose from an alien brass bed. A bouquet of red roses hemorrhaged on a table. The floor was hardwood planks– he couldn't be in a hospital. He took a step, felt dizzy, and steadied himself by touching a wall. French doors flung open to a balcony. He staggered toward the breeze. Thudding down to the mist-covered seat of a wrought-iron chair, he looked out over gardens that fell away, in the distance, to the sea.

Navigate. Long Island. He bolted up and returned inside. He took in the walnut shade of the beadboard paneling. The implacable white porcelain sink and tub hinted of a fading stylishness. The drab wallpaper clinched it. He couldn't be in The Garden City Hotel. He could not possibly be anywhere else.

Communicate. He reached for the black telephone with no buttons but No. 106 inked on its center dial. "Hello, could you send some breakfast up?"

He was standing on the set of the movie *The Spirit of St. Louis.*

Which Hunter knew hadn't done well at the box office. Viewers suspected Jimmy Stewart, 47, couldn't play the 25-year-old Lindbergh with any sort of believability. Never mind that Stewart was a World War II bomber pilot, starved himself neurotically thin, and dyed his hair Nazi blond. Invited to casting meetings, Lindbergh felt uneasy, too. He wanted to go in a different direction. He suggested Anthony Perkins, star of *Psycho*, might be better in the role of Slim.

Hanging from the ceiling of the Smithsonian Institute, the original *Spirit of St. Louis* cost $10,580 in 1927. For the Cinemascope movie in 1957, Warner Bros. paid $11 million to create three full-scale flying replicas. After shooting, one of them disappeared.

Hunter heard three knocks on the door. He saw the mocha porcelain knob barely start to spin, then stop.

"Room service."

"Come on in. It's unlocked."

Still the waiter didn't come in. Feeling a little woozy, Hunter crossed the carpet and swung the door open. The deep, rich aroma of eggs, ham, and blueberry waffles filled the room. He looked around. His breaths grew shallow.

"What day is it?" Hunter asked.

"Tuesday."

"And you're sure."

"Yes, sir."

Taking out his wallet, Hunter gave him a little something.

"Thank you, sir. Thank you. I've never received such a generous tip." He stared at the thousand-dollar bill in his hand.

When he left, Hunter got onto the telephone. "Can you connect me to Berlin?"

"Berlin, Germany?"

"Here's the number: 011-49 389-1238."

The telephone made the low burr of a transatlantic call. He heard the secretary pick up. "*Grüß Gott, Schröder & Neumann.*"

"May I speak to John Abel Smith, please?"

"One moment. Is this Commander Dauger?"

"Yes."

"Are you all right, sir? Mr. Smith was quite concerned."

"Yes. Thanks."

Now Smith's voice wafted across the Atlantic. "Hunter, is that you?"

"Yes."

"Where did you go? You excused yourself, walked out of our office, and never returned."

"Smith, do you have my dog?"

"Yes. No. Rolfe took her with him when we realized you left."

"Ask Pia to watch her instead. Rolfe has no rights to Dido. Sorry I had to run off like that, Smith. It was an absolute family emergency."

"When are you coming back? You know, we've still got to finish with Rolfe."

Hunter hung up.

He finished eating, downed a second cup of coffee, and surveyed the room to see if he'd brought any things. He'd brought nothing. He double-checked the closet and the bathroom. With a touch of elegance, he looked behind the bathroom door. Still nothing. He descended the stairs into the lobby and paid his bill. At least he had his wallet. He walked out onto the great porch and down through the gardens. Below the gardens was a street. He banked around some parked motorcycles, then descended from the hotel property to a busy thoroughfare. He took a single step into traffic.

With swerves and honks, cars blew around him, the escaped lunatic. Judging the closure rates, he loped across the northbound lane and easily made it to the grassy midsection, across which blew the scattered fragments of a newspaper tolling *10 Dead, Toxic Shock*, apparently the next new thing in the annals of medical horrors. *Britain Victorious in Falkland Islands War. Vic Morrow and Child Actors Perish in Helicopter Explosion* while shooting *Twilight Zone, the Movie*. Hmm. Had to be the *Post*.

Railroad tracks ran across the southbound lane. Below, a hobo jungle flourished. Hunter skirted the soggy boxes, looking for a sign of Dido. With a soft sadness he caught sight of silhouetted indentations in the tall grasses, a place of wary sleep. Where did hobos go by day? The hairs stood on the back of his neck. Dido might be among them, lost in the dark wing of her amnesia. He felt her presence near.

He kept walking, the long strides of a vagabond. Except his socks were wet, so the sides of his shoes cut into his ankles. Keep going.

Now he hit a modest, vinyl-sided neighborhood of reconsidered porches and milk bottles. This was the crowded part of Long Island, far from exclusive. When he slipped through a line of trees, the huge tarry expanse of Roosevelt Field Mall opened in front of him.

Eight a.m. There were only a handful of cars here amid thousands of empty painted spaces earmarked for patrons of Bradlees; Woolworth's; and Fabulous Zayre, where discounts were king. He turned left and walked along the edge of the woods below streetlights big as spaceships. The last time he'd seen the moon–when was that–it was on fire. Now it slept in suburban gloom over Bloomingdale's.

He caught sight of a security truck driving straight for him. Best to focus ahead and keep moving with a normal gait, not looking back but hearing its growling engine grow closer.

"Hey, hotshot!" a voice said behind him.

Hunter turned, got his bearings, but said nothing.

"Are you lost?" the mall cop asked.

"An interesting question," Hunter said.

"If you're going shopping, you've got to head that-a-way. Then you've got a two-hour wait till the stores open up. If you're planning on pissing in this parking lot, Caballero, think again. I have my eye on you."

"I have no such plans," Hunter said.

He started from the truck and walked another 150 feet. The truck, with its glassy eyes, kept staring at him. Noiselessly, it followed. Hunter looked at the leaves of the trees on the far side of the lot, lifted as if for rain. He looked half a mile east at a low-slung set of telephone and power wires. He shifted ever so slightly to his left, as though he were in a dance, with memory loss his partner. He licked his index finger and held it above his head to catch the breeze.

A solitary tree in a black field. The security truck drove a circle around him, giving him a wide berth. The driver rolled down his window. Hunter heard him snapping pictures.

Say, are you a perv?

"You sure you're all right, buddy?" the cop asked. Behind him, updates from last night's baseball game played on the radio.

"Sure, but I could use a ride to the rent-a-car kiosk." He pointed toward the Hertz sign in the distance.

"Jump in. Anything to get you off my watch."

The silence grew as they traveled across the tar desert toward civilization. "Any family around here, buddy?" Hunter's driver finally asked.

"That's not as easy a question as it seems," Hunter said. The throb of the *Spirit of St. Louis's* engines still rang in his ears. When it got too quiet again, Hunter said, "Do you know who Roosevelt Field Mall is named for?"

"Sure. Franklin D."

"No," Hunter said softly.

"Teddy?"

"No."

"No?"

"It's named for Teddy's youngest son, Quentin, a World War I aviator shot down in a dogfight over France when he was just 20."

Hunter leaned back in his seat. Quentin had launched on early-morning reconnaissance to hunt for Boche observation planes, only to be jumped by seven Fokkers over Coulonges-en-Tardenois approaching the Marne. His squadron mates couldn't come to his aid because they were being gunned themselves by the swarm, but what they saw… He maneuvered longer than was humanly possible. 'He certainly died fighting.' No fewer than three German aces claimed the kill–'two machine-gun bullets in the head.' Even the enemy reported he 'met the death of a hero. Conspicuous gallantry, attacking again and again.' Posthumously, Quentin earned the Croix de Guerre with palm. The 95th Aero squadron sent the medal to his dad. Teddy so loved his son he never got over his loss. Here's to the hidden man.

"That's how you can have an airport named for you, and still nobody knows your name," Hunter said. Hopefully, the mall cop wouldn't realize he'd been on a reconnaissance mission of his own. Hunter wondered if Lindbergh had felt strange taking off from this field named in honor of his school chum from Sidwell Friends.

"Just hang in there, fella. We're almost there."

They were out of Jaguars at Hertz. Out of Ferraris. Hunter drove through the throat of Long Island in a light blue Ford Escort automatic, crossed the Williamsburg Bridge, fought the cabs on Bleecker, then turned onto Fifth and Park. At the Waldorf Astoria, he gave his keys to the valet ("Love the wheels," he said), and registered for Suite 712.

He tossed his duffel on the marble shelf in the bath, took out a clear plastic kit, and brushed his teeth.

He took a long shower to stab memories of the last few days back to him with its sharp knives of heat. He turned it up until he nearly cried out in pain. He dried off with a soft towel, dressed, and slipped up to the Starlight Roof, where Xavier Cugat still showed up occasionally to lead the band. Inside the ballroom, the French blue walls rose to the glass ceiling. To the left of the stage, a piano slept in the horse latitudes of afternoon. It was Cole Porter's 1907 Steinway grand from when he stayed at the Waldorf Towers. Now, like a high-performance aircraft forgotten in a hangar, it waited for someone's touch.

It had been years. Hunter hit an A and let it throb in the silence, a lament. It was a squash ball bouncing in an empty court. He hit a D, and an E. Closing his eyes, he took a stab at "I Concentrate on You."

The last time he played it, Dido was listening. Or at least he thought she was, dangling a glass of cheap Chablis and looking at him with deep brown eyes that went with her soft, soft hair and long legs. Back then he used to smoke Gauloises, serving only to confirm the suspicions both his Navy friends and civilians had for him. No need to think like this. He closed his eyes as the silence grew ears and a tail.

"Hey, Mozart," a voice said behind him. "Are you lost?"

"Hey," Hunter said.

"The ballroom's closed," the porter said.

Hunter stood. "I was just leaving."

He walked through the lobby into bright sunlight, turned left at the street, and stepped into the glittering cave of Grand Central Station at 2:11 p.m. *Take two*. It was exactly as crowded as it was before, when the 'Carrel people,' or whomever they were, put him in their crosshairs. The rush of memory magnified his steps. His substitute briefcase felt heavier. Every hair on the back of his neck bristled and stood on end. He wavered in the footlights of what was about to happen.

Movie adverts flashed on the screens: *Tootsie, An Officer and a Gentleman, E.T.* Slowly, the shoeshine station wheeled closer to him, as if on a conveyor belt.

"Shine, sir?" a man asked him. He was different than the one before.

"Next time," Hunter promised and quickened his step. Grand Central whirled with immanence. He pulled the key out of his wallet and looked at its tag, N-X-211. He walked to Locker No. 211; no joy. The rest of the lockers were strangers. Number 1927 didn't work. Would he have to try them all?

The attendant took an interest. "Can I help you find anything, sir?"

"No," Hunter said. "I see it right here." He walked straight to No. 1932, inserted the key, swung the door open, and took out the single black box inside. The attendant still hung around, so he waved. "I'm all set."

Just don't look at him. See, he's already gone back to his desk. Walking to an unoccupied library table–the dark green writing surface whispered government issue, but it was really just obsolete railway inventory–he lifted the top off the box and placed it to one side.

What was in here, a Mexican jumping bean? Didn't Ned have a sense of humor. Inside a Mexican jumping bean, the larva of a moth develops in the seedpod, wakes, and rattles the shell in terror. But this tiny sarcophagus wasn't brown. It wasn't a bean. What lay so listlessly at the bottom of the box did not contemplate any movement at all. Hunter gently held it to the light and turned it this way and that. It appeared to be a glass ampoule of potassium cyanide with its rubber cover cracking, World War II vintage or older. Just like Smith's. Could someone other than Smith have treasured such a deadly hobby? In the bottom of the box was a business card. On the front of the card was a name below Olympic rings. Henry Breckinridge, Captain, United States Fencing Team, New York Athletic Club. On the back of the card was an address scrawled in shaky handwriting that wasn't Smith's, wasn't Lindbergh's, wasn't Ned's: "Radium Crystallization Laboratory, Orange, New Jersey." The inventors of Undark.

Back to the Waldorf. Never had Hunter walked toward a parked Ford Escort, or any vehicle, with such purpose.

Chapter 25

Manhattan, New York

An airplane will fly if a bit overgross.
But it sure won't fly without fuel.

CROSSING THE GLITTERING steel span of the George Washington Bridge from New York into New Jersey, Hunter looked to his left and saw the Empire State Building, the Chrysler, and the rest of Manhattan shimmering in the heat waves above the Hudson River, stalled in time. Ahead were the Palisades of New Jersey, immense cliffs above the water, much of it parkland still owned by the Rockefellers.

Turning right along Palisades Parkway, he drove past The Rustic Cabin, the nightclub where Frank Sinatra was discovered, and continued into a hidden enclave of 1920s mansions. All had views of the water. Cut deftly into the ledge, they hung in midair. Between gaps in the leaves, he caught sight of sweeping views of the dark river from the New York skyline to the Tappan Zee Bridge. Maybe God didn't live up here, but some distinguished devils had once called this place home, including Lindbergh's inside man, Henry Breckinridge.

Hunter turned down a sloping driveway toward the cliff's edge. The Escort purred as he coasted on idle past not one, but two signs marked "Private" so a trespasser couldn't possibly claim not to have seen them. Briefcase in hand, he walked to the front door and rapped on the knocker, a cross of swords fashioned out of heavy brass.

"Back again? I'm warning you!" he heard a woman's voice with an English accent cry from above. Hunter stepped quickly to the left as a bucket of gray water was spilled toward his head from the second floor. The splash back darkened his knee and left droplets on his shoes.

"You can take your bloody Census straight to Hell," she called again, more softly. "I know my rights. I don't have to answer any of your questions."

"My name is Hunter Dauger," he said. "I'm not from the Census; I'm a fellow fencer, and an admirer of Henry's."

Her face appeared in the window. "Go away," she said.

"I have a five-thousand-dollar check that I've made out to the U.S. Olympic Committee in Henry's name. I met your husband at Hotel Beau Rivage. I've been carrying this donation for over a year because I wanted to give it to you personally to pass on."

There was a pause.

"I've been to the Beau," she said. "It would be better if you came later. My son-in-law will be here then."

"Secretary Graham?" Hunter asked.

"Oh, do you know him, too?"

"I've heard him speak." Graham, former secretary of the Atomic Energy Commission, was a gifted storyteller like his cousin, *Gone with the Wind* novelist Margaret Mitchell. "I look forward to meeting him again, but I'll only be in town for an hour."

"Oh, all right, I'll be right down," she said, then faltered. "Is that your car?"

"I'm saving up for it." The Ford Escort wasn't that bad, though Hunter made a mental note to return it to the agency in favor of a Jag before he penetrated anyone else's privacy. He'd met members of the Nomenclatura in Rumania who deeply coveted their *Escortăs* in order to stand out from the boxy brigade of black Soviet Zis and Zils. He knew first-hand that Valentin Ceausescu was tooling around in a white Escort just like this, but with four on the floor–it had cost a free-speech dissident an arm and a leg to get it to Bucharest for ten times the U.S. retail value. Lindbergh, countervailingly, had flown the Atlantic with no *escortă*. It didn't matter if it was sheer bravery or savant foolishness. Impossible to know.

"How do you do?" Hunter said, sketching a bow. "I'm pleased to meet you, Mrs. Breckinridge."

HOW SHE'D HATE to know he was thinking, "Mrs. Breckinridge *No. 3*." If the Illuminati were members of the secret society directing clandestine events in Europe since the Crusades, it was the Society of the Cincinnati, strictly descendants of Revolutionary War heroes, who pulled the strings behind America's passion play 200 years after the Siege of Yorktown. None of these descendants was more poised for stardom than Henry Breckinridge: Princeton and Harvard Law.

Mrs. Breckinridge the first was Ruth Bradley Woodman, until *shhhh*–the divorce. Number Two was Aida de Acosta Root, the leggy brunette daughter of a Havana steamship millionaire. Aida was of noble blood, a child of the House of Alba in Aragon, Spain. *Mas fascinante*, she was aviation royalty. At nineteen, she was the first woman ever to fly a machine-powered aircraft on her own–a solo in a dirigible over Paris–after charming M. Santos-Dumont out of his silk bag. While he chased her shadow in his sportscar, she zoomed over the countryside from X to Y. *"Mademoiselle, vous êtes la première aero-chauffeuse du monde!"* After she ditched him, he lovingly placed her silver-framed snapshot on his library table beside a bud vase quickened by a single orchid. Only death would end his despair (and rumored celibacy).

Hungry for fresh meat, Aida married and quickly divorced Oren Root III, whose uncle was Nobel Peace Prizewinner and former U.S. Secretary of State Elihu Root. Waiting in the wings was Henry Breckinridge, Esq., the former U.S. Undersecretary of War. In 1927, she plighted her troth unto Henry forever, or until 1947–whichever came first.

By 1928, Henry was Lindbergh's lawyer. Naturally, Lindbergh was sweet on Aida as a fellow child pioneer of the air. She was 44, Henry 41, Lindbergh 27. All of which became vivid for Hunter when he stumbled across letters to Aida that Lindbergh had penned on U.S. Embassy stationery, the envelopes postmarked Mexico City. That took some nerve, Daddy. Was it a thrill to flirt with your "Dear Mrs. Breckinridge" under the roof of Ambassador Dwight Morrow's "Casa Mañana" in Cuernavaca even while you were sparking with his daughter Anne and still in the flush of your romance with Elizabeth, she of the tragic heart? It was Aida who was Henry's wife when Buster vanished, Aida who was your go-between with Henry, Aida who kept you flying on the straight and level when your world was no longer on the up and up. It was more than just disturbing that Aida and Henry were guests at Highfields the weekend before the abduction. Not that there was a dress rehearsal for the kidnapping.

HUNTER LOOKED hard at this final Mrs. Breckinridge. Widowed since 1960, she was gamine but less flashy. Still stunning at 70, she seemed a true English flower, with pretty eyes for a splasher of gray water. If only he'd brought Dido with him, she might have warmed up this meeting.

"Margaret Breckinridge," she said, with a strong little handshake.

"Commander Hunter Dauger, United States Navy, retired. Please call me Hunter."

"Oh, an Annapolis man."

"Harvard. Like your husband, I fenced with epees, though I could never have held a candle to him." He handed her the check in an envelope addressed "To the USOC" and blessed the little voice in his head that told him to prepare it in advance. "It's so nice of you to speak to a complete stranger who's intruded upon your privacy." He smiled, recalling the awkward silence he'd so often suffered when talking with one of Dido's friends. "I was going to ask you a further favor, but I find I haven't the nerve to ask you to see Col. Breckinridge's Olympic medals, even if this is the chance of a lifetime. To think that he fenced against Nedo Nadi!" He turned to leave.

"Wait," she said. She gave a firm nod. "I'm about to have lunch. Are you hungry?"

"I could eat," Hunter said.

HE FOLLOWED AS she sailed through the salon, with its green Nichols carpet, French chandelier (a touch of Aida?), and rosewood vitrines filled with Rose Medallion china emblazoned with the Breckinridge coat of arms. The enormous library gave way to the gun room.

"I can feel him in here," she said.

But not in the bedroom? "I'm sure you sense the whole Breckinridge family," Hunter said. "What is it, a Vice President and two Senators?"

She smiled, a debutante again. "Two Navy ships have been christened with the name *Breckinridge*. Not to mention a pair of U.S. senators, six congressmen, the Ambassador to Italy, the Minister to Russia who attended

Nicholas II's coronation, two Revolutionary War generals, two Confederate generals, the U.S. Attorney General under President Jefferson, one U.S. Secretary of War, one Suffragette, and two Presidential candidates, including my husband." She smiled when a black servant materialized with cucumber-and-watercress finger sandwiches, crusts removed, a pitcher of tea, and sterling-silver spoons, all of which he balanced gracefully on a Chinese Chippendale table. "Henry used to joke he was the underachiever in the family."

While she took a morsel delicately off the plate, she nonetheless sat rigidly at the front edge of the chair, demonstrating she was well 'schooled in posture and empathy.'

For a moment they were silent. Then she blurted, "He didn't talk about it much, but I think it weighed heavily on Henry that Frank Roosevelt, whom he'd known since childhood, beat him in the Democratic National Primary."

In all of this she'd deftly avoided mentioning Henry's flamboyant cousin John Cabell Breckinridge. "Bunny" had traveled to Denmark in the 1940s in search of sex-change surgery. But it never panned out. S/he achieved cult status in *Plan 9 From Outer Space*. "How did your husband feel about *Myra Breckinridge*?" Hunter asked.

By now Margaret's eyes had frosted over and she was in full scold mode. She smoothed her skirt, crossed her legs. "Mr. Vidal was a good friend. None of us knew he had so cruel a sense of humor."

Hard to believe we were talking about the same Gore Vidal. Had she ever read any of her 'good friend's' books?

He looked at Margaret, so stony, so sphinxlike. He shouldn't mention Lindbergh so soon. Just wait. Plan your work and work your plan. The next step was to dare to call her Margaret directly. He rose and walked to a shadow box in a gold frame.

"Margaret. Your husband's medals. Remarkable. This is his Olympic participation medal from Antwerp in 1920?"

She nodded.

"These are priceless." He looked closely at the Bronze Medal Henry won in the 1928 Amsterdam Olympiad in team foil.

As for his own awards, Hunter hadn't been as careful. In a drunken rage after losing the IC4As during his senior year to a certain fencer he disliked so intensely he wouldn't repeat his name–and who bore an infuriating resemblance to Radu–Hunter impetuously threw his silver medal and all his swords into Long Island Sound. It was a hard moment to live down, though traveling light had its rewards. If you're not the world's best piano player, shouldn't you burn your pianos?

"How did you and Henry meet, Margaret?"

"Charles Lindbergh introduced us."

Hunter nodded slowly. He reached for a sandwich and took a bite. The cucumbers were fresh and cold, the bread textured with privilege, the watercress crisp and spicy. "Most toothsome," he said and raised his eyebrows.

"The best you've ever had," Margaret said. "The secret ingredient is celery salt. Henry and Charles designed this sandwich together. Not only was Henry Charles's lawyer through thick and thin, he and Charles were birds of a feather. Henry was Charles's best friend."

"Not many people can say that," Hunter said. Fewer than thirty thousand. He looked at the early Zuber et Cie wallpaper, the Niagara Falls panel of *Vue de l'Amérique du Nord*. While it wasn't from the first block printing or even the 1875 release, it was from the 1920s printing. It was real.

"Henry was Harry Guggenheim's attorney until Mr. Guggenheim, who so loved aviation, asked him to look after Charles's interests personally. Henry and Charles first met at the Army & Navy Club in Washington D.C., where Henry was speaking about the role of aviation in warfare.

Henry's father, Gen. Joseph Cabell Breckinridge, founded the Club, you know. Henry told me that night was one of the rare times Charles ever indulged in spirits. This was way back–1927, 1928, I don't know. I'm not sure. After a few of the famous daiquiris, their kinship took off. It was as if they shared the fear that one lifetime was not enough for either of them to explore the spirit of invention. They used to go hunting in the woods near the Hudson. Two loveable kooks. At Charles's suggestion, Henry removed a rusty iron spiral staircase from the back of our garage and installed it in the forest as a deer blind. It's probably still out there." She paused. "It's hard to believe, but they were haunted by the men they might have been."

"I'm a member of that club."

"They let commanders in? Henry and Charles were both colonels when they ran into each other at the Club. Henry and I always loved the library, with all those donated books full of sea stories. But old stories begin to carry an impossible weight. Henry stopped going to the Club after he had to drink four cups of Sanka with Omar Bradley. It was too hard on his kidneys." She finished her tea and rang a small bell. A second later, her servant came and took away the tray without a word.

"So, Charles and Henry," she said. "Two singular men. Charles needed someone like Henry, worldly and jaded, to fence off the investment offers and invitations to join businesses as a trustee. In the end, they settled on Pan Am and Juan Trippe, in spite of Juan's having gone to Yale. When Charles got interested in medical research, Henry helped him with the fine print to protect his interest in that first artificial heart. Charles was on the cover of *Time* Magazine multiple times, and not always as an aviator. Once for his inventions."

"We fly in the shadow of giants," Hunter said. He looked into her eyes, violet in this light. He'd misjudged earlier. She had been a great beauty. Was The Lone Eagle ever lovely to you? "The world hasn't been the same without them." He waited a heartbeat. "When was Charles's last visit here?"

"Henry died in 1960. Charles surprised me by stopping here between Christmas and New Year's, 1973. He said he just wanted to be near Henry. I'm afraid he wept when he saw Henry's swords. He was sitting in exactly the chair you're sitting in now."

Hunter said nothing.

"I can tell you, Henry didn't worship Charles," she said. "It was the other way around. It was Charles who begged Henry to teach him how to fence. He asked him how to address correspondence, how to behave at parties. I even think he tried to talk like Henry. Whenever possible, they went everywhere and through everything together." She paused. "Henry told me that even on the black day when little Buster was kidnapped, Charles called him first. They talked long and hard, and then Henry got into his car and drove all night to Highfields to be at Charles's side."

"Considering their deep friendship and your husband's insight, I'm not surprised Charles would have considered it essential to consult with Henry before he went to the state police," Hunter said. "A moment of calm before the storm."

"If you let the police just barge in, crashing around like a herd of bison without any background, who knows what will happen. Henry was there to protect Charles, to handle things and ensure the family's privacy. This was a most delicate matter. Henry told me he and Charles spent ten straight days and nights together at Highfields, huddling and directing the kidnapping investigation with Col. Schwarzkopf."

Hunter smiled. "Now it was three Army colonels. But of course, the FBI entered and started calling the shots."

"Not so fast," she said. "Henry and J. Edgar Hoover were both in Woodrow Wilson's cabinet, so it was still

Henry's game. Everything went through him. Henry told me the state police and FBI were afraid of Charles because of his fame."

"It's true the investigators were young," Hunter said. "Col. Schwarzkopf, a West Pointer, might easily have slipped back into the long gray line and favored Lindbergh's position without even realizing it. Here's where I'm coming from. Every one of the family servants suffered intrusive and heated questioning from the FBI and the State Police, but Lindbergh himself was never asked to account for his whereabouts. If people were so shy around Lindbergh, or bedazzled by him, don't you think Henry should have insisted he be interrogated? The smallest detail might have helped."

"*Henry* interrogated him. They didn't have time for investigations. They were trying to find his boy!"

"But Henry himself was a delay, wasn't he? No one could fault him for that. That was his job, as Charles's counsel."

"Henry was a lawyer. Lawyers specialize in delays. But there's no question Charles was above suspicion. He deserved to be. He earned that. Though the first moments at Highfields did come back to me when Chappaquiddick happened, and Teddy Kennedy consulted with his advisors so long before reporting the drowning of that poor little Polish secretary. Nobody wants to talk about it anymore, now that Teddy is the king of Washington." She dropped her voice. "Would you want a president who can't keep his trousers zipped?"

"Mary Jo Kopeckne," Hunter said. She deserved the dignity of a name. Her very syllables plunged the soul in despair. He studied Margaret. "In both cases, skilled navigation was required, though second-guessers might wonder, what stopped Kennedy and Lindbergh from going to the police sooner? Aren't the layers of insulation incriminating?"

"In Charles's case, calling Henry first was *better* than going to the state police. Tell the locals and they go off half-cocked, putting the child at further risk. Tell the FBI and they'll make a federal case out of it. In the worst of times, great men are unhurried. Henry and Charles had the crowds and the press to worry about, and they needed to consider the ransom note so they could proceed under the radar. A great light was shining on Lindbergh's wings, and it was important not to tarnish them because a black-hearted foreigner stole his child. Everything Charles and Henry did was deliberate, including Henry's contacting underworld individuals like Mr. Capone and Mr. Moretti, Longy Zwillman and Joe Adonis." She closed her eyes.

"Now there's a Christmas card list," Hunter said. "It must have been a privilege to be Charles's dearest friend."

"You understand, I wasn't married to Henry then."

"Yes, but did Henry ever talk to you about those crucial early hours when the baby was missing but the world didn't know about it? Those moments when Henry guided Lindbergh and deftly prevented him from being questioned. To trained investigators, every second counted."

"I can't see why," she snapped. "The baby was gone!" She looked quickly at her watch. "This crime was so horrible, and so unspeakably evil, that it upset Henry whenever it came up– even years later, in our marriage. If ever I brought it up, he'd say "Hark" and hold his finger to his mouth. He knew little Buster very well. He loved Charles so much; it was like losing his own son."

Don't rush. Be a great man. Conduct your life with unhurried grace. Like hell. "Did they ever talk about Buster's barely perceptible imperfection? The web of skin between his big toe and the next toe?"

"I never heard of such a thing," she said. "I think we've talked enough."

"It would have looked something like this." Hunter unlaced his shoe and slipped off his Interwoven sock.

All the color drained from Margaret's face. "Get out, you filth."

Chapter 26

Englewood Cliffs, New Jersey

Faced with a forced landing at night, turn on your landing lights.
If you don't like what you see, turn 'em back off.

WHEN HUNTER RETURNED to the Escort, the gentleman in black was sitting in the passenger seat. Instinctively, Hunter looked for Dido behind him before he remembered, *Dido isn't here.*

"Where to?" the man asked.

"Orange. The Undark factory," Hunter said. "Maybe a 20-minute drive."

"Let's go," the man said. "Um, have you had lunch?"

"Yes, she gave me a little something."

"Oh."

Hunter started driving and entered the ramp for the New Jersey Turnpike.

After fifteen minutes, the man said, "Do you mind my asking what she gave you?"

"A cucumber sandwich with watercress and celery salt," Hunter said.

"I mean, did she give you what you wanted for information?"

"I know."

Hunter took the exit for I-280W.

"Have you ever been to Undark before?" the man asked.

"No," Hunter said. In fact, he'd never been to Orange. An innocent traveler would have to be tricked into going into Orange, or make a seriously wrong turn into the ugly side of Newark while looking for the international jetport. Ahead were signs for Rhinegold Beer. No lack of telephone wires. The Passaic River curled around the suburban community where Newark businessman went home to sleep. Not exactly a garden spot.

MARIE CURIE may have withered away and died of radium poisoning, but not before she blessed the world with her research and cursed Orange with her deadly touch. It was she who tempted humanity with the need to see bedside alarm clocks with hands and numerals that glowed in the dark. The Undark plant led the industry.

With paintbrushes glimmering, unlucky young women worked night and day to decorate the dials. When these girls started to perish from exposure to the radioluminescence, some with x-rays revealing skeletal glow because shift leaders looked the other way when they licked the tips of their brushes for accuracy, it was Henry Breckinridge who defended the corporation bigwigs against the dying Undark girls.

En garde. No settlement was made to the radium victims during Henry's watch. No doubt the girls still lit the dirt six feet under.

"One thing the third Mrs. Breckinridge didn't tell me. Henry Breckinridge earned a quarter million for his first successful defense of Undark in the late 1920s. He was just wrapping up the case when he met Lindbergh."

HUNTER TOOK THE OFF-RAMP to Route 10, turned on High Street, and kept driving until he reached the United States Radium Corporation at 422-432 Alden Street. Like a scene in a movie, the lost Patent Application Building shimmered into view with its pass-through to the Crystallization Laboratory, defunct since 1970. Looming behind it, the Warehouse lay eerily quiet as he drew near. Like Avernus, there was a palpable godlessness here.

A rat the size of a longshoreman slipped under a pile of rubble directly ahead. Hunter felt the gentleman in black staring at him.

"What?"

"You might have bought me some lunch," the man said, "even if you were no longer hungry yourself."

"I do have a little something," Hunter said. He opened the glove compartment. "It's fresh this morning." Just after dawn, Jacques at the Waldorf had conjured it and tossed it to him as he dashed through Palm Court. Even now it was fragrant with roast turkey, walnuts, and cranberries on sesame bread from the hotel bakery. The tidbit was preserved inside an embossed linen napkin, then gently placed in a Waldorf *paquet* finished with a blue, gray, and gold ribbon.

"Nothing gets past you. Hand it over."

Hunter obliged. While the gentleman in black gingerly took a nibble inside the car, he got out for a look around. A metal-fenced pathway led to the warehouse, now covered with vines.

"Surely you have Grey Poupon?"

"No," Hunter said. He was surprised at his own irritation at the stale joke. "Please don't hurry on my account."

"You have a lot of hate for Lindbergh, don't you?"

"How can I hate someone I never knew?"

"You never knew your father."

"You've got that right."

"Is that why you're here?"

"When I interviewed Emily Sharpe about her sister Violet, the maid who killed herself before the Lindbergh kidnapping trial, she told me they had friends who worked here who were very ill. Lindbergh had an unhealthy interest in their deterioration caused by this distinct environmental factor. He was fascinated with deformities that appeared in their offspring."

"I get it," the man said. "You know Lindbergh kept haunting this place, and you're dying to find out why."

"Haunting," Hunter said. "That's your department."

The warehouse grew larger as they approached. A faded sign on the walls of the corrugated steel structure boasted "Undark" in letters the height of a human being. Below that, "A division of the United States Radium Corporation. Radium luminous material. Shines in the dark."

Though formidable, the padlock on the great sliding door was a decoy, because a smaller door hidden by being built into the slider caved open when Hunter pushed it with his shoulder. Darkness rushed the two intruders as they stepped inside. After the door creaked closed behind them, the silence joined the darkness and numbed Hunter's brain. In the illusion of infinite space, he lost track of the black box's ceiling or corners. In their random disorder, pin-sized nail holes in the roof looked like stars in the night sky. He looked down and couldn't see his own shoes.

Switching on his pen light, he showed the man Breckinridge's card with the word Undark on it. "How am I to account for this?"

"Looks like your handwriting, if you ask me. How do *you* account for it? Come on, think." The man dusted off his hat. "You know, I'd feel sorry for you, son, if I didn't know you already felt sorry for yourself every day. You're so busy wondering who you are, you forget to be grateful for who you aren't. Relax. Just slowly put it together in your mind."

"When I look at you,' Hunter said, "I can hear the first shovelful of dirt hitting the top of my coffin."

Hunter was startled by a scare-up sound. It was a pair of swifts, lifting and flapping past the invisible I-beams near the roof. A single shaft of sunlight caught their purple wings.

"You're getting to be a full-on Pretender now, aren't you?" the gentleman said.

"Whatever you say, especially since I'm not quite convinced you exist," Hunter said. Who else had ever really seen this guy but Pia?

"Interesting, your insisting I don't exist," the man said. "No doubt you do it to convince yourself you're more solidly here. Are you listening to me? This is exactly how you made your wife disappear."

Chapter 27

Washington, D.C.

Flying is hours of boredom punctuated by moments of stark terror.

SEVERAL DAYS LATER, Hunter was headed toward the Army & Navy Club on the corner of Northwest 17th and I streets on Farragut Square in Washington, D.C. when he saw the gentleman in black walking crisply toward the same club from the opposite direction, unaware of Hunter completely. This was too much. Hunter was floored. He hadn't imagined the man might have a separate existence. He had to find out if he were a figment of his imagination.

But when Hunter hurried his step to draw near, his quarry wheeled round. "Hello Commander."

"What are you doing here?"

"I'm going to see a man about a horse. After that, I'm going to see my old friend Norman Schwarzkopf. It's no secret you're investigating Lindbergh. So am I. Want to tag along?"

Hunter knew the gentleman in black knew what he suspected, but he realized he had no idea of what motivated the gentleman himself at all.

"All right," Hunter said. They glided below the shade of the Club's entry canopy and climbed the stairs to the door. "Let's do this."

Chapter 28

Washington, D.C.

No one has ever collided with the sky.

"IT'S A PLEASURE to meet you, sir," Hunter said in the chestnut-paneled dining room of the Club. A quiet bartender neatly placed a daiquiri in front of him without a sound. He would never have chosen this cocktail anywhere else, but the rum-and-sugar concoction was first introduced to the United States in precisely this location, so it always felt right. Opposite him, in midnight blue Army service dress with ribbons, was General Norman Schwarzkopf Jr., with his own daquiri. Seated beside Schwarzkopf was the gentleman in black, who had nothing to drink at all. The general seemed completely engaged by the gentleman. It was Hunter he couldn't see.

"It's so good to see you again, Norman," the gentleman said. "Does your family still have the house in Trenton?"

"Yes, but it's for sale," Schwarzkopf said. "When I started commanding the 24th, there was no time to keep it up anymore. But I remember your visiting, all the way through World War II."

"Your parents were very dear to me," the man said. "All those Christmas parties. The last time I saw you, you were ten. I was so proud when you went to West Point, Norman. Just like your dad. I know your life has been full." He paused. "I guess your dad told you why I left the police force."

Schwarzkopf's voice was warm. "He told me 'Uncle Stitch has a drinking problem. It makes him imagine things.' He said you would never let go of that Lindbergh business."

Hunter kept silent. Let them grow younger, closer.

"You have that exactly right, son," Stitch said. "It was the one thing about which your dad and I disagreed. I was for drinking on duty. He was against it." Stitch paused. "He did so much for me. I was honored when he made me his right-hand man on the investigation team. In those days, there weren't a lot of Cuban detectives in the New Jersey State Police."

Schwarzkopf straightened. "My dad said you could have been the greatest detective ever to join the force, but that you let things get to you too much."

"Still do."

"Is it really not over for you, then?"

"I thought maybe it was, but now this guy has made me start wondering again. I don't mean any disrespect to your father, and I'll always be grateful for what he did for me, but something still doesn't feel right. Can you remember, when did your father last talk about the Lindbergh case to you?"

Schwarzkopf reddened. "Are you talking about a deathbed confession? He warned me. He said you might come around sometime."

"I'm sorry, son. Please tell me what you know. I swear to you it will not change my opinion about your father."

The waiter floated by. "Would the gentlemen like another daiquiri?" Dead silence. "No? Then can I get you some coffee?"

"Yes," Schwarzkopf said. "Sure."

"It will be an honor, General," the waiter said and departed.

The three waited for the interloper to get out of earshot.

"God help me, I was 24 years old and headed for Japan when I stopped in at my parents' for Thanksgiving in 1958. Everything seemed fine at first, but then our get-together was interrupted by my father clutching at his throat. He'd get that look when 'The Weakness' hit him, as if someone were siphoning air from his windpipe."

Stitch half blinked his crocodile eyes. "To be gassed and survive during World War I is far from being weak. Major General Norman Schwarzkopf Sr. was a hero." He turned to Hunter. "He scared the Mafia straight in New Jersey."

Schwarzkopf shrugged. "He always coughed, but this was one of the bad times. Then he looked like he was going to be coming around. He went to the head of the table to start carving the turkey. When he signaled to me and made a joke about passing the baton, we all laughed, but as I watched him during the meal, he ate almost nothing, which wasn't like him. After supper, we all got up to go to the living room, but he just sank to the floor. We called an ambulance, but by the time he got to the hospital he could barely keep his eyes open. As he lay dying, he called to me and said your name. 'Never talk with Stitch,' he said. 'A great number of secrets are going with me, things I'm not proud of.' By then I was already familiar with your typical trench confession."

"So, Norman, this means more now because he specifically mentioned me," Stitch said.

"I'm not sure where you're going with that," Schwarzkopf said.

"From what I've learned," Hunter said, "your dad's difference with our friend Stitch may have more to do with his never interviewing Charles Lindbergh as if he were a suspect and then realizing, with a lump of guilt, what he hadn't done. Lindbergh's story could have been checked for inconsistencies if he were interrogated freshly after the child went missing."

"Does that phrase bug you like it bugs me?" Stitch said. "'Went missing.'"

Schwarzkopf scratched his chin. "Are you suggesting that if the New Jersey State Police and their investigation teams had made it to the crime scene ahead of Henry Breckinridge, who knows how much better they might have done?" He shook his head. "Lawyers. But factoring the lawyer out, it would still have been unthinkable to put the hot lights on the grieving parents back then. Especially *those* grieving parents. The first local police to arrive at the scene were young guys. They literally handed a torch to Lindbergh. He headed up a frenzied search from house to house, knocking at neighbors' doors, asking if they heard or saw anything. Lindbergh was too busy leading the chase to be questioned himself. Of course, that sounds ridiculous today. The more grisly a kidnapping, the sooner the newspapers try the family members until they're cleared by an alibi."

"Norman, you probably don't want to hear this, but you understand it wasn't just the younger guys. Once your father was involved, he himself never questioned Lindbergh."

Schwarzkopf took a breath. "Col. Lindbergh was the Army's stardust poster boy. Col. Breckinridge was Army. My dad was West Point to the bones, a survivor. So, it's fair to say they were of one mind. Then you factor in the interruptions. Calls were coming in from all over the world. So many people wanted to help. President Roosevelt called, the Sheik of Araby. Celebrities crawled over celebrities to show the greatest concern."

Hunter nodded. "Buster got lost in the shuffle."

Stitch looked sad. "I was there at Highfields. I was nobody then. I'm nobody now. But I myself should have spoken up about what I knew was happening. At least two days were being thrown away. Imagine letting a fox loose for a hunt and then mounting your horses dozens of hours later. You have to believe Breckinridge knew that time was being lost. Lawyers bill by the hour. But like I said, I was a nobody. So were the members of the FBI, who failed to interview Lindbergh–I've read the FBI files. We were nobodies crawling over nobodies." He inhaled. "Plus, I started drinking then."

"Being a great leader means making it possible for those around you to be great," Schwarzkopf said. "So, my father failed you there. What do you think happened, Stitch–or *didn't* happen–because Breckinridge deflected suspicions away from Lindbergh?"

"Again, I mean no disrespect to your father, but during my fleeting moments of sobriety, those lost hours began to eat away at me," Stitch said. "Especially at night, when self-doubt kicked in. I'd begun to suspect the man I looked up to so much had deliberately chosen me for the honor of a leadership position in his investigation because he knew I wouldn't question anything he did."

"Flaws are everywhere; painstaking methodologies are illusions," Schwartzkopf said. "These hours seem to weigh heavily on the two of you, and it turns my stomach to guess at why. I'd prefer you didn't tell me any more. But I can tell you this. Right now, this second, you have a chance to go on with your lives. We have a programmed text in the Army: *The Professional Army Officer and the Human Person*. Jesus, I've been to so many touchy-feely seminars. But in this case, it's instructive. The Human Person in me is whispering to both of you that you have a big lump of crazy on your backs. You seem like nice enough guys; both of you are obviously gifted. As a fellow officer, I'd like to thank you for your service, Commander Hunter, and for the secrets my family would rather you didn't disclose, but that I know you will probably have to. From your service jacket, I see we came very close to meeting in 1967. By my count there were at least three occasions when we were maybe two or three clicks away from each other. So, while I don't know you, I know you. I consider what you say very seriously. Sadly, there isn't enough of a chaplain in me to confide to you we need to look for justice in the next world. Life is short. What would it take for the both of you to drop all this, go forward, and enjoy life? Long story short, many of my young officers don't know who Charles Lindbergh was anymore–actually, that's not true. But it's hazy to them, like King Arthur and his knights, an unclear recollection of something half remembered from their boyhoods. Some shiny, invisible thing. Like F. Scott Fitzgerald said, 'Show me a hero, and I will write you a tragedy.'"

An Army captain with an aide's brassard pierced their private space and dropped to Schwarzkopf's ear. The aide whispered, nodded three times, and left.

Schwarzkopf lifted his hand as if to get up, caught himself, and methodically drank from his cup of deep, dark coffee slowly, with unrushed grace. He made it seem so good; Hunter gave his own cup another taste. The general turned to him: "I'd like you to know, I'm sorry about your wife, Hunter. It's not as though I have no intelligence. Just a beautiful woman. So often those who serve their country with distinction lose those who are dear to them just as they're finding themselves."

The general lifted his eye to catch his aide, who was waving urgently but somehow respectfully outside the window. Then he shook hands and left, the circles in the center of his coffee spreading out like waves. Hunter watched Stitch's Adam's apple rise and fall from a hard swallow. Covertly, Stitch wiped a tear from his eye, as if he'd just won a vacation to the most disappointing place he'd ever fled from.

Which for Hunter was Cuba and that last look from Streak, the recollection of which could wrench his stomach to the edge of vomiting. No, it was the tableau of Dido's bedroom, the windows flung open, the moment when a second had turned into forever.

Sun flashed on the Club's wrought-iron door as the general entered the shafts of light heading up 17th Street. Crossing I Street, he dissolved into Farragut Square.

"Good old Stitch," Hunter said finally. "Do you mind telling me what you know? I'll even settle for what you don't know."

"I don't know why I've always been called Stitch. My name's Louivet Macedoine. My mother was a waitress from Havana, my father a dockworker from Morne-à-Chandelle. But you know this. It's your curse to need to check things out. Maybe I'm just a function of what you know. All we really do know is, you're in trouble."

"Tell me something we both don't know."

"I don't mind telling you, Commander, that's flattering." Stitch cracked his knuckles rudely. "I mean, your asking me for an opinion." He glanced around. "Do you think there's more coffee?"

Hunter connected with the waiter's eyes and flashed him the international hand sign for the devil's brew. Then he took a deep breath and looked at Stitch as if he were seeing him for the first time.

"So, it looks like both of us are still working on the same case."

Chapter 29

Washington, D.C.

May your lift always exceed your drag.

HUNTER TOOK A GOOD look at Stitch because he realized they were going to be getting closer. He was exactly Hunter's height, though his arms and legs seemed longer, like the boxer–what was his name– Ezzard Charles. Weight was likely 179 pounds. Age roughly seventy-five. When he smiled, crows landed in branches around his eyes, a sign of genuine warmth. While his suit had the lightest of shines, it was in perfect condition, flashes of white shirt at the ends of his sleeves. Stitch leaned forward, about to speak. Hunter let himself believe he was there when he mirrored the motion.

Surely Stitch wasn't a dream. Schwarzkopf had seen him and addressed him directly. The trouble with wondering about everything was, it put you in wonderland. When you thought of it, how happy was Alice when she stepped through the looking glass? The little pin on Stitch's lapel–covering a small moth hole?–declared "It's Sinatra's world–we just live in it." Or was this just part of Stitch's costume, a way to hide, like his black suit and hat. Hunter took another deep breath. Why had it taken him so long to get a first impression of him?

"Let's go back to the shadowy time when Charles and Anne became the parents of Buster," Stitch said.

"Yes, let's do." Hunter nodded his head encouragingly and opened his palms. *The less you say, the more he'll tell you.*

"We're on solid ground there, a terminus if you will," Stitch said. "Let's take a leap and say this boy is you."

"Nothing doing," Hunter interrupted. "You don't steal up on the incredible to discover what's credible."

"When did you first guess he was you?"

"I love the unknown, but there's something to be said for the known. I've never made that guess. In a way, I've refused to make it. I remember something stirring in me while reading *The Boy's Book of Lindbergh, the Lone Eagle*." Hunter stopped himself. "Please understand, Stitch, the part about who you think I might be–keep it dark, won't you, especially in a place like this."

Stitch smiled. "If nothing else, you and Buster luxuriate in an oasis of coincidence."

How long had he rehearsed that line? The waiter appeared with more coffee. "Is there anything else for the two gentlemen?"

"In about ten minutes, I'd like a little cognac," Hunter said. "Have you any of the Richard Hennessy?"

The waiter looked quickly at his watch, then looked back to a black walnut door behind the bar, with its listening glasses. "The really, really good stuff? Four hundred dollars a bottle?"

"Unless you serve it by the glass." Hunter turned to Stitch. "How about you, *mon ami*?"

A scowl. "I'm on the job."

The waiter vanished.

"Here's what I've got, Hunter. You were born June 22, 1930, well after your Lone Eagle came under Carrel's spell. You've noticed Lindbergh could focus acutely on instrument panels, or lose himself in the scientific contemplation of undreamed-of engineering whirligigs? Well, he really was a savant. And for every glittering achievement of a savant, there's an empty space where his personality should have been. In today's language, this malady is called autism. You know the famous story about your dad entering an empty theater with your mother."

"Let's just call him Lindbergh," Hunter said.

"Among the 500 empty seats in the semi-darkness, a lady had left a white sweater, apparently to save her place while she stepped out to the restroom. Lindbergh walked in and sat directly on the sweater. What compelled him to choose exactly that seat in an otherwise empty theater? Was he out to steal the sweater?"

"He would have determined, upon entering the room, which seat had the best view, the best acoustics. He'd have factored in the gallery, the grandstand, the sound absorption of the cushions, all on the fly. He'd have held up his finger and caught the breeze of the place. He'd even leave a little room for intuition. Yes, there would have been just the one seat for him."

"And why didn't he pick up the sweater and take it to the lost and found?"

Hunter felt a tremor in his leg. "He wouldn't have seen the sweater. Not important enough, because it involved an insignificant person. In the rush of important data, the sweater would have been swept below the tidal wave. But where are you going with this?"

"Carrel knew from the start what the world *didn't* know about Lindbergh. He didn't give a damn about Lindbergh's flying feats, only his autism, which begged to make him his robot whom he could exploit. Carrel was a Svengali, or what have you."

"I'm waiting," Hunter said.

"It was only after Buster was born that Lindbergh began sifting through Undark. What did Emily Sharpe tell you?"

Slowly the memory took shape. It was during the lost days before he saw Dr. Feelia that Hunter had visited Emily Sharpe, Violet's sister. He held up his hand, remembering.

"She told me…something she heard from Violet while they were working in the Morrow household. Violet eavesdropped on Lindbergh and Anne fighting about his visiting Undark too much. Violet's impression was, 'Miss Anne was sure he was seeing somebody.'"

Stitch laughed. "How often women doubt our 'scientific curiosity.' Lindbergh would have tried to convince Anne he was intrigued by radium dials for night flying, but Anne knew better, though she was wrong about the nature of his disappearances. Lindbergh's fascination with Undark was tied up with Buster's syndactyly. No one in the Morrow household was permitted to speak of it. For Lindbergh, it was deeper than unspeakable. He and Anne had flown so much together, he feared she was exposed to solar radiation while pregnant. Or was the weakness in her heredity? He was studying the girls at Undark to learn the birth defects that radiation exposure wreaked on their children.

"By the time Buster was born, Carrel had crept into Lindbergh's head and made him deeply repulsed by any imperfection," Stitch said. "The little man cultivated Lindbergh's ego until he really started to believe his responsibilities were on a rarefied plane. The gene pool must be kept pure. Any ethical roadblocks, any sense of loyalties to 'lower' humanity Lindbergh might once have felt, were swept below the excitement, like the sweater. My theory is, Lindbergh entered a psychic thunderstorm. Buster became a puzzle to solve, not a person. Lindbergh's own child was a freak, something to hide from Carrel, who'd whispered to Lindbergh that he was a perfect specimen."

Hunter felt his own toes tingle, then burn. "My psychotherapist could explain you away, like that," he said.

"You'd better hope I exist," Stitch said. "Otherwise, I'd be magic, a stereotypical hallucination, something nice people are no longer allowed in our enlightened world. More likely, it's just that I'm beyond you. As Carrel confided to his tall protégé, 'Most civilized men manifest only an elementary level of consciousness. They take pleasure in watching, among great crowds, athletic spectacles, in seeing childish and vulgar moving pictures, in being rapidly transported without effort, or in looking at swiftly moving objects.' Think of how the *Spirit of St. Louis* fits into all of this, and the crowds that swarmed him at Le Bourget. 'They are soft, sentimental, lascivious, violent.' And faceless. Can't you just see Lindbergh's slow nod of agreement? 'They have no moral, esthetic, or religious sense. They are extremely numerous. They have engendered a vast herd of children whose intelligence remains rudimentary.' And here you are, Lindbergh, their king, their Superman, invisible as Careu Kent, passing through the looking glass as you inseminate half of Europe. They cannot grasp what an earth induction compass is. You're not their celebrity—you're too famous to be a celebrity. By primitive man's measure, amplified by radio squawkings in the electromagnetic spectrum, you are a god. What's wrong?"

Hunter shook his head back and forth.

"What?" Stitch sighed and stretched out his arm. "Go ahead and pinch me."

Hunter twisted the skin on Stitch's good hand until he squawked and slapped him in the face.

"Okay? And Hunter, do you want to know the funniest part? Just one in three thousand people have syndactyly. But what really would've gotten into Lindy's craw is that it's much more common in darker-skinned races than in whites. Wouldn't Lindbergh have hated *that* to get out! He was desperate to prove the imperfection that 'spoiled' Buster was in Anne's bloodline, not his."

"If what you're saying is true, then all those bastards, all those Lindbergh babies, were, in a way, my fault," Hunter said. "In other words, the fault of my fault. Lindbergh was conducting an outrageous scientific experiment of his own to see if other children he fathered with other women would receive that defective gene. There would never be enough children to create a suitably scientific study group. It was the only way he could let himself off the hook."

"The experiment stretched into the 1960s," Stitch said. "You must've thought it strange Lindbergh would desire children from the two Hesshaimer sisters, both of whom were born cripples. Both use canes to walk. What was that about? Then I realized how deeply Carrel's demonic assumptions had seeped into his mind. From the earliest days of their friendship, the great Nobel laureate isolated Lindbergh's weakness and systematically trashed the last part of his innocence. I hope Carrel rots in hell for it. Too bad his son is out to kill you."

"Carrel never had a son. You're just fishing, aren't you?"

"Carrel and Ann-Marie-Laure Gouriez de La Motte had no children," Stitch said. "But on the wrong side of the blanket, he might easily have been a father. Go with me a second. Let's suppose there is such a son." A wistful light entered Stitch's eyes. "Or a daughter. Why do you suppose he or she would want to kill you?"

"The patents again. You and John Abel Smith."

"Fine," Stitch said. "But the perfusion pump is nothing to sniff at. Lindbergh worked two years on it, almost three, in absolute secrecy. Fewer than thirty were made. Four are at the Smithsonian. Millions saw one of the pumps at the

1939 World's Fair. *The glass heart.* In front of huge crowds, it kept a dog's isolated thyroid alive."

"Tell me something new."

"I've had a change of heart. I'd like a daiquiri now," Stitch said. "They invented it here, and I'm having one."

Hunter signaled to the waiter, who gave a solemn nod.

"In case you're wondering, Lucky Lindy didn't kill you. He may even have loved you. But because of Carrel's lies, he couldn't stand the sight of you. So, it was he who arranged for you to be abducted, with a little help from his friend Henry Breckinridge. The night of the kidnapping, Lindbergh was in neither of two places he was supposed to be. According to his schedule, he was supposed to be delivering a speech to wealthy NYU alumni at the Waldorf Astoria. But he never showed. Henry Breckinridge, his man at the Waldorf, made telephone calls to 'find' him. When Breckinridge reached Lindbergh, Lindbergh told him to make apologies and to call ahead to Anne at Highfields to let her know he was arriving late.

"Lindbergh's excuse for staying at the Morrow's house in Englewood the night before was to be closer to Manhattan for the Waldorf appearance. So, it was nothing less than stunning for him to 'forget' about the Waldorf gig. With Breckinridge smoothing everything over, Lindbergh started his drive to Highfields at 6 p.m., arriving at 8: 25 p.m.

"Little Buster had a chest cold, so he'd been put to bed before seven in a pale blue pair of Dr. Dentons with an electric heater glowing beside his crib.

"Lindbergh was in his library directly below Buster when the caretakers saw the door to the nursery was open. They felt an icy cold breeze coming through an open window. They walked in. You'd expect a scream, right? But the first sound was a giggle. Infamously during the last two years, Lindbergh had made it a sport to play "hide the baby" to embarrass and fluster the young girls and steadfast older couples who were babysitting. It tickled Lindy to see them tearing their hair out, looking for the missing Eaglet. You know, humor is a tool that great leaders use to relax the troops. This practice of making his child disappear shouldn't be looked at as incriminating."

"So, we're not to look at the practice as something more heinous," Hunter said.

"It wasn't a matter of seconds but instead a matter of long minutes, maybe twenty, before it dawned on the caretakers that it wasn't a prank."

The daiquiris arrived. Stitch raised his glass in a toast.

"Bruno Hauptmann didn't drop you; rather, he faithfully filched you from your bedroom window at Highfields; delivered you to a fourth party through underworld connections hand-picked by Breckinridge; had no idea you were cleansed by the anonymity of the adoption process; and unwittingly made you the man you are today. Hauptmann's fatal error was to accept the $50,000 ransom money Breckinridge set him up with."

"You're one corpse short of believability."

"It was dark work, but it was Breckinridge who arranged for the replacement cadaver and the quicklime for the shallow grave. Don't imagine the former Undersecretary of War had no access to a body, however small. I cannot tell you who that little boy was, or where he came from. Your stand-in, of course, had the great good fortune not to suffer from your webbed toes; hence the quick cremation, a brilliant stroke of playing fast and loose with evidence. When the Eaglet's body was formally identified by Lindbergh–and in private–he was there to make sure the corpse *didn't* have your special, and most distinguishing, feature."

Something passed over Stitch, and he locked onto Hunter's eyes. "From where I'm standing, there were exactly seven degrees of separation between Lindbergh and

Ned and Nora Dauger, the real heroes of this story. Ned and Nora loved you without knowing who you were."

Hunter said nothing.

"When I say Ned knew nothing about this, I mean he knew absolutely nothing," Stitch said.

"While you seem to know something more," Hunter said. "Especially about Ned."

"Let's put it this way. The closest point of approach between Lindbergh and Ned was Raytheon, where Ned worked and where Lindbergh did some early consulting. I spent the better part of the winter of 1954 trying to measure the degree of Ned's innocence, which was quite startling. A detective doesn't run into that every day. Have you ever reflected how lucky you were to grow up with him as a father?"

Hunter felt a deep ache for Ned. His heart thumped. He'd loved Ned with all his might, but he was devastated to understand that a stranger like Stitch could feel that wasn't enough.

"Breckinridge was another matter entirely. Lindbergh's 1927 Atlantic crossing was old news by the time you disappeared. A modern PR guru would have been going crazy with the lost opportunities. Was Lindbergh's celebrity sliding away? What to do to keep your audience share? Not that Lindbergh could ever rekindle the frenzy of those crowds in Paris and on Wall Street–that was a once-in-a-millennium stunt. But realize–if he couldn't get any more credit from flying, all that was left to him short of notoriety was…frightfully…sympathy. He and Anne were sliding off the world map when you vanished. A heartbeat later, they became international stars the moment there was no you."

"You mean the better part of a lost week after there was no me, if ever it were me, which I've never said. I get what you're saying about Ned. I wish I were his son."

"Your wish has been granted. You were his son. Are you so hung up on bloodlines, or is it just karma?"

Another round of daiquiris floated in. Stitch, a spectator in Hunter's misfortune, took a sip. "Now this is nice. This place is a bit stuffy, though."

"That's what I like about it."

"All this suit-and-tie stuff in a changing world. It makes me kind of sick. And don't forget, the women have their own 'smart separates.' So many rules." Stitch lowered his head, reflecting. He started to say something, then stopped. He sighed.

"What?" Hunter asked.

"I know it's a shot in the dark, but did you ever consider Anne Morrow Lindbergh might have had a hand in Lindbergh's loss of faith? To be an autistic narcissist was a deadly combination. We'll never know how early she started dividing her attentions away from him. You're so interested that the police never interviewed Lindbergh. You've never interviewed her."

"No. Absolutely not. Just absolutely no." Hunter had refused even to consider driving to her home on the coast of Darien, Connecticut, to ask her. It was every investigator's secret: some things are better not known. He couldn't bear to imagine his own mother turning him away.

"I'm sure every woman in the world wondered what it was like to be her, before and even after the kidnapping," Stitch said.

"You mean rich, a famous novelist, photographed at all the best events, the greatest designers in the world clamoring to dress her, and married to a god?"

"With the world watching, she won the ultimate love match: the shy, self-effacing Lindbergh. She even snagged him from her older sister Elizabeth. There's no modern-day equivalent for landing Lucky Lindy. Joe Namath? Donald Trump? Steve Jobs? Warren Beatty? George Lucas? Ted

Turner? Don't make me laugh. What was she going to do, cheat on Lindbergh by finding a better pilot?"

"I know where you're going with this," Hunter said, "and I don't like it."

"Antoine Saint-Exupéry wasn't just a Lindbergh. He was two or three dimensions more sophisticated. How could Anne have resisted such a figure, a world-class novelist and philosopher, not to mention a stunning hero of aviation? Short story long, if anybody were a more natural pilot than Lindbergh, he was it. When Saint-Exupéry made a harrowing escape through occupied France via Portugal and North Africa to come to the U.S., he was the toast of New York for *both* of his talents–as a war hero and as the legendary author of *The Little Prince*.

"Talk about *Le Violon d'Ingres*. Since the suave Frenchman and his wife were estranged, they led separate lives in separate apartments–she in the Bevin House in Long Island, he in a hideaway he kept at Beekman Place in Manhattan. Regardless of their sex, every writer of any description wanted to have cocktails with him. Anne Morrow Lindbergh was just a face in the crowd. It wasn't that he was savagely handsome–quite the contrary. He had a sharply unsettling face. But he was irresistible. He dazzled lovers and jealous enemies with understatement. Every word he uttered was a magical incantation. *Would you like a cigarette? Have you considered…taking off your dress?* He didn't just have love affairs with women, he had a love affair with everything. What a man. I say, do you research?"

Hunter said nothing.

"From my notes, Anne Morrow Lindbergh visited Beekman Place unescorted 27 times between January, 1941 and Easter, 1943. Saint-Exupéry had just won the National Book Award for *Wind, Sand, and Stars*, rendering Lindbergh's stabs at writing almost childlike. How flabbergasted Lindbergh must have been when he realized his wife and Saint-Exupéry were lovers."

"There's no way for you to know this," Hunter said.

"Unless I were the detective Lindbergh hired to check it out," Stitch said. "Why do you think Lindbergh booked Room 512 here at the Army & Navy Club in Washington for three weeks running without an engagement? Because he couldn't bear the humiliation of being in New York, knowing what was going on. That's a lot of daiquiris. Probably while his wife was taking off her blouse for Saint-Exupéry. Look at this, from an early draft of one of Anne's diaries."

Hunter glanced at the photocopy of a discarded galley proof. Something told him not to touch it. "This has never come to light."

"Correct." Stitch grinned. "But just listen:

> *It was very exciting…Perhaps it was only because it was almost the first time anyone had talked to me purely on my craft. Not because I was a woman to be polite to, to charm with superficials, not because I was my father's daughter or C's wife; no, simply because of my book, my mind, my* craft. *I have a* craft! *And someone who is master of that craft, who writes beautifully, thinks I know enough about my* craft *to want to compare notes about it, to want to fence with my* mind, *steel against steel….Summer lightning.*

"Hell, *I* almost fell in love with Saint-Exupéry. Here he is, a war hero, daring to convince the U.S. to get into the war against Germany, and here is Lindbergh, a stooge on the radio, warning his country to stay out of the fight."

"Millions of Americans were isolationists," Hunter said. "Anne Morrow Lindbergh agreed with her husband."

"In public. But see, I was acting as a private detective."

A fly in the fuselage. Hunter stiffened. "This is unkind. It isn't right for you to have brought this up." Was it Stitch's daiquiri or his own? At least two sheets to the wind, he reached into his pocket and popped a Xanax Dr. Feelia had given him "for emergency use only." It was as if one part of his life were losing its stability and decanting into another. Now the entire Army & Navy Club began a 45-degree bank to the right. The chandeliers leaned.

"Hunter," Stitch said. "Why do you have so much trouble coming to terms with yourself? You've suspected for years who you really are."

"I like to keep things simple. Answer my question. Who do *you* think I am?"

Stitch reached for his hat.

"The moment I disclose who I think I am, I turn myself into a Pretender," Hunter said. He looked down. His hands were jittery, vibrating out of their cuffs. *Where was Dido?* "Let sleeping dogs lie."

A strange look stole over Stitch's face. "If who you are is in your heart, why don't you tell Pia?"

"I cannot ever tell Pia."

"Then tell yourself."

"Now there's a thought. I'm a world expert on Lindbergh. But what if I don't dare to believe my own claims?" It was what had kept him from turning his analytical abilities inward. But was it also what kept him from deducing Dido's whereabouts? *Aviate.* He put his hands on the table to keep the world from flipping over. *Navigate.* He eyed the silverware into place. Slowly, the water glass stopped moving. *Communicate.* "Besides, the moment I isolate myself as the heir, I'm a target, with billions of reasons to kill me."

"Do I have to remind you, you're already a target," Stitch said. "I have to tell you, and this decision is not based on casual inquiry but instead decades of research. You've spent your whole life not knowing who you are. You've spent a lifetime in the dark. You are the Man in the Iron Mask."

Chapter 30

West Berlin, West Germany

I'm not speeding, officer. I'm just flying low.

HUNTER TOOK THE OVERNIGHT flight to West Berlin, deep in thought. Maybe the path to self-discovery was to learn less about himself in favor of learning more about those dear to him. Like they said, pray to God but row to shore. All of which suggested Pia. He'd tried to keep up with her with postcards and by phone, but there was no substitute for the real thing. As his rental Jaguar flashed through the streets, he felt an alluring sense of getting closer to her.

Pia's new apartment was near the top of one of the lofty sky rises, the Steglitz-Kreisel. The glassy monolith was pure Philip Johnson, though the design was credited to Sigrid Kressmann-Zschach. All told, the cigarette lighter was 118 meters to the pinnacle. Pia's digs were barely at the 90-meter level.

"Come soon," she'd written, including a new telephone number. "I can't wait to see you."

Hunter looked up at her building from across the busy street. The lower floors were occupied by a hotel and high-flying couture shops. The middle floors were given over to financial concerns. Near the top, a lucky few got to call this place home.

He was challenged by security but satisfied he was on the list. The elevator hummed as he headed up. Released on Pia's floor, he entered a hallway glistening with white tiles, the devil to clean. He was happy to hear the sound of Dido scratching at the other side of the door, and approaching steps.

Pia, dressed in a clinging winter-white cashmere twin set and white capris with a silver belt, surprised him at the door with a deep kiss. Dido danced but restrained herself from jumping up on his trousers. Inside, with sweeping views of the city below, the decoration was white couches on white ash floors against monumental, blue-filtered windows. "Where am I?" Hunter laughed. "I like the new blonde hair. But who are you, Virna Lisi?"

"I thought you would."

"How'd you ever end up here?" he asked, then stood stupefied that he'd rashly posed a question for which he didn't want to know the answer. He'd careened in with three successive risky questions in a row.

"There was a three-month space between long-term tenants," Pia said. "My advance from my next movie was enough to cover it, along with what you sent. Radu heard about it while researching material at the Frankfurt Book Fair and thought it might be a perfect place to film a couple of the scenes."

Ah. *Aviate.* "Why didn't he snap it up? I mean, it's fabulous."

She laughed. "It's so unHunter of you to say fabulous. Radu is a Biedermeier type. I'm the one who likes the *avant*. Do say fabulous again." She walked up to him and kissed him before he could. "Hold me tighter. It's like I can't get close enough to you."

When they came up for air, she said, "I have a present for you."

"Your taking care of Dido is present enough," Hunter said, "though I do accept gifts graciously."

"No, I want to show you," she said, swinging open the glass-and-stainless refrigerator. Lined up like little soldiers were bottles of La Tropical. Behind them were takeout cartons from Havana Sexy. Hunter started breathing faster. It was strange enough without coincidences intruding.

"Let's have one of these, and then you can tell me why you disappeared into thin air."

Now Hunter's footing was more sure. He'd been covering for his absences for close to two decades. After he told her he'd blacked out and found himself in the Garden City Hotel, she asked to see how the bullet wound in his leg was doing, now nine weeks healed but still tender. She traced her index finger around the point of entry, bent down, and kissed him. When Dido jumped onto the couch, Hunter started to shoo her off, but Pia said, "Let her stay. She and I have an understanding."

"You both make friends easily," Hunter said. "I'm so glad to see you, Pia."

"Come out to the balcony," she said and picked up a pad of paper and a pen. "You can see everything up here. It's like flying." She slid open the door. Far below was the sound of children.

"Okay," Hunter said. "I was kind of enjoying this couch, though." He picked up his beer (what a relief that she had it there, waiting for him) and followed. This high above the ground, the first monument he looked for was the Berliner Funkturm, the onetime Nazi radio-broadcasting tower where the first television signals in the world were transmitted. Built in 1926, this was one of the marvels Goering showed Lindbergh as his guide to the New

Germania in 1936. Hunter drank in the sight. Strange to be at the same height as the tower's restaurant, bombed and burned twice during World War II.

"What are you staring at?" Pia asked.

"The first time I was in the Funkturm, I ate in the restaurant so I could get my bearings and understand Berlin. I was a Lieutenant in the Navy, working as an aide to Admiral Leighton. Later I was there many times, because the admiral had a thing for lobster. They still serve fresh Maine lobster."

"I can see you in uniform. It's almost as if you're still wearing it."

"With the gold brassard. That was in the 1960s. The food, as I remember, was great. Have you ever been there?" What he really wanted to know was, had Radu taken her there yet.

"No, but it sounds really fun," she said. "A trip back to your past. Since the tower is always staring at us, we might as well stare back. I'll just have to change."

"You look great," he said. "How could you improve on this?"

"I'm a bit too comfy."

"This won't ruin the Cuban food in the refrigerator, will it?"

"Actually, that food isn't ours."

Radu's?

"Dido adores it as much as you do. I don't know what that says about your taste. Why would a Scottish dog ever take to Sancti Spiritus chicken, low on spice?"

"She's from England."

"'She's a border terrier,' Radu says. He says if something comes from a border, you always credit it to the northern side, which would be Scotland."

"Quite an encyclopedia, our Radu."

"Hunter, he means nothing to me. Look, it's getting dark. At night, they light the bottom half of the tower a pretty indigo shade. The upper half is magenta. I'm going to wear something dark and sparkling."

"That's perfectly all right with me."

"It's a little number from my new movie, about Marilyn Monroe and Kennedy."

"Happy birthday, Mr. President."

"I'm not the lead, Hunter."

"Well, who are you, then?"

"Jackie's sister, Lee. Radu says we *could* be sisters. He recommended me for the part."

"But he's not directing. You mentioned some money was involved here, which doesn't seem to be his cup of tea."

"In this case, he is my agent."

"A new career. How many clients does he have?"

"Just me so far."

"Ah."

Pia walked through the open door. Hunter listened for the *thresh, thresh* of her moving hangars.

"Hunter, could you help me with my outfit?"

From around the side of the door she held out a clingy dark blue dress with two deep Vs. He took the gauzy silk garment cut on the bias. Holding it by the sequined straps, he turned it front to back, marveling. "An extraordinary feat of engineering. Does it require a brassiere?"

She reappeared in the doorway in sheer black stockings fastened to a silk garter belt.

"Not yet."

Dido hid her eyes.

WHEN THEY STORMED into the taxi, late for their reservation to the tower restaurant, the driver barely took his eyes off Pia.

"Funkturm," Hunter said.

"A place of heavenly gourmet seduction," the driver said, looking back through the rear-view mirror at Pia as she touched up her lipstick. "They've just redecorated it with a nostalgic twist to mimic the 1920s. Rosewood bars, long black tables."

"Berlin should be careful about being too nostalgic," Hunter said.

Pia shifted in her seat until her presence warmed his side. She'd pulled her hair back into something new. "How many women have brought you here before?" she asked.

While Hunter might still be in a post-coital stupor, he wasn't going to touch that bait. When she pulled Hunter's face in for a kiss, he decided to give up seeing if the driver was still watching. He inhaled her fragrance and kissed the pearly back of her neck. *Navigate*.

"Here's your funkturm, Mr. Funky," the driver said when they pulled up. "English?"

"Yankee," Hunter said. "Here's your tip."

"Oh, my God," the driver said. "You must be mistaken."

"Hush money," Hunter said. "When you pick us up at 2200 hours, you will be a little more polite."

"Yes, sir," the driver said. "You enter through here, the Palais am Funkturm."

They entered the vast lower level of the tower, designed around a circle and arrayed in blue. It seemed almost to be moving. How long would it be before Stitch showed up? Maybe it was best not to think about him, so he wouldn't keep slipping in. Just now, it was better not to share Pia's attention with anyone.

Then why had he talked unnecessarily to the cab driver and given an exorbitant tip? Had he crossed over to the north side of the border between stupid and crazy? *Communicate*.

"You said you were hungry. Are you thirsty, too?" he asked Pia.

"Famously," she said in Radziwillian. "Darling."

"Still in character?" Hunter asked.

"Sometimes people prefer the Pretenders to the originals," Pia said.

"With jewelry a singular exception." Hunter looked at her black pearl mabe earrings, which must have cost a fortune. Too bad they weren't fake, because now he'd have to consider who'd given them to her. "Isn't it funny that jewelry is often a downpayment on a future."

"That's a good one," Pia said and laughed. "A fifty-year-old talking about the future. I like it."

"The future is what you make of it," Hunter said.

The maître d' led them 270 degrees around the tower until a new sector of Germany shimmered below. Tiny cars honked and spilled their headlights on black boulevards lined with lindens. Stars above the horizon kept moving—jets lining up for final approach to Berlin-Schönefeld airport. He looked across the table. Pia was in her element. Again, he was unable to pierce her thoughts, which made her all the more intoxicating. Don't doubt her or your feelings for her. If you doubt her, she'll disappear. Just enjoy her company, for once in your life. Take your hands off the stick and let someone else fly.

He imagined himself flying over Berlin the way Lindbergh had over Paris, looking for Le Bourget. If the tower were a plane that was about to flame out, where could he make a dead-stick landing? A seven-to-one glideslope might take him over there, to the dark farmland on the edge of the brilliance of Berlin.

Bad idea. That blank area was a lake. Lake Nymphansee, famous for the lovers who strolled along its shore on Karl Marx Road. The lay of the land was coming back to him. Extraordinarily clear by day, it was a horrible black pit to drown in at night. Or was he still suffering from his encounter with the devil at Lake Averno out of displacement? He had to stop thinking like this. Better to drown in Pia.

The waiter brought the menus and two flutes of champagne.

"Are you still serving the grilled zander filet?" Hunter asked.

"With the almond butter, the sweetheart cabbage, and the sautéed baby potatoes. And for the Fräulein?"

"I'd like the King Trumpet Mushroom Stroganoff," Pia said. "Don't spare the sour cream."

"Let the chef choose the wine," Hunter said. "Afterward, we'll have dessert and coffee with the Remy VSOPR."

"Of course, you will," the waiter said, turned on his heel, and marched off.

Pia stroked Hunter's shin with her toe. "Isn't it already afterward?"

When Hunter just smiled, she said, "Hunter, a penny for your thoughts."

"I'm not sure I'm thinking of anything. I'm glad to be here. I am so sorry about my long absence. So much strangeness has been keeping us impossibly apart."

"You're after something, aren't you?"

"Isn't everybody?"

"Yes, but you seem somewhere else."

"It's just the opposite, Pia. I want you to feel safe with me."

"Like you're flying the plane?"

"It almost feels like we are now, up here." Hunter leaned closer to her, reached, and brushed her cheek, so warm, so Pia-like. That would be his new imperative. Live in the moment and nowhere else. Or was that too Lindbergh-like? "I'd like to take a drive in the country tomorrow."

"Can Dido come?"

"It was Dido's suggestion."

"Where are we going?"

"Across the border to France. There's something I'd like to show you."

"Won't they give us trouble with Dido?"

"I'll insure her with blanket coverage."

THE NEXT MORNING, the drive through Potsdam was so bright the castles and trees seemed cut with scissors. Pia wore a long scarf like Isadora Duncan, while Hunter seized the occasion not to wear a suit–the first time he'd taken that liberty in months. Instead, he wore black chinos and a gray-ribbed turtleneck.

"Hunter," Pia laughed. "You're dressed like a grad student!"

"Continuing education."

"What's next?"

"Hanover, Dusseldorf, Cologne. We'll be approaching the border when we drive through a place called Trier. It used to be the largest Roman city this side of the Alps. The Romans called it Trevorum."

Pia stretched in a way that would have halted a column of centurions. "It's always instructive when an American tells me about Europe. Should I be taking notes?"

"Once we're across the border, it'll be less than two hours to Paris."

"I guess that's making the best of a ten-hour drive. You still can't tell me where we're going?"

"They say most dead pilots are found with their hands around the microphone instead of the controls."

HOURS LATER, Pia was asleep, drowsing on his shoulder, with Dido on her lap. Both breathed so evenly, with warm ease, that Hunter was tempted to pull over and sleep himself. Just then Pia jerked up. "If it's so far, why didn't we fly?"

"Did you just have a bad dream?"

"Yes, I guess so."

For lunch they stopped at a half-timbered restaurant by a river that featured "Trout From A Lively Stream." Then they were back in the Jaguar, chasing the sun to the west. Dido barked at a flock of crows as they approached the northern entry to the medieval city of Trier. The Porta Nigra or "Black Gate" blocking entry to the town was a marvel in gray sandstone designed to instill supernatural fear in any offcomer.

"There are Roman baths here, too," Hunter said. "The thermae."

"You're quite a little tour guide, Hunter," Pia said. "But Dido and I have had enough. Where is our surprise?"

Chapter 31

Paris

Keep the shiny side up and the greasy side down.

A S THE SUN faded to twilight, they drove through vineyard after vineyard, tunnel after tunnel of trees. By the time the tip of the Eiffel Tower was visible in the shadowy horizon, they were deep in suburban farmland that slept in a mantle around electric Paris.

"Almost there," Hunter said. He turned down a narrow drive and through the darkness approached a long, low series of buildings with corrugated steel roofs. The commercial oasis was painted with words dissolving in rust. Surrounded by gorse and ivy, a stucco house waited silently nearby, blinds closed. Hunter looked at its door. No light flashed on. No one called out.

They left the car in front of the smaller of the two warehouses, which was fitted with ancient wooden doors on rollers held shut by a combination lock. Hunter flicked on his penlight and handed it to Pia. "Hold this, please."

"What are you doing?" she said warily. "Where are we?"

"Shhh," he said, though it obviously annoyed her. "I'm sure of the combination, but it didn't work the first time. I'm going try it again."

"Maybe the lock was made to keep us out," she said.

"What's in there is mine."

"Really."

He rolled the lock again, feeling Pia's impatience, one hand now on her hip.

"So, what's the combination?"

"One, nine, twenty-seven."

"Here, let me give it a go," she said. "I'm good at this."

Now this was more interesting. In the near pitch darkness, it was sensual nigh unto intimate. He watched Pia's slender fingers deftly spill the tumblers left, then right, then left. She closed her eyes and with a triumphant sigh pulled down on the lock, which gave way with a click.

Hunter wheeled the great door open, exposing yards of dark inside and a rush of cool, fresh air.

"A great surprise, Hunter. A big box of sleep."

"Use the penlight."

She flicked it around and gasped. There with its shiny Wright 223-horsepower, 9-cylinder, air-cooled radial engine; its quaint, cambered struts; its machined engine cowling; its hard-rubber tires; its moderne, riveted empennage; its supernatural essence breathing with the conviviality of all 1920s machines, was *The Spirit of St. Louis*. "His aircraft!"

"Almost," Hunter said. "It's the missing plane from the *Spirit of St. Louis* movie. Lindbergh test-flew it for accuracy, but not in 1927. Nineteen *fifty*-seven." He paused. "It's the real deal, but it's a replica. One of six. Most are in museums all over the world. One didn't fare so well."

Hunter paused. "Japanese plutocrats ginned up a dead-perfect copy of the *Spirit* in the jealous weeks after the 1927 crossing. Built for the Mainichi newspaper empire, their zircon *Spirit*, accurate in all details, lacked only an accurate pilot. It crashed in 1928, an event not thoroughly covered by its parent publication. This particular model is known as The Missing *Spirit*."

Looking the monoplane up and down, Pia almost became her stare. "How can it be so…alive?"

"It better be, for what I paid for it."

"What did it cost you?"

"The original *Spirit* cost just under $11,000."

"I bet this one cost more."

"Sure."

She strode to the plane, and he put his hands around her slim hips as she hopped up the step and entered through the door to the cockpit. Inhaling her fragrance, he sensed her body move beneath her clothes as she settled into the brittle wicker seat. Her skirt shifted ever so slightly upward as she reached for the rudder pedals. Nobody who ever strapped on the N-X-211 looked as good as Pia did now, in the fermenting darkness.

"How do you like it?"

"Come on, girl," she called, so he handed Dido up to her. She caressed the instruments with her fingertips. "Will this fly now?"

"You mean *this second*?"

"Yes." Her eyes sparkled.

"It will, but I've never flown from this grassy runway before, and it's unlit. It would be dangerous." As if matters of danger had ever mattered with the *Spirit*. "Not to mention, it has five gas tanks. It's a flying bomb."

"I thought you were a pilot."

Hunter nodded. "You understand, it's not a passenger plane. The seating arrangement couldn't be more selfish. Remember, it's all about flying alone." He ran his hands along the fuselage and felt a shiver. "Just you and all that sky."

"It is perfect, Hunter. Look at its exquisite, miniature instruments."

"They're not so tiny." Hunter looked at the dash. Something swept over him until he was so overcome with emotion, he didn't know what to say. He looked up at the stars, which had come into view above the city of lights. It was purple above the big glow, then indigo, then blue, and finally cobalt and black.

"Hunter, you're crying."

"No," he said.

"Maybe…maybe we could come back in the morning and look at it in the daylight. What did you pay for it?"

"The steepest costs were for completely breaking down the engine on a test stand, lubricating it, re-engineering corroded parts, tuning it up, and recalibrating the instruments. Something north of $3 million. I'm not finished paying for it. The invoices are still coming in for the reconditioning. They threw in that sachet with the pine fragrance. It was free."

"Well, it's a beautiful surprise," Pia said. An impish grin stole over her face. "After all these years, my father's plane."

"Thought you were over that," Hunter said. "We shouldn't live in illusions."

"Well, what the hell do you think this is?"

"This is not your surprise. Your surprise is behind the seat."

"Let me see."

She slipped to the ground, stretched with unconscious allure as she reached around the seat with her left hand, and pulled out a brown paper rectangle held together with twine. She shook out her hair.

"Do you have a knife, Hunter? Oh, it's in your hand." The twine popped off, and Pia pulled the paper away. "It's a lovely…something-in-a-frame." Just then the moon came out. "It's... No, it can't be. It's too exquisite. Paul Klee?"

"It's called *Keep Moving*. He painted it in 1961."

She headed into the car and turned on the map light. She pulled off the rest of the paper. Was it a black tree in a white sky, or a white tree in a black sky? "How did you know? I love it. Is it a perfect replica, like the plane?"

"No, this is the original."

"How did you know my favorite artist was…Oh. Of course, you know. But…*I've seen it before*."

"Of course, you have. It was in that conference room where we first met." He'd bought it from Smith. "It's for you. The lawyers don't get to keep everything."

THAT NIGHT, they stayed in the Ritz near the Opera in Paris. Pia liked it because everything was white in the room. She took the floral print down and replaced it with the Klee, which jumped off the wall like the musical drop of water that puts the world in tune. *Plink.* She stretched out sideways on the bed so she could see it better. Dido jumped up and curled beside her, as if she, too, were going to study the painting.

Just blocks away, the cobbled Rue de Lappe in Bastille beckoned with Havanita, where the food was great, and a live band played *guaracha*. Hunter dashed over in the light rain and returned with *Filete de Tiburón*, green rice, *maduros*, two Cuban coffees with a kick, and some extra *maduros* for somebody special. If closed eyes and a low growl meant anything, Dido liked it when Pia slipped her some of the baby shark, too.

Was heaven intertemporal? That night Hunter felt young and also very old as he thought of the *Spirit of St. Louis* crouched in the dark like a sparrow, waiting. After he and Pia spent some time getting very close together, long after he was sure she'd fallen asleep, she turned to him.

"Tell me why you like me, Hunter. Why me?"

"You have the grace, even the courtesy, to find me interesting. You're excited by things I have no idea about–

different things–even wrapped up in them, like your acting. You have the courage to love surprise." You are an inexhaustible reservoir of mental health. You have a magnetic attraction to Dido, and to me. All compass needles point to you now.

"So, it's not just that I resemble anyone?"

Hunter peered into her eyes, saw down deep she was Pia, and felt a wave of relief. He'd never felt so strong in years. "It is not."

Pia was a lighthouse he could travel to across an infinite darkness. But first he'd have to earn her. That wasn't something she could give to him but more like something he had to learn to give himself. "What I respect about you, Pia, is few actresses have the talent to portray themselves. I feel more myself when I'm near you." But this was radioactive talk, like Radu.

Pia smirked. "And who are you playing right now? Like all men, the successful lover? Wait a minute–I'll get you your silk bathrobe."

"Dido and I both find you impossible to resist." He waited. He hadn't dared ask before. "Why do you put up with me?"

She scowled, thinking, then laughed. "Three little words: 'Not Lindbergh's daughter.'"

"But plenty of people aren't Lindbergh's daughter," Hunter said.

"Hunter. You've helped me see that I, most singularly and especially, have no need to be just somebody's daughter. I am me."

THE NEXT NIGHT, they returned to Berlin in a lightning storm, the streets full of deadly sparkles. Pia and Dido were halfway up the elevator when she said, "Oh, my gosh. Your painting is still in the car."

"It's your painting," Hunter said. "I'll get it."

In the parking garage, he ran into Stitch, never in a rush, always with that look on his face.

"You've been busy," Stitch said. The roar of the rain made it harder to hear him.

"Correction. Happy," Hunter said.

"For someone who has autism."

"Once again, you are off the mark, my friend. At worst I'm displaced, and who in the world isn't displaced?"

"By a dead child? How can you possibly be jealous of a dead child? I hope you know what you're doing, Hunter. You're living an illusion."

"Who isn't? Let me see your driver's license."

"How fast was I going, officer?"

"Just tell me. Is your real height and weight the same as what's on that little piece of plastic you keep in your wallet? Or, like anyone but Pia, do you carry around the illusion of who you used to be?"

"The past is what you make of it," Stitch said.

"Everyone has a second identity, stalking us across time. Most of us don't have the guts to confront it."

"Right you are, Hunter. But when are you going to learn that being right isn't the answer to anything?" Stitch touched his finger to his brim and stepped away. This time he didn't disappear around the corner. He got lighter and lighter until he wasn't there at all.

Just...*keep moving*. Hunter found his car, picked up the painting, and came to a halt when he realized the storm had grown quiet, too. Stitch was nothing more than a specter of himself, insubstantial and not exactly agreeable. The voices in his head could at least be more encouraging. He started walking again, concentrating on the sound of his own footsteps, which now grew Hitchcock-loud and sounded strangely wet in the bone-dry garage. Step, step, step. After two more strides, he stopped and let the bruise of darkness grow around him, filling everything. Then he heard the bronzy snap of a switch being thrown. The lights went out.

Hunter widened his stance, waiting for nothing to arrive. His fight with Nothing was a return grudge match, and he'd stopped training for it. Somebody was going to get it.

In the continuum of night blindness, there was gray, black, jet black, blue black, and then a whistling shade that sought a lonely harmony with nothingness. Hunter stood still and waited. Then he heard something faintly. It was the roar of headlights and the bouncing sound of a car. He heard it rising through the lower levels of the garage. It ripped into the quiet and lurched toward him.

Hunter stepped behind a stanchion before the headlights stabbed through him. Then the metallic Biscayne-blue Ford Sierra pulled up beside him, with its ultramodern styling for low wind resistance. The Germans never dropped their romance with Hitler-loving Henry Ford. The doors opened. Four thugs in suits piled out.

"We bid you greetings from Dr. Alexis Carrel," the first man said.

Was it Stitch who put them up to this? Or John Abel Smith. "Carrel's been dead since 1944," Hunter said. "Before that, he was insane. Before that, he was a traitor to his country, a collaborator, the kind of smiling grandfather who would smother a baby. By the way, what rock did you crawl out from under?" When they didn't say anything, he said, "Nice car."

"We have something for you to sign. Just a quick signature, and then we're gone. It revokes any claims to the Carrel family's earnings from heart-transplant patent revenues the world over."

"No can do. Besides, you'd need a witness."

The man looked hurt. "I am an attorney. My three friends are disinterested witnesses."

"You'd have to deal with the authenticated descendants first," Hunter said. "Why me?"

"They've already signed, with handsome compensation. Your signature will also restrict you from identifying any further Lindbergh children."

"Whom do you represent?"

A second man came forward, agile, well groomed, with dark hair and an ironic smile. Hunter caught his breath when he realized he was looking into the eyes of Rick Streak. Or could it be his son? Maybe it wasn't about money, or even Lindbergh. Maybe the world turned simply on revenge. In a rush he remembered Streak hadn't been extraordinarily sympathetic to blacks in flight school, a drawback Hunter now regretted he hadn't had the courage to call him on. Had Streak, in the bloom of his insanity, been a member of the Klan? Negative constituencies massed like dark constellations. Hunter swallowed. "Have we met?"

When the second man said nothing, Hunter said, "It only takes a generation before the high principles of science are dropped and we're back to money. Or are you Lindbergh Nazis, actual corporeal beings grown out of the sincere but misunderstood friendship Lindbergh had with Goering? You think I'm the son of Lindbergh, and you consider me a traitor."

The men held their ground.

"I just had a thought. Do you know a fellow named Stitch?" Hunter asked. Then he ran. The suits followed suit, firing their automatic weapons at him, *blip*, *blip*, as he slammed into the glass stairway, threw the fire-alarm switch, and raced higher to the top. As the hapless suits (dressed, unfortunately, like Hunter himself) pursued him through the endless glass building, Hunter closed his eyes and stopped. He realized he was in Pia's first movie. He took a deep breath and stared at them; weapons raised. Like Stitch, they slowly melted away. What was the price of self-identity? He remembered the Klee, still in his hand. Was the world as dumbfounding in white and black as black and white?

WHEN HE TOOK Dido for a walk later, he went down the same stairs and spilled into the parking garage. He did his best to keep his feet because the earth was moving below him so quickly. His skin moved in slow waves on the back of his hands. The azure Ford Sierra still wasn't there, though the rest of his life had taken on the fragrance of a new car.

Did Lindbergh's authorized children experience these hallucinations? Worse, probably. Anne Morrow Lindbergh loved her husband enough to share his lies and even believe in them–an astonishing achievement–or at least make us believe them. Like her two daughters, she'd insulated herself with lyricism and distance. Hunter paused. Was it Lindbergh or Carrel who was his great white whale, and how might he spear it across time? Before the white whale, there had to be a black whale. Was it the sky itself, scoffing at his timid shore?

This time when he went upstairs with Dido to Pia, he took the elevator. At two a.m., in his arms, Pia sat bolt upright and screamed. "Hunter, no! Don't do this!"

"What's the matter?" Hunter asked. He held her so close she had to gasp for breath. "It's all right. You've just had a bad dream."

"No," Pia said. "It's not all right. I know what you've got in mind."

Chapter 32

Brooklyn, New York

Speed is life. Altitude is life insurance.

TWO DAYS LATER, Hunter stared at a withered plant in Michelle Feelia's newly polished copper *cache pot*. It was as though she'd buried her telephone in a bowl of dirt, expected it to grow, and then carefully tended the coffin. "I like what you've done with the place."

"I've never claimed to have a green thumb." Michelle stood and poured steaming water from the kettle. "I must say, it was strange of you to ask to meet me on a Sunday, and before noon, too. I hope this doesn't become a habit."

"The double whammy," Hunter said. "Sorry."

"I'm suspicious of people who use that term." She handed him a mug. "Chiefly because no one has ever defined a single whammy to my satisfaction." She studied him more closely. "You look good, Hunter. You don't have those bags under your eyes. You haven't been recently bandaged."

"The trick to mental health is to set the bar low," Hunter said. "This is new, too." Above her mantel was a print showing a woman in a black dress with a bouquet of flowers rushing hopefully toward a window. As though she'd summoned him from a dream, a liquid, narrow man with a green tunic, black slacks, and black shoes flew over her head, twisting his neck impossibly around to kiss her at the last second. Very French. That's how it must have been with Anne Morrow Lindbergh and Saint-Exupéry. No actual indiscretion but something flying in her heart, undisclosed, impenetrable. It wasn't the dead who tell no tales, it was the living. He recognized the artist as one of the Surrealists and knew this painting, but he couldn't remember who it was just now. No one else painted surfaces like that. It would keep him up at night. Who had painted it?

His eyes moved to another print, black and white. A print of Pia's painting. Funny. "The Klee wasn't here last time, either."

"He called it *Too Early on a Sunday Morning*," she said. "If you were my patient, I'd be charging your insurance double, so please, Hunter, how can I help you."

"I think I'm ready," Hunter said.

"That sounds encouraging," Michelle said.

"I know," Hunter said. "I used to think nobody's ever ready. They're just filling a sudden gap. Everybody's caught off-guard, or pretends to be. The accidental tourist, the field-commissioned general, the amateur detective. It's time I decided to go pro."

"What brought you to this conclusion?"

"I've had a chance to spend some real down time with Pia."

"Where have you been?"

"In West Berlin."

She pursed her lips.

"You don't really like Berlin, do you," Hunter said.

"Not my idea of a place to recover. The Wall and all. I lost family in Germany. But this isn't about me. It's about you. I know I'm not your therapist, but I am Dido's. Hunter. Have you ever considered you're just lonely, on a cosmic level? Loneliness begets loneliness. It breaks you down cell by cell and puts you in danger. If you're the loner type, you already have undeveloped monocytes, which haunt the blood of lost souls–not just in spirit but literally. I mean there are studies. From the days of the cavemen, who had to exist socially or die, loneliness has tinkered with the human blueprint. It takes you into a black pit, and it's hard to dig your way out. It's not for nothing that the lonely seek out the company of doctors."

"Michelle, you crack me up. Such poetry, and on a Sunday morning. Correction. You *were* Dido's therapist. Remember, we were talking about Pia."

"Do you remember my recommendation to take things slowly?"

"I do," Hunter said. "But my question for you is, what do you do if things take you quickly?"

"Hunter, as much as I like you, we've got to set some boundaries. Either I'm talking with you as a friend, or you need to sign some paperwork."

"You're taking a risk, aren't you?" Hunter said.

"Hunter, why do I have the sense that you're saying all of this is about you and Dido or you and Pia, but I keep getting the feeling there's someone else and you. Someone you won't talk to me about because you don't even want to talk to yourself about it."

Chapter 33

Garden City, Long Island, New York

"*Unknown airport with Cessna 150 circling overhead, identify yourself.*"

"WOW," THE DRIVER SAID. "Thank you, sir. Don't you want some change?"

Hunter waved him off and stepped out of the taxi. The cupola on top of the Garden City Hotel surveyed the slope to the Atlantic the way it always had. He heard a flapping sound and looked up. Above the flower gardens, the hotel's flag, a crowned lion rampant on a field of blue, rattled in a light breeze from the northeast. Perfect. The sky darkened with stars.

"Have you any luggage, sir?" the bellhop captain asked as he passed under the *porte cochere*.

"I'm all set."

The captain backed out of view. In the lobby, where once there was paneling and potted plants, now there was a glitzy gift store and the sunken entrance to nail and hair salons. Elizabeth Arden Red Door Spa. Aromatherapy. The latest in skin care. Retail boutiques. The reception area was about a minute old in this constantly changing resort. Wearing a double-breasted blue blazer, the desk clerk looked up and took him in slowly. A reinforced smile. "Hello, may I help you, sir?"

"Sure, thanks," Hunter said. "I have a reservation for Room 106."

"Yes, I see that." A probing glance. "You aren't…"

"Yes. I'm Hunter Dauger."

"It's uncanny. Has no one ever told you you look a lot like Michael Moriarty? I admit to kind of a crush on him. I mean, you could be his brother. Remember the S.S. officer in *Holocaust*, the lawyer? There was Meryl Streep and James Woods, but Michael Moriarty–he could chill you to the bone. That ice-blue stare of his, yes, the kind of look you're giving me now. But of course, your look is much warmer–you know what I mean. Sorry if I'm gushing. I have show business in my blood. Here's your key, Mr. Dauger. I guess you know Room 106 is kind of a famous room?"

Hunter grinned. "Yes, but the only thing famous I'm looking for right now is a good night's sleep. I'll need a wakeup call."

"Absolutely, sir. We're computerized. What time would you like?"

"Three twenty-seven this morning. How's the room service?"

A full step back. "Sir, our head chef is a graduate of Johnson & Wales."

"Any messages?" Hunter asked.

"A moment please. He flipped through a book of carbons. "Yes, it looks as though someone sent you a letter. I'll get it right away for you." He went into the back room, pulled out a drawer, and returned with a plain business envelope stamped in blue.

"Many thanks," Hunter said, and slipped it into his vest pocket.

"I hope you have time to try the new pool," the clerk said. "It's very classy. And we have a PGA Tour golf course."

"Yes. The sign behind you reads it's not for nothing that since 1874 you've been called Long Island's most luxurious hotel."

The clerk stood on tiptoes, looking past Hunter toward the incoming crowd. "Maybe you're here for the concert, too?"

Hunter stopped at a landing halfway up the grand stairway, looked down through the lobby, and counted twelve mammoth crystal chandeliers in the ballroom. Carts carrying stacks of gold-gilt folding chairs were being wheeled inside.

Room 106 looked exactly as it had when he'd awakened in it months before. The crystal decanter and water glass. The lurid wallpaper. He tried again to summon a memory of the two black weeks that led to his turning up here, but he came up with nothing.

He tossed his duffel on the sink, kicked off his loafers Pia had picked out, took out the letter while he hung up his jacket, pulled back the bed clothes (not a healthy idea to lie on the spread, nor would Lindbergh have), removed his socks, and stretched out to rest. Cool sheets tickled his toes.

The envelope felt heavy in his hands. He tore off the top and blew the letter open. The return address was Midtown Precinct South.

> *Just thought you'd like to know. Your case is wrapped up.*
>
> *You weren't the target at all. It was a drug deal gone bad.*
>
> *You were caught in the crossfire. This was a simple case*
>
> *of mistaken identity.*
>
> *Respectfully,*

Lieutenant Snark

Hunter picked up the room-service menu from the side table and had a look. Nothing but your usual steak-and-lobster hotel fare. He reached for the telephone and hit the button with the miniature waiter. "Hello, I'd like to order dinner."

"Yes, Mr. Dauger. What would you like?"

"Actually, I'd like to order some Cuban."

"The bellboy could get you some. It would take an additional thirty minutes. There will be a delivery surcharge."

"Any good?"

"I don't know, because I can't handle spicy food. But the word here is, it's the best Cuban this side of Flushing Meadows."

"First time I've heard that before."

"I'll send the menu right up."

Hunter placed an order for the *Boliche*, with its deep, satisfying flavor of beef stuffed with chorizo browned in olive oil; salad with watercress, avocado, and sweet pineapple; and a bucket of ice. "I'll just raid the mini bar. Oh, and *two* used packs of Orisa cards. Not new cards. Used."

"Yes, sir." There was a pause on the line. "That may take longer than just the additional thirty minutes. But you're dining alone?"

"I might not like my first fortune."

After dinner, Hunter watched an episode of *Mannix* on television. Men in suits were running to and fro from late-model cars all strangely built in the same year, tumbling over hoods and trying to run each other over. Automatic double doors opened and closed. That strange sense of waking in a hospital, not knowing where you've been. Then the romantic part, a little bossa nova and champagne, Joe

Mannix leaning confidentially into the female lead for the episode, wondering, "When will you leave me, Dido?"

"I can't leave you if you've never known me."

Hunter shut the TV off. No station identification. The room went black. He'd once spent the night with a carabiniere named Isabella Vieira who after lovemaking intrigued him with, "Could you open the TV please?" and "Could you close the TV?" As though you could open or close the third dimension, or the illusion of depth, that a TV seduced you with. So strange to hear it from a policewoman.

"Is that an Italian thing?" Hunter asked her. He so loved her name. It made her sound like an opera singer. Isabella had beautiful eyes. Not ice-blue like an assassin, but Mediterranean and sensual, warm like the water in the Blue Grotto in the caves below Capri. A blue you could swim in. He heard two soft knocks on his door.

Aviate. He was back in Room 106, in total darkness. He hadn't remembered turning the light off, but he must have. He slipped on the hotel scuffs, opened the door, and Stitch walked in, followed by a waiter pushing a cart with complete tableware set for one and the bag of takeout sitting on a china platter. The waiter vanished with his tip.

"This is the second time you've called me from here," Stitch said.

"I've never called you."

"If you had, I mean. It would have been the second time. I'm sure you know what you're doing, or what you think you're doing. Of course, you're away with the fairies."

"I suppose you're hungry."

"I could eat," Stitch said. "I'll agree with this. You won't be whole until you work this out. Your problem is, you ache for the approval of the person you most detest. You've spent most of your life denying it. Which by my account means you're normal."

"Like some rum?" Hunter asked.

"Precisely my point. You undercut what I say as though you're an American."

"I am an American."

"I'm sorry, no. You don't have the predatory innocence. Your big voyage is across the unconscious, and that's a Caribbean point of departure. Careful, buddy, you're about to leave the shore."

If only he weren't such an eavesdropper. For fifty minutes they did not speak but instead ate in the dim light of the table lamp. When the floor started to buzz, Stitch asked, "What the hell?"

"It's music," Hunter said. "'Midnight at the Oasis,' I think it's called. Maria Muldaur is performing in the hotel tonight."

"I don't care if she's Maria Callas, that's annoying. What do people pay to hear something like that? Your room should be soundproof. I'll bet in my room you can't hear it."

"You should try it and see," Hunter said.

"Not until I have my fortune," Stitch said. "Cut the cards."

Hunter pushed a deck in his direction. No reason to tense inside. He heard Michelle Feelia saying, *relax*. "I am relaxed," Hunter muttered.

"How's that?" Stitch asked. He cut the cards and furrowed his brow. "Ha! Listen to this. *You're almost at the top. That means you have further to fall.* I think that's yours, Hunter."

"Nothing doing." Hunter raised his chin.

"What's yours, then?"

Hunter gazed out the window, as if he could fly into the dark. "Let's see." He cut the deck and looked. "'*Ignore previous card.*' Interesting. Luck has a do-over!"

But that wasn't what it really said.

THE DOOR SHUT behind Stitch when he left. Hunter stared at the ceiling. Time curled up like Dido and started to drowse. Hunter removed the slippers and looked down at his toes. The purple webbing. They said a foetus in development went through all states of evolution. At one point he was a bird before becoming a human. He caught his breath. How could this tiny difference have meant so much to a stranger, much less one who might have been his father? He imagined he could see the veins pulsing in the webbing. His heart thumped. Lindbergh had checked out the dead substitute to be sure he *didn't* have the webbed toes. To be sure the victim was normal. His real son, the greater embarrassment, would be moved far away from him in the dark, by a Breckinridge, whose family had a history of moving things in the dark.

If not you, who? If not now, when?

He thought he'd be anxious, but instead he melted into his bed. With slow, even breaths, as slow as the sea, he disappeared into the deepest sleep of his life.

Chapter 34

Garden City, Long Island, New York

Please don't tell mum I'm a pilot. She thinks I play piano in a whorehouse.

BEFORE DAWN, HUNTER strolled down the hill through the gardens to the parking lot of Roosevelt Field Mall. There he approached the faded auto-parts warehouse that had started its life as a hangar, the last vestige of the old airfield. The triple-bay truck doors to the warehouse were flung open. Inside it was dark and empty as a canyon. Outside its mouth was the spitting image of the *Spirit of St. Louis* replica from Paris, its engine in a warm hum. The beautiful old taildragger. So far, so good.

"Morning, Hunter," a man in a scarred leather jacket said above the roar. "It was a long trip, but she made it just great on the freighter. She's as good as new."

Hunter smiled at Hank Roula, the retired Ryan Aviation mechanic who supervised her manufacture, care, and appearance for the film and knew this plane better than anyone. Just as he had on the telephone, Hank sounded as if he were calling through the mist from an offshore dory.

"She has 29 inches of manifold air pressure. All five tanks are topped off. The magnetic declination machine works. But sorry, she's too heavy for takeoff. We're a no-go this morning."

"Perfect." Hunter stared across the empty parking lot as its tar 'runway' rolled past the neon sign of Bloomingdale's. The department store loomed in the dark, the *Spirit's* image reflecting in the display windows, so everything seemed framed in a movie screen. The stars felt hot on the back of his neck.

Hunter checked his charts and tucked a greasy paper bag behind his seat. Two roast beef and two ham sandwiches. The liturgy continued, checking the pavement for oil drips, plucking at the control cables to the flaps and ailerons in the manly quiet. How many times had he preflighted in the predawn darkness? He'd spent half his years in the Navy flying at zero dark-thirty. "We'd better hurry," he said to himself. "Better if I don't slalom around shoppers."

"This is nobody's airport, Hunter," Roula said. "I wonder how Approach Control at Kennedy is going to respond."

"They'll have to scramble some jets to let me know," Hunter said. "I'm not carrying a radio." Down to two: *aviate, navigate.*

"How are we doing on insurance?" Roula asked.

"You mean, do I pray?"

"I didn't mean that. But do you?"

Roula reached into the cockpit to take out the heat shield that had been placed inside the windscreen for transport, but Hunter shook his head no. "Leave it there."

"You're not serious. Hunter, no. There was a reason this replica has a winder, unlike the original. It's an *improvement.* You're supposed to *see* where you're going."

"Lindbergh didn't." Hunter produced a long metal stick with eyes. "I'm going to use a periscope like he did because of that extra fuel tank in place of his windscreen."

"Two wrongs don't make a right."

Hunter pulled out a flask of brandy and took a deep, strong shot. "How about three wrongs?" He entered the plane and strapped in.

"It's more like ten wrongs." Roula made the sign of the cross as he stepped closer to lean into the window. He reached in and grabbed Hunter's necktie, part of the full suit he wore beneath his Nomex flyboy togs. "You be careful, sir. Godspeed."

"Hank. I want no fuss about this. If I don't make it, don't breathe a word about it. If I do, don't breathe a word about it." He scanned his instruments, simple as the dash of an early Pierce-Arrow. "Four hundred forty-eight gallons, check. Let's go!" Though it began to drizzle, the canopy of cumulus began to lift above the advection fog. Ahead, to the left of Bradlee's, power lines sprang out like snakes. His eyes snapped open, full and bright. "Chocks!" Hunter screamed out the open window. Slowly his senses expanded to include the entire *Spirit* like a second skin. The engine vibrations became his circulatory system. Man and machine became one.

From inside the warehouse, a dark figure slipped past Roula, scrambled across the disturbed air mass around the *Spirit*, and disappeared below the wings toward the struts and wheels, agile and confident. A most familiar face. *Aniq*. In a few seconds, Aniq emerged and staggered away, holding the chocks up in his hands and grinning. He dropped the chocks and cupped his mouth megaphone-style. "Go set the world on fire!"

Hunter nodded and jammed his boots on the brakes as he did his run-up. Everything was perfect. He looked out the periscope and picked out the shapes of rent-a-cops walking toward the plane from all directions now. Time was running out.

At 35 inches of mercury in the manifold-air-pressure gauge, this blithe *Spirit* was bursting out of her skin. Hunter closed his eyes and took a deep breath. Then he eased his feet off the brakes as he hurtled forward, skidding slightly left. Just the softest of corrections. The airspeed indicator climbed. Thirty miles per hour, thirty-five, forty, forty-five… Come on. Fifty. Fifty-five. Rotate!

Nothing happened. He jammed the stick forward. He was the pilot of a lead sled, a coffin whose weight, 5,150 pounds, would seal his death. Sixty knots! Rotate! The *Spirit* climbed into the gray drizzle, the shopping-center lights illuminating the power wires ahead. Hunter could hear himself breathing. Don't pull up too much, or you'll stall. He actually aimed the nose down to gain airspeed, then popped the stick back. With a sickening lunge, the *Spirit* cleared the first set of wires, with two more to go. His port wheel dragged into the second wire, but it snapped free from the pole, sparks flying behind the dark silhouette of the monoplane. *That'll cost us.* Then the *Spirit* felt a gust of wind from the ocean, and she easily cleared the third wire. Hunter started a slow turn to the northeast and headed below 400 feet for the dark coast. He was already going to hear from the FAA about being so low (the minimum was 1,500 feet), but he didn't want to give the air-traffic controllers at Kennedy a second cow.

He banked a little more, just 20 degrees. No need to give this old bird aerodynamic overloads. He looked at the houses, rooftops, pools, trees, the sparkling dreams. He was in the moment, doing something rash–flying a high-wing monoplane from New York to Paris–a crazy ecstasy.

Ahead was the Long Island coast, purple and dark, pointing north. Michelle's last words had been, "*We all carry a shore inside us.*" He now knew what she meant. Death is a crossing of the darkness like Lindbergh's. Each of us, at the moment of reckoning, makes the flight across the dark ocean toward a place where there is no time. Lindbergh long ago ceased to be a human being but rather a projection of our desires. Hunter was chasing a radio phantom.

Chapter 35

Transatlantic

Lack of planning on your part does not constitute an emergency on mine.

HUMMING UP THE COAST in the *Spirit*, securely strapped into the unreality of the situation, Hunter craned his neck around to hear the "fly" zooming around the greasy lunch bag and found none. Nor had there ever been a "fly." The nightmare fly was invented for the movie version of *The Spirit of St. Louis*. Director Billy Wilder was convinced it would be too psychotic for Lindbergh to talk to himself all night, lost between the darkness and the dawn. Somehow, there had to be a 'listener.' So just before takeoff, Wilder slipped a housefly into the script. A secret sharer, a little cockpit companion. Hey, buddy.

Jimmy Stewart so despised this indulgence that halfway through shooting he said he'd walk off the set if the fly were his co-star. Finally, he and Wilder made a deal. The fly could encourage interior monologue only to the last twinkle of Newfoundland's Cape Race Station, before the dark crossing. Then, without curtain call or explanation, the fly would disappear. He wouldn't even get to buzz off.

Wilder cast an insect in the movie to humanize you, Daddy. *Hey, we've got to have at least one sympathetic character onscreen.* Hunter resumed his scan and checked the lonely spaces behind him. If there were a fly in this cockpit, it would appear right here, stealing scenes. *Right...now.* In the movie Michelle was watching, no doubt she'd have him name it Pia.

WITH THE BEACH stretching below, Hunter looked west to the hazy mainland where Lindbergh first disappeared from public view after marrying. Hundreds of reporters plotted to chase the newlyweds after learning of their secret Englewood ceremony inside the Morrow mansion, but Breckinridge used decoys so the 'lovebirds' could slip through Manhattan unseen inside a long dark car.

The car sped to the Connecticut side of Long Island Sound, where a rowboat lay covered with brush by the shore. It was among Lindbergh's first successful brushes as a nowhere man.

Lindbergh took off his jacket and started rowing Anne toward their sleek new power yacht *La Mouette*, anchored gently in the mist. What better wedding present than the privacy of a luxury craft? That night on *La Mouette* would be Charles's and Anne's first time together.

While the filthy reporters screamed, expostulated, sent irate telegrams, and jammed the phone lines to their editorial offices, the couple ditched them and grew clean. Not until *Mouette* was well underway to the Morrows' vacation mansion on North Haven Island, Maine, did the world suspect where they'd been.

Newlyweds Believed Heading For Morrow Summer Home

Associated Press, June 7. The cruiser *Mouette*, with Col. Charles A. Lindbergh and his wife, the former Anne Morrow, aboard, was "going East" along the Maine coast today. It was thought that the young couple might be heading for the island of North Haven and the Summer home of Mrs. Lindbergh's father, Ambassador Dwight W. Morrow.

The little cruiser made York harbor last night, and Col. Lindbergh took

on supplies sufficient to run him to North Haven, about 100 miles

up the coast.

The *Mouette* was tied up but an hour and then cast off and finally

anchored off Cape Porpoise, some 15 miles east of York harbor.

"Going East" was the colonel's reply to an invitation from

Republican National Committeeman Joseph W. Simpson that he

spend the night at York Harbor.

Lindbergh devoted himself personally to each of the design specifications for *La Mouette*, the 'seagull.' How out of character of him to christen his cruiser after the first living things he saw at the end of his crossing. Or had Anne, with her softer sympathies, named it? What music more mellifluous than the complaints of sea birds? They had a soft call, the sweeter to wake to. For God's sake, Hunter, you don't want to be sleeping right now.

Built in 1929, *La Mouette* was a 38-footer–long, low, and still afloat on a lake in Wisconsin when Hunter last visited it. Per Lindbergh's request, the boat's cabin was built with more headroom so he could stand up straight at the helm. The original blueprint called for two staterooms.

For his honeymoon, he insisted they be combined into a single love nest. It suggested you had a sentimental side, Daddy. Who got to you? You were still a year away from meeting Carrel.

During World War II, the Elco division of General Dynamics constructed hundreds of similar sleek gray yachts for Gen. Douglas MacArthur. Lieutenant John F. Kennedy commanded one of them, *PT-109*. Young Kennedy was fast asleep when enemies on the bridge of a Japanese destroyer spied the dark outline of his Yankee patrol boat, bore down on it, and sliced it in two.

How deep and sweet JFK's sleep must have been in that somnolent lagoon, the prelude to his later disaster. What do you do when an enemy destroyer slices you in two?

AVIATE. Hunter banked softly to the left. The Connecticut seacoast town of Darien rose into view. In the 1950s, the authorized Lindbergh children grew up here, watching no TV and traveling under assumed names while their father grew more deeply eccentric and profoundly absent. And yet, Darien was a sentimental choice.

Lindbergh, who drove a Volkswagen to 'keep it dark,' who still said 'Hark' years after it fell out of speech, chose Darien in midlife because he could catch a glimpse of his old friend Harry Guggenheim's ocean palace on Long Island across the Sound.

It was in the seclusion of Harry's mansion that Lindbergh wrote *We* in 1927. Time was short. The exclusive story of the first solo transatlantic flight was demanded all over the world. When his ghost writer lost his nerve, Lindbergh rolled up his sleeves, yanked the manuscript back for himself, and tackled it solo in the library of *Falaise*, surrounded by Roman arches and cobblestones.

We was printed 28 times the first half year it was out.

Lindbergh and Harry met when Harry (a World War I flying ace) and his wife Carol showed up before one of the *Spirit of St. Louis's* test flights in New York. "Look me up when you get back," Harry said, a brotherly encouragement only. Deep down, he was sure Lindbergh would never return. It was among the last things Lindbergh heard before heading into the blue.

Not only was Harry educated (he left Yale to earn two degrees at Cambridge) and incomprehensibly wealthy (in 1917 he bought his first Curtiss flying boat, which he kept in Manhasset before entering the Navy), he was starkly brave, having flown in dogfights over France with the First Yale Unit, established by Admiral Robert Peary, the polar explorer. The dozen boy heroes of the First Yale Unit would go on to rule the world, from William Rockefeller to Juan Trippe, founder of Eastern Airlines and Pan Am. Harry himself would serve as U.S. Ambassador to Cuba; open mines and ore-smelting factories in Mexico; and climb to the top of Manhattan finance, funding not only art museums but the future of his first love, aviation, which beckoned with glowing promise for the human race. With Lindbergh whispering at his side, Harry underwrote all of Dr. Robert Goddard's rocketry and liquid fuel experiments, the doorstep to space.

It was Harry who introduced Lindbergh to Henry Breckinridge.

The trouble with Harry was, he was Jewish, Daddy. There really was a dollar amount where a conflicted Anti-Semite like you would drop any objections to feel the icy thrill of cash passed from the warmth of a helping hand. What a phony.

Harry named his castle *Falaise* after he saw the shadow of his Sopwith Camel move, during World War I, over a magnificent Normandy pile set in the cliffs. The 10th century Château de Falaise in Calvados, immense waves crashing at its feet, was the birthplace of William the Conqueror.

Hunter circled above the rooftops of the clubby, Edwardian space where *We* took shape–the cross outs, the redrafts in the windless paneled library.

NAVIGATE. New waves cried for attention. As Hunter resumed his northern heading, he saw the tip of Long Island sliding toward him before it fled beneath his wings. He saw *Witchcraft*. He half-reached out the window to wave but felt the cold rejection of his sister. Had she ever been his sister? He saw the sweep of sand; the lighthouse; even Montauk Public, his old high school, a.k.a. MonPu. He thought of Manfred in mid-stroke, cornered and lonely. It was still dark, still before sunrise. There was still time to turn back. No, there wasn't.

Chapter 36

Transatlantic

Think ahead of your airplane.

WITH LONG ISLAND behind, there was nothing but blue to the east. Still cloaked in the pre-dawn, New London beckoned from the west northwest, hazy with future, wavering in the young heat waves across Block Island Sound. Hunter could barely make out the silhouettes of the white church spires and the mouth of the Thames River, where in 1921 as a prep-school student, Howard Hughes paid $5 to take a ride in Harry Guggenheim's seaplane.

Here, now–the first rays of sunrise! The world was shoveling sunlight on all sides. Skirting left of New Shoreham Island toward East Greenwich, Hunter followed the Old Post Road north as it hugged the rosy coast through Narragansett, Shelter Harbor, and Blue Shutter Beach. Approaching the Coast Guard station at Point Judith, he saw the Block Island Ferry in transit to the mainland from the island's purple shadow. Over Newport he could easily make out the crashing surf below the castles of the Cliff Walk and three shades of red tile on the roof of The Breakers, the Vanderbilt mausoleum so monumental the wind whistled through its upper loggia. The shadow of the *Spirit* moved across its emerald lawn.

Dividing the center of Buzzard's Bay, he banked over Cape Cod's scorpion tail and soon caught sight of Plymouth, where blueblood historians conspired to agree they'd invented the first Thanksgiving. Yachting, sailing, and flying–all seemed connected somehow and all rigged, like religion, politics, and science. What explorer's club wasn't a private smoking room for privileged men.

Aviate, navigate, pontificate. Best just to *Aviate*. The good news: the *Spirit* was tight as a top, humming musically. Never had Hunter felt so in harmony with a plane before. While this radial engine was loud, it was no worse than a Navy T-28 trainer and a great deal softer than, say, the RA-5C Vigilante spy jet he'd flown with the Cuban coast rushing below. That's what he could use, a few shots of Cuban coffee, with the caramelized sugar exhilarating on his tongue–rocket fuel.

Things were going so well that a maniacal cheer took hold of him. It sparked his senses, even without a single cup of coffee. As a cautionary measure, he'd slipped a thermos of java into the food-container compartment behind his feet, saved for the night leg only. He looked away from the compartment lid and hummed to distract himself inside the hum of the fuselage. Perfect. A replica being flown by a Pretender. The Clown Prince of Pretenders, if you like. And this was surely a replica among replicas, with no one to watch its soundless passage.

Hunter looked at the earth inductor compass at the top of his instrument panel, approved of the gentle quiver of the needle in its center, and continued his scan in a second sweep from shore to sea. Oil-pressure gauge, oil-temperature gauge, turn-and-bank indicator, airspeed across the top level. Lower row: the tachometer, landing lights, compass & level, altimeter.

Still more: control lock for automatic pilot, inclinometer, gas mixer, gas cocks to select fuel tank, primer, clock. Keep the airspeed between 70 and 120 miles per hour or you'll find yourself swimming, the last thing on Earth you want to do.

Hunter looked down again. Bickering sea birds careered below him, their calls not so poignant as the *mouettes* he hoped to hear on the other side. To the east, like Odysseus, he watched the last rays of dawn rise above the wine-dark sea.

Chapter 37

Transatlantic

Superior pilots use superior judgment to avoid situations
where they have to use superior skills.

THE *SPIRIT* FLEW on, with southern Massachusetts flashing below in lovely sunshine. It lit the tips of pine trees, etched shadows in slashes of rocks. Maybe there was a genetic predisposition for feeling elevated by the joy of flying. Though Hunter still had physical, electrical, and even mystical control of the *Spirit*–balancing its flight, checking its fuel, and dead reckoning with startling intuition–still another part of him was terribly lost. Unknown dangers lurked ahead.

Boston, the hub of the world, now rose into view over the dark green water, the Prudential Center easy to pick out among the skyscrapers. Hunter checked his altitude and reduced it to 500 feet. Charles, father dear, I am looking for you. Do you sense me? Maybe a real man must be a hero and a villain at once.

Calvin Coolidge launched Lindbergh's godhood when he gave him the Medal of Honor in 1927, a dumbfounding gesture for a feat involving no military combat. Nor was Lindbergh precisely an explorer. Instead, he was, the President said, "a boy who did a man's job." A common man magnified by radio to a mystical beatitude–a man made into a god.

Hunter scratched his forehead, though there was no fly to brush away. In flying the *Spirit*, was he a man doing a boy's job? How the children loved Lucky Lindy. Lindbergh actually invented a hobby. The model-plane phenomenon shaped the future of young boys in the fawning years following Lindbergh's miracle. Lindbergh's influence was so deep he literally changed the nature of boyhood, created echoes where there were none before.

Salem; Gloucester; Rockport, with its Good Harbor Beach and Sandy Bay. Banking west, Hunter flew over the Isles of Shoals, a necklace of six islands and tidal ledges six miles offshore. During his Harvard days, he slipped up here for a weekend but didn't last the first night. New England had a way of staring him down. Nowhere was this more savage than on the Shoals. Hunter dipped his wing for a better view of the lonely green World War II observation tower on Appledore Island; the bleak rockiness of Smuttynose; and Star Island, home to a lonely hotel and Betty Moody's Cave, where in the cleft of a cliff, hiding during an Indian attack, a young Colonist mother accidentally smothered her daughter, muffling her mouth to keep her silent. *Aviate, Navigate…* Maybe the little girl got off easy.

With a shiver, he flew along the icy coast of Maine. Dropping to chase the shadow of a whale, he saw rocks swiftly approaching and popped up to 300 feet, having nearly hit the lens of Boon Island Light. How long had he been flying now? Hello, fuel indicator. There was gas enough to reach the Bay of Fundy before he switched tanks.

Forty minutes later, Hunter overflew North Haven Island and the Morrow estate. Kind of a nostalgic place–no wonder the Lindbergh family still came here every summer. A boy on the porch waved as the *Spirit* buzzed overhead. Poor kid. A new generation explored the rocks and seashells here, unaware of secret branches snaking from their family tree. With a pang, Hunter looked down at the harbor where Charles and Anne took off in their seaplane to begin their North-to-the-Orient flight. How deeply you believed you loved each other then.

With his shadow tracing over Bar Harbor, Acadia National Park, Castine, Eastport, and Franklin Roosevelt's Campobello Island, Hunter entered Canadian airspace. Suddenly all was blue below him–the Bay of Fundy. At 12:23 Atlantic Time he descended low enough to read *Meteghan, Nova Scotia*, on a water tower. He checked his chart. The Eaglet was a full two minutes ahead of the Lone Eagle! By 2:58 p.m., he cleared Mulgrave. Now he was seven minutes ahead of Lindbergh, but this wasn't a race. It was a flight to the death. Lloyd's of London refused to give odds on Lindbergh's surviving his crossing. Slow down and conserve fuel.

Soon he'd mirror the Great Circle route Lindbergh followed through the night. But time crawled very slowly. It was twilight before he saw St. John's below his wheels. Ahead was Cape Race and its huge cliffs. Beyond that, stars and more stars wheeled infinitely into the unknown.

Hunter said a prayer of thanks for the lack of cloud cover. Lindbergh's flight notes confessed to a void in the pit of his stomach when he saw clouds towering into deadly castles while crossing the tip of Newfoundland at dusk. Below and to his left, Hunter saw Cape Race wireless station. The White Star liner *Titanic* tried to reach it with her Marconi when all was lost, but she failed. She slipped into the ink, never to be seen again.

No wonder you dropped your radio, Daddy. Better to vanish in silence than let your last action be a soft tapping, so mouselike, answered by Nothing.

Aviate. Altitude is 500 feet. Now, ease down to 100 to reach the thickest air and feel the thrill of your closeness to the sea. *Navigate*. From here, Witless Bay looks on fire, backlit by the last dying gasp of the sun.

Hunter abandoned all hope and turned into the brutal dark.

Chapter 38

Transatlantic

Experience is a tough instructor.
First comes the check flight, then *the lesson.*

NEXT STOP, IRELAND. In the numbing blackness, Hunter wondered if he'd ever see sunlight again. What was left of it shrank behind him, a green sparkle. He checked his watch. Eleven hours and twenty-five minutes since takeoff. You are now two minutes behind Lindbergh's pace. Did you become distracted while trying not to think about Pia all this time?

Aviate. Block her from your mind. Right. Their parting had chilled him, so angry was she that he'd decided to make this flight without getting her input. The storm rose to dark heights inside her. She shook out her hair, just like that:

"Why would you ever do this? You'll just die."
"We all just die."
"Will you have a rescue patrol?"
"This is just something I have to do in secret."
"But do you have to do it all alone?"

"I didn't tell you because I knew you'd react like this."

"Well, that's a great basis for us to relate."

"I knew you wouldn't give me your blessing."

"You're wrong. You have my blessing."

Lights out. She walked into her bedroom, slammed the door, then returned.

"Hunter, is this going to work? You look at me as if I'm a full-scale replica of someone else. I am so much younger than you. Where would our happily ever after be, and when?"

Hunter's mind rushed to cover Pia's question, stopping nearly at random in his passport's fragrant almanac. "Key West," he said as she turned away. "A tropical breeze carries the coolness of the water to you. The breeze never lets up." At least it didn't in 1961. Back then, 10,000 spooks were on the CIA payroll in Miami. One weekend he slipped down Ocean Highway to stay at the Dolphin Inn and Marina on Little Torch Key.

When Castro lit the exploding cigar for Uncle Sam during the Bay of Pigs invasion and 'we' decided to get the hell out, the CIA cut ties with Miami and hightailed it back to Washington. Misery lingered behind and settled in. Left in the lurch, desperate families made the dark passage from Cuba to Florida without hope of a U.S. welcome. Their heroism actually meant something, with everything on the line. Lowering into handmade boats, rafts, and floats that didn't float, they paddled bravely to their dream of freedom. All night you could hear the immigration patrol boats out there, very fast, picking off the Cuban families who were only trying to make it to the safety and shore of a new land by at least getting their toes on the sand. Before they changed the laws, to set foot in Florida meant you'd set yourself free. At Little Torch Key, Hunter saw their exhausted silhouettes being pulled from their boats like spent butterflies.

At night, the crunch of tires and headlights meant the U.S. Immigration patrols were surveilling the coast from the shore, too, looking for new arrivals–sets of eyes hiding below mangrove roots. Interrupting people's desperate dreams was just a job. Blaring from their jeeps, their fascist radios were loud, frightening. In a short span of time, Hunter came to despise the dream killers.

Who were still out there, no doubt. In Key West, there was no future or past, just now. Panther tracks in the sand. Loads of coral. Cracked conch residents so dissipated the tropical breeze robbed them of all ambition. Forget about the alcohol, which flowed in abundance. Key West was drunk with wind, which cosmically tied everything together and tore it apart. Wind, sand, and stars. What you wanted to do with your life became a matter of nostalgia. Looking at Pia, Hunter felt strongly he should buy that marina, go out at night, and help the families get to shore safely. When he tried to tell her about it, he sounded like a crazy person.

"Why would you want to go to Key West with me, Hunter?" She looked out the window at the dazzling lights of Berlin.

"You wouldn't have to do it, Pia. We could do something here, too. Berlin has its own dark crossings." But surely not as temperate. "Let's talk about it when I get back."

"*We*. Go to hell, Hunter. You don't care about me. There is no more selfish act than what you're about to do. Your keeping it a secret makes it more absurd and selfish. I can't even look at you right now." She turned and walked into the bedroom, Dido trotting behind. The lock on the door clicked.

He walked softly to it. "I know how this sounds, but this shall be my last selfish act."

Shall. Why the grandiloquence? He tapped softly. No one answered. So, he made up something she said next, through the door, inaudibly. Something like, *It's easy playing Lindbergh. Not so easy to play yourself.*

GET IT STRAIGHT in your head. You're flying this high-wing monoplane from New York to Paris because the only way to get past a father–even a father you've never met, even a hero who in no way is your father–is to do what he did so you can dump his memory. Stomp on his footsteps. Bury him. *Move on.*

Hunter stared at his black windshield. Pia would be waiting for him on the other side, except she never offered to meet him in Paris. Of course, he was too cool to ask. Before and during World War II, there were men. A generation later, Hunter and his ilk were just guys. Pia must, and surely would, forgive him, though there was no one here to give him assurances, not even a cinematic fly. Or was there? He thought he felt something on his face, but he had no mirror. The entire Atlantic Ocean was his mirror.

In the darkness beyond Cape Race, unheard and unseen, Hunter set his mind back on course. This outing was just between himself and Lindbergh. A father-son deal.

The task was simple. A thirty-three-hour flight. What made it easier for you, Daddy, was the gigantic wall of non-engagement that separated you from fear. The way you were wired, there was no fear.

Keep moving. It was so eerily quiet out here. Hunter had refused to check the weather before his flight because Lindbergh had no way of really knowing what weather was ahead of him. Worse than that, Lindbergh's slim forecasts betrayed him during his hours of darkness. Lindbergh's moment of truth came barely out of sight of land off Labrador. He'd flown into the teeth of a sleet storm.

In Hunter's case, without the delusion of a forecast, it was the magnificent absence of violent weather that began to work on his mind. When would the weather hit? It was like waiting to catch a shark at night.

A shark doesn't put up a fight when you hook it. There's nothing but lassitude, even indifference, as you slowly reel him in. Only when his malignant eye crests the surface does all hell break loose. Not a good idea to think of sharks at night when you're heading out over the ocean.

Best not to ponder bad luck. Lindbergh's 'bug' protected him from bad luck. Later in life, his indifference to bad luck showed more deeply with his careful selection of an unmarked grave in Maui, Hawaii, atop a bluff of black lava, the better to elude supernatural autograph hunters. It put an exclamation point on your eccentricity, Daddy. In death, insist on the privacy of your corpse, even submitting a drainage scheme to your undertaker to keep your mortal remains high and dry. Your wicked wick, Sir. Your funeral planning spoke eloquently to your gap in understanding the prime directive of no longer being alive. A headstone is for the comfort of those you've left behind. Someplace to visit, to work into a regular routine.

Unless you were immortal, flying above the radar. Unless you, like Careu Kent, were the answer to everybody's dreams. How dare anyone think you insane?

> *Oh dutiful for spaceship lies*
> *Newfoundland in the rain*
> *The devil's wavetop majesties*
> > *So distant from the Seine,*
> *Atlantica, Atlantica*
> *You look so dark to see*
> *Misunderstood my drowning good*
> *From me to shining me.*

Suddenly Hunter couldn't breathe. He felt an intense impulse to turn back. With 3,000 miles of scary ahead, he banked and reversed course so he might one last time set eyes on the lost cliffs of Cape Race–just to see the sun grow brighter again. To say goodbye.

With Canada reassuringly ahead, Cape Race grew larger and re-defined itself, warm and beckoning. No one would know, or even care, if you turned back. *I would know.*

Why cross the darkness unseen? Regrets and reconsiderations floated into his mind like dials in his instrument scan. It was precisely because it meant nothing that he had to do it. Fireworks over a graveyard. Hunter looked below and to the left to see the last specks of rock and sand before banking hard to the northeast to resume his dead-man's heading for Ireland. His final sight of land taunted him. Below the mute radio tower of Cape Race, below the white spume of waves, a green light twinkled from what looked like a sand bar. What was the light source? The water around it reflected a tricky shade of bronze which warned of submerged rocks.

Drive into the dark, and keep driving. The Atlantic shelf slouched toward the Labrador Current–an angry man in black boots stalking into his basement to check on the remains of his human captive.

In the clarifying night Hunter now made out black dots of fishing boats with their maritime lights in jade and ruby. In the dying light, shafts of bright gold reflected from the wavetops so impossibly it seemed to connect with a flash in the back of his 'brainpan.'

What a Lindbergh word. 'Skull' was somehow too live, too human, for him. Hunter caught his breath when he saw the last brushstrokes of sunlight hit the water at a great distance in ever more gentle stripes to the horizon.

Above the horizon there was a gap. Then the low ceiling took over, with shadows on the bellies of clouds, phantasms streaked and shot through with threads of gold. Above the dark curtain, gaps of blue flickered below the ionosphere's ultraviolet whispers. Still higher was heaven, or what passed for heaven.

Many pilots, while climbing to a higher altitude to penetrate a cloud layer with its threats of rain, feel more religious or at least more diffidently atheist when they see the sun dazzling above the clouds blinking in the unseen upper atmosphere, bright and endless. Again, Hunter experienced the shiver of feeling what Lindbergh felt, seeing what he saw.

Maybe this was the real key to Lindbergh. He wanted to feel something, anything, even fear, and spent the rest of his life disappointed he wasn't allowed even that. Incomprehensible to Hunter were the sullen souls in passenger jets who slide their observation windows closed while bright air rushes inches from them—screaming, even giddy, with life.

Now the lower clouds parted and the whole sky turned blue with the reveal. In the caprice of thirty seconds, Hunter wondered if he might be too warm in his electrically heated flight suit. Sun sparkles danced across the entire sea until he felt ridiculous with reflection and the ocean turned harder and harder, like something carved.

The minute atoms of the Earth were disappearing with the sun, a blur made motionless by its very movement, wind currents picking up because of the temperature differential between the vanishing rays and the cool blue of the sea. Though he'd flown so many times before, Hunter allowed himself to wonder if things would get holier the higher he climbed.

The adiabatic cooling rate was a two-degree drop in Centigrade temperature for every 1,000 feet you climbed. Icarus, flying toward the sun, would have frozen to death at the icy altitudes long before the sun's rays could have melted his wings.

No wonder weather was the backdrop to the greatest music. It was as if the weather wrote the music. *The Planets*. The daybreak reverie in *Carmen*, with its doomed beforeness. The *Grand Canyon Suite*. The last fading sun, fighting to stay in the sky, beat mercilessly on the back of the *Spirit* and diffused across its wings, tail, prop arc, and black windshield, the monument he'd erected to his stupidity.

Hunter looked at the water again and gasped. It had shifted to Caribbean blue, with indigo beyond it. It was Aruba! Maybe all the colors of all the water he'd seen was something he carried around in his head. The blue green was a shade that…would look good on Pia, setting afire those coppery glints in her dark hair. But what didn't. What was ecstasy? A sexy way of feeling tired of feeling tired.

When all the light went out of the sky, he felt very small. *Oh, my God, forgive me for what I've started.*

There was barely enough moonlight to see the edge of the sea through his periscope. His concentrated reality was the artificial horizon in his attitude indicator. *Move your scan around. Aviate.* Even this disturbed, he held the joystick with the relaxed confidence of a lover. The Atlantic was a wicked siren who didn't care if he made it across or not. *Navigate.* What hour was this? It was dark as an elevator shaft outside.

He was approaching hour twelve. It was hour fifteen when Lindbergh went goofy. Hunter divined this from reading between the lines of Lindbergh's flying notes. *Watch out for hour number 15.*

Every uneventful second of this black night brought Europe, and landfall, closer. Hunter felt his ship moving forward with its reassuring hum, sparks and vapor from its radial engine spinning off the circle into infinity as his consciousness advanced, advanced.

He reached behind his seat, took out the paper bag, unwrapped the roast-beef sandwich, and took a bite. Wait a minute; this was the ham. Breaking the magic sequence– would this be unlucky? If Lucky Lindy didn't believe in luck, he wouldn't, either. The ham was dark and mysterious, and he tried not to think of the last living seconds of the pig, its last upward turn to the knife, its eyes. *If you're going to kill me, hurry up and kill me.*

Two HOURS DEEPER into the dark, Hunter caught sight of a ship. By now, to save fuel, he was flying barely above the wave tops so he had to look up and to the left to see the watch station on the bridge. A rusty old thing, with moonlight glinting on its ladders. About 450 feet long. He flew around it, rocking his wings to be seen.

People think rocking wings is what pilots do to show off, but it's what we do when we're lonely. No joy. He kept his bank in, doing a level sweep past the transom, and read, in Norwegian, the word *Delta*.

How strange. Didn't the Norwegians have fjords? Slow as a slug, he crept up the ship's starboard side at 100 knots. He looked down the long end of his left wing, its navigation lights flashing. He blinked to make sure. There were no shadows, no moving figures, in the bridge. He could see the empty wheel. A deserted freighter, charging into the dark. I am the Hunter Gracchus.

He swept his stick over and felt the wind catch his wing as he banked into another circle and saw that the freighter's wake was disturbing, and therefore stimulating and igniting, phosphorescent plankton as it knifed forward into the dark. He caught his breath the illumination was so stunning. No one in the world was seeing it but he.

Like a party guest who didn't take the hint, he flew a third circle around the *Delta*. Were they all asleep, rocked by the hand of the deep? Would no one be at the navigation table, verifying its course? Maybe they'd gone down the ladder for more coffee and would be right back. Surely the captain wasn't up. Around the freighter and its lights was an aura of holy blue that shifted in its penumbra to green, then purple, and finally to gray and black.

Hunter didn't circle the freighter a fourth time. He was afraid he'd look into the bridge and see the face of Rick Streak.

He tossed the sandwich wrapper behind him. It rattled in the empty space where Lindbergh had stored his pneumatic life raft and three days' worth of U.S. Army rations in case he had to land at sea.

Hunter hadn't bothered to carry the large pair of shears Lindbergh brought in the event of ditching. Ever handy, Lindbergh might then have cut the fabric from the fuselage or one of the wings of the *Spirit* to make a primitive sail. No *Kon Tiki* here. Nor did Hunter believe in a kite, another bit of Lindbergh's survival ingenuity. For Hunter, and even for Lindbergh, who knew better, it was all or nothing at all. Anything else was just for show.

Hunter felt the light of the freighter recede behind him as he descended into the well of blackness, deeper and deeper, as though he were a spelunker. *Aviate*. Airspeed 100, altitude 100. *Navigate*. Check your passage along the Great Circle Route every 100 miles, once on the hour, stitching your way with course corrections every 100 miles, never accounting for wind. That's what made dead reckoning deadly. You plunge into the darkness presuming your last position was believable. While praising Lindbergh for his courage, weather experts had marveled that his ocean transit with net-zero wind was the greater miracle. That *was* luck.

Still blacker outside, a throbbing darkness. As if Hunter's black windscreen weren't enough, the *Spirit's* overhead wing blocked his view of all stars like a silk blindfold, making celestial navigating impossible. So much for the relic on Hunter's wrist, a 1931 Longines-Wittnauer hour-angle watch invented and patented by Lindbergh. The watch depended on calculating displacements of longitude from known stars. Naturally, it helped if you could see them.

The need for sleep echoed in Hunter's head. Losing the feeling in his hands, he bore a hole in the night until everything went dark like a switch snapped off in a basement.

What was blacker than black? A numinous black, reflecting the absence of something. Any darker than that and you're in the Spirit Cave.

Chapter 39

Transatlantic

Never let an aircraft take you to a place your brain didn't get to five minutes earlier.

THE SPIRIT CAVE is black on either side of your wings. It's black below you, floorless. No one who hasn't flown across a great ocean can ever understand. You go from the experience of feeling there's too much space around you to sudden claustrophobia. Pitilessly, the walls of night move closer. At its blackest, you're surrounded. The Spirit Cave is deepest black in a hoary whirl of stars. It was what Hunter had come here for. He flew straight in.

The walls seemed moist and black in his imaginings. They shone from underground streams as if they'd spent millennia underwater in a lake that had disappeared. The decomposed outlines of bog bodies and mummies lined the walls. The roof of the cave was glossy black and leprous with scales, as though it had once been a living thing.

Hunter flew further into the cave of spirits, the maw, the hearth of the dead. Far more deeply he could make out a candle at the end of an enfilade of black doorways, and he felt the temperature dropping.

He was only the lights in his cockpit, his wings invisible as he flew deeper into the cave. He was the thrum of his engine. Dreading who he might find here, he couldn't stop the downward drift of his heavy eyelids as he heard the voices of Santoria deities, a blue circle of figures who sat while conversing gently around Louivik Macedoine.

"Hello, Stitch," Hunter said.

Stitch scowled and pointed to a young, slim boy sitting beside him with the playful innocence of Krishna. "This is Ellegua."

Hunter trembled. It was dead 'Buster' Lindbergh, the baby who had taken his place in the shallow grave. In the place of eyes, the grizzled child had cowrie shells and a beatific smile that turned beastly when he spread his lips. Stitch flew into agitated Creole chatter while the spirit looked beyond him and carefully regarded Hunter.

"Quick, give him something scarlet," Stitch said.

Hunter snapped off a red Bakelite safety switch and held it into the darkness. The little child reached toward it.

Stitch moaned. "He needs three things. He believes in threes."

Hunter unwrapped his roast-beef sandwich, ripped it in two, and held the two pieces toward the windscreen. The red insides began to glow.

"What's that?" Stitch leaned toward the boy, who whispered to him. "He remembers you."

"From when I was a child?"

"No. When you were in Cuba. He is the Règle of all crossroads, the king of the lost. He has something for you."

Out of the darkness, a purse made from the mortal remains of a baby alligator swam into the cockpit with the stamp "Cuba" painted on it. Intensely red. Hunter reached for it. The last time he'd seen it, it was in his locker. He'd bought it in Cuba to give to Dido, but somehow he'd never gotten around to it. Had she seen it as just one more slight, one more evidence of her incompetence? Had he bought it for a daughter they'd never had? Now the purse disappeared, and all was dark again. The stars in the cave began to spin.

Hunter gripped the stick. "Father?" he called gently. "Are you there?" He looked ahead and realized he'd flown so low that a wave two hundred feet high towered over him. He was hundreds of miles east of Iceberg Alley–where could it have come from? He could hear its thunderous fathoms, its malignant green as it arched sickeningly over him.

Aviate. He went to full throttle and pulled his nose up so sharply he cleared the wave but wound up inverted, so he rolled into an Immelmann. *Navigate*. He felt so much fright that he climbed higher and higher as he banked back to his Great Circle course and checked it against his magnetic induction compass. *Communicate*. Then he prayed to God to deliver him from the spirits that governed the deep. How high was he now? He looked at the altimeter and saw with alarm that he had crested 13,000 feet. He felt so cold, the air so thin. He plunged the nose down until blood rushed to the back of his head so he could get below 10,000 feet. Otherwise, hypoxia would steal his consciousness from him. At 9,000 feet, he tipped his wings, looked above, and saw what Saint-Exupéry must have seen above his plane while flying suicide routes as a mail-delivery pilot in the Andes, an ice palace in the halls of the dead. A place you can never return from unchanged. Saint-Exupéry had described night as a black bottle of tequila that would empty itself by morning, leaving a single pilot still out there flying–a corpse with diamonds for eyes.

Hunter swallowed. When the night drained, who would find his skeleton? Saint-Exupéry had never learned. After his interlude with Anne Lindbergh, after they'd said their final goodbyes, he'd gone back to fly for Free France.

Even then jealousy closed, rather than opened, doors. When General Charles de Gaulle stripped Saint-Exupéry of his wings under suspicion of being a German spy (he'd refused to renounce German writers and artists among his friends), he'd taken to drinking; it took nearly a year to clear his name and earn the right to fly again. Finally, Saint-Exupéry accepted the deadliest patrols to show his courage and patriotism. Taking off in his Lockheed P-38 Lightning from a secret base near Erbalunga, Corsica, he crashed and drowned near Marseilles, farther from where his mission directed than the inexplicable frozen snow leopard mountaineers had discovered near the icy summit of Kilimanjaro. In a twist of fate, he was flying P-38 Lightnings over the turquoise Mediterranean while his rival Lindbergh was flying precisely the same model aircraft, swooping and diving to gun down Japanese Zeros above lonely palm-tree atolls in the Pacific.

Loved by the same woman, both took their secrets to their graves. When divers discovered Saint-Exupéry's plane on the ocean floor, experts determined it exploded on impact with the sea and that its last maneuver had been a vertical dive, straight down. Had the suave Frenchman killed himself? Hunter thought back to the locker in Grand Central Station. Beyond the Undark card, had the ampoule of cyanide been Saint-Exupéry's gift?

What would it have been like to have had Saint-Exupéry for a father? He closed his eyes, then snapped them open. For a 'real' pilot, the miracle of flying was more moving than the miracle of birth. To hell with both of them. Nowhere in Lindbergh's voluminous *Wartime Journals* did he make mention of Saint-Exupéry's death. How deep did that jealousy go? *Just keep moving.* When nothing makes sense, maybe a little coffee will help. Surely a brush with death entitles you to unscrew the coffee thermos.

Hunter locked his stick and rudders into autopilot, then opened the mercury picnic thermos decorated in plaid. The top of the thermos was red–that might have made a better present for the child. He lifted it to his nose and smelled the dark, earthy fluid. He inhaled it and let the warm fragrance fill his chest, remembering how he'd first come to enjoy coffee with Ned.

Maybe Ned was out here, too, among these specters of manhood. On Sunday mornings, Ned would light the deep-spiced Black Mallory tobacco in his ebony pipe, flap open the *New York Times*, and read aloud to him. In moments like these, curling up by Ned's chair was more fun than a barn full of swallows. Ned took his coffee black. After his sister was born, no one objected when Hunter drank coffee, too. At first, Hunter spooned a little milk into it, and two lumps of sugar (three if Ned turned away), but as time wore on, he thought of the drink as something very different from dessert.

Steady at five hundred feet. Fifteen hours since takeoff. What astonished Hunter was how different Lindbergh's two accounts of the same flight had been. When he was twenty-five years old, in his bestseller *We*, Lindbergh described everything by the numbers.

But decades later, his alter ego Careu Kent indulged in some self-exploration. Whereas hour number fifteen passed uneventfully in *We*, that same hour spread its vans and preened like a peacock as a supernatural encounter in the sequel *Spirit of Saint Louis*. In the middle of the Atlantic, presumed dead by the rest of the world, the strangely earthbound Lindbergh now saw pixies.

He was dead tired, finally penetrated by self-doubt, when he heard noises behind him near his life raft and all the supplies. Tuned as he was to monitor every engine shudder with exquisite sensitivity, this was a disturbing development, so he set the controls on lock, unstrapped, and crawled aft to see what was going on.

He surprised two little monsters who were discussing his fuel lines. They gave him a thumbs up and some helpful navigational advice. They were green, with green fins. And webbed toes.

Chapter 40

Transatlantic

You can't be a pilot if you don't love the sky.

WHAT NONPLUSSED HUNTER about this Atlantic crossing was, things were going perfectly. Syncretized Santorini deities excepted. Had he syncretized himself with Lindbergh, Pia with Dido? He didn't think so. A solution can't rashly be substituted for a problem. More likely, Lindbergh and Dido were syncretized with the unknown.

If navigation were the occult, and who out here dare say it wasn't, then its medium was the earth inductor compass.

Unknown to voyagers like Magellan and Cook, a magnetic aura more invisible than radio waves surrounds the Earth. Like a mystic, the great Glasgowegian scientist Faraday sensed this electromotive force as he watched a smaller magnet assert itself within the earth's magnetic field. As this smaller magnet moved through a larger set of magnets, its magnetic relation to that field changed instantaneously with its movement.

It was a beautiful woman walking into a courtroom full of old men: their eyes follow her as she walks past them. Not a word has been spoken, but so much has happened. Who was to say the woman herself wasn't changed by the passage?

Frighteningly, it was more reliable than the North Star.

In a deductive universe, the one we're convinced we're living in; things make sense–logic is king. But in an inductive universe, you have to take a leap of faith and subjugate yourself to the larger, invisible lines of flux around you. You have to accept unseen forces and give yourself up to the magic that is magnetic induction.

Mounted just behind the wings, an anemometer whirling in the dark on the spine of the *Spirit of St. Louis* powered the inductor compass by turning a generator shaft that electrified two magnets on gimbals, one of them set at 90 degrees to the direction of the Earth's poles. The other magnet was locked into the position of Hunter's selected heading. The floating magnet sensed the changing differential between the world's magnetic field and the path of the plane, expressing the electromotive force by wire to a dial on the *Spirit's* instrument panel.

Lindbergh, by checking and correcting his position every hundred miles, reached the coast of Ireland having never been more than 10 miles off course. Across 2,000 miles of blue water, secure in his blindness, he believed he was crossing a Godless ocean with the vaunt of 20th century science patented in 1912. Everything was unknown if you didn't bother to know it. The adoring crowds saw Lindbergh as a Nordic god, dazzling in his Aryan aspect, incapable of deceit. Throw in a little magnetite between his eyes like a homing pigeon to bring the myth home.

Fifty-five years later, Hunter was less sure, even about magnetism. When you're halfway across the Atlantic, you're more open to suggestion. Who was to say that the stunt Lindbergh pulled off wasn't…he took another long sip of coffee….beginner's luck. No, magnetism wasn't going to take him to landfall, or even skill. Best to stick with the holy trinity. *Aviate*. Four hundred feet, wings level, oil pressure good, control surfaces in their desired positions. *Navigate*. Hunter took out his pencil and checked the next hundred miles. Seven miles off course. *Communicate*. Turn down the voices in your head.

Growing up with Ned, Hunter hated it when his bedroom lights were switched out. The worst was when someone left his closet door open. Things grew long and deadly in the night. Who or what might come out of it? He worried he might be sucked inside. A foretaste of death.

As a young man, he walked through that dark closet and found Cuba on the other side. He slipped in again, looking for Dido. Now he was up here, where no one in the world knew exactly where he was.

Maybe it was Lindbergh who stayed still during those 33 hours in flight, while the rest of the world moved. Not that it mattered. Every night all of us muster more moxie than Lindbergh ever did just by closing our eyes, not knowing if we'll wake in the morning. The dark crossing. Will this be my last night on earth, or will I wake at landfall?

How could one human being be so honorable and dishonorable at the same time? What was this need to take additional risks and have secret families in the face of huge public adulation? Thomas Jefferson was seduced into believing he was a superman–why shouldn't he keep a wife and his slave wife happy just steps apart. Something was always off with the truly extraordinary heroes of this world.

Hunter sipped again from the thermos. If only he were wrong about being Lindbergh's son. If only science could prove him wrong. But science had suggested otherwise, if Kerry Banks Mullis, the Nobel Prize winner, held any weight. Hunter had come across a sample of Lindbergh's hair–a souvenir clipping a barber saved after the 1927 flight. When an immortal floats your way, you're going to want a piece of him. Something in Hunter directed him to buy it and treasure it.

The Eagle's first haircut after the transatlantic hop was in London. According to the *Times*, he dropped in unannounced to a shop on St. Martin's Lane. When the barber died, his son soldiered on, with the shadowbox of blond locks still up on the wall. When Hunter stopped by, the son was getting ready to retire, so he was glad to have one less thing to clean up. A 500-pound note did the trick.

"You're a collector, eh?" the son asked.

"In a manner of speaking," Hunter said. "Not that Lindbergh means anything to many people anymore."

When Hunter went to see Dr. Mullis and give him the box, he included a sample of his own hair. Three weeks later, the doctor took him back into his laboratory.

"Well, dog my cat," Mullis said, a glass of wine in his hand. "I did the test twice. Are you sure this sample has never been tampered with?"

"No," Hunter said. Who was to say it wasn't Pretender hair in the glass box? The barber might have wished he'd taken a sample when Lindbergh had visited. A blond customer was sitting in his chair. What the heck? Who'd ever know? Snip. The barber wouldn't even have told his son. Hunter smiled. Maybe it wasn't even the barber's son who'd sold the locks to him. Maybe the son wasn't a real barber by any stretch but the imposter son of a barber.

"Well, I'll tell you what I think," Mullis said. "It seems impossible, but–"

"I don't want to know," Hunter said. "I just want the opportunity to have known."

A negative would mean nothing. A positive would mean nothing–though maybe it might have offered some relief for unmoored Manfred. If Hunter were the monster's son, then Manfred wasn't. While Hunter seemed motionless on the outside, he was in a firestorm of emotions. He thought back to Anna Hauptmann. Would her peace bring his ruination, or would his settling the question once and for all leave an open, gaping feeling in himself that would never go away? He had the luxury to refuse the results now, but he knew he'd have to know soon. Because it wasn't just about him anymore. It never had been.

"What you're talking about is a quantum superposition," Mullis said.

"Is that a Steinway?" Hunter asked, peering into his living room.

"One of the square ones," Mullis said. "Doesn't it look like a coffin! When they invented the baby grand, the Steinway company put 500 of these outdated models onto a barge and dumped them in the middle of New York Harbor to dramatize they were turning away from them forever. This was one of the few that got away."

"Thank you, Dr. Mullis."

"You take care now," Mullis said.

Hunter stopped. "Dr. Mullis, please send the results to this address." He handed him his card from the Beau.

HUNTER KEPT FLYING. He flew through the shadows, waiting. The night so starry and malignant it seemed to rush toward him and swallow him whole, connecting him backward to other black moments best unremembered, the past and future tunnels that drain into the same inky well.

He looked at the gauge to see his artificial horizon. Perfect, as if his wings were painted into the straight-and-level position. He rocked them just to make sure the gauge was still working.

Now the emptiness of the sky began its enchantment, a lush, roaring silence. The *Spirit* continued drilling a hole through Nowhere, with time stopped. No pixies here; they'd have had to face the anxiety of being re-enactors. Hunter took another swig of coffee. Best to keep moving.

He looked into the thermos and saw to his surprise that it was completely full.

Just hold on. He remembered his last spirit card, the one he wouldn't tell to Stitch: "*You can't love life until you live the life you love.*"

With dead reckoning, he did another 100-mile calculation. Just two miles off course. This was dazzling, impossible. Afraid he was dreaming, he put the plane in a slow bank to the right. The *Spirit's* wing dipped into the abyss as it began a slow turn into total darkness, descending in a deadly circle, the light of the world high above. The devil was down here, lounging. *Tick.* For a ghostly second Hunter sensed his father turn back with that million-dollar grin. "Next stop, Canyon del Muerto."

Time to switch fuel tanks again. Where had the last five hours gone? Now it wasn't just Lindbergh for whom time disappeared. Hunter opened his eyes and realized he'd been lulled into a full dive. He'd entered a storm, he'd stalled while sleeping, and now he was beyond rudder shaker. He was going down.

He split into two Hunters, one gracefully accepting what was happening, the other fighting for his life.

Three hundred feet. The *Spirit* was deeply stalled; he had no choice but to aim the nose straight down counter intuitively to build up airspeed. There would be just one chance.

Two hundred feet. Was he smiling, or was it a grimace? More rudder shaker. The whole plane mushy, slamming toward the ocean like a hammer. One hundred feet. The beat of his heart. The need for love. Fifty feet.

Communicate. Dear God, please bless everyone. Thank you for this life. Please accept my spirit into the deep. Please bless Pia and Dido. For a flash he saw them looking up quickly from a couch. He closed his eyes as he pulled the stick back with all his might.

The explosion was seen by no one. Seawater crashed against the shattered fuselage as the fire leapt into a five-hundred-foot flame. The deep boom reverberated over the blackness that waited in every closet, insinuated itself into every lonely night, every set of eyes that turned away. "I'm here, Hunter." It was Ned's voice, the prize he should have held more dear.

His left wing was ripped off the ship. The call sign N-X-211 hung on the waves for three minutes as three black sea birds swept over. Then down, down, the *Spirit* spiraled toward its final resting place, Hunter's charts and sandwich debris popping to the surface. Ten feet below, the door swung open, and he fell out, his arms spreading wide as though he were swimming. The green sea darkened, and a ray swam past him as he fell deeper into nothingness.

Thoughts swirled as the current carried him down. He remembered talking to Pia in the car, driving to Switzerland.

"For this sparkling second we are relevant, moving together. Something could go terribly right between us," she said.

"When?"

"Just wait."

"But what's going to happen, Pia?"

"The best part is, we don't know."

A LANTERNFISH and two burbots vibrated past him as he continued his gentle descent. Then a ling and a canopener smoothdream erupted from the soft silt on the ocean floor as he hit the shelf of Irish coast, against which the waves were washing barely two miles away, soft as an old song.

The night continued its music above him, the fetch of wind barely discernible, its whispers across the waves a radio station no one but the dead could hear.

The *Spirit* lay broken in four pieces: the cockpit, fuselage, and empennage were flipped over and piling up with sand. The Wright Cyclone engine was on its back, cylinders shiny, sparkling and new. The monoplane's signature wing lay akimbo, its silver fabric ripped. To the west, an underwater mountain range with valleys pulled everything toward a greater dark.

During their honeymoon, in Deruda, Italy, Hunter and Dido had been treated to coffee in painted cups. *When you taste this, your morning will never be the same*, the server told the happy couple. The decorated image of Rafaelesco grinned in agreement on the mug's side. Hunter tried it, and it was true. The best he'd ever tasted. By saying it, she'd made it true.

Hunter sensed a disturbance passing over his watery grave, a tiny rush of water, a cleft in the North Atlantic. It was early morning on the next day, with no one in the world aware he'd gone down. It was the sole of a tiny sailboat, long and lovely with a raked-back mainmast that meant it was either a Herreshoff or a Sparkman and Stephens, its pure white hull and Hood sails running with the wind. The saloon was made of pure mahogany, the cleats in eternal bronze. What could something as lissome as this be doing over here, among these Irish fish?

It was the sloop he and Dido had pretended they might one day own together–after the F.A.A. took away her pilot's license forever. Even then, Hunter felt his future regret. The substitute dream would never be good enough.

He watched as the sloop was swept away by light air. At the wheel on its coppery deck, the vessel's blithe sailor pulled back her hair to feel a great breeze cooled by the supernatural. It was Dido. She lifted her chin into the wind and embraced the chill.

Chapter 41

Transatlantic

I'm from the FAA, and I'm here to help.

DIDO RACED HOME to her thatched cottage high atop a cliff looking out over the sea. *So, this was where she'd slipped away to.* The housekeeper had already cooked dinner, the sweet smell of lamb and rosemary etching into a memory that would curl up in front of the fireplace forever.

"Hunter," she said. A blond nine-year-old boy should have looked up, but did not look up, from the couch. With ferocious intensity, he was tinkering with a toy plane in four parts. "Hunter," she said again. He picked up two of the pieces, ran over, and hugged his mother. She shook out her hair. "Dear son, are you still playing with that beastly thing?"

BUT HUNTER wasn't in a Chekhov story. None of this happened. He woke and pulled up at the last second. We fly to our funerals with the moon on fire.

He came to consciousness flying straight and level at 100 feet, 70 knots. He increased it to 100 knots. Up ahead was the coast, clouded with birds. Having cast his soul to the care of the Eternal, he felt oddly refreshed.

Great cliffs lay ahead, hundreds of feet high. The surf pounding the shore seemed distant and porcelain green. It was already late afternoon in Ireland, five hours of sunlight deeper into tomorrow than Newfoundland. Shaggy sheep dotted thatched, whitewashed farms scattered across the countryside. He looked down and saw a collie chasing a liquid flock of lambs as it rushed this way and that, moving with the shame of the shocked.

Slowly, Hibernia moved below him as he watched the shadow of the *Spirit* advance over the fragrant, spellbound Earth. Indulging in a shallow bank, he buzzed what had to be Dunguaire Castle with its Norman tower and massive portcullis softened by ivy. From this height, no one would question why this was called the Emerald Isle. The cliffs grew great and black as he approached the limits of County Cork on the southern tip of Ireland. His eyes followed a single road that twisted and turned along the last barren peninsula before the blue gulf that led to Albion. The road got narrower and then went straight to its final stop. The end of the line. White brick with a red coursing, Galley Head Lightkeepers House in Rathbarry was built on the very last green slope to a soaring cliff of kärst. Only a formidable white stone weather wall held it safely above the monster waves. No car was parked in the gravel lot. Where did lighthouse keepers go when they needed a moment alone? What signal do you shine when you need to find yourself? *Dido. Just because you're dead doesn't mean you don't have to answer me.*

Suddenly, he felt his heart race. In the blue distance to the east, he could see England. It grew and he covered the blue gap below him, birds whirling, whitecaps dancing because the fetch–the distance the wind traveled–was so great. Maybe that's why women were called fetching. It wasn't just their warmth; it was the interior distance they traveled to be close to you. Wasn't trust just a function of distance? He leaned his head out the window and felt the breeze. A gentle hand descended on him, and in the vast intimacy of the tiny cockpit he started to cry.

What coffee was left was growing colder with each tick of the clock, like a corpse. Because he couldn't look forward, he scanned the lost cluster of islands below his right wing and caught sight of St. Martin's, Grimsby, and the castles Cromwell and King Charles built to ward off invaders from the south. They should instead have concerned themselves with their internal revolutions, their involutions, blue water revolving with cyclic certainty toward the place where like children, time and gravity shyly venture their first kiss.

He'd been to Grimsby before, where the hamlet of Old Grimsby, with its Ruin Beach Café, was being challenged by New Grimsby and all its superior amenities–its startling curve of fresh beach, its nearly Caribbean water along the Quay, its liquid women and television celebrities, the pub at the Inn where they brewed their own stout. Here was a place where the devil could kick off his loafers.

Aviate. The cliffs of southern England grew and fell away like the gates of the undreamed. In geographic harmony with Ireland, more couthy collies chased their flocks beside more unmanned lighthouses.

Navigate. He felt a chill when he realized he was passing over the same village Lindbergh promised he'd overflown. A thrill seized him when he realized he had a chance to make true all the private lies his father had perpetuated. The Eagle was dead now. "Daddy, you bastard, I'm through." But maybe everyone's a bastard. I hold no more myths about you. It's so easy to judge your parents harshly when you're younger, but when you catch up, suddenly they're not so incomprehensible. Maybe you 'losted' me, and maybe I can't judge you. All I can do is find myself.

Assuming he could hang on and make it. Rough with fatigue, he stared down at Sevenoaks Weald, flew over Riverhill House, and picked out the turkey tree and the light-blue Triumph parked beside it. More lives suspended in the glimmer of Lindbergh. The thatched roofs clustered as he flew over Hastings and Truro and leapt over the English Channel at twilight with his motor running perfectly. He thought of banking along the White Cliffs of Dover but elected not to because it might make him think of the sentimental song of the same name.

No need to take unnecessary risks. Once he started humming it, it would take days to get it out of his head. That was one of Ned's tunes, and Ned was dead. Get out the lead. You've got to wash that song right out of your head. Jesus, another stupid song.

Next stop was France in the uneven glow of the sun's last fading rays behind him. Beyond Le Havre, Haute-Normandy twinkled distantly to the north, docks and factories amid the dusting of a brand-new city. The mouth of the Seine lay invitingly ahead, tracing a serpentine path toward Rouen, but he was over Jersey now, and the quickest course was direct to Paris. The pink and purple glow around the cities deepened to cobalt and black. Those lights ahead and to the left would be Caen, the target of every Allied bomber flying out of eastern England when it was Germany's rocket stronghold during World War II. This was the central base where the buzz bombs were launched by teenage terrorists who dreamed of killing crowds, smashing Albert Hall, exploding Big Ben. The sound of the V-1s vibrated over London until the drones cut to silence and the bombs fell. The souls below held their breath.

There were so many kinds of silences. If he were lucky enough to make it to Le Bourget, he hoped to land in a silence as deafening as the uproar was when Lindbergh had circled and followed the runway lights to infamy, the ineluctable shadow of celebrity.

He would fly through darkened France as quiet as a buzz bomb in final flight, unseen, even by himself.

Lit to the hilt, astounding in its nerve, here was the sparkling Eiffel Tower atop a cloak of lights dancing across the darkened buildings of the Seine and ebbing toward St. Denis. By now, Approach Control would be trying to reach the *Spirit* across its radar screens, asynchronous with time.

Electromagnetic waves were fondling his plane as they probed the black shape and tested it to see if it were friend or foe. Following the heat trace of his engine through the night sky, Exocet missiles shifted, precessed on the gimbals of their launch carriages, and aimed their streamlined tips along his undisclosed flight path. There were rules about flying over this capital city without a calling card. French aviation officials were waiting to welcome Lindbergh, with reports called ahead by ships and observers in Ireland and England, but this second *Spirit*, without a flight plan filed, sinking lower and lower to the treetops and streets of Paris, could be hostile. Aware that air-defense missiles had no sense of humor, Hunter, exhausted as he was, still couldn't resist the temptation to fly so close to the Eiffel Tower he could read the menus of the diners at the 90M restaurant halfway up.

He glanced at his watch. Thirty-three hours, 14 minutes. Oil pressure good. Ailerons working. Off the tower, he set a course of 031 degrees and lined up with the lights of Le Bourget. His triumphant return to a place he'd never been. As a final step, he turned off his position lights to avoid discovery. See no evil, hear no evil, speak no evil.

Suddenly he felt the invisible thunder of a Concorde Supersonic Transport behind him, so he banked hard left and went to full throttle, peeling off in what amounted to a wingover. Two hundred feet. One hundred feet but still buffeting, nearly inverted. Kick the rudder, stick over.

Come on, power. His stall buzzer sounded as the *Spirit* woke back up and responded. He heard a crash of leaves from a treetop and felt a sickening drag as a branch ripped at his starboard wing, but he dragged his way up, checked the pattern for more aircraft, and snuck closer to the runway behind the disturbed air mass of the Concorde, the *Spirit* shuddering but alive. The supersonic transport, a giant hole in the darkness, would be the perfect shield that would allow him to turn off the runway and pull into the grass beside an inactive taxiway, without even blue lights for company.

He flared above the invisible tarmac, crabbed for a mild crosswind, and wondered again if he were falling asleep. With his body so disconnected from his mind, how would he know? All he really knew now was a ragged anger for sleep. He'd slake himself with it. Easing the power back, he waited for his wheels to hit. On the best landings, you never feel them. Pilots treasure the moment before they've 'greased' a landing, a suspended animation. It was two seconds before he was sure he'd really grabbed the Earth. Dear God, couldn't we keep this *entre nous*. His heart beating out of his chest, he slowed quickly with the control tower unaware, turned short into the unlit taxiway, and crept across the night grass toward a black patch in the woods. What were those things rushing away in the grass? Rabbits.

Three figures walked quickly toward him in the dark.

Chapter 42

Paris

The Seven P's. Prior planning prevents piss-poor performance.

Hunter parked the rental Jaguar in the lot of an invisible hotel fringing Le Bourget, checked into a room, and downed a single shot of Canadian Mist before falling deeply asleep. In his dreams, he was still flying. He woke up during the night of the next day, jubilant but trembling. He bought a yellow Bic razor and a newspaper in the hotel gift shop. The only cologne available for purchase was English Leather, in the little wooden box. When in Paris.

He took an ice-cold shower and shaved. Flapping open *Le Monde*, he caught up with world events. At that moment, according to the press, no one was having a ticker-tape parade. He couldn't shake the strange feeling of *dépaysement*, of being somewhere without actually having arrived.

It was dark again when he drove into Berlin, following Unter den Linden and its lights toward Pia's high rise. He would tell no one. If you're a real pilot, if you fly through the spirit cave, it's not something you break out at cocktail parties. Better to be what you'll do than what you've done. How many days had he gone without Cuban food? He'd try a new place. No need to darken the doorstep at Havana Sexy. Feel the thrill of this moment. Drink it in.

He walked into the elevator and hit the up button, feeling dizzy, happy. He knocked on the door. Radu opened it.

"Things have changed," Radu declared. "Her silence is mine, her eyes mine. It is as if she knows everything about my childhood, my present, my future, as if she can see right through me."

"Ah, Chagall," Hunter said. "Have you ever written anything yourself? I can see right through you, too." He looked past Radu at Pia, who was watching him across the room. Hunter tilted his head and grinned in his offhanded way, the way he might have as a young man. He stepped in, grabbed Radu's hand, shook it, and said, "Radu, I'm so glad to see you!"

He laid a big kiss on Radu's mouth while the director struggled to get away. He held him harder.

"Hunter!" Pia laughed. "You've found your funny!"

He released Radu, flew over to Pia, and gave her a deep kiss from an awkward angle. She pulled away. "Hunter!" And then she stood up and leaned in for another.

"I want you to know," Hunter said as Dido wriggled between them and crushed herself against him. "I want everyone to know. I'm back." It was time to say goodbye to Dido forever. Like that, Hunter's nightmares disappeared.

This was the secret that escaped Lindbergh. You don't fly across something; you fly to someone. For however long it lasts. Finally, Hunter was flying home.

Postscript

THE PUBLIC has long been fascinated by the Lindbergh family story. The opening of The Lindbergh Baby Murder Investigation exhibit in 1983 drew a record crowd of curiosity seekers to the New Jersey State Police Museum in West Trenton. The featured displays included the homemade ladder purportedly used by Bruno Hauptmann and a reliquary containing hair and bone fragments labeled to be those of the kidnapped and murdered "Buster" Lindbergh recovered from the woods surrounding Highfields. In 2001, forensic DNA testing conducted on the artifacts was inconclusive. In 2003, in accordance with the final wishes of Anne Morrow Lindbergh, all possible future testing of the remains that survived the cremation was blocked by the family, who took possession of the fragments and buried them. United States family members have declined to provide samples of their own DNA for testing.

In 2003, DNA tests confirmed that the three children of Brigitte Hesshaimer were the offspring of Charles A. Lindbergh.

According to
https://www.mnhs.org/lindbergh/learn/family/double-life,
the direct descendants of Charles Augustus Lindbergh are:

With Anne Morrow Lindbergh:
Charles Augustus Lindbergh Jr.
Jon Lindbergh
Land Morrow Lindbergh
Anne Spencer Lindbergh (Perrin)
Scott Lindbergh
Reeve Lindbergh (Tripp)

With Brigitte Hesshaimer:
Dyrk Hesshaimer
Astrid Hesshaimer Bouteuil
David Hesshaimer

With Marietta Hesshaimer (Brigitte's sister):
Vago Hesshaimer
Christoph Hesshaimer

With Valeska, Lindbergh's secretary (surname
unknown):
a son (name unknown)
a daughter (name unknown)

Acknowledgments

THIS STORY is a product of the imagination.

Chasing the shadow of Careu Kent has taken me from Little Falls, Minnesota; to Washington, D.C.; Long Island and Manhattan, New York; North Haven Island, Maine; Hopewell, Trenton, Englewood, and Orange, New Jersey; Stockholm, Sweden; and multiple Lindbergh haunts in France; England; Italy; and Switzerland.

I'd like to thank Reeve Lindbergh, Charles A. Lindbergh's youngest American daughter, for the insights she gave me during an interview on the Lindberghs' North Haven Island summer retreat for *Portland Monthly* magazine.

I'm grateful to A. Scott Berg for corresponding with me regarding Lindbergh the scientist. Few 21st century readers are aware that beyond being the first human being to fly solo from New York to Paris, Lindbergh also developed the "first artificial heart." It is merely a coincidence that Lindbergh's 'heart' was made of glass.

At Long Barn in Sevenoaks Weald, England, I met Rebecca Lemonius, the present owner of the house where Charles and Anne Morrow Lindbergh hid from the world's press when Bruno Hauptmann was electrocuted for the kidnapping of the Lindbergh Baby in 1936. In this luxuriant setting south of London, Charles and Anne entertained some very controversial pre-War guests as part of the frightful 'Cliveden Set.'

I'd also like to thank Mark Falzini, who took time out of his busy schedule to show me artifacts from the Lindbergh Investigation evidence at the New Jersey State Police Museum.

The sources for the flying chestnuts that launch each chapter are 'traditional,' some from squadron notes I've taken over the years, some from my Navy flight manuals, and many verbatim from resources such as the Wits Flying Club's Facebook page. Sometimes, real wisdom is hidden in colorful language. Full of faded magic, these sayings are the stuff of Navy flight school in Pensacola and were central to the exotic private language I attended to as editor of the Navy's flying magazine, *Approach*, from 1981-1983, when this novel takes place (1982).

About the Author

Colin W. Sargent, Ph.D., is the founding editor & publisher of *Portland Monthly* magazine as well as a novelist, playwright, and poet.

A former Navy pilot, he teaches writing at The College of William and Mary. His novel *Red Hands* was released in the U.S. earlier this year.

Photo credit: RHONDA FARNHAM.

OTHER HELLBOUND BOOKS

Goodbye Stranger

Another gripping noir thriller from the bestselling author of *The Gentleman's Choice* and *Dark Beauty*

Danielle Harrington has the life many women envy: She's beautiful, rich, has two wonderful children, and is married to the Preston Harrington - the handsome, charismatic, retired quarterback who won two Super Bowls.

Unfortunately, something is very wrong with Preston. Having suffered more than his fair share of injuries and concussions, he becomes quiet, withdrawn, and distant.

As Preston spends more time away from his family, Danielle begins suspect an affair without realizing her husband is involved in something much, much worse…

Following a series of tragic incidents and the return of an old nemesis from the past, things begin to spiral out of control for Danielle as Preston's dark side puts her and their children in terrible danger.

Colleen

"Sexy, intriguing, terrifying - Colleen has it all! " - James H. Longmore, author of *Tenebrion.*

Lacey, a goth introvert with sketchy people skills, befriends Colleen, a dazzlingly beautiful ghost, during a solo Ouija board session. At last, her loneliness comes to an end.
An eclectic pairing indeed, but they form an odd-but-satisfying and far-from-platonic friendship.
When Lacey begins work as a stripper, she and Colleen find themselves with a conspiratorial mystery to solve in the strip club.
Unfortunately, Lacey's newfound supernatural lover has a secret… or two and isn't what she seems to be at all.
Colleen is not a ghost at all, but a succubus with an unfortunate habit of killing people.
Accidentally.
It's not long before the mounting number of deaths occurring around Lacey draws the attention of a tenacious homicide detective…
Can Colleen uncover the shady happenings at the club and keep her beloved Lacey out of jail?

Playground of the Dead

Playground of the Dead is a macabre tale set in a seaside California community of Clear View.

There have been a number of unexplained deaths of the town's citizens - all related to tragic incidents involving its children.

The police chief, Braden Powell, a man dealing with his own troubled, tragic history, has been investigating the mysterious occurrences with frustratingly minimal success,

Gradually, he comes to realize there may be a sinister, supernatural connection too horrifying to comprehend.

<u>Pede</u>

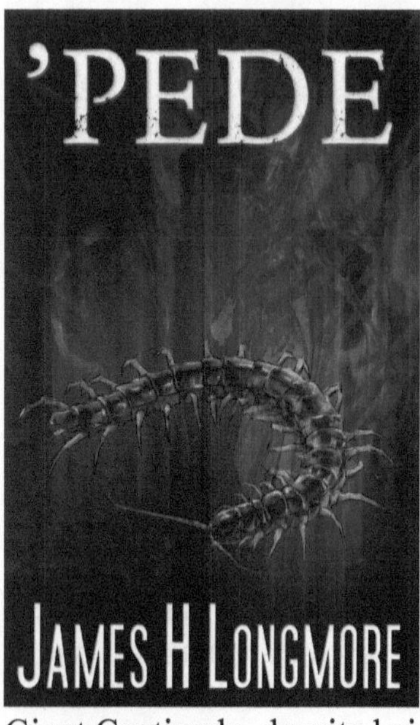

"A brutally affectionate homage to the creature feature!

The once luxurious Mountainview Spa Hotel in the heart of California's Coachella valley lies decaying, abandoned and heavily boarded up - the site of a radioactive, "dirty" bomb explosion five years' previously. Zoology Professor, Jane Lucas, harbors a lifelong phobia of *Scolopendra gigantea,* the Giant Centipede, despite being the world's leading authority on the creature.

Following the savage deaths of two teenagers who broke into the hotel to cavort in the natural underground spa and the discovery of centipede remains almost three times natural size, the professor teams up with four of her students to investigate.

Their expedition soon becomes a fight for survival when they're trapped inside the hotel with a gang of violent thugs and a voracious swarm of oversized centipedes that infest the place - and then discover another creature even more terrifying is hunting in the Mountainview's deserted hallways: a centipede of impossibly monstrous proportions... ravenous and desperate to feed.

Crimes of Hate

"In compiling this anthology, it was my intention to focus on stories of crime motivated by hate. Not racially, politically, or religiously motivated violence, even though these are labeled 'hate crimes' in contemporary media. Edgar Allan Poe's *The Casque of Amontillado* opens the anthology and *The Interlopers* by Saki (H.H. Munro) provides an appropriately hateful bookend as the final tale.

In between these two classic stories you will find seven very imaginative and original creations by incredibly talented contemporary authors:

Jennifer Trumbull gives us her take on what happens when a privileged young woman with everything going for her decides to kill someone in the aptly titled *I Hate You*.

Randall Smith cautions *Don't Be Stupid* in his disturbing tale of an eleven-year-old boy who's not quite right.

Psychopaths, Grieving and Timeslips is a most unusual novella from P.K. Kleypas. It deals with hate and the ensuing guilt it can arouse in 'normal' people forced to deal with psychopathic family members.

SF by Steven Purselley is a coming-of-age tale of profound darkness.

The Last Ray of Summer by Anthony Ferguson is another tale of family drama and the extreme measures required to end the acts of a sociopathic father.

Che Trujillo offers an inside look at the initiatory practices of an urban gang and a glimpse into the mind of a victim turned killer in *Cherry Boy*.

Crepuscular, my own contribution to this collection, tells of the lingering consequences crimes of hate can generate even decades after the fact.

So, immerse yourself in the strange situations and states of consciousness we have conjured for your amusement.

And, be cautioned against unleashing your own crimes of hate on the unsuspecting world."
Bret McCormick

**A HellBound Books LLC
Publication**

www.hellboundbooks.com

www.ingramcontent.com/pod-product-compliance
Lightning Source LLC
Chambersburg PA
CBHW062014190726
48285CB00001BA/282